Demand the World

DEMAND THE WORLD

Graham Shelby

BARRIE & JENKINS
LONDON

First published in 1990 by Barrie & Jenkins Ltd,
Random Century House, 20 Vauxhall Bridge Road,
London SW1V 2SA

This book is a work of fiction. Any resemblance
between the characters portrayed and real persons,
living or dead, is purely coincidental.

Graham Shelby has asserted his right to be identified
as the author of this work

British Library Cataloguing in Publication Data
Shelby, Graham, *1940–*
Demand the world.
I. Title
823.912 [F]

ISBN 0–7126–3463–0

Phototypeset by Input Typesetting Ltd, London

Printed and bound in Great Britain by
Mackays of Chatham PLC, Chatham, Kent

This is for four good friends, four firm pillars:
Bob and Brigitte in Vauhallan,
Geoffrey and Josephine in Heaton Mersey.
And for Sallie, the keystone . . .

Travel, not with banners furled,
Ambition shadowed by a shield.
But snatch the day. Demand the world.
Claim all the foreign field.
Leave the timid to cower together at noon,
Then shiver alone at night.
Glory was never meant for such as they.
Only to those with the courage to fight
Can The World be a part of The Way.

From 'Harvest of Brave Hearts and Single Minds'

CONTENTS

PROLOGUE

Paris: 1886

His condolences muttered with uncaring haste, the black-dressed official turned to the question of payment. He wanted to know who would settle the bill for the *char funèbre*. The services of the driver and his three assistants. The grave-digger and *his* assistant. The priest. The paperwork. The government seal of authentication.

It had to be understood, he said, that what with the rain and the need for a canvas awning over the grave, certain extra costs would be incurred. Everything was listed here on the docket. Immediate payment would be greatly appreciated. The total came to twenty-eight francs and fifteen centimes, though should Monsieur care to add something as an expression of his gratitude . . .

Baron Enrique von Wisner de Morgenstern roared to make the man blanch. He struggled to bring his long, cadaverous frame forward from the deep leather chair, his fine ashen hair in disarray, sunken eyes glaring, a sinewy arm extended.

'You bloody rodent! The deceased not yet buried, and you talk to me of tips and – *gratitude*? And what if you don't get your money, here and now? Will you leave the coffin there in the parlour and take the hearse away empty? Abandon the body to smaller rats than you? By God, but you're a mean-minded creature.'

The official blinked, aware that he'd retreated in the face of the old man's outburst. 'I would have you know,' he said lamely, 'I am a public servant in the pursuit of my official duties. Your remarks are an insult to the municipal authorities.'

'Then submit a report,' von Wisner snapped. 'But you'd better do it quickly. I am seventy-five years of age and I am dying. Perhaps, in a month or so, you'll have *me* for a passenger. Oh, don't look so worried; the money will be over there in that escritoire.'

'As for the matter in hand, Monsieur – '

'It's Monsieur le Baron.'

'Yes, well, I'm to remind you that, all formalities having been concluded, the deceased will be buried near the east wall of Père Lachaise cemetery at five o'clock this afternoon. No provision has been made for mourners, though we could, I suppose, erect a second awning. That would bring the total cost to – '

'It will not be necessary,' von Wisner told him. 'I alone shall be there.'

'No friends?' the official queried. 'No relatives?'

'That escritoire,' the old man repeated. 'Right-hand drawer. Be good enough to bring me the brown leather purse. It's time you were given your, what was it, twenty-eight francs and fifteen centimes?'

Scenting money, the official crossed to the writing desk and took out the purse, couching it in his hand. It was satisfyingly heavy. Time to sweet-talk Monsieur le Baron.

'All bereavements bring great sadness,' he murmured. 'The more so perhaps on such a dismal day as this. The rain seems set to continue; Heaven's tears, as I've heard it said, though flowers do bring a refreshing glow of colour . . .'

Von Wisner had taken the purse, loosened the drawstring and was counting out the sum he intended to pay. Exactly twenty-eight francs and fifteen centimes. Not from meanness, but because he knew the deceased would be furious if he allowed himself to be manipulated by the rodent. '*Nearly thirty francs for the ditch, and he all but baldly asks for a tip? Mother of God, Enrique, you tell him to go hang! The days when we had money to throw around are long since over. Oh, sure, there were times, and I blush to think of those wild excesses. Mine more than yours. But that was a different world, my dear friend. A far-away country. Another life entirely.*

'*If you really want to please me, save your money, then book the plot next to mine. We've still a thousand reminiscences, a thousand fresh topics to explore. Now live out your days until they grow too heavy, and the light too dim. Then join me there, protected from the wind in winter, and shaded from the sun. If you want to know the truth, Enrique, I've had all the sun I can stand!*'

'I was saying, Monsieur le Baron . . . A fine bank of flowers to offset this dismal day?'

The old man glanced up and growled: 'What? Flowers? I hadn't thought – '

'For no more than a few centimes.'

Torn between his reverie and the official's soft-spoken blandishments, Enrique von Wisner de Morgenstern remembered the flowers in that other world, that far-away country, where all was pungent, exotic, brilliant to the eye.

He saw no harm in agreeing; a touch of colour would not be amiss. Foolishly, his mind distracted, the old man handed the purse to the servant from Père Lachaise.

The man pretended to cough, stooped and turned, clawed a handful of coins from the bag. Von Wisner's eyes were already downcast, his thoughts turned inward, unaware of the shabby deceit. He told himself yes, I must do that today. Book the plot next to hers. Who knows, but I might be alongside her sooner than I think, for her own death has certainly sapped my will to continue.

'*Voilà, Monsieur le Baron!* A few centimes, as I said. Now you just leave things to me. But don't forget; five o'clock near the east wall. And of course I won't submit a report. It was just a misunderstanding. The sadness of the moment. Here, Monsieur le Baron, here's my hand.'

Once again von Wisner growled: 'What?' then wrapped his skeletal fingers round the official's fleshy palm. The man winced and pulled free, hurrying out of the room to call the carriers from the hearse. They stumped up the steps, shouldering their way along the corridor, tracked mud from their boots into the parlour and hefted the black varnished coffin by its handles. It had taken the boss a damn long time to call them . . . Stuck out there on the *char funèbre* . . . Near drowned in the drizzle . . .

Von Wisner heard them curse, heard them spit, heard the corners of the coffin bang against the walls. He snatched at his brass-topped cane, anger driving him awkwardly from the chair. But his left leg was partially paralysed, shards of shrapnel buried in his thigh. Coming to his feet, the towering Hungarian adventurer toppled and fell against the door. By the time he'd pinned the cane for balance, the carriers had taken the body of Elisa Alicia Lynch from the house and out of his life.

He called: 'Wait!' But none of them heard him. He called: 'Treat her with care! Treat her with respect!' But the nervous snorting horses had been whipped on their way, plunging through the mud of Rue de Charonne. He limped along the corridor and out into the rain, in time only to raise the black malacca cane like a flagless pole, its emblems and blazons left in that distant world, where so much had been delightful. Yet all of it, eventually, destructive.

With Elisa taken from him, the baron gathered his strength for what he suspected would be his final dignified sortie from the house. He might limp out again in the weeks to come, but he would never be dressed as he chose to dress today.

This was to be his tribute to the woman who'd been his friend, his companion. His last determined exercise in pride. The chance for Paris to see – if Paris cared – that an old man could still look good in cavalry boots and high-buttoned tunic, medals and ribbons on his shallow chest, his belt as tight now as when he'd been twenty, his oiled Hungarian sabre slick in its scabbard.

Everything Von Wisner did was now painful. Climbing the stairs without Elisa's shoulder to lean on. Fumbling with the hooks and eyes and buttons of his uniform, yet with Elisa no longer there to help him. Everything he did seemed clumsy, and he glanced from time to time at his heavy, steel-case watch, fearing he'd be late at Père Lachaise.

He dragged a razor down his long, commanding jaw, combed his hair and bushy moustache, buckled on his belt and sword-hanger. Then he hooked on the sabre and edged his way downstairs again, leaning on the thick black cane, praying he'd find a cabriolet in the street.

The baron twisted the key in the door and lurched down the steps, scowling as the rain turned his uniform from summer blue to mauve. He waited stoically until a cab splashed up from the south, then waved the cane to arrest it. As the driver reined in, Von Wisner grunted with horror at something he'd forgotten. Something he feared he might now have left too late . . .

'Tell me,' he demanded, 'do you know of a mason's yard? I need a headstone cut, but it must be done now. Without delay.'

'Well, let's see,' the young driver mused. 'There's a place across Boulevard Diderot, near the railway station, or if you only want something simple – '

'Simple, yes. And I need it before five.'

'Then we'd better try Jean-Christophe. He did my mother a nice clean headstone, and his yard's a lot nearer than Diderot. But don't expect cherubs, or pages carved like a Bible. Jean-Christophe's a good workman, but not what you'd call artistic.'

'Take me there,' Von Wisner directed; 'then stay until it's done. I shall need you again.'

'Suits me,' the man said cheerfully. 'People say it's hard to find a cab when it rains, but I tell you, *mon Colonel*, it's just as hard for us to pick up a fare. You think anyone wants to stand out in the street, mud sloshing about? I'll say they don't.'

He chattered on, the old man hunched beneath the stiff tarred canopy of the light, bouncing conveyance. The baron said nothing, preoccupied now with the words to be chiselled on the headstone – words for the world to read in Père Lachaise.

*

The bearded Jean-Christophe jammed his tongue in the corner of his mouth and painstakingly copied down the inscription. He showed it to the tall, stooping Von Wisner, who gazed at it and sighed and said: 'That's correct. But without decoration.'

'Well, that's the thing,' the mason told him. 'I'm not much up on angels.'

The driver of the cabriolet smiled and suggested *le Colonel* wait in the bar across the street. 'I'll come and tell you when it's ready. That be all right?'

He's a pleasant change from the official, Von Wisner thought, nodding once, then limping towards the welcome warmth of the steam and smoke-wreathed bar.

The aged adventurer sat there for an hour, bony fingers twisting a glass of absinthe, memories spilling tears across the ridge of his cheekbones and down into the magnificent tangle of his military moustache. Customers glanced across, concealing their smiles at this quaint, almost comic character in his musty uniform, with his cluster of medals, the sabre that threatened to trip the waiters in passing. *What a funny old fool . . . Wonder where he got all those decorations . . . But he looks the part, looks like a man who's been around a bit . . . He could tell a few good stories, eh . . . And turn the air blue with some of 'em . . .*

Their amusement tinged with respect, they left him alone. Had they cared to think about it later, they would have admitted that the old man's presence made them feel at ease, both protective and protected. If his uniform was, well, yes, a bit of a circus turn, his air of sad authority was undeniable. Stooped by age, he could yet, they acknowledged, haul himself to his feet and silence the room with his roar. And maybe still show them how to go at the enemy with a sabre.

The owner of the bar sent a waiter across with a second glass of absinthe and the message, '*C'est moi qui paye.*' Von Wisner listened as the waiter relayed it, then turned towards the bar, half rose and nodded his thanks. The owner tried to match the courtesy of the nod and sent an empty beer glass spinning to the floor. Von Wisner smiled and sat down. *How many times have I bowed,* he mused, *and in how many courts of the world. It's not so easy if you've not had the practice. Or are pinned behind a bar.*

He sat where he was until four in the afternoon. Then the cheerful young driver came over to tell him the headstone was ready, and did the *Colonel* want him to load it aboard the cab?

15

'Please do so. When I've settled things with the mason, I'd be grateful if you'd conduct me to Père Lachaise. The eastern gate.'

'Right. But I think we should hurry. With the mud and that, and most of it being uphill . . .'

They reached the cemetery at four forty-five.

The single awning had been crudely strung with flowers, a cheap bouquet wired to the wooden coffin. Whatever the official had clawed from Von Wisner's purse, no more than a few centimes had been spent on the promised touch of colour.

The rain continued to wash across the city. Elisa Alicia Lynch was buried, the Baron Enrique von Wisner de Morgenstern standing guard. His right hand couching his brass-tipped cane, he raised his left to his mouth and licked his finger to loosen a ring.

It was something he'd been given for services rendered more than twenty years before. A beautifully fashioned miniature of the great South American vulture, the condor, the bird was studded with rubies and emeralds, chips of diamonds, clasps of solid gold.

He twisted it from his skinny finger and tossed it on to the coffin. 'For you,' he murmured. 'You always admired it, my dear Elisa, and now it is yours for ever.'

The priest – who had anyway seemed invisible – had now gone.

The black-dressed official had long since scurried away.

The grave-digger and his assistant had loitered, retreated, vanished.

And yet, at a distance, the young cab driver stood unprotected in the rain, unable to say why he'd stayed there, yet somehow glad the old man wasn't alone. What he *should* have been doing was drumming up trade. Slowing at every street corner and shouting out he was free. Yes, he mused, earning a bloody crust is what he should've been doing, 'stead of hanging around in the largest graveyard in Paris.

Von Wisner coughed as the chill invaded his chest. He knew he was old for his time – 'Old and old-fashioned' – and he sometimes regretted that he'd never kept a diary of his exploits, of the times when he'd *not* been so old. *A full enough life . . . Twenty countries . . . The company of presidents and prostitutes . . . Dancers and diplomats . . . Missionaries and murderers . . . Half the Old World, and half, perhaps, the New . . .*

But in all that time he'd never met a woman like Elisa Lynch.

History would judge her as what? As heroine? As harridan? Well, fine, let history shuffle its papers and reach its verdict. The world to

16

come could see her as it wished . . . though, frankly, to hell with whatever it decided. To the Baron Enrique von Wisner de Morgenstern the woman he'd come to bury had been a friend. No more than that – and let drab, grey historians sort *that* out, if they could – but certainly no less.

To others the russet-haired, green-eyed Elisa had been temptation, salvation; a chirpy, thieving magpie, or a flagstaff jammed firm in the earth.

She had ruined the greedy, and impoverished the ignorant, plucking their purse and laughing at the glandular stupidity of men.

She had also, given her outstanding beauty, razor-sharp wit and flexibility of mind, raised and ruined a nation . . .

Von Wisner leaned on his cane, feeling it sink into the ground. He tugged it free, made his way round the grave, and balanced his six-and-a-half-foot frame to peer at the words on the headstone. Good workmanship, yes. And simple, as he'd asked for.

ELISA ALICIA LYNCH
1835–1886
WIDOW OF FRANCISCO SOLANO LOPEZ

'So there you are,' he murmured. 'The condor ring and the title you always deserved. Never his wife in life, you can now be forever his widow. And with a friend not long in coming, for this icy rain gets to the marrow of my bones.'

PART ONE

Cork: 1847

1

As soon as she heard her parents stirring beyond the partition wall, the girl prepared to face the still-dark day. It was late November, and would not be light for another two hours . . .

Swinging her legs from the narrow, rough-hewn bed, she reached blindly but accurately for one of the sulphur-tipped matches, dragged it across a serrated metal plate, then lighted the small oil lamp on the table beside her. The stench of sulphur mingled with the smell of the crude, black oil. Shadows flickered, and the girl could see frost on the window.

She stood and removed her plain cotton nightdress, naked now but for calico drawers. Tall for her twelve years, she was under-nourished and underweight. Shivering, she pulled on a similar garment, though this at least with a flower-embroidered collar. The ill-fitting floorboards cold underfoot, she snatched at a pair of coarse woollen stockings, a pair of wooden-soled shoes. Finally a shawl, her all-purpose source of warmth. Mended and patched in a dozen places, it was, ironically, more colourful now than when new.

The girl did not linger in the room. She would wash when the chores had been completed, scour her teeth with salt, comb her springy red hair. There'd be plenty of time for that later. The first thing to do was to light the fire in the kitchen, then heat some water so Papa could shave.

Passing her parents' door she called out a greeting, turned to descend the staircase, lifted the cold iron latch and entered the kitchen. Behind her, a second door led through to the parlour, though that room had not been used for more than a year. A second room meant a second fire, and the family were hard-pressed enough to find fuel for one. Besides, the parlour was designed to receive visitors, which meant tea and sweet baked biscuits, a mug of ale or a glass of foreign wine. But all these were pleasures of the past, the parlour itself a museum of memories, best kept closed today.

She put the lamp on the table, then used the flame to light three tallow candles, taking the last to the fireplace. Crouching there, she levelled the ashes in the grate, scooped handfuls of twigs and wood chips from a wicker basket, set them carefully on the glowing embers, then blew slowly, gently till they caught. Practised at her task, she broke pieces of cut, dried peat, scattering them evenly on the fire. When they, too, had begun to burn, she suspended a cauldron of water above the slowly mounting flames.

Her reward was to stay there then, warming herself at her own creation, waiting until her parents came downstairs. An avid reader, she sometimes imagined herself in a distant country, though her dreams were not of wealth or jewelled gowns. All she wished was that the hunger pangs would cease, and her house in that far-off land be always warm . . .

'Good morning to you, Elisa. You sleep the night through?'

'Slept well, Papa. Though you'd best wrap up tight today. There was frost on the glass, did you notice?'

Cavan Lynch nodded, crossing the room to embrace his daughter and steal some heat from the fire. Now forty-five, the quiet-spoken Cavan looked older than his years. At least two stone underweight – though which grown man was not, in this blighted island? – his narrow face was pinched, skin sallow, pale hair fast receding. Never physically dominant, he had earned the post he held through intelligence and a calm, likeable nature. Those who worked with him in the Port of Cork found him level-headed, progressive, and blessed with a certain dry wit. His employers regarded him as reliable, strangely honest in a place where opportunities abounded – in short, a decent man to be Senior Clerk of Shipping Affairs near the mouth of the River Lee.

'I'll set out your razor and soap,' the girl said. 'And please let me try again to hone the blade. I've watched enough times, Papa. I'm sure I could do it right.'

But Cavan Lynch smiled and shook his head. The last time she'd tried, well, her slender fingers had slipped and she'd all but cut through the strop. Yelping with alarm, the girl had then dropped the razor, though it was the curved bone handle that hit the floor, not the blade. 'There's not much I wouldn't trust you to do, young Elisa. But bringing an edge to my razor is one of 'em, may Heaven preserve the man you marry.'

'Very well,' she sniffed. 'Then I'll find myself one with a beard, how's that? Maybe one of your sea captains. As a matter of fact, why don't *you* grow a beard? Then you wouldn't have to shave every morning, and I could stay in bed.'

'I'll tell you why,' a voice murmured from the doorway. ''Cause

22

your father would look ridiculous, my dear, and I won't have him mocked just so *you* can lounge the morning away in the covers. That's a good bright fire you've set. Switch the pots and I'll see what's for breakfast.'

Elisa grinned, and came forward to kiss her mother. Returning to the fireplace to lift the cauldron with a rag, she filled a bowl with hot water for Cavan's shave.

Adelaide Lynch – promising always to see what was for breakfast – made her way to the larder, dipped a ladle into a sack of husky oatmeal, mixed the meal with water, then skimmed the husks from the pot.

They were clinging, even now, to a way of life that had changed.

A year ago they would have had a choice – bacon or herring or simmered potatoes; dense brown bread with butter and cheese; soup, if the weather was cold, as it was today. But the blight had reduced them to a diet they must supplement with lies. There was no more bacon to be had. No more butter or cheese, honey or sugar, no more buttermilk, or fruit or fresh green vegetables.

The wholesale collapse of a single crop had affected everything, and now both Cavan and Elisa pretended not to hear when Adelaide said she'd see what was for breakfast . . .

Just three weeks earlier, Elisa's routine had been different.

She had still left her bed at the sound of her parents' stirring, still lighted the lamp and clambered downstairs to heat water in the cauldron, though when Cavan had shaved she'd taken her place at the shallow stone sink, washing her face and combing her hair, ready to leave for school.

Cavan had much further to go, and left the house before his daughter. But soon after seven, Elisa Lynch followed the selfsame route, stamping along the track that led to Miss Gardiner's General Day School, a mile to the north of the river that flowed through Cork.

She'd attended the school for the past four years, finding friends and making enemies, as any child must.

Encouraged at home by a father who'd been educated in Dublin and Bristol, a mother who'd been born in Vienna, Elisa had shone as the brightest pupil in Miss Gardiner's damp, drab schoolroom.

The teacher had quickly recognized the girl's abilities, though several of the other children disliked the way Elisa paraded her knowledge. She was too clever by half, was the red-haired Lynch.

23

Liked to show them up, so she did, always sighing, she was, as they fumbled with their answers.

The Sullivan brothers had one day pounced on her in the playground, torn off her dress and yelled to know if she thought herself so special now, for she sure 'didn't look no different' from anyone else.

Sometime later, Mary Reardon had accused Elisa of making eyes at the boy she, Mary, one day hoped to marry. 'You think yourself so smart, you Lynch, just 'cause your father's an office man! But all he is, he's just a spindly clerk. Couldn't dig his own peat, or his arms would break! Why'n't you keep away from here, an' leave our lads to us?' She'd then slapped Elisa's face, earning a grin of approval from her friends.

Two years ago, when Elisa was ten, a girl called Biddy O'Brien had joined the class. Shy and uncertain, the diminutive Biddy had been rejected by the Sullivans, scorned by Mary Reardon, bullied by the likes of James Murley and the three O'Donnells. Sensing that Elisa Lynch was also alone, though at the other end of the spectrum, the eight-year-old Biddy had plucked up her courage and sidled onto Elisa's bench, leaving a respectful distance between them. She half expected the girl to wave her away. After all, they had nothing in common, for wasn't Elisa the daughter of a Port Official, whilst Biddy was but the child of a cotter, with three unschooled brothers, a father who drank, a mother who sprayed the air with her incessant coughing?

It astonished the eight-year-old when Elisa said: 'Sit all the way down there and you'll fall off the end. I've seen you on the walk to school, and back. Don't you live in the Kilbreen hamlet?'

'So I do.' Biddy nodded. 'We go different ways at the crossing.'

'No need to whisper. Move in closer. What's it like, Kilbreen?'

Biddy shrugged. 'I ain't much with words. It's just a track, with dwellings along by a stream. Not stone-built, like yours, or this one. I seen yours once . . . Glass in the windows, an' all . . . An' tiles on the roof, like here . . .'

'I'll tell you something,' Elisa murmured. 'Two things, if you want to know them. One is you've got the sum wrong on your slate. The answer's twenty-four. The other is we could come to school together if you want. Meet at the crossing, then go back when the bell strikes noon. How'd that be?'

The younger child had bitten her lip, brought suddenly close to tears. It wasn't that Elisa had yet invited her friendship, but Biddy knew that she could stay on this bench now and have companionship on the lonely walk from the crossing. 'That'd be all right,' she said quietly, licking a finger and changing the answer on the slate. 'I wouldn't mind that at all.'

They had soon become inseparable, Elisa Lynch seeing Biddy O'Brien as a younger sister, someone to be protected, encouraged, her lack of confidence bolstered. If Biddy sometimes failed to grasp the problems Miss Gardiner gave the class, then Elisa would murmur assistance, or shamelessly tell Biddy what answer to chalk on the slate, what response to offer the teacher.

Cavan and Adelaide would probably disapprove, though Elisa could see no wrong in helping a girl who wore clothes that would surely be next year's rags, a girl who lived in a mud-brick cabin, with turf as its roofing, earth and straw and the excrement of animals on the floor, its only furnishings a wooden board that served as a table, a cauldron in which they cooked their endless, meatless soups, and split wooden bowls into which they dipped split wooden spoons . . .

All this Elisa had learned from Biddy's lips, for the child of Kilbreen did not invite the daughter of the Senior Clerk of Shipping Affairs in the Port of Cork to her home.

For her part, Elisa had asked Biddy to the house, though the girl would just smile and say maybe, it sounded nice; perhaps when her mother was better. There was always an excuse, the simple truth being that Biddy was frightened to go.

Yet their friendship continued, though physical closeness ended at the crossing. The division of the road was a daily reminder that Elisa lived in a semblance of comfort, her father paid a regular wage. As for Biddy O'Brien, whose bed was a pile of straw that sucked damp from the ground, hard times had turned to granite. Nationwide, the potato crop had failed, then failed again. And hers was a family – along with hundreds of thousands of other families in Ireland – who relied for their total sustinence on the easily planted, easily nurtured potato.

At the age of eight, Biddy had dutifully spooned the boiled or mashed potato from her bowl.

At the age of ten – with the one pig the O'Briens had owned now slaughtered and salted and eaten – the girl made her weary way from the crossing to the hamlet of Kilbreen, resigned to the fact that the

25

cooking pot would now contain nothing but the gleanings from the hedgerows.

No wonder she felt unable to invite Elisa home.

The potato blight had struck with terrible rapidity. A matter of weeks, a matter of days, in some parts of Ireland in a matter of hours, the broad green leaves withered, the stems collapsed, and digging up the year's crop revealed a putrid pulp. To the skeletal, starving millions, it was as though God, beckoning His angels, had deserted the land; and then, as if the news of this had drifted down to Hell, stirring the Devil, it had brought scaly-winged demons flapping to the surface.

With the Powers of Light departed, the Forces of Darkness had swooped across the unprotected country, searing the crop with their rancid breath, clawing the ground with their poisonous talons; then, swirling away and down between the clefts and fissures of rock, they thrilled to know that such damage had been done, such a range of dying assured.

The potato famine was everywhere. Striking first among the impoverished inland peasants, it encroached upon the villages, isolated the towns, spread its disease to the very cliffs of the island.

It raced throughout the south-west county of Cork, rotting the plants in Mallow and Macroom, Kinsale and Conakilty, Bantry and Kilbreen.

With neither meat nor vegetables, with salt and flour too expensive, cheese and buttermilk but a memory, the tenant farmers, and the cotters who rented an acre or so of their land – all these desperate folk – began to starve.

By September 1847, Miss Gardiner's General Day School class had been reduced from an average of twenty to ten, then eight, then only as many as could be counted on the fingers of a hand. Elisa still came, assisting the scrawny Biddy from the crossing. But the Sullivan brothers had fled their home, and James Murley had died, as had two of the O'Donnells.

Rumour had it that Mary Reardon was walking the banks of the Lee, offering her thirteen-year-old body to sailors from the continent of Europe, and that the boy she had hoped to marry had hanged himself, preferring the rope to the clutching pangs of starvation. Someone else had drowned in a peat bog; others succumbing to typhus or pneumonia.

Elisa Lynch was herself now skinny and ever-hungry, and would rather not have stamped the winter track to Miss Gardiner's school. But Biddy O'Brien needed help on the journey from the crossing: weak and breathless, the younger girl was mutely grateful for the grasp of her friend's slim hand, her thin, encircling arm . . .

Then three weeks ago, in early November, the Inspector of Education had travelled up from the city. On entering the schoolroom, he had scowled at the unoccupied benches, made his way to Miss Gardiner's desk and interrupted the lesson.

'You're teaching a near-empty room, seems to me. There were ten pupils the last time I called, yet all I see now are five. Should have told us that, Miss Gardiner. Should have kept the Education better informed.'

The weary young mistress had attempted to calm him. 'You *must* know,' she murmured, 'these children only come now to eat. The Education allows me a ration of biscuits, and that's really why they're here. You say there used to be ten, and it's true. God knows, there used to be twenty, sometimes more. But surely you'll let me feed these pitiful few who can still find the strength to attend. I implore you, sir. Have we not lost enough of Ireland's offspring to the blight?'

The man sucked his teeth, then glanced round the mildewed schoolroom, hoping he would not catch cold. 'Your plea is well made, Miss Gardiner, and I appreciate your concern. But with three-fourths of your class no longer present, you cannot expect to continue drawing your wages. Nor, indeed, to be granted free fuel and food.'

Wan and depressed, the once-pretty teacher asked if the Inspector intended to close the school.

'I see no other choice,' he told her. 'It pains me to do so for, were I myself married, I'd doubtless have children of my own. But you must understand, Miss Gardiner. The resources of the city are stretched beyond their limits. We've a dozen minor establishments like yours. It simply isn't possible to sustain such places for the sake of a handful who, by your own admission, are only here to keep dry and swallow down biscuits.'

'You make it sound quite cheerful,' the woman retorted. 'Almost festive.'

'Such bitterness does you no credit, though I'll not have you think me heartless. I'm empowered to let you distribute what's left of the oatmeal, and here – here's a full week's money. All this, of course, on the understanding that you close the school today.' Then he nodded at the mistress, winced a smile at the children, turning to

27

call back, 'Leave the keys in the porch, if you will. Someone will be sent . . .'

He was in a hurry to continue his rounds. Miss Gardiner's General Day School was but one of many he had to condemn.

Elisa and Biddy waited for their share of the hard baked oatmeal. The three remaining boys had snatched at the flattened cakes and made for the door, choking and coughing as they crammed their mouths with the food. Given more today than ever before, they promised themselves they'd take some home for their families. But a head full of good intentions was no match for an empty belly.

The girls stayed where they were near the desk, struggling to find words of farewell for the teacher. They heard the school door slam shut behind them, then watched as Miss Gardiner manufactured a smile. 'Well, now. So we're all of us sent on our way. I admit, I feared it might happen, though I did think they'd give us more time. But who are we, after all, to fight the Education?'

'Where will you go?' Elisa asked, Biddy echoing yes, where would Miss Gardiner go.

'To Youghal, I suppose. My mother's there, and I daresay she'd welcome the company. It's no more than thirty miles, and who knows but I'll meet some strapping lad who'll be willing to convey me.' She attempted another smile, though without conviction, too many years spent here in this damp, grey school, the woman aware that her looks had paled, the dream of a lover or husband beyond attainment.

But Elisa Lynch said sure she would. 'Or maybe you'll find a gentleman in Youghal.' Biddy nodded, wheezing as she said: 'An' both come back here, and open the school again.'

Still clutching their oatmeal biscuits, the girls crowded close, pressing against their teacher. 'Of course I'll be back,' she told them. 'With or without a feller I'll be back. And meantime you take care of each other, you hear me?' Then she told them to hurry on home, and not slam the door.

Glancing back along the room, Elisa saw that Miss Gardiner had moved to a shelf where the slates and chalk were kept; she was stacking the slates just so, ready for the next time.

An hour later, the children reached the crossing. They had walked the track together for the better part of two years. The O'Brien girl was now ten, the Lynch girl twelve, and the parting was hard to accept.

They sat for a while on the verge of the road, exchanging silly remembered stories. Then Biddy surrendered to her tears and Elisa held her, promising to visit her in the hamlet of Kilbreen.

'It's not like we're far apart. It's only two miles. We walk that twice a day. You should ask your papa to bring you to the house – how many times have I said so? And I'll ask mine. I might even bring you some ribbons, how'd that be? Now I suppose we'd better get home, like Miss Gardiner told us. Sky's clouding over, and I can't hear half what you say these days for your wheezing!'

Biddy O'Brien agreed, and the two girls waved their drawn-out farewells till the hedgerows intervened.

2

In the weeks that followed the closure of the school, the tracks and byways around Cork became dangerous as starving peasants trudged towards the city, driven from the hinterland by the dual terrors of famine and eviction. Sometimes alone, though more often in groups, they ambushed travellers and stripped them of whatever they possessed. Threats turned to violence, common assault to murder. With the failure of the potato crop, and no foreign enemy to blame, the Irish waylaid the Irish, villagers closing ranks against their neighbours.

Elisa begged to be taken to visit Biddy. Adelaide demurred, but Cavan refused point-blank. 'You know perfectly well I work six days a week at the port. I leave home at dawn, and return with the last of the light. The roads are beset by ever more desperate men. God knows, things are bad enough in the daytime – '

'I'm not asking to go to Kilbreen after dark,' the girl asserted. 'But you're with us all Sunday, Papa. Couldn't we please go one Sunday?'

Cavan sighed. 'Do I need to remind you I spend Sundays here at the table, writing up the accounts for our landlord's estate? It's fortunate for us all that I'm employed on his lordship's behalf, else we'd lose the right to live here. You'll see your friend, I promise you. But not until the roads are better patrolled, and the books written up.'

Elisa was forced to accept her father's refusal. She knew the house stood at the south-east corner of an Englishman's estate, the property of Lord Charles Cassel Natesby. Resident in London and Shropshire, the man was an infrequent visitor to the 32,500 acres he owned in a broad horseshoe encircling Cork. But word was out that Lord Natesby was even now on his way to Ireland, intending to spend Christmas in nearby Carrick Manor. So, yes, the girl could see the accounts must be ready, and that Papa had no time to spare for the two-mile walk to Kilbreen.

As for the roads being dangerous, that too was true; a recent experience still fresh in Elisa's mind.

It had happened – when was it, ten days ago? – when a weak, itinerant beggar rapped on the door. Papa was at work in the port, and Adelaide slipped the bolt, touched by the man's plea for food.

She sent her daughter to mix the beggar a bowl of meal and warm water, then watched in horror as he lurched from the doorway, turning to beckon a dozen others from the isolated track. Gaunt and uncertain, yet armed with sticks, they advanced on the house, Adelaide screaming as she struggled to close the door. Elisa returned along the hallway from the kitchen, dropped the bowl and threw her own frail weight against the wood. As luck would have it – luck they could never count upon again – they managed to turn the key and ram home the bolt, listening then to the rain of maddened blows.

The beggars did not dare break in, staggering away instead towards the city. But who could say that others, even more desperate, wouldn't storm the house, smashing the windows and clambering in, bloody and hungry, crazed beyond all caring?

When Cavan Lynch learned what had happened, he brought a carpenter up from Cork, paying the man twice what the job was worth to make solid, iron-strapped shutters. These were now in place, the parlour dark, the kitchen admitting light from a small, south-facing aperture, though too small for the passage of a man.

It seemed a terrible thing to do, and Cavan felt bowed by the weight of his cruel decision. *Barricade the house against my own people? Deny them meal and water, these folk who have nothing?*

But what if I leave my wife and daughter unprotected? How, in God's name, could I stay at my desk in the port, with my family at the mercy of dull-eyed marauders?

Forgive me or not, Heaven must understand. Bad enough that my women are imprisoned, though at least they'll be safe in their gaol.

Cavan had gone further, and discussed the problem with the merchant captains who brought their bills of lading to his office. They had always thought well of Cavan Lynch, regarding him as a man who wore his position lightly, fair in his dealings, uncorrupted by bribes or the easy profits of his station. If they sometimes smuggled in cognac or wine from France; lace from the Netherlands; rich, sweet sherry from Portugal or Spain – if they did so, they would keep the knowledge to themselves, aware the Senior Clerk would not condone their actions.

He would check their vessels with quiet impartiality, then warn the discovered smugglers to slip anchor and be gone. 'I'll allow you clearance on the next outgoing tide. Otherwise, it's up to you and the Excise.'

A pity, they thought, there weren't a few more like Master Lynch. You knew where you were with him, easygoing though he seemed.

So they had listened to his problem, discussed it amongst themselves, then presented him with a brace of pistols. They assured him it wasn't a bribe, but a damn necessity, so it seemed, if he was to walk the track in safety.

They showed him how to load and prime the handguns, asking if he had fired a pistol before. He told them yes, though the fact was he hadn't, and hoped he never would. Yet common sense made him learn what they taught him, aware as he was that even a clerk might soon be called upon to pull back hard on a trigger.

One of the pistols now lay on a high shelf in the kitchen, the other thrust into a deep flap pocket in Cavan's winter coat. The one on the shelf was ready to fire, should Adelaide ever need it. But his own was not, the shape and bulk sufficient to make him feel he was armed . . .

November rain gave way to the snow of December.

Adelaide Lynch schooled her daughter, opening one of the shutters in the kitchen, though she was careful the hooks were within easy reach should footsteps be heard.

Born in Vienna, the drawn yet still elegant Adelaide Katherina Lynch was at ease in her native language, in Latin and French and, for twenty years past, in English. The daughter of a charming confidence trickster, she had been sent to Bristol at the age of nineteen, not knowing that her father would then write to say he'd been advised to leave Vienna, advised to leave Europe, and would contact her again when the freighter docked – 'Though at which Pacific island is yet to be determined'.

Adelaide had never heard from him again. She had met Cavan Lynch, fallen in love with the slim, gentle Irishman, and returned with him to his birthplace, the city-port of Cork.

There, in the slate-grey house, she had given birth to two boys, now both senior ratings in the British Navy; then a girl, Corinne, who had not much enjoyed her life in the house on Lord Natesby's estate, dreaming instead of a more romantic future.

At the age of sixteen, Corinne had eloped with a Frenchman, a musician, returning with him to Paris. It seemed, from her twice-a-year correspondence, that her husband was much sought after by the orchestras and *conservatoires* of the capital, and that Madame Corinne Barachin could view with disdain the life she had left behind.

No more than six when her elder sister decamped to Paris, Elisa became the *only* child to Cavan and Adelaide, who determined to share all they knew with this, their late-born offspring . . .

No wonder Elisa Alicia Lynch had shone in Miss Gardiner's General Day School. No wonder she had annoyed the Sullivan boys, upset Mary Reardon, found herself alone on a bench until she was joined by the timid Biddy O'Brien.

Born in this rent-free house on the outskirts of Cork, the red-haired, green-eyed Elisa was truly Irish. Her thoughts, however, already stretched beyond the bleak, snow-smudged horizon.

It was she who suggested her mother study the letters again. 'I mean, Mama, she *did* say we could visit her, if we wanted. Said she's got rooms to spare. And surely the people of Paris aren't starving, for don't they live on cakes, and all drink wine?'

Down in the port, the Senior Clerk of Shipping Affairs crouched over his desk, gazing dully at his own spread of papers. The same words seemed to blaze from the documents – 'Import of Indian corn . . . Careful handling of Indian corn . . . Generous gift from the Irish Relief Society of Boston; 220 tons of Indian corn . . .'

All right, he thought, so it's true. Ireland's firmest allies *are* the Americans, and they were among the first to respond to the famine. They've sent Lord knows how many clippers and freighters, sloops like the USS *Jamestown*, still anchored within sight of the office, and most of them bearing this gift we don't yet know how to handle, this flint-hard Indian corn. Generous indeed, but they might as well send us pebbles for the beach.

Also known as maize, this American foodstuff had been loaded aboard in New Orleans and Galveston, the grain unmilled, the assumption being that the Irish would grind it themselves.

But the Irish did things differently. *Their* staple diet was the lumper potato, dug with a spade, then boiled in a pot. The climate wasn't right for flinty corn, and they didn't have the mills, the grinding wheels, the blades. The well-meaning Americans were sending parasols to the Arctic; fishing rods to the Sahara.

But the problem didn't end there, for Indian corn travelled badly, with a tendency to overheat on the voyage. The friction of the husks would cause it to smoulder; the juice steamed out from the grains. At the end of its six, eight, ten-week crossing, the corn had to be off-loaded without delay, cooled and dried, turned and sifted, raked and cooled again. Some seventy hours of careful attention were needed before the combustible grain could be safely stored.

Even then, it was still inedible, shrinking and growing harder by the day.

Cavan Lynch pushed the documents aside, groaned and straightened his spine. There was nothing more he could do today, at least not here in the office. The sky was heavy with impending snow, and his team of clerks had asked if they might leave a half-hour early. He had nodded and sent one of them to alert the driver of the outside-car, their conveyance along the river road to the city.

Instructing another to extinguish the lanterns and lock the door, Cavan left the chilly wooden office, to make his rounds of the night guard.

Exchanging a greeting with the muffled men who stood beside braziers in the cold, it seemed odd and contradictory that their task was to remain there all night, breaking ice that might form in the buckets placed along the quay, the water ready in case one of the warehouses burst into flame, thanks again to the self-combusting Indian corn.

Left to me, Cavan thought, I'd dump the stuff in the Lee.

He remembered something he'd read in the *Cork Examiner*, a journalist's wry comment on the problem: 'We accept America's gift in the spirit it was sent, yet would call on a Higher Power than even that spry nation, so we'll learn how to turn their stones into bread, and their applejack into whiskey.'

Yet better America's effort than England's.

Comfortable in London, the man in charge of the so-called Relief Programme for the Irish, the Permanent Head of the Treasury, Charles Edward Trevelyan, had already, so it seemed, grown weary of the problem. Trust the Irish to complain that their gifts weren't wrapped in pretty paper . . . That they'd neither the mills to grind the corn, nor the knowledge to build the mills . . .

Fuming at what he saw as apathy and ingratitude, he wrote to one of his officials: '. . . Charity must not be made an *agreeable* way of life'.

Awaiting Cavan's return, Adelaide and Elisa sat together near the low peat fire, taking Corinne's letters one by one from the table, then holding them to the light of the small, unshuttered window.

'She does rather boast,' Elisa remarked. 'I don't much like her tone.'

'Well, she's met with success,' Adelaide said gently. 'Married a fellow she loves – and a talented one, by all accounts – and they're both of them doing fine. You're not to be jealous. Your sister is, after all, ten years older than you.'

Elisa shrugged, reaching for one of Corinne's more recent letters. 'It just seems to me she's talking down her nose, is all. Listen to this.

' "We've had a remarkable Autumn here, Jean-Pierre and m'self. He's performed in several concerts, more than my memory retains, and is ever so well respected. As for me, I continue to lay out designs for the finest *couturiers*, and was just last week presented to a relative of His Majesty, Louis-Philippe. I curtsied nicely and was told she approves of my work. *Quel succès!*" '

'She's enjoying her moment of triumph,' Adelaide murmured. 'Wouldn't you be pleased if you'd stitched some fine garment, then been complimented – ?'

'Why would *I* stitch it?' Elisa queried. 'What *I'd* have is someone make the gown for *me*.'

She found another letter, and said again, 'Listen. "*Les enfants vont bien*. Both girls speak perfect French, and are pretty as a picture. Not nearly as dumpy as Elisa when she was their age!" '

Adelaide reached to comfort her youngest child. 'It's a reason for going to Paris,' she said. 'We'll buy cakes the moment we step ashore in France. Cakes and good, wholesome food. Build you up before we get to the capital, and then you can show her how truly pretty you are.'

'I'd need a new dress,' Elisa said quickly. 'Something in green. I think I'd look well in green.'

Her mother nodded; where was the harm in allowing Elisa her dreams? She said green seemed right; green would contrast nicely with the russet of her hair.

'I think so too,' the child nodded. 'And a bonnet with ribbons, the kind as would stir in the breeze.'

Adelaide smiled and agreed again, watching Elisa now upright in her chair, skinny hands moving to button the unbought dress, settle the unbought bonnet . . .

'Fetch me the pen and ink, if you will. And those sheets of paper your father brought back from the city. We'll compose a letter together, how's that? Then see if Papa agrees.'

'Oh, he will, you bet.' Elisa grinned. 'He'll find passage on the

soonest ship, then buy us both gowns and bonnets and, well, everything! He'll get himself a job in the Port of Paris – hope there is one
– and you and me, we'll just go around in our gowns, nibbling now
and then on sugary cakes! You know what, Mama? I'm really going
to try and be nice to Corinne.'

Seated three on one side, four on the other on the outward-facing
benches, the clerks huddled deep in their capes and coats, sleeves
hanging loose over scrawny wrists, their gloves now too large for
their hands.

All of them had lost hair in the past twelve months. Most had lost
teeth. Three complained of deafness, whilst one of them – who dared
not admit it for the sake of his job – feared he was going blind.

A year ago they had sung songs and bandied stories, twisting round
to clutch at the backrest of the bench. Someone had suggested they
call themselves The Carolling Choristers of Cork. Maybe give concerts, why not? They were good enough, weren't they, singing along
on the cart?

But a year ago the world had been more cheerful, the outside-car
bearing twelve, where now there were seven.

These literate young men had paid the same price as the pupils of
Miss Gardiner's school, two of them victims of typhus, two others of
pneumonia. The fifth had watched his wife curl aside in bed and die;
then he had walked from the graveside, murmuring his prayers, and
drowned himself in the Lee.

There were no songs tonight on the outside-car. Nothing but the
rasp of breath as the clerks inhaled the chill winter air, coughed it
out, or turned to spit the dreadful yellow bile that congested their
lungs. Jolted along on the one-horse wagon, they wondered how long
they themselves could survive, privileged as they were to have a job,
and money enough to keep them this side of starvation.

At the second halt in the city, Cavan Lynch dismounted from the
cart. The conveyance would go on alongside the river, though the
Senior Clerk was now left to climb the flight of icy steps that led to
his homeward road, the road which then became no more than a
rutted track.

He wished his clerks Godspeed and good night, gloved hands
raised in weary acknowledgement, the outside-car jouncing on.

His dark woollen coat changing colour beneath the flecks of evening snow, he pulled down the brim of his low-crowned hat, hitched his collar and started to tackle the long, steep climb.

. . . Something had to be done about the corn. Ditch it in the river, or find some way to mill it . . . Contact the bakeries, the smithies, the nearby army barracks . . . Appeal to them all, explaining the need to shatter the grains and somehow release the flesh of the maize from its iron-hard husks . . .

No longer fit, he paused for breath, leaning on the handrail of the steps. Gusts of wind brought snow from the heights, scorning his ability to climb. Yet Cavan Lynch had done this six times a week, summer and winter for twenty-five years. So what you do now, he told himself, is take the steps slowly, ten at a time, then pause for breath and turn away from the gusts. Then another ten and another pause. The days are long gone when you'd race to the top, energy fuelled by good red meat or fresh white fish.

Ahead of him lay an ill-defined street, beyond it a mile of petering road, its final building the now deserted schoolhouse. After that was the track he travelled every day, the track Elisa had travelled with Biddy, the rutted width framed by briars and hawthorns, skeletal and black against the snow.

Releasing his grip on the rail, he set off through the bite of winter, pleased to be on the level.

Fifty yards from the head of the steps, three men lurched from cover. The skittering snow was bright enough to show him the men were armed, this one with a cooking knife, those two with clumsy clubs.

Cavan halted, his heart again racing, the innocent clerk admitting the onrush of fear.

He peered at the men, glanced back at the slippery steps, and heard himself mutter, 'Get home before it's dark.' It seemed suddenly important not to run.

Without weighing the risks, he dug in the pocket of his coat, hauled out his unloaded pistol, and levelled it at their heads. 'First one who comes against me's blown to the ground! And don't think I ain't got a second, primed to fire!'

A foolish and empty challenge, though they weren't to know it. The pistol was real enough, and the man was coming forward –

The trio backed off, muttered curses wreathed in the vapour of their breath. *So they'd wait for the next one . . . A woman, maybe, or a man with nothin' but a single, hickory cane . . .*

37

Swinging the gun, Cavan cleared the trap. Then he hurried on, turning from time to time to make sure he wasn't followed.

Grateful for the gift of the pistol, he was nonetheless pleased it hadn't been loaded, else maybe he'd have fired it in panic. And, by doing so, killed a man he knew. For the one with the cooking knife was the son of a nearby farmer, a lad he'd often stopped to chat with, a once-cheerful youngster who'd offered Elisa a kitten, shrugging as the child had squealed her thanks.

It's a hell of a thing, Cavan thought, that kittens have now come to knives.

Having skirted the side of the house, he rapped on the kitchen door. No ordinary knock, but part of the new-fangled code he'd learned in the port; a recent invention of the American, Samuel Finlay Morse. A single tap – then another – then two more in quick succession, spelling out the letter L.

Adelaide had smiled when he first suggested such a theatrical precaution. 'Don't you think I know your voice well enough after twenty-five years?'

'That's not the point. With the shutters closed – Well, suppose I'd been waylaid near the house by men who were intent on gaining entry. They'd expect me to use a key, or failing that call out in the normal manner. This way at least, with Morse's code, you'll know it's safe to open up.'

'It's an odd way for a man to come home,' she remarked, Elisa then pestering to be taught her own name in the dots and dashes of the code.

But there was nothing to smile about tonight, as Cavan recounted the incident near the steps. It just served to underline the need for caution.

Taking her husband's wet coat, Adelaide hung it on a peg near the fire. Elisa fetched him a concoction of herbs and hot water, and the foul-tasting drink dulled the ache in his limbs.

'Thank God you had the pistol,' Adelaide said. 'I pray you'll carry it loaded from now on. Though perhaps it won't be for much longer, for we've something else in mind, Elisa and I.'

Nursing the thick stone mug, Cavan Lynch felt the bitter infusion relax him. Hunched on a chair, he said: 'Tell me . . . Are we to join your father on his far Pacific island . . . ?'

'For all his cunning, I doubt he's still alive,' she murmured. 'But part of what you say is true. Our salvation lies abroad.' She told him

38

then of the letters she and Elisa had spread on the table; the summer and winter missives from Corinne. She reminded him of their daughter's offer – 'How we can, if we wish, stay with her in Paris. It seems she has rooms to spare, furnished and waiting.'

Cavan glanced up, and his wife continued quickly. 'It's surely the thing to do, my love. Get Elisa away from here while she's still in some health. And you, yourself, for you cannot climb those steps every night, weary as you are, and at constant risk from brigands.' Standing gaunt near the fireplace, Adelaide gazed at her husband, his balding head dipped low. 'Full winter is not yet upon us,' she added, 'and hunger has already turned to starvation. You must know – you *do* know – that the worst is still to come.'

'I don't dispute . . . But it isn't that simple. How can I just – ?'

'How can you what? Leave your desk? Resign your position? Leave his lordship's accounts uncompleted? I'll tell you how – look at me, Cavan, look at me long and hard, then look at Elisa. And after that I'll bring you the mirror, and you can look at yourself!'

Her voice had hardened, urgency sharpening her tone. Cavan raised his head in obedience, then blinked as if struck, seeing his wife and daughter with a sudden, terrible clarity. *God, but the elegant Adelaide looked old. And Elisa so scrawny, her red hair lank, her once-vivacious expression shrunk and pallid.*

He had no wish at all to look at himself. Adelaide alone was a sufficient reflection of the truth.

He heard himself speak, the words tangled in confusion. 'Allow me a few days . . . Things to arrange . . . One of the clerks will have to be promoted . . . And most out-going ships are already crowded, bound for the Americas . . . I'll need a few days to secure us passage across to France . . . and finalize the accounts, pass over all the ledgers . . . A few days at least, for I can't just abandon – I can't just up and off.'

Elisa sank down to sit at her father's knee. Adelaide moved to stand beside him, her hands on the tight-strung sinews of his shoulders. 'We are not going to flee,' she told him. 'You're a decent man, and it's not within you to flee. You've held your post with honour, and I wouldn't wish to go till you were ready. All I'd ask now – May I write to Corinne and say we accept her offer?'

His wife's fingers were as bone on his own bony shoulders. Elisa's upward gaze was that of a green-eyed cat, trapped in the thorns, and begging to be released.

39

May God forgive me, Cavan thought, that I've allowed them to come to this.

'A few more days. But yes. Write the letter and I'll see it sent on the next available boat. I've been too nailed down by vanity, it seems – '

'Not vanity. By loyalty, maybe, to the county where you were born. And all those responsibilities that are part and parcel of your job.' She kneaded his neck, and smiled, remembering other times, when the touch of her fingers had aroused him so wonderfully well.

Then the twelve-year-old Elisa said: 'When we get there, to France, will you buy me some cakes? And a dress and a bonnet? Mama and I have discussed this, so I'll look my best for Corinne. And what's-his-name, her husband.'

Cavan Lynch shook his head, though with pleasure at his daughter's greedy demand. Leave the port and the house and take passage to France, and the rest of it seemed easy. The girl would have her cakes, and her gown, and maybe, in time, recover her fine good looks.

3

The coach had been due sometime in the morning. But it was not until almost two in the afternoon that the look-out rode back to the manor to say it was coming.

The servants and staff were hastily assembled on the steps, the women shivering in their thin black uniforms, the footmen and butlers protected in livery and gloves. A south wind carried snow up from Kinsale. The employees of Carrick Manor prayed the look-out had been right.

And then they could see it, a lumbering carriage drawn by six plunging horses, the driver and guard huddled on the high, blanketed box. Encrusted with snow, the distant figures seemed shapeless, inhuman, the horses snorting clouds of steam as they trampled up the rise towards the manor.

The staff were drawn to attention, the major-domo reminding the men to bow with precision, the women to bob without slipping on the ice. 'Anyone lets me down, they'll be packed an' away by night-fall.' Then he took up his position at the foot of the swept stone steps.

The coach gave a final lurch and came to a halt. The major-domo waved one of the footmen forward to open the door, but an angry voice barked, 'Leave it! Stand away!' Then a heavily built man slammed down on the catch, pushed at the door and kicked it with his boot, releasing the outside step.

Lord Charles Cassel Natesby descended to the snow.

'It's a pleasure to see you again, my lord. Though we'd hoped you'd be here sooner.'

'Then we're all in close agreement,' snapped Natesby, clearly in a foul humour. He stamped the snow, as if the ground itself should have been swept clear, turning to help his wife from the leather-lined carriage. 'Come gently, my dear. We'll soon have you settled in comfort. It's all been a bloody pig of a journey. And I'll see heads roll for it, don't you fret. But it's over now, so catch my hand – well, catch it, woman – and it's into the warm with us all.'

'I can't say I feel my best,' Lady Natesby wavered. 'All that jolting, and then the wheel . . . I do believe I should go straight up to my room . . .'

41

'We'll put you where you like,' Natesby said curtly, glaring with irritation as another voice bellowed from the far side of the coach.

His nineteen-year-old son, Robert Grenville, had debouched and was yelling at the driver to go easy with the baggage. 'And mind that fowling-piece! Cost a fortune, that did! A damn sight more than *you've* earned, or ever will!'

The bullish, leaden-faced Natesby assisted his wife up the steps. The servants were ignored, though the major-domo was summoned by Robert Grenville: 'We've a few scores to settle with the driver here, and those who hired us the coach.'

'I should really see to his lordship, her ladyship, Master Grenville. Perhaps, in a while or so – '

'Good Christ,' the young man said, 'don't you think they know their way? Now listen to me, whatever-your-name-is. We weren't but twenty miles from Lismore, where we spent last night, when this bloody contraption shed a wheel. Can you imagine how long it took those idiots on their box to tap on a new one? *Nothing less than two hours!*'

'Seems excessive,' the major-domo murmured, 'though with you there to help them – '

'With me there to *what?* On a country track, with the sky itself frozen? You imagine we'd leave the carriage, and scramble around in the mire?'

'All I meant, Master Grenville – lighten the coach? Just while repairs were effected?'

Natesby's son dismissed the suggestion as stupid. Then he told the man who controlled Carrick's household that demands and claims must be sent to Lismore, the cost of hiring the carriage reimbursed, and punitive sums imposed for the hardship they'd suffered. 'My father wants them to know they're a damn shoddy outfit, and must pay for not checking the wheel.'

More than twice Grenville's age, the long-jawed major-domo smothered a sigh. 'I heard the Lady Elizabeth remark on the jolting. So the track wasn't always smooth?'

'From Lismore to here? Worst stretch of road I've ever travelled! Hip bones felt they was comin' out of their sockets. It's a wonder the roadside's not littered – ' He stopped abruptly, realizing the Natesbys had lost their case.

The major-domo said nothing. Leaving the slim and arrogant Robert Grenville to chew his fleshy lip, the master of the household

42

walked round the carriage and up the steps to the forty-room mansion.

An hour later, the servants and staff were all about their business; the Natesby family grouped in the drawing room, Elizabeth deciding her own room upstairs would have been too lonely. Better to stay down here on a couch, her legs draped with a rug, sherry and biscuits to hand.

Wealthy enough to own more than thirty thousand acres of County Cork, a string of thoroughbred horses, herds of cattle and flocks of sheep, Lord Charles Cassel Natesby voiced his deep dislike of the Irish.

Aware that he would one day inherit the property, with its dominant manor, its outlying villages and hamlets and isolated houses, Robert Grenville nodded agreement.

Elizabeth sipped her sherry and nibbled her biscuits, convinced the men were right, else why would they say it? After all, would Charles accuse the Irish of being lazy and apathetic if they weren't? And would Grenville say they were starving out there, 'cause they didn't know a potato from the toes on their feet, unless there was truth in the statement? Quite funny that, toes and potatoes; she giggled at his joke.

His own flask of whiskey within reach, Lord Natesby said he hoped the journey from London would prove worth it. 'A bloody pig of a crossing on the ferry, that's for sure. And I didn't take much to the general accommodation, coachin' across from Wexford. You'd think our own friends were running short too, the little they gave us to eat. And their conversation's dried to dust; famine here, and famine there; rents not paid, and stories told as would make a statue weep. I'll be glad to see our bailiff. Learn if things are as sad and sorry here.'

The arrogant, full-lipped Grenville amused them with a story of the cleric and the prostitute. The characters might have come from anywhere, but Grenville made them Irish, earning a belched-out laugh from his father, a titter from Lady Elizabeth. *Well, there you are . . . So typical . . .*

Then the major-domo knocked on the rosewood door, entered the drawing room and told Lord Natesby the bailiff was waiting in the library. 'The fire's unlit in there, my lord, though I took the liberty of setting a few candles. I didn't know how long you'd care to receive him.'

'Send in one of the maids,' Natesby commanded. 'Tell her to put a match to the fire. I've personally no time for the man, but there's things I need to hear. Give him some port. Make him feel welcome. Tell him I'll be along soon.' He glanced at Grenville, assuring his son that the bailiff would know if the journey *had* been worth it. 'And let's hope to God it has been, or we've all been jounced for nothing.'

White when she'd entered the manor, Elizabeth now showed the high bright flush of drink. She extended her glass to Grenville, asking if he'd 'Enact the gentleman. Though no more than a hard-travelled lady deserves. As much as you deem is right.' She blinked vacantly at him, then smiled as he filled the glass.

Charles Cassel Natesby turned his blocky face away, pretending not to see. His thoughts were anyway centred on the bailiff's report; in hoped-for obedience to the orders he'd sent from London.

If the Irishman had fulfilled his duties, then all would be well with the Englishman's estate. If not, then Lord Natesby would set more heads rolling than a hay-cart could ever contain . . .

They were closeted together for an hour. The ruddy-complexioned bailiff did most of the talking, his report speared through by occasional, piercing questions from his leaden-hued master.

'Are you sure the stocks are safe? And sealed?'

'They are, my lord. And well away from the channel.'

'And departure fixed? You say things are safe, but how will you see them transported – ?'

'I meant to say the *main* channel. There is, however, another. What it does, my lord, it runs close behind – '

'Spare me the details,' Natesby dismissed. 'If you've done your job right, then we've nothing to concern us. The stuff will be taken out as arranged, and I'll see you well rewarded.' He grunted to back his promise, gazed round the library at the books he'd never read, then motioned the bailiff to the door. 'You'll report to me again when the stocks are gone, Master Conor. At which time I'll see you well recompensed.'

Each man big and broad-shouldered, though Natesby's skin had been spared the whiplash of branches, the dagger thrust of thorns, the scars of the country, they bade each other good night.

The bailiff set out on the moonlit descent to his house, as Charles Cassel Natesby crossed the hallway and banged open the rosewood doors of the drawing room, happy to tell his wife and son the bloody pig of a journey had been worth it. The produce of the estate would earn them a profit. Orders had been followed. The Irishman had done what he'd been told.

'I still think we should claim our money back from Lismore,' Grenville insisted. 'Tell 'em the wheel spun off on the flat. Blame it on the coach.'

His father stepped forward, cuffing the young man with a mixture of severity and affection. 'Why do you always think small, my dear Grenville? How can Lismore possibly matter, with our incomes from Cork assured?'

'Don't bully the boy,' Elizabeth appealed. 'I count on him to top me up.'

Increasingly concerned about the welfare of her school-friend, Elisa begged to be taken to Kilbreen. But Adelaide now sided firmly with Cavan, reminding the girl of the dangers that lurked in the hedgerows.

'Oh, please! We could take the pistol Papa left for us. I must see how Biddy is. She's the only friend I've got! I won't go to France till I've visited the hamlet!'

There were tears and tantrums, and a growing determination to make the two-mile journey . . . The girl was convinced that Cavan would return from the port one evening and tell them to pack. '*I know we've had no reply from Corinne, but it's becoming daily more difficult to get passage out of Cork. If we don't go soon . . . Anyway, I've secured us tickets aboard a packet that leaves on tomorrow afternoon's tide. We may each take one small valise.*'

Inventing her father's words, and ignoring the fact that the Senior Clerk of Shipping Affairs would never leave in such haste, Elisa panicked. She waited until Cavan had left for work and her mother was in the kitchen, airing the night-damp bedding. Then she raided Adelaide's sewing basket, stealing scraps of coloured cloth and lengths of ribbon. These would be her gifts to Biddy O'Brien.

She baulked at stealing food, though what was there to take but a bag of oatmeal, a sack of poorly milled flour? Yet even if they'd had more to offer, the girl knew she would never have robbed her mother's pantry. *So all I can hope to do is cheer Biddy with these few bright patches.*

A little later, when Adelaide was upstairs, Elisa pulled on a pair of thick-soled boots, wrapped herself in her cheap, hooded cloak and slipped the bolts on the kitchen door. Consumed by her desire to see Biddy, she was unaware of the gravity of her action. Not only had she ventured from the safety of the house, leaving Adelaide to cry out with alarm at her daughter's absence, but she'd left the door unbolted, her mother at the mercy of marauders.

Careless of the risks to herself, Elisa Lynch stamped awkwardly through the snow towards the crossing.

Less than half a mile from the house, and struggling for balance on the unseen underlay of ice, the girl heard voices drifting from the snow clouds to the south.

She clambered on to the road verge, then down into the ditch beside the hedgerow. Cold and frightened, she already regretted her foolish, well-meaning attempt to visit the hamlet. Her father had been right, of course, for who else in the family ventured along the track every morning, stumbling back at dusk? If Cavan said his wife and daughter were better off within the prison of their small, shuttered house, then who was Elisa to countermand his orders?

It occurred to her now – *I left the door unlocked!*

And the voices were louder, low and ill-tempered, as tall, swaying shapes emerged from the snowy mist. 'Oh, please Heaven, they don't see me,' she whimpered. 'I promise I'll never again – '

'Over there. Ain't that one of 'em? I tell you, Captain, they're linin' the whole bloody road!'

The voice had a coarse English accent, the shapes now revealed as soldiers on horseback, the riders muffled and buttoned against the cold. The one who had spoken jabbed a gauntleted hand at Elisa, the captain telling the man to pitch her in. 'Another three and we'll call it a day, eh, Sergeant? Drop them off at the poor-house, then get on back to the warmth. But make a proper search of the ditch, if you will. They've a way of crouching like rabbits.'

Elisa stared. The first pair of riders was followed by two others, then by a narrow, canopied wagon. Insufficient leather curtains slapped with the movement of the cart, snow scudding in on its piteous passengers, all of them children, all of them huddled in rags.

The sergeant sent his horse trampling close to the verge. 'Well now, missy, you seem better dressed than most. Borrowed the cloak from your sister, eh? So where's the others?'

'Others? What others? I don't understand.'

The soldier leaned down, his pock-marked face flecked with snow. 'Now listen, girl. We ain't got no time to play games. Either you dig out the rest of your brattish family – though we only take children – or we leave you to starve. Leave you to freeze. Leave you to your

46

own bloody kinfolk.' He spoke without emphasis, his tone hard and level and unfeeling. He could not care a damn if the girl came aboard or not. His job was to patrol the roads, shoot anyone who carried a weapon, and fill the cart with all the starving brats he happened to see. Or leave them snivelling in the ditches. Up to them.

'Get a move on,' the captain snapped. 'England's doing enough for these people, God knows. Put her in and have done with it. I've a card game waiting, and how will I deal the pasteboards with frozen fingers?'

By now their intention was clear, and Elisa said no. 'I don't need to go with you. My parents – We've a house – I'm grateful you'd save us – ' Then she backed away, glancing now at the angry riders, now at the gaunt, collected children in the cart. Their eyes streamed with tears, mucus running from their noses, their skinny shoulders quaking with the cold that cut round the curtains.

One of her own chilled limbs gave way beneath her, and Elisa fell to the ground. Then she forced herself up again, pleading with the driver of the cart to wait – 'Not for me! But here! Here's some ribbons and stuff! They were meant for a friend, but these other children – surely they could share them?'

The sergeant clicked his tongue with irritation, barring her way with his horse. The driver of the wagon lashed his mounts into action, the captain kicking in angrily with his heels. They were really unbelievable, the Irish. All the time offering silly little presents, yet with dwellings you wouldn't put your servants in, and a diet of food you wouldn't give your dogs. They really had a lot to learn, the Irish. Amusing enough with their songs and that, but otherwise terribly backward.

The patrol went on, the children carried still further away from the poor-house.

Elisa looked at the swatch of coloured fabric in her hand, then thrust it across her eyes. Blindfolded, alone on the winter road, she wept for the children, wept with shame at her own foolhardy venture, wept at the way she'd left the house unlocked.

She turned to find Adelaide standing beside her with with one hand raised as if about to slap her, the other outstretched as if to lead her gently home.

'Next Sunday,' Adelaide murmured. 'Your father will take you then. It's not really the time to make promises, but I'll see you're taken to Biddy's next Sunday.' She watched as Elisa let the coloured scraps fall, and felt the girl's skinny frame press hers for comfort and forgiveness. Then mother and daughter, silent and thoughtful, trudged home through the snow.

4

Aware that he would soon be resigning from his post, Cavan Lynch decided to make a final inspection of the warehouses that lined the quay. A task that had, since his promotion to Senior Clerk, been his special responsibility.

In keeping with the Orders of the Port, he had checked them at the beginning of every month, his hips weighed down by a broad, buckled belt, hooks riveted to the leather, each hook bearing a bunch of heavy, iron keys.

It was a thankless job, this verification and updating of the stores. It should really have been done by the Excise men, though everyone knew how they hated to get dirty, strutting about in their smart blue uniforms, cockade-trimmed hats and cleverly pleated sashes. Prowl around in the dust and grime of a warehouse, and they'd emerge with their plumes wrapped in webs, tasselled boots scuffed, uniforms snagged or torn. It wouldn't do at all for the port's vain peacocks to besmirch their finery. So it was left to Cavan to make the rounds, for all the world like a music-hall gaoler.

A double row of dark, tarred warehouses loomed above the river. Fixed wooden gibbets extended from the ends of the buildings, pulleys suspending ropes that would hold the incoming barrels and bales. Thirty feet high, the sheds were a maze of ramps and balconies, partitioned storerooms, passageways and shelves. The wooden dividers could be dismantled, then stacked against the walls, space rented by the cubic yard.

Shadowed by the warehouses, the quay was littered with fishing nets, horse-drawn sledges, caulking pots that bubbled on braziers, the stinking black smoke slapped this way and that by the wind. Shouts of command were answered with sullen grunts of obedience, the air filled with curses, warnings, the snatch of a popular song.

Sailors walked sure-footed along the bouncing, unrailed gang-planks; soldiers patrolled the cobbles, bayonets screwed to the muzzles of their rifles; civilians clamoured at the gates, pleading for food, a strip of canvas with which to make a shelter, an open-deck ticket to America.

It was bedlam now, and Cavan preferred not to see or hear what was happening, his own home shuttered, his workplace enclosed by solid, protective fences.

He checked the contents of Warehouse One, pleased to see they conformed to the grey paper docket. As did Two. And Three. Four and Five, too, both rented by government agents, the sheds now filled with Indian corn. And the husky grain sitting cool . . .

He started on the second row, these towering sheds set further back from the river. It was colder here, in the snow-filled alley between the weather-boarded buildings, all shouts and curses smothered by the keening of the wind. He consulted his papers, studying the Declaration of Contents for Warehouse Six.

'Eighteen Gross Red Brick Tiles. Fourteen Tons Construction Bricks: Red/Grey. Six Tons Flooring Tiles: Plain/Spanish/Speckled. Thirty sacks Grouting. Five Cases Masonry Trowels, Stone Chisels, Levelling Cords and Chalk.'

He removed his gloves, fumbled for the key, told himself a glance would be sufficient. I'm not here to *count* the tiles. Not here to *weigh* the bricks. There are four more sheds to be checked after this, and the cold's damn near biting my bones as it is. So let's take a look and get on.

He struggled to fit the key in the lock, twisted it hard, then removed the hasp, pushing against the door. As he did so, he dragged a scarf across his face, masking his nose and mouth. Brick dust could leave a man choking for days, the tiny shards embedded in his throat.

Yet no red dust was stirred by his entry, and the Senior Clerk false-footed with surprise. He frowned and went forward, the winter light finding its way through a hundred chinks and knot-holes in the walls. Then he stumbled again, the scarf falling free, his intelligent eyes blinking stupidly at the wonderland of Warehouse Number Six.

The building contained no tiles, no bricks, no sacks of grouting, tools or cords or chalk. What it *did* contain – and these he could see immediately – were sides of beef and mutton, encrusted with salt and suspended, row upon row, from long iron bars . . .

And heavy slate chests, stamped with the warning LEAVE AS BE, and below the warning 'Butter (500 blocks)' or 'Cheese (100 blocks)' or 'Salted Bacon; Pork Bellies; Joints and Trimmings' . . .

Moving deeper into the shed, Cavan Lynch discovered pyramids of sacked-and-stacked oatmeal, enough to feed every tenant family in the region. He saw bins of wheat, vast wooden pens heaped with turnips, boxes of salted mackerel, a second row of butter chests . . . More cheese . . .

Foolish thoughts ran through his mind. *It's the Government's doing –* *Christmas approaching – They've decided to show some mercy. It's been shipped* *in secretly as a gift for the people – Stored here ready for general distribution.*

A fine dream, and he clung to it for a moment, until reason tore it away.

These were not the generous imports from England or Europe or the distant American continent. These were the produce of Ireland herself, famed for her cheese and butter, the mackerel trawled from the fishing grounds off Cape Clear. The corn was a local tillage crop, unaffected by the blight and grown only on the big estates, where extensive acreage made it worth the yield.

As for the beef, the pork, the mutton – these too were part of the richness of County Cork. *More precisely, the part that formed a horseshoe* *round the city.*

Stand here till you freeze, Cavan told himself, but you cannot deny the truth. Nothing in this warehouse was ever grown or raised abroad. Nor is it intended for the starving population. It's been stocked here in secret, ready to be exported, a cornucopia with its trumpet-mouth facing the sea . . .

He forced himself to inspect the remaining sheds. No more than an hour's work, for their contents matched the dockets. It was only Warehouse Six that had failed to conform.

Stamping snow from his boots, he re-entered the office, then spent a further hour consulting chits and invoices, tallies and ledgers, the mass of papers that serve as the wrappings of commerce. One of the clerks aproached him with a query, and was brusquely told to find the solution himself. 'If not, then leave it till tomorrow. And don't disturb me again.' The clerk withdrew, exchanging a glance with his colleagues. Don't often see Master Lynch so ill-tempered. Must've had a run-in with the Excise.

Little by little, Cavan's suspicions were confirmed. Various documents were missing, though a careful study of the Shipping List revealed that meat, butter and cheese were to be loaded aboard a Norwegian vessel on 16th December, less than two weeks from now. Her holds floored with ice, the *Ottar* was destined for Southampton, the Port of London, the Belgian port of Ostend.

The cereals were to be shipped a few days later, along with the mackerel and turnips.

Examining the papers, Cavan peered at the stamps and seals, some of them lightly inked, others blurred, the signatures all but indecipherable. Names written in haste? Well, perhaps so. Or

51

scrawled in the hope that they'd pass unremarked, the Senior Clerk of Shipping Affairs not recognizing the hand.

But he did, for he now knew what to look for.

The smeared seals of Lord Charles Cassel Natesby, the Englishman whose estate supported cattle and sheep and pigs, game and poultry, grew root crops and cereals – and, aside from these, a stable of hunters; an aviary of fine, exotic birds.

Who else could have stocked Warehouse Six if not Lord Natesby? Who else owned so much of the county, his products untouched by the blight? Oh, yes, it was Natesby's cornucopia, yet Natesby's right to dispose of it as he wished. If he preferred to ship it abroad, to be sold at a profit, he was free to do so. Morally shameful, maybe, but legally justified, and no more than a matter for the Englishman's own conscience.

But Natesby could not have arranged all this from his town house in London, his country house in Shropshire. He needed a man on the spot, an Irishman he could trust; and who better than his steward and bailiff, the ruddy-faced Conor?

The man who'd found the money to send Cavan to study in Dublin and Bristol. The man who'd appealed to Natesby to let the newlyweds have the small, stone-and-slate house on the corner of his estate.

The Bailiff Conor – Conor Egan Lynch. Cavan's uncle.

The truth was undeniable. Scrawled though they were, the signatures were those of Conor Lynch. Here, on this form; there, on that. Renting the warehouse. Countersigning the payment until the end of December. *But signing for bricks and tiles, sacks of grouting and tools.* And not ever admitting that the great tarred shed would contain the food all the tenants and cotters would need to survive through the winter . . .

Sharing the same legal cloak as his master, Conor Lynch had stayed within the law. But the knowledge that one of his family had seen fit to collaborate with a foreign, absentee landlord, to accept Natesby's money, and ignore the country-folk who were dying around him – the bitter awareness of this was too much for Cavan to take.

His clerks gaped in alarm as ledgers and papers were swept from the desk, spewing across the floor. Leather-bound files broke their wings as they hit the boards, smaller documents fluttering like feathers.

'You,' Cavan said. 'Tip some ashes in the stove. And you, Master

52

Rory, fetch the outside-car to the gate. We're going home early today. I've someone to see.'

Happy to be off work – at what was it now, only three in the afternoon – they wanted to thank Master Cavan for their liberty. But how could you thank a man who hurled his documents aside, and was trying to pull his coat on with his fingers turned to fists?

Mother and daughter heard the coded rap on the door, both of them turning instinctively towards the bevelled face of the wall-clock. 'He's home to tell us to pack,' Elisa blurted. 'I knew it would happen like this. I knew I'd never see Biddy!' Scowling, she thrust a poker at the low, smouldering fire, rebellion plaited with obedience.

'Let's just wait and be sure,' Adelaide counselled, though her voice lacked conviction, for the girl was likely correct. Why else would Cavan leave his desk early, unless to tell them he'd secured passage to France, a chance that might never be repeated? She wondered how much time they'd have to prepare, sparing a thought for Corinne, who would not yet have received her mother's letter. Would she truly be pleased to see them, her gaunt and enfeebled parents, her wary younger sister?

Slipping the bolts, she urged Cavan into the house, then locked the door behind him. Out of habit she reached to take his coat, misunderstanding as he shook his head. 'Are we *that* pressed for time? Must we sail on the very next tide?'

'What? Sail where?'

'For Paris, of course,' Elisa said sullenly. 'Or wherever ships go to, over there.' Crouching beside the invigorated fire, the girl looked angry and insecure, convinced her promise to Biddy O'Brien would be broken. 'It's why you're home early, isn't it, Papa? Why you won't even shed your coat? 'Cause we've now to pack and leave?'

Cavan Lynch gave a gesture of weary comprehension. 'The only reason I'm home before time – Well, it's important I see Uncle Conor. I could have walked on, but I need a filled lantern, a few spare matches; the wind has a way of cutting round the glass.'

Adelaide asked: 'What is it that's so important? It's only Sundays we go there, or him to us. Please, my dear, now you're with us, can't it wait?'

'I regret to say it cannot.' The man sighed. 'Things have waited too long as they are.'

'At least let me heat the infusion. It's more than a mile across the hills – '

53

'Heat it then. And will you, Elisa, fill the lamp? But quick as you can, if you please. It's a visit I wish to get over and done with.' He seemed ready to say something else, but changed his mind, leaning instead towards the fire, a gloved hand braced against the mantel-shelf, warmth driving the pallor from his face.

Adelaide gave him a mug of the foul-tasting herbal drink. Elisa carefully filled the base of the lantern, lighted the wick and closed the smoke-smeared glass. They wanted to ask him why – Why did he have to trudge the snowy hills tonight, then make the sudden, steep descent to Conor's dwelling? What on earth could be so urgent that he had to stand in his damp wool coat, sipping in haste at the infusion, his fingers that cupped the edge of the mantelshelf drumming against the wood?

Elisa decided to ask him outright, then felt Adelaide squeeze her shoulder. The wife knew far better than the child that Cavan had already left them, and was deep in conversation with Uncle Conor . . .

Aware that his daughter had moved to stand beside him, holding the lantern suspended from its short, hooked pole, Cavan brightened to ask if they'd keep some soup simmering on the fire. 'Uncle Conor's a generous man with the drink, though I doubt he'll invite me to eat.'

Elisa said quickly she would. 'I'll stay up as late as matters, Papa. Oh, and don't forget the matches.' She pushed them into one of his side flap pockets, then waved at his thin, stooped back as he unlocked the door and thrust the lantern at the dark.

It was fitting, perhaps, that Carrick Manor should hold the highest ground on Lord Charles Cassel Natesby's horseshoe estate. And that his steward and bailiff, Conor Egan Lynch, should live on the slope of the master's ridge, high enough to be within a fifteen minute summons, yet low enough to be out of Natesby's sight. If the bailiff was needed, the bailiff was there. Otherwise, the crude and ruddy-faced Irishman could be ignored.

Elsewhere, fringing the Englishman's vast holdings, were a dozen hamlets and villages, all of them hidden in the folds of the hills, a decent and necessary distance from Carrick Manor. 'Neighbours is one thing,' Natesby would say with a smile, 'but we wouldn't care to bump knees with 'em, after all! Do that an' we'd all be *kneebours*, what!'

He enjoyed this play on words, and recited it often to his friends.

It was his own creation, though he had so far failed to match it with another. Never mind. His friends could be counted upon to tell a few jokes of their own, and the clubs in St James's echoed with the raucous guffaws of anti-Irish humour. Like the priest and Sexagesima Sunday . . . The farmer from Wexford who put his boots on the wrong feet and spent the day walking round in circles . . . The ever-popular story of the convent and the novice from Connemara . . .

And when hilarity lapsed, there were always insults to be laid against the Irish in general; their apathy; their ignorance; their stupid, unquestioning love of a coin, 'Though you could paint a flat pebble and watch 'em run off to spend it! God, so you could!'

His dislike of the Irish given full rein in London, Lord Natesby was intelligent enough to blanket his feelings in Cork. After all, a sad and sorry lot though they were, they were needed to run the estate. And one you could trust, bullish great lump though he was, was Bailiff Conor.

Skidding as he descended the slope, Cavan saw the smudge of light in his uncle's window. Then he heard the dogs, baying and barking, and the door swung inward, candlelight staining the snow.

'Who's there? Stay where you are, or I let the hounds free!'

Cavan raised his lantern, identifying himself by its light. 'You've a fine way to greet your callers, Uncle. Is that how you'd do it, if sent for from the manor?'

'No reason to be sent for tonight,' Conor replied. 'Though what'd you be doin' here on a weekday after dark, Master Cavan? Sunday's been our day, since I ever remember.'

'Keep your dogs inside, and I'll come and tell you.'

Conor grunted, turned to kick the animals back to their straw, then beckoned his nephew across the yard.

The bailiff found it difficult to settle his expression, for why indeed was Cavan here, risking his skinny frame on the icy, unmarked track? Elisa taken sick, perhaps? Adelaide gone back to, where was it she'd come from, Orstia, Ostria, some damn place like that? Or was nephew Cavan here on his own behalf, sorry to think his uncle lived alone, and with Christmas around the corner . . .

'Come in! Come in! Get up close to the fire. Take some brandy. Picked it up from the Frenchies. Passed me a dozen flasks of the stuff, out near the mouth of the Lee. Talk bloody funny, the Frenchies, eh, but they know what they're up to with drinks!' Barging about the gloomy, ill-furnished room, Conor Lynch roared at his dogs to sit quiet, then slopped the fine foreign brandy into cheap, unwashed glasses, and thrust one at Cavan. He settled his muscular hips in a chair across from his nephew, tipped back his glass and spoke through the rivulets of heavy, glistening liquor.

'Surprises me no end, Nephew, you riskin' your way in the dark.'

'I do it every night in winter,' Cavan said quietly. 'Out and back to the port.'

'Well, course you do. Course you do *that*. But comin' across the hill with your spectral lantern. That's a thing I ain't known you do before. So why tonight? Stare though I will, I see no seasonal gifts!' He swallowed the rest of his cognac, frowned as he saw Cavan's glass was untouched, then shrugged and refilled his own. 'So tell me. What's the struggle been for? Accounts not finished, and you're worried that, now Lord Natesby's here – '

'The accounts are up to date. Anyway, those you gave me. And far from being worried about Natesby – '

'*Lord* Natesby,' Conor reminded him. 'A man of his station – '

'Very well, Uncle. Lord Natesby. But far from being worried by his presence at Carrick Manor, I'm delighted to know he's here. It'll give me the chance to talk to him. Inform him of what – '

'Just a minute,' Conor interrupted, lurching forward in his chair. 'You've not said yet why you've come to see *me*. But now you're on about visiting Lord Natesby. I'd be pleased to know why you *are* here, Nephew. And all outside of a Sunday.' He stared at Cavan, droplets of cognac dripping from his glass.

The younger man's call had unnerved him, but he held his gaze until Cavan said: 'It's all about bricks and tiles, Uncle Conor . . . Though you might know them better as salted beef and bacon.'

The bailiff blinked, and turned for comfort to his glass. 'Don't know what you're talkin' about – '

'I've reason to think you do. After all, your name's been scrawled on all kinds of papers. Though God knows it was hard enough to make sense of them.'

'I don't know what – ' Conor began again.

'Oh, but you do!' Cavan shouted. 'You've signed your name in deceit. And you're filling your purse with foreign coin. And for all your attempts to stay secret, you've handed your loyalties on a plate to the English, leaving the Irish bowl empty. Huddled up close to Natesby. Forgive me, *Lord* Natesby.'

'You ain't makin' sense,' Conor blurted. 'All this talk of deceits and secrets. It don't explain why you've come here now – '

'Then I will,' Cavan levelled, 'for it's all on account of Warehouse Six. The burgeoning Warehouse Six.'

Lord Natesby's steward kept the cognac close by, refilling the glass with dull repetition, then belching the fumes from his belly. The more he drank, the more he mumbled, Cavan listening hard, the nephew leaning forward, the uncle slumping back.

'I'm sixty now . . . Been Lord Natesby's man for these past thirty years . . . Treated me decent, Lord Natesby . . . Set me up here – allows me the dogs – free wood for the fire – fruit in the springtime – rights and permissions – all sorts of rights and permissions . . .

'Say he's got my loyalties on a plate? Well, yes, I've stood loyal to Lord Natesby, and it shames me none to admit it. Been Lord Natesby's man . . .' He reached a broad, scarred hand for the flask, grunted as the cognac slopped, then waved it at Cavan who said nothing, shaking his head.

'Picked this up from the Frenchies . . . Told you that before, maybe, how the Frenchies talk funny . . .'

He rambled on, justification interspersed with sudden barks of anger. His nephew was told to forget what he'd seen in the warehouse; it was none of his business. Lord Natesby's affair, the Englishman's alone. The landlord's stock, to dispose of as he wished. And Cavan would do well to keep his mouth shut, 'less he sought to be evicted, tossed out on the track.

'There's places already on the list. Cotters who can't pay his lordship what they owe. Stupid peasants who clamour to be fed, crying 'cause they ain't got their potatoes. Low Rising'll go. An' Macrill, an' Kilbreen, an' Glanderry. An' all along the edge of Dunsannon . . . Don't know how well off you are, Nephew Cavan, comfy in your stone-built house . . .'

The bony clerk then re-entered the conversation. His drink untouched, he asked Conor if he truly meant what he'd said. 'Stay silent about the contents of the warehouse?'

'That's it, boy, that's the way.'

'And allow Lord Natesby to ship the stuff out, selling what's needed *here* at a profit abroad?'

'None of our business. Keep what we've got. Every man for himself in times like these.'

'So you'd have me do nothing? The food sent overseas? And the villagers evicted? And then you'll squat here with your hounds and your wine, and to hell and damnation with our countryfolk? Is that how you see it, Master Conor? Is that how you'd have us behave?'

'Be a damn fool to do otherwise,' the bailiff slurred. 'Now, get you on home, and I'll put in a good word for you, next time I see his lordship. Pretend you never inspected the storerooms. Oh, by the way, help yourself to a flask. Find one out there on the sideboard . . .'

Conor Egan Lynch blinked vacantly as Cavan came to his feet. He was still trying to focus his gaze as his nephew lighted the lantern and left the house.

Preoccupied by what he'd heard – and by a name that scratched for admission to his mind – Cavan Lynch stumbled through the snow, the jaundiced lantern wavering on its pole.

Ten minutes on and he floundered in a drift, no longer sure of the track. He'd veered too far to the right, he decided, swinging the lantern in a slow, exploratory arc. He'd need to regain the ridge . . . Up there . . . Keep above the snow banks . . .

He retraced his steps, dug his boots sideways at the slope, climbed in what he believed was the right direction. *The man who helped finance my studies in Dublin and Bristol, when my father drowned, leaving sheaves of debts unpaid? Welcomed us back to Cork, and encouraged me to tackle the port exams? Have I truly just spent time with that selfsame man? Or is it all a part of some vile, demonic plan, with once decent men diseased by greed –*

His attention lapsed and he skidded, his left foot wrenched between two deep-buried stones. The lantern fell, though mercifully upright, cushioned by snow. Pain flared in Cavan's ankle, bruised flesh quickly swelling against the unyielding leather of his boot. He groaned as he pulled his foot from the pincers of rock, and crawled to reclaim the lantern. It seemed his thoughts were well-founded, *for didn't the whole world know the devil never slept?*

He limped, then hobbled, then all but dragged his way to the house.

In defiance of his orders, Adelaide had opened the shutters that faced the road, and set a row of candles along the sill. She stood shivering near the gate, gasping as he laboured from the dark. After she had helped him inside, relieved at least that he'd not been waylaid, she ignored his protestations as she cut the boot free from his foot.

The swelling was ugly, the only remedy to bathe it in tepid water, then bandage it painfully tight. And attempt to assuage the pain with a strong infusion. They would know soon enough if he'd broken or fractured a bone, for the agony would soar above the dulling of the herbs.

Cavan refused to be helped to bed.

With Elisa asleep upstairs, he preferred to remain in the kitchen with his wife. He recounted the story of the warehouse, then told her of his meeting with Conor, admitting the need to get their daughter to the place he now remembered – the third place his uncle had mentioned – the hamlet of Kilbreen.

'God knows when they're to happen, these evictions. Conor talked of several, and among them Kilbreen. I'd have taken her myself, but in all honesty I don't see how – '

'Be calm, my love. Save your concern for the warehouse. The roads are well enough patrolled for Elisa and me to go there tomorrow.'

'Oh, no. I'll not have you out there, unprotected.' His frail body sunk in a wheel-back chair, his injured foot extended towards the hearth, Cavan Lynch twisted in frustration to his wife. '*Your* place is here! And hers! The hell with Biddy O'Brien! It's everyone for himself – ' Then he stopped and stared, listening hard to the echoes of a voice that could surely not have come from his own dry throat . . . *It's every man for himself in times like these* . . . Uncle Conor's phrase . . . The Devil's disease . . . And already, so it seemed, on Cavan's lips.

'We won't be unprotected,' Adelaide reassured him. 'We'll wait until one of the patrols is in the vicinity; maybe even ask if they'd escort us. We'll go there in daylight, and be home again well before dark. And I'll take one of the pistols, or both if you insist. Now tell me – Am I to warn the folk of Kilbreen about Lord Natesby's intentions? God forbid I should panic them, but isn't it only right they be alerted?'

The question added strength to Adelaide's suggestion that *she* accompany Elisa to the hamlet. It was no longer just a matter of two children meeting, but of warning an entire community that their landlord planned to drive them from their homes. The same held good for the others Conor had mentioned, Low Rising and Macrill and Dunsannon, though these were several miles away to the west. When Cavan's ankle had healed he'd do what he could to get word to them. But for the moment only Kilbreen could be reached, the cotters put on their guard.

With reluctance, he consented. 'I can't say the idea sits easy. If it weren't for what my uncle told me . . . But you'd better take what you can spare from the pantry . . . And if things are as bad as I fear

59

over there . . . Well, you might decide to bring the O'Brien girl back home.' He shrugged then, Adelaide placing a gentle hand on his shoulder. Such a casual, murmured invitation, she thought, was the very essence of Cavan Lynch. Appalled by the discovery of the foodstuff in the port, then shocked by Conor's turncoat slurrings, the man could still find the heart to say if need be they'd adopt the child of Kilbreen. Not in so many words, for that was not her husband's way. But clear enough for the woman to understand, the way she'd understood most things about him, since they'd first met on that beach below Bristol . . .

Moving away, she collected the pistols, an oilskin bundle of wadding and percussion caps and shot. 'Here,' she said. 'Seeing as you're lounged in the chair, you can show me what your navy friends taught you about guns. Do I hold the thing at arm's stretch to fire it, or what? All the weeks we've had one up there on the shelf, and you never thought to instruct me. It seems to me now's the time.'

Perhaps it is, he thought. And if Elisa were threatened, I don't doubt she'd shoot to kill.

5

Next morning, Adelaide entered her daughter's bedroom, shook her gently awake, and told her that Papa was still sleeping, and would spend the day at home.

The girl rubbed her eyes, squirming upright in the bed. 'Is he ill? I can't ever remember a time when – '

'He'll be fine. He took a nasty fall on his way back from Uncle Conor's. Twisted his foot. But it's nothing that nature won't heal. Now listen. We've an errand to perform. And I'll thank you not to squeal and shout when I tell you. We're to go to Kilbreen, you and I. So you'll get your way at last, and visit Biddy.'

As Adelaide had known and feared, Elisa yelped with delight. Then she clapped a hand to her mouth, mumbled her apologies, and set her expression in what she hoped was one of attentive obedience. 'But Papa's not coming? He'll allow us to go together?'

'Dress for the cold. Find that rag doll you've been making. I hope it's finished, for there's no time left to complete it.'

'Oh, it is,' the girl claimed, scrambling from the bed. She rescued the doll from a chest, and presented it to her mother. 'Well, all right, I meant to put lace round the collar, but it doesn't need it anyway. Or do you think it does?'

Meaning it, Adelaide said: 'I think it looks fine. Biddy will surely adore it. Now dress and come down and get washed. We're to wait till we see a patrol on the road, then trust to their protection.' With a firm nod to her daughter, she went to rekindle the fire, to boil water for their oatmeal breakfast. She filled a five-pound sack with flour for the O'Briens, a smaller sack with hard, salted fish, and another, bulkier bag with meal. A knotted rag contained their smallest, yet most important, offering – unmilled crystals of salt.

The twelve-year-old Elisa descended the stairs in slow motion, setting each booted foot with exaggerated care, anxious not to waken the sleeping Cavan. She told herself she was doing so in order that Papa's injury would heal, undisturbed. Then she blushed in the dark of the staircase, for it wasn't just that. It was also to be sure she'd get to see Biddy, and watch as the younger child hugged the bright rag doll.

*

Adelaide linked the sacks of flour and oatmeal, suspending them from a cord around her neck. Elisa was given the bag of stiff, salted fish, the knotted container of salt. The woman's slim hips were made bulky this morning with the brace of navy pistols, her daughter's underfed belly pushed out by the splay-limbed doll.

They stood on the track near the house gate, eyes half closed against the glitter of freezing snow. There were clouds to the west, solid as mountains, though the sky above County Cork was an icy, unfractured blue. Silence and stillness held the land, pinning snow to the hedgerows, daring a bird to fly, a mouse to dart.

'I'm cold,' Elisa complained. 'Why can't we just *go* there? You think we'd be waylaid on a day like this?'

'Then you wait indoors,' Adelaide directed. 'I'll call you if – No, listen! Do you hear . . . ?'

There was the crunching sound of hoofbeats approaching from the north, then the snort of horses, and the rough exchange of curses and comments as a detachment of English cavalry, their blue and gold uniforms bright against the snow, trampled back from the limit of their patrol.

The officer in command gazed down at them, snapping out questions, amused by Adelaide's foreign-tinged accent, Elisa's shivering impatience. 'Well, you're a cut above the usual rabble, though ain't you a bit foolhardy to be carryin' sacks of food?'

'That's why we've not set off yet,' Adelaide reasoned. 'I was hoping you'd escort us, Captain. You're bound for the crossing anyway, it seems, and Kilbreen's not far – '

'Sorry, Mistress, but we ain't permitted to detour. 'Gainst the rules'

'Could you at least allow my daughter to ride behind – ?'

'Out of the question. Sorry. Pretty little thing though, ain't she?'

'I've no doubt she'll treasure the compliment,' Adelaide retorted. 'As I've also no doubt you won't let us hold the bridles, to steady our balance.'

'Sorry,' he repeated. 'But out of the question. Military issue, these mounts. Act of aggression to touch 'em. But tell you what. Why don't you follow in the hoof-prints? Horses don't often tread wrong.' Then he flicked a finger towards his tall, cylindrical hat, turned the gesture into a forward wave and led his troopers down the slowly descending track towards the crossing, the city, the barracks.

He had not even offered to relieve the woman of the burden of her sacks. Probably a rule against transporting civilian effects . . .

As they stumbled in the wake of the patrol, Elisa hissed: 'Should have shot him, Mama. And you could have done so too, for his own holster's all strapped up. Then we'd have taken his horse and galloped – '

'Watch where you're going. Keep to the prints.' Then she glanced at her daughter and said: 'Don't think it didn't occur to me.'

The girl grinned up at her, and they followed the fading sounds of the patrol.

By the time they reached the crossing, the riders had vanished. Mountainous clouds still loomed in the west, though static, as if they themselves were frozen. Adelaide slapped her gloved hands together, Elisa copying. When they spoke, the words seemed visible, softened by the feathers of their breath.

'It doesn't look like much of a track.' The girl frowned. 'Have you ever been to Kilbreen, Mama? I never have.'

Adelaide shook her head. 'It shames me,' she started, then preferred not to think of the places she might have visited, had she cared to know her neighbours better. But life had been sufficient with Cavan and her sons, then with Corinne, and most of all perhaps with Elisa. Far from rich, the Lynches had been content to keep their own company, envying no one; a quiet family who derived their greatest pleasure from being together in their slate-and-stone house, reading or talking; exchanging ideas; their sense of humour more apparent with a smile than a shrilling laugh.

Without the blight, the famine, the devil's dance in Ireland, they would likely have continued as before. Cavan would have served his years as Senior Clerk of Shipping Affairs; Adelaide sharing her knowledge of languages with her late-born daughter; Elisa eventually leaving as Patrick and William and Corinne had left, the greying and ageing parents then moving, perhaps to a cottage closer to Cork.

But who knows when the devil will choose to start dancing? Who has ever heard a satanic, warning overture?

'Let's get on,' Adelaide urged. 'That doll of yours will be frozen as *we* are. Biddy won't thank you if the doll gets there all shaking.'

Elisa giggled. It was one of the things she best loved about Mama. Strict words; the demand for obedience, then out of the blue a remark like that. Like saying she'd given some thought to shooting the arrogant English captain.

She held Biddy's gift tight beneath her coat, hoping her friend wouldn't ask why there wasn't lace around the collar . . .

Flanked by thorny, untrimmed hedgerows, the path was pitted with icy puddles and swamps of freezing water; hillocks that belied their firmness sank beneath their feet. Mother and daughter floundered together, Adelaide struggling for balance as the sacks dipped and swung, Elisa yelping as salted, finny fish banged her leg. It's as well we set off early, they agreed. Take us longer than we imagined, getting home.

Then Adelaide stopped, drawing her daughter to a hump at the edge of the path. 'I'm not sure,' she said, 'but I think that's it. I think that must be Kilbreen.'

Elisa stared, felt her head twitch in disbelief, and moved a cautious step forward as if to clarify her gaze. She saw hutments of twigs and branches; walls made of earthen clods that a child might slap together in an aimless afternoon; a double row of these pitiful dwellings – *and no more than two or three spirals of smoke in all the silent hamlet.*

'Well, she told me . . . Said they didn't have bricks or slates . . . But I never supposed . . .' Then she swung around, shouting that this couldn't be so. 'It's not possible! It *can't* be where Biddy lives! Kilbreen must be further on!'

They entered the hamlet as explorers might venture on to some ominous, foreign shore. Her shoulders chafed by the hempen yoke that held the food sacks, Adelaide clutched Elisa with one hand, the other thrust in the pocket of her cloak, ready to draw the pistol.

They saw no one in the street, heard no voices.

In the first windowless dwelling they found two women dead, their bodies shrivelled by cold and starvation, yet with flesh enough left for the rats . . .

After that the girl was told to stay back. 'At least until I think we've found young Biddy.'

A wise decision, for the second hovel contained the sprawled and bloated body of a man, his emaciated wife on a stool beside him, a bundle couched in her arms. As Adelaide's shadow filled the doorway, the woman flinched. Her lips pulled back from a fence of rotting teeth, she clutched the bundle tighter, and from it a baby's arm lolled. There were rats here too, scurrying close to the walls. Biding their time.

They found Biddy O'Brien in the fourth house along; the first in which smoke spiralled from the roof. As with the others, the single room was devoid of table and chairs, the mud floor puddled with water that dripped from the thatch overhead. Straw laid directly on the ground served as their only bedding – and as concealment now for yet more startled rats.

The child and her parents lay huddled together near the hearth, drawn like animals to the hissing vestige of warmth. The man groaned. The girl twitched. The woman lay stiff and unmoving, her glazed eyes open in death. There was no sign of Biddy's three brothers.

Adelaide brought her daughter into the room, then called gently: 'Biddy O'Brien?'

The child twisted round, all but pinned by her parents' efforts to warm her body with their own. She said nothing until Elisa came close, then licked at lips disfigured by cold sores, her voice rasping dry in her throat. 'Miss Gardiner come back . . . ? You here to fetch me . . . ? Share the same bench, like before . . . ?'

Elisa stared at her friend's bloodless face, at the terrible hollows that ringed her milky eyes. Never much of a size when at school, she now seemed reduced, as if by some act of sorcery; cursed to grow ever smaller, ever more wizened.

'That's right,' Elisa lied. 'Miss Gardiner's back from Youghal. But first you're to come home with me. Oh, and look. It's for you.' She offered her the splay-limbed doll, watching in horror as Biddy reached to claim it. *The doll's arms were thicker than Biddy's.*

Adelaide had meanwhile discarded the food sacks and ducked through the rear door of the hovel, returning with fragments of wood, an armload of briars. She knelt beside Biddy's father, easing the man to one side of the hearth. He groaned again, though seemed to know he was being moved with kindness for his lips stretched in the stricture of a smile.

Aware of her mother's intentions, Elisa lifted Biddy from the fading warmth of the fire. 'Only for a minute. Here. We'll share the cloak. You and me and – You thought up a name for the doll yet?'

Avoiding the dead woman's eyes, Adelaide dragged her from the hearth. Then she crushed the brittle thorns, piled them against the embers and smouldering peat, and heaped the fragments of wood on top of the briars.

Her plan was simple, but time was scarce. She would go out again, scavenge for wood, and build the fire till it caught and held. Then she'd find water, or snow, and set above the blaze a cooking pot filled with oatmeal and salted mackerel – a crude and hasty soup for the folk of Kilbreen.

God alone knew how many were still alive, still able to swallow the coarse, salty liquid. But even if there were only a dozen . . . only five . . . only one . . .

The thorns crackled and spat. Adelaide glanced at Elisa, who was hugging Biddy close, the two of them crouched on a dry patch of the floor. With a nod of approval she left them, ducking again from the hovel, then tearing her gloves to shreds as she dragged at the bushes, wrenched away parts of a small, sagging outhouse. It must once have sheltered pigs, for Adelaide found herself mired in filth, the hem of her skirt and cloak weighed down by the viscous mud.

Inside the dwelling, Biddy rasped: 'I don't *care* if she ain't got a collar . . . Best friend I ever had . . . Well, 'part from you . . .' Then she coughed and choked and the doll was speckled with blood.

Redmond O'Brien died without the children knowing; their heads together, whispering names for the doll. A lady, of course, so why not Lady Kilbreen? Or Lady Rose, since a patch on her left leg showed the flower and petals of a rose?

And then the wizened child said no. She'd decided. She knew the right name. 'She's to be "Miss Elisa". An' that way, when we ain't together, we always sort of will be . . .'

Gasping and coughing, she claimed Elisa's friendship for ever, the patchwork companion there to listen, to say what the real Elisa Lynch would likely have said . . .

Returning again, Adelaide heaped fuel beside the hearth. A long, steady gaze was enough to tell her that Biddy's father was dead, the girls crouched in ignorance, heat at last permeating the room.

She found the O'Briens' cauldron – the one essential possession among the impoverished families of Ireland – and stopped to wipe the mud from the hem of her cloak. Then, having hauled the pot outside, she scooped a tattered glove in the snow. The cold bit at the scatches that laced her hand, though she forced herself to fill the cauldron, pleased that the fire would turn the snow to water for the soup.

A feeble attempt to help those of Kilbreen, it might be, but it was all she could think of doing. It was all a person *could* do in the depths of winter; the pantry bare; the wells frozen over; the devil performing his dance.

The snow now heaped in the cauldron, Adelaide frowned and listened. For the second time that day the silence was broken by the trample of hoofs, though the intrusion was more than just the muffled approach of an ill-tempered English patrol. Along with the hoofbeats was the creak of leather, the groan and squeal of a wagon. And the dull stamp of men, growling their complaints, filled the air to the east of Kilbreen with the noise of imminent danger.

Adelaide Lynch hefted the scorched iron pot, carried it in, and hooked it above the fire. Then she moved to interrupt the girls' affectionate murmurs, telling Elisa to stay where she was until called, and keep Biddy close by at all times.

'I heard it too,' Elisa said. 'You think it's someone coming to save Kilbreen?'

'Why not? Who knows? But until we're sure, you just stay here and keep Biddy by.'

Elisa nodded, and the children once again dipped their heads close together, the younger girl too entranced by her doll to spare a glance for her parents. The last time she'd looked they were sleeping; they were probably sleeping now.

'And then the prince . . . An' what does the prince do next . . . ?'

Adelaide went no further than the doorway to peer along the street. The low, worm-ridden lintel of the hovel made her stoop, but she wanted to see who was coming before admitting to her presence in the hamlet.

Well-intentioned philanthropists? Gentlefolk from Cork, here to dispense largesse to the starving cotters? English agents, sent to comfort their weakened Irish cousins? Or was it, perhaps, something harsher, something closer to the fears Cavan Lynch had recounted last night? Not aid for the hamlet at all, but the promised eviction.

Set shoulder to shoulder, ten across the street, the men stood three rows deep, hammers and axes at the ready. They grunted and muttered, cheap boots penetrated by the cold, eager to get the job done. Paid by results, why the hell were they kept waiting?

Behind them, and higher up the slope, a six-horse team had been reined in tight, the brakes applied to a massive, flat-bed cart. Fixed to the cart was a branched oak cradle, its four steepled arms suspending a twenty-foot, iron-tipped ram. If the hammers and axes failed, there was always the ram . . .

Gazing through the brittle winter air, Adelaide saw the triple row of labourers shoved aside, and a man barging forward, stained leather hat tipped low.

Moving clear of the work-gang, the leader dug inside his jerkin, withdrew a folded sheet of paper, then raised his ruddy face to scan the street. And, by doing so, revealed himself as Lord Natesby's steward-cum-bailiff, Conor Egan Lynch.

Adelaide gasped, Elisa choosing that moment to tug at her mother's cloak. The bid for attention was rewarded with an angry rebuff. 'Stay back inside! There's someone we – someone I know out there, and I need to hear what he says. Now keep quiet.'

The girl retreated, feeling shamed in front of Biddy. But the younger child was busy admonishing her doll for some imagined impertinence. 'Such manners! I really don't know!'

Her face shadowed by the hood of her cloak, Adelaide remained unrecognized in the doorway, intent now on hearing what Conor had to say. She had an excellent memory, and knew she could repeat it later, word for word. Cavan would wish to know.

'People of Kilbreen! I'd have your attention! Empowered as I am by his lordship, Charles Cassel Natesby, I command you to vacate your dwellings, an' remove yourselves from this place. None of you's furnished the rent to which his lordship is entitled, an' are thus in contravention of the law. Your continued presence here is therefore illegal an' – ' His own memory failed him, and he was forced to resort to the paper. 'Yes, an' your tenancy terminated forthwith, as of this date, December the ninth, Year of Our Lord, Eighteen Hundred, Two Score and Seven. An' forthwith means you leave this place *now*.'

He had a strong, carrying voice, did Uncle Conor, and the stillness of the winter day was well-suited to public announcements. Whether or not the inhabitants of Kilbreen understood what he'd told them, the measured-out words brought them from their hutments, though like the newly dead from their graves . . .

Gaunt and ragged, those who could walk at all shuffled to the street, fissured lips working soundlessly, eyes blinded by the glare. Some of them tried to smile, believing sustinence was at hand. Others wavered in welcome. Most stood listless, already too close to death to comprehend or care.

Then one of the work-gang growled: 'We come 'ere to do it, let's get the damn thing done!' There was a mutter of approval for this anonymous desire to set about the task, and a restless stamping of feet. Finish up lookin' like *them*, if we stand around much longer. Get a move on, Master Bailiff. Ain't you revelled enough in the echoes of your voice?

Adelaide had meanwhile turned and crouched to be level with her daughter. 'Now listen,' she said urgently. 'You're to stay here with Biddy. I'm off to talk to – to that man down there, but I need to know where to find you. So keep near the door, but out of sight of the street. Whatever else, you're to stay here till I call you.'

Elisa nodded. But a deal was a deal, and she demanded confirmation. 'And then we'll bring Biddy home?'

'Crowd you up tight in your bed, you and young Biddy and the doll.'

Elisa hummed with pleasure, warning her friend to warn her namesake not to keep them awake all night, rag legs kicking. 'And the same goes for you!'

They ignored her departure, and Adelaide straightened as she strode through the slush of the street. She threw back her hood, and tipped her chin high so Conor could see who was coming. Gave *me* a surprises when I saw who it was. Do the same for him.

But she was still no more than halfway through the hamlet when the work-gang surged forward, permission granted for the clearing of Kilbreen. So Adelaide did what she had never in her life imagined she would be called upon to do; she fumbled in her pocket, dragged out one of the navy pistols, raised the barrel and pulled back on the trigger.

The report made less noise than she expected, though it was loud enough to stop the work-gang in their tracks. It also jarred her wrist, and Adelaide winced as she walked onwards, through the smell and smoke of the shot.

It pleased her to see the men hesitate, uncertain of what to do next. *So here. Show you I mean it.* And she tugged the second gun free.

Slowed by the glutinous mixture of snow and mud, she was nevertheless close enough to Conor and his gang for an errant shot to kill. If she stumbled, for example. Or squeezed the trigger too early. Her grip was unsteady enough, God knows . . .

For a moment, farce replaced tragedy as the brutish labourers cowered and cringed, their heads turned away, hands raised as if somehow to deflect the bullet. Those in the front row collided with those behind, the men cursing as axe handles cracked against kneecaps, hammers numbed shoulders. They retreated in confusion, thirty men at the mercy of this single, lunatic woman.

Then Conor went forward to meet his nephew's wife, swung his arm and swept the loaded pistol aside. There was a second flat bark, a gout of snow, the pistol drowned in the street. 'Bloody madness!' he roared. 'And from you?'

'Yes, from me. I heard all about it last night. About Dunsannon and Macrill and Low Rising. How you'd sold out to Natesby – '

'Get out of the street, Mistress Adelaide. I'm warning you. Move aside.'

'You're full to the brim with warnings, so it seems. Warn the villagers to leave. Warn your men to make ready. Warn me now – '

'Very well. So here's the way it's to be.' Aware his work-gang were watching, the bailiff snatched at the woman's arm, then used the weight of his body to herd her from the street. It was no time to be out-talked and out-witted by the clever Adelaide Lynch. Now was the time to get the gang moving; do the job they'd been brought here to do.

He thrust her forward, leaving her to stagger against a house wall. A bellow to the labourers, and they went about their business, each man pretending he'd stood jaunty in the face of the madwoman's threats.

Her gloves ripped apart by the briars, wrist and arm bruised, food sacks brought here for nothing, Adelaide Katherina Lynch watched the men barge round her. All right, so she'd tried. *But where is the virtue in trying, if I fail?*

Common sense told her to move back down the street and reclaim her children. The word made her blink – my *children?* Though how else could it be now, for of course they were both hers. Not just Elisa, but the scrawny, diminished young Biddy. After all, with the child's parents dead, she had no one else to turn to. Nowhere else to go.

Ever an O'Brien, she'd be treated henceforth as Elisa's sister, the shoes for one no brighter than the shoes for the other. Always an O'Brien, well yes, for why should Biddy not honour her family name? But in every other way Elisa's sister. In *every* other way.

Edging along the street, the woman left the work-gang – Conor's labourers, the *wreckers* – to their work.

They hauled bodies from the hutments and dumped them in the snow. Then they slammed at the walls with their hammers, bit at the props with their axes, called for the ram if the dwellings dared to resist. The flat-bed wagon was backed into place, the cradled trunk swung backwards and forwards, thatch and turf and timber subsiding in a dull, dampened cloud.

'It would not do at all,' Lord Natesby had told his steward, 'if we just snap our fingers and send 'em on their way. The only method – as we've seen before, and you're bound to agree, Master Conor – is to drive 'em out once and for ever. Heave-ho their hovels. Level 'em flat. Break 'em all to kindling. If we don't do it right they'll be back again next morning, fixin' themselves little shelters in the ruins. And after that – need I tell you, my dear Bailiff – they'll come knocking on Carrick's door. Not a penny in cash between them, but imploring me for comestibles, cart-loads of peat – Heaven knows where it'll end.

'I tell you, Master Conor. This blight's been the damnedest nuisance. Workers I thought I could rely on . . . And what are they now, but beggars on the whine . . . ? So off you go. Chase 'em away. An' make sure they ain't lured back. Get it done quick, and I'll see you don't want for necessities . . .'

The weft of command was bound tight with the warp of reward. And it made good sense, for his lordship hadn't bought thirty thousand acres so he could be charitable to the cotters. Business was business. A man could understand that. And the weak must go to the wall.

So the ruddy-faced bailiff controlled the destruction of Kilbreen, wading from this side of the street to that, his wreckers hewing and smashing at the hutments, then catching their breath whenever the ram was called in.

The dead were tossed back against the ruins, the living abandoned among the wreckage of their hamlet. Later today they'd deal with Dunsannon, and Macrill, if time allowed . . .

Elisa had heard the first pistol shot, but had been too busy nursing Biddy to see its effect on the wreckers.

The second shot – when Conor had swept the pistol from Adelaide's hand – had drawn the girl to the door of Biddy's house, and she'd watched the man – 'But that's Uncle Conor!' – bully her mother to the far side of the street.

Elisa had then gaped as the thirty hired labourers set about their task. Biddy clung close, anxious to tell her friend that the doll had a secret to whisper in her ear.

'In a minute. She can tell me in a minute.' *But what's happening out there? Was it Uncle Conor who'd been shouting? And why did he push Mama like that? And why did she fire off the pistols?*

'She wants to tell you now!' Biddy insisted. ' "Miss Elisa" wants to tell you – '

'I said in a minute. Mama's coming back.' *I don't understand what they're doing, those men. They're breaking down the houses!*

71

Her attention frayed, Elisa watched as the wreckers razed the hutments; as Biddy badgered her; as Adelaide angled towards them. Standing bemused in the doorway, she saw charnel-house figures sagging in the snow. The ram was now blocking the street, the iron-tipped trunk see-sawing in its cradle. *What's going on? Why are they doing that?*

'Oh, come on back quick, Mama! But watch for the wagon! *Watch for the wagon!*'

Jammed between the buildings, the six-horse team plunged and snorted, trampling sideways in an effort to stretch their harness. Placid enough in the open, they tended to panic when trapped.

And trapped they were now, the broad-shouldered dray-horses stamping around, nudging the woman off balance. She fought to drag her cloak and skirt from the mud. But her boots were mired and she fell to her knees in the filth.

Elisa shrieked, 'No!' and ran out from the hutment.

Biddy dutifully followed, hugging her doll.

Struggling to her feet again, Adelaide Lynch screamed at the girls to go back. But Elisa would have none of it. *Leave Mama floundering, shadowed by those great snorting brutes?* So she forced her way forward, one arm raised to ward off the towering horses. Steam blew down from their nostrils, the sweat of fear turned to vapour on their flanks. And now the mud slowed her, oozing round her legs, and shouts that were meant to comfort her mother shrilled to cries of alarm. 'I can't come further! I'm trapped! Mama, I'm trapped!'

Adelaide reached her, caught the girl round the waist, wrenched her from the glutinous swill of the street. Lurching like drunkards, they veered away from the horses, and Adelaide then pushed Elisa towards the shelter of a wall. 'Stay there . . . I'll see to Biddy . . .'

The cold air seemed to sear her throat as she turned again to the street. She knew that only God had allowed her the strength to rescue her daughter, and prayed He'd permit –

But by then it was all too late.

Buffeted by the sounds of the wreckers, Adelaide saw the wagon-master lash angrily at his team, the frightened beasts milling beneath the whip. They pulled violently to one side, the six great dray-horses swinging towards the western end of the hamlet, unaware in their terror that a child stood glued in their path, her doll held high so it wouldn't get spattered with mud . . .

Biddy O'Brien and the splay-limbed 'Miss Elisa' were trampled and crushed in the black and white smears of the street, the animals

72

storming over them, and panting with relief when they saw the track beyond Kilbreen. It calmed them to know there was open country ahead . . .

But nothing could calm Elisa. Her child's mind fought to reject the horror of the scene. *Biddy's fallen in the mud, but she'll get up again, so she will . . . I can't see her because of the horses, but I bet she's climbing out, all sticky and cross . . .*

. . . Need a proper good washing, that Biddy . . . And 'Miss Elisa' too . . . Into the tub with you, Biddy . . . Oh, do stop wailing; you'd think you were being drowned. I said stop wailing. Why do you scream so? Why do you scream to deafen me? I'm your friend!

But it was not Biddy O'Brien who wailed and shrieked. It was Elisa herself, eyes blinded by tears as her mind now told her yes, what she'd seen had been true, and her schoolmate would not be clambering from the mire.

Someone else must have witnessed the tragedy, for men were yelling, the wagon-master leaning far out from the bench. As he bellowed to learn what had happened – 'Damn it all, *what* child? *Where?*' – Adelaide clutched her daughter close, in an effort to smother the sounds. She felt the girl shake uncontrollably, choking on her tears, small fists flailing in hopeless agony.

'Why didn't you get her too? You should have known she'd follow! She was my friend, and you should have *known!*'

'Yes,' Adelaide murmured, allowing Elisa to squirm and struggle within the comforting folds of her cloak. 'Yes, mayhap I should. And yet, God forgive me, I'd only the strength for you . . .'

Little by little, ignoring the nightmare sounds of Kilbreen, mother and daughter mastered their anguish, Elisa unclenching her fists and reaching to stroke Adelaide's face. 'I did not mean what I said, Mama. You told us to stay in the house. You told *me* to stay with Biddy. It's not your fault at all. It's mine. *I'm* the one – '

'Now stop. It does no good to apportion blame. We both know the fault lies with none of us here. We are all victims of harsh times. Young Biddy is gone, as are thousands of others, each as innocent as she. It's a terrible tragedy, and we'll never forget it, but two of us have survived, at least for the while.' Turning her head, she winced with pain as she pushed herself erect beside the wall. Her cloak hung heavy on her tall, half-starved frame. Her boots were like shackles round her feet, mud making them as limiting as chains. 'Wait here. I must first have a word with Uncle Conor.'

73

'Ask him – ' Elisa started, then paused before trying again. 'Ask him – well, to let Biddy keep the doll. You know, Mama? For ever? I'm sure they'd both get fresh clothes in Heaven. Even a silly doll.'

'Dressed just the way Biddy wants,' Adelaide assured her, though the words came out dry and listless. It was hard to believe, standing here amid the filth and clamour of a village being wrecked, that Heaven much cared about the cleansing and costume of a child who'd been crushed, let alone a patchwork doll.

Conor Lynch appeared round the rear of the ram, signalled to Adelaide, then stamped through the mud towards her. He'd heard about the death of the O'Brien girl; he'd flirted with sympathy, but shrugged it aside. This was neither the time nor the place to sit and sob. The wreckers had been summoned, and the hamlet had to be wrecked. The last thing the steward needed was his nephew's wife come calling with her daughter.

'All right,' he said quickly. 'So now you know what can happen. Cavan should've paid heed last night. Owned to what I told him. Now get you off home, you an' Elisa, and let's have no more interfering. It's each man for himself at times like these.'

Numbed and exhausted, Adelaide murmured: 'You'll at least see she's decently buried?'

'Do what I can,' Conor grunted, then broke off to bellow fresh orders.

'And her doll? Will you try and find it and – ?'

'What doll? You want me to trawl the street for a *toy*? Now listen to me, Mistress Adelaide. You were never asked to come here, and I dare say that child would still be alive if you hadn't. Cavan has his job, and I have mine, and I doubt you bang on *his* office door to see how he's doing. I'm sorry the girl got trampled, but your intentions were badly misplaced. She should not have been in the street, and you should not have been anywhere near Kilbreen.' Then he moved aside, the wagon masking him from Elisa's sight, and he stooped and dragged a sodden lump of fabric from the mud. 'This the thing? This what mattered so much to her? All right. Just for you . . .'

'For Elisa.'

'For Elisa, then. For both of you. I'll see it put under the pump and laid with the body. But will you now please get your daughter away from that wall? We're about to demolish it. And I'd hurry if I were you; the ram's swingin' round . . .'

*

74

With no more battles to be fought – and lost – Adelaide and Elisa trudged westwards from the remnants of Kilbreen, the two hunching forward against the spirals of the wind.

'Did you ask him,' Elisa insisted, 'about the doll?'

'No need to,' Adelaide told her. 'Someone had found it already, and washed it clean, and tucked it in Biddy's grasp. It surprised me that men like that could be quite so gentle.'

Elisa nodded, loving her mother for the comfort, not just of her cloak or her voice, but for assuring her that Biddy would never be left alone.

Then they made their way together through the silence of the snow, pretending not to hear the thud of hammers and axes, as another Irish hutment was brought to ruin.

6

On 11th December, Cavan returned to the port, where he once again checked the contents of Warehouse Six. Nothing had been moved, though the *Ottar* was due to sail in five days time, taking the meat, butter and cheese.

Tomorrow was a Sunday. He would visit Lord Natesby in the morning, and plead with the man to let Southampton and London and Ostend get by without this particular cargo, dispensing it instead to the starving Irish.

The chance of persuading Charles Cassel Natesby was negligible, but the effort had to be made.

I do not much believe in miracles, Cavan told himself, though they are, I suppose, by their nature, unexpected. Anyway, we'll see.

Sunday found Carrick Manor in turmoil. It was one of Elizabeth Natesby's well-intentioned, ill-thought-out ideas; invite Sir Richard and Lady Lucinda Fitzalan over from Millmay, and with them their daughters, marriage in mind for the gangling Robert Grenville.

Pouting his displeasure, the nineteen-year-old Grenville did what he always did when confronted with hard work or filial duty. He took to horse. He'd not been seen since breakfast time, refusing to say when, 'if ever!' he'd be back. 'It ain't the first time you've set these snares for me, Mother, and I damn well wish you'd not do it! The Fitzalan girls are far too *ordinaire* for my taste, and so what if they're pretty? Get pretty girls of me own in London. Snap me fingers, *et voilà!*'

Elizabeth doted on her son, and decided not to contradict his boast. It was true, of course, though she wished they weren't so exclusively shop girls, actresses, ladies of, well, one might think, questionable virtue. No doubt they revelled in Grenville's wit, but they certainly emptied his wallet . . .

Lord Charles was less enamoured of his selfish, spiteful, posing, peacock son. Matter of fact, he dreamed of the occasions when he'd been tempted to reach for the riding crop, or place the squared-off toe of his boot –

But no. Elizabeth would have created a God Almighty fuss, and Grenville would have snivelled like a foreigner sent to be hanged.

So on Sunday morning the family had gone their separate ways. Lord Natesby to the sanctuary of his study. Grenville to the far corners of the estate. Elizabeth to the kitchens, where she'd plagued the staff, insisting that the sauce tasted salty, the pork too bland, the cakes just plain uninviting. 'I do understand,' she told the cooks, 'that fate has deprived you of any continental training. But this sauce – it really won't do. I mean to say. Now why don't *I* supervise, whilst we try again?'

The staff said nothing the woman would ever hear, all of it expressed with their eyes . . .

Alone in his study, the leaden-faced Natesby perused the past year's accounts for the 32,500-acre estate, broke off to stir the fire, paused to drink his whiskey. He was not looking forward to the midday meal with Sir Richard and Lady – what was her name, Lucinda? – though his wife's insensitive matchmaking contained at least a particle of sense.

Get Grenville espoused to one of the Fitzalan girls, and the boy would stand to inherit a further 26,000 acres of County Cork. A nice parcel of land, the Fitzalans'. Damn good cattle; plenty of riverside grazing; a well-run estate, from all he'd heard.

But Sir Richard was a reader, and Natesby was not.

Lady Lucinda was forty-something in line to the throne, and Elizabeth was the daughter of a well-to-do timber merchant – but for God's sake don't mention *that* at the table.

And as for the girls, they were not just pretty, but quick as a whip-crack, and as much at ease with the locals as with the gentry.

Not really something you could say about Robert Grenville. Not much *at all* you could say in favour of Grenville. *And where was he anyway, the visitors due in an hour?*

The major-domo knocked on the door, allowing Lord Natesby time to set aside his whiskey glass, pick up his papers and pretend to be surprised.

'Hmm? What? Yes, come.'

'I regret to disturb you, my lord –'

'Well now you have, so what?'

'A gentleman to see you, my lord. Leastways by his manner. A

77

Master Cavan Lynch. Ain't he something in the port? And relative to the bailiff?'

Natesby tetched. He'd met Cavan before, their talk devolving on facts and figures, projected profits, an increase in fuel for the cotters, a special plea for the aged and infirm. *Another bloody reader.*

'All right. Send him in. But warn him I'm cut for time. Fifteen minutes is all – tell him ten – say it's all I can spare.' Then he gulped down his whiskey and papered his knees, his head down over the documents as the caller came in.

Cavan Lynch had not been here since last April, though he retained fond memories of this book-lined study. This and the library . . . Pity Lord Natesby never took the volumes down from their polished mahogany shelves.

'I apologize, Lord Natesby; I intrude upon your work. I'm Cavan Lynch, clerk of the port –'

'So you are,' the Englishman agreed, 'though what's with this modesty? You're the *Senior* Clerk, as I recall, an' been so for some distinct time. Pleasure to see you again, Master Lynch. I'll just set these papers back in order and – let's see, what's the time now? Eleven an' some. Too early to offer you refreshment?'

Having already seen the flask and the glass – *and Lord knows, am I not here to win him over?* – Cavan said a whiskey would surely beat back the cold.

'Does it every time,' Natesby approved. 'Get you a glass m'self, Master Lynch. Not much point in ringin' the bell, for a little thing like that!'

Even so, he made a fuss of it, his actions reminding his visitor that the master of Carrick Manor did not usually bestir himself for his callers. But at least *this* Lynch spoke properly. And nodded his thanks.

'Chair over there. Sit for a moment. Tell me why you've come. But I must warn you – I'm most awful skinned for time. Guests an' that. One of Lady Elizabeth's doings. I'm sure you know how it is when the wife sets a spread.'

Cavan swallowed a decent measure of the fine, matured whiskey – and yes, it did send the warmth to his limbs – then said why he'd come here, ignoring Natesby's suggestion that Adelaide could ever, these days, set a spread.

'The thing is, my lord, the region's out of balance. Kilbreen and similar wrecked hamlets on the one hand; the contents of a certain warehouse on the other. So I've come to ask for your help in the matter, counting on both your personal and Christian generosity.'

Then he waited, watching as the slate-faced Natesby acknowledged the discovery of the foodstuffs.

They each played the game impassively, the Englishman concealing his surprise, the Irishman his anger. Be patient, Cavan told himself. Don't provoke him .

'You're aware, of course, Master Lynch, that the warehouse is private property. On public land, but duly rented –'

'I am, my lord. And its contents remain untouched. However, the Authorities require me to check them all on a regular basis, which is how I discovered –'

'Very well. But how does that make it any of your affair? I'm a businessman, my dear sir. I struggle to turn a small profit. Those logs in the fire there, candles in their sticks, money for the servants, the ostlers, money for every damn thing here at Carrick – it all comes out of my own meagre coffers. Yet now, it seems, you're out to make me feel guilty.'

'Far from it, my lord. You must heat and light your mansion as you will. And it's in Ireland's interest you retain all the staff you can afford. But I repeat, if I may: things seem terribly unbalanced when we've Kilbreen on the one hand – You do know what happened at Kilbreen?'

Charles Natesby was about to say yes, oh, yes indeed. A bunch of dull-eyed peasants, without the brains God gave to trees. Potato-gobblers, all of 'em, but quickly reduced to whining and wailing when the crop they lived and died by happened to fail. Oh, yes, he knew all about Kilbreen and Macrill and the others whose names he'd forgotten. Just an endless line of gaping mouths and outstretched hands, and all of 'em plaintively crying to be kept by Carrick, nurtured by Natesby.

But he said instead: 'Let's see now. See if we can't come to a sort of compromise. Regard each other as the decent fellows we are. For example – well, here's a thought. Suppose I sell off the turnips, right there in the port? And a quarter of the wheat stocks? Would you call me ungenerous then, Master Lynch? Would you still say things were unbalanced?'

'Not at all,' Cavan told him. 'I'd be grateful to you, my lord, as would all those who could afford to buy your produce.'

'Well, there we are then – '

'But most of them cannot. And you've made no mention of the beef, the cheese, the bacon.'

'Now hold hard!' Natesby laughed. 'I do believe it's *you*, Master

Lynch, who's toppled somewhat off-balance. Sell off the meat and butter an' that? Halve a year's profits? Have the vessels I've hired sail away again high in the water?'

Cavan shook his head. 'I'm not suggesting you sell it off at all, Lord Natesby. I'm suggesting – pleading, if you will – that you distribute it among the thousands who are starving. But sell it cheap, no.'

'Glad to hear it.'

'I'm asking that you *give* it away, and not let this county die.'

Natesby lurched to his feet, pulled the study door open and roared for the major-domo.

'This man – this uninvited caller – he's now leaving! Show him to the steps!' Then he saw Cavan Lynch from the room, mouthing at him to stick with what he knew best. 'You're a clerk, Lynch, and that's all you'll ever be. Now get on back to your pens and papers, and don't ever dare tell *me* how to run my affairs! Give the stuff to your indolent bloody kinsmen? I'd rather burn it where it sits!'

Limping from the manor, Cavan was beckoned by a frantic Lady Elizabeth. She was out on the steps, fumbling with wreaths of holly and mistletoe, part of the decorations for her imminent guests, the Fitzalans.

Then she saw he was walking with difficulty, frowned and said: 'No value in asking *you* for assistance. A cripple's no good to *me*.'

He left the major-domo to hang the wreaths, and was nearing the end of the drive when Robert Grenville thundered towards him, thrashing at the haunches of his wild-eyed stallion.

The young man shouted at Cavan to move aside. 'Call him Pegasus; so where's his bloody wings?'

By the time the Senior Clerk reached home, he knew what he had to do.

It frightened him to think of it, the mild-mannered man now called upon to show courage. But there was no other way, for how else could he keep his self-respect; how else could he fight for those who could no longer fight for themselves?

Well, he thought, I'm still in charge of Shipping Affairs. Still with some authority in the port. And still with the keys.

That Sunday evening he told Adelaide that things had gone well with Lord Natesby. 'Though it's time we considered leaving for France, for you know how winter can churn the English Channel.'

His wife sensed things were not as Cavan described. His smile was too stiff, his explanations evasive. He was telling her what to do, but not why. Staying too long in the parlour, yet leaving his favourite books on the broad wooden shelves. And reminding Elisa of the life that lay ahead; 'A wonderful city, Paris, from all Mama's told us. A girl couldn't wish for better. And you speak good French already, so she assures me.'

'Are we going soon?' the girl asked. 'You make it sound as if we're going soon.'

'Likely we will. Before the Channel gets rough. So decide what you'll pack, for we'll only be allowed what we can carry.'

Elisa went upstairs to tackle the problem. And Adelaide gazed at her husband, aware that lightning – a rarity in December – might suddenly cleave between them.

The next morning Cavan limped along the track, down the railed steps, and clambered aboard the outside-car, which jolted along to his office. Then he talked to a number of people he could trust, each of them willing to help this man they thought honest and decent.

In the evening he returned to the house and told his wife and daughter he'd booked passage to Roscoff. A gig would come and collect them tomorrow, around two in the afternoon. 'I'm sorry it's hasty, but I think now's the time to leave.'

There were tears and regrets as Adelaide and Elisa bade farewell to their home. But they packed in obedience, mindful of the surprise they'd give Corinne.

'Her letter must still be somewhere in the post,' the woman accepted.

'But what if she says no? What if she says she can't have us, Mama?'

'Oh, I'm sure she will. I'm sure she'll find space. Told us what a fine house she's got there. And all those rooms to spare.'

'And when we get to Roscoff, can I have that gown?'

'I don't see why not' Adelaide said, though the words seemed to lock in her throat as she added, 'You'll needs get the francs from Papa.'

On Tuesday, 14th December – two days before the Norwegian freighter was due to sail from Cork with its cargo of salted beef and

81

bacon, butter and cheese and whatever else could be packed in the refrigerated holds – Cavan Lynch used his authority to unlock the doors of Warehouse Six.

Word of mouth had already spread the message, and the approach to the port was seething with the hundreds of townsfolk and country folk who'd made their way there, hoping without expectation that the rumours were true.

And so they were. With a military detachment on hand to control the crowd, the Irish were admitted ten at a time to the warehouse and laden with food enough for weeks to come, sent staggering on their way. Grown men wept without shame, or sank to the cobbles, thanking the Family in Heaven. Then they hauled themselves to their feet, hefted the sacks, and made light of the long miles home.

There were others who came, though not in search of food . . .

For several weeks now the port had been filled with four-and five-masted schooners, eager to take the Irish from their homeland. The majority would go to New York and the eastern seaboard of North America, at fares ranging from £5 to £15 per person. As many as twenty-five in every hundred would die before the New World was sighted.

Yet America was their goal, their Eldorado. Survive the churning Atlantic, the maggot-ridden food, the contagious diseases in the cramped and insanitary quarters below deck, and the fleeing masses would rediscover skills they'd forgotten, a sense of adventure kindled within them, the nightmare of stagnant Ireland replaced by dreams.

As the famine dug its talons ever deeper in the weakened body of the country, those who could somehow raise the exorbitant fare pushed their way past those who could not.

Although the majority would sail to America, others chose the English port of Liverpool. And a few, just a few, the continent of Europe . . .

At three o'clock, Adelaide and Elisa were deposited at the port. Tinny whistles shrilled in the air, smothered by the deeper boom of horns. A thousand orders were bawled from the decks, a thousand answers roared up from the quay. Baggage carts cut a swathe through the crowd, uniformed officers jabbing directions, the terrified emigrants herded into line.

Multicoloured tickets were waved aloft; this for First Class; that for Second; a drab dark brown for Steerage. Then a sudden swirl as a ticket was snatched, the thief dodging away, the passenger stranded and ruined. A fight for a place on the gangplank, fists and baggage flying, children lost and left wailing. Hasty farewells as families were torn apart, the old staying behind, the young not wishing to leave them. 'We'll see each other soon,' they said. 'We'll send for you to join us.' And the old ones said: 'Aye, that's it. Or you'll come back home, soon as the blight's off the leaf.' Then the clang of a bell, shouts of command, a final snatched embrace. 'Off you go now. God bless. Keep warm.' And the old ones watched as the young ones fought their way aboard the great swaying schooners, all of them unaware that fortunes were being made with every sailing.

'So what if they're packed a bit snug?' the shipping magnates remarked. 'They're desperate enough to quit Ireland, are they not? Willing to abandon their families. And what do they care if they're hip to hip, and shoulder to shoulder on the voyage? How else are the rats to leave their sinking island?'

Justifying their profits, the ship-owners saw themselves as selfless humanitarians, and boasted of the way their vessels plied the Atlantic, bent upon saving the Irish.

And so what, they repeated, if the price of the outward passage continually increased? And the passengers were kept battened below deck? Who was going to lodge a complaint? Certainly not the shivering, sickly emigrants.

Further along from the schooners, a battered, 30-foot *chalutier* nudged the quay.

The trawler's captain leaned from the wheel-house, espied Cavan Lynch and yelled above the bedlam of the port. '*Dépêchez-vous! La marée descend. Il est grand temps de partir. Ils viennent ses passagers? Oui ou non?*'

'*Une minute. Je vais voir.*'

The Breton captain watched as Cavan climbed a flight of black-tarred steps bolted to the weather-board wall of a warehouse and then peered north towards the gate. The crowd surged and swayed, Excise men pouncing on those they thought worth the effort, cynically charging them an Embarkation Fee – 'Five shillings coin. What do you mean, you haven't got it? Well, what the devil *have* you got?'

Then Cavan saw his wife and daughter and beckoned them urgently. They jostled their way along the quay, Adelaide carrying two worn valises, Elisa with a bag of her own.

'*Ça y est! Elles arrivent.*'

The captain of the trawler *Mariette* acknowledged Cavan's shout. The balding clerk scrambled backwards down the steps, forcing his way towards the *chalutier*.

An Excise man blocked his path. 'You. You paid your Embarkation Fee? Five shillings by Order of the Government. Can't let you aboard without –'

It gave Cavan Lynch the chance to say what he'd long dreamed of saying to one of the port's fancy peacocks, though he'd rather have had more time in which to measure his riposte.

'Don't be such a damn fool. You're addressing the Senior Clerk of Shipping Affairs for the Port of Cork. And there is *no* Government Order. There is *no* Embarkation Fee. You're a pilferer in plumage. A tasselled-up tout. Now leave these people alone.'

The man gaped and backed into someone's sharp elbow. He winced, and Cavan barged past him, enjoying the faintest tug of a smile. *Been wanting to say that for years . . .*

He reached the foot of the *Mariette*'s gangplank in time to greet his wife. 'You must get aboard now,' he said, voice raised to combat the blare of the horns, the shriek of the whistles. 'Captain Leguelec's anxious to leave. And you're to tell Corinne – '

By then Elisa had crowded alongside her mother, the girl shouting up at him, 'Why's Mama to – ? Surely *you* can – I mean, you're coming too!'

Adelaide told her daughter to hurry aboard. 'Kiss Papa, but be quick, then get on the boat.'

'But wait! I don't see why – '

'*Will you, please, for one time in your life, do as you're told!*' Adelaide's voice broke as the tension and truth of the moment swept across her.

Cavan was not coming with them.

He stooped and embraced his daughter, turned her skinny shoulders and sent her stumbling into the care of a deckhand, gesturing to the man to guide her aboard. Elisa said no, twisted round, and fought to be free of the man's firm grasp. She was now sharing the terrible truth with her mother.

Papa would not sail with them.

'*Embarques-la vite*,' Cavan said. '*Prends soin d'elle.*' Then he reached for his wife and said he was sorry, but he must stay here for a while –

'Oh, I realize now.' Adelaide nodded, her eyes filling with tears. 'From the moment you first told me, I think I knew. You were ever the type to sit quiet, brewing on a challenge. Then would rise, like good beer – And now you've opened the warehouse, am I not right, and shared out the food – '

'Leguelec's growing impatient. It's time you were aboard.'

' – and you're staying here, so the Excise men won't chase us in their cutters – '

'Off you go now. Elisa's at war with half the crew.'

'They'll send you to prison, my love. Or they'll ship you to the colonies. Or worse than that, if Natesby demands it – '

'Swing me off? No, he won't do that. He'd have half the county marching up to Carrick. The funny thing is – but I must surrender you to the captain – I've been, what is it, twenty-five years as a clerk, and now it seems I'm a hero. But if Lord Natesby's friendly magistrates point me to the gallows, I might well become a martyr. And I can't see the English, blinkered though they are, being quite as blind as that.' Then he kissed the woman with whom he had fallen in love in Bristol, and loved ever since, and handed her over to the sailors, reminding them not to forget the two valises.

The mooring ropes were lifted from their bollards, and the *Mariette* drifted from the quay.

Adelaide stood near the wheel-house, elegant still for all she'd shared in the famine.

And then Elisa came to stand with her, what looked like a clasp-knife waved urgently aloft, the girl's free hand brushing her flawless cheek.

The *chalutier* was already well out into the Lee, the suck of the tide drawing it away. But Cavan understood what his late-born daughter was trying to make clear.

She'd packed his razor.

And then Lord Charles Cassel Natesby arrived in person, accompanied by his son, Robert Grenville, and his steward-cum-bailiff, Conor Egan Lynch.

Grenville had armed himself for the occasion, riding down with a rifle across his knees.

'So we've been robbed in broad daylight, eh? A year's work gone for nothing? Well, you just leave that bloody accountant to me! Blow his hairless skull off, see if I don't!'

It upset him when Lord Natesby wrenched the rifle from his grasp and threw it into the river.

'But he's a thief! He's given away what's ours!'

Conor Lynch pretended not to hear as Lord Natesby said: 'Not ours, my greedy Grenville. Mine, without doubt. And my wife's, by cohesion. But not yours at all till we die. So not *ours*. Now why don't you stay back here and swap stories with the horses? Steward Conor and I will see if the thief's to be taken.'

Leaving Grenville to sulk, they barged their way past the lines of those still waiting to board the schooners. Conor jumped up to peer above the crowd, then said: 'There! He's along at the end.'

'Makin' ready to escape?'

'No, my lord, not so's I can see. Just stood there quiet.'

'More fool him,' Natesby muttered. 'Maybe he's frozen with fear.'

They found Cavan Lynch gazing southwards at the distant, rust-coloured sails of the trawler *Mariette*, loath to turn as Natesby bellowed his name.

'I've had word,' the Englishman told him, 'that you've done away with my stock. It's a hard thing to credit, Master Lynch, and I hope to hear you deny it. Well, sir? Well?'

Cavan left the dipping *chalutier* to her voyage, nodding at Natesby and said yes, the message was correct. He'd taken it upon himself to open Warhouse Six, and had emptied it – 'Leastways, I hope I have' – to the final grain of corn. 'It should now be the cleanest shed in the port. And ready for your bricks and tiles . . .'

Hands reached out to grab him, two voices raised in fury. Conor's first, the bailiff enraged that his nephew had rejected his advice. 'I warned you to mind your own business! Who do you think you are to go against Natesby? I mean to say, *Lord* Natesby! The damage you've done to Carrick – '

'Perhaps, though I doubt it. As I doubt they'll starve in South-ampton, or Ostend.'

Then the second voice, Natesby calling to the soldiers and the Excise men, appealing to anyone in uniform to take this man in charge. 'I want him arrested! Held for trial! He stands condemned from his own mouth. Yet look at him! Where's the remorse? He's just happy to stand and watch the vessels sail by!'

'Only that one,' Cavan corrected, his arms pinned tight. 'Only the one bound for France. She rides well, don't you think? Trust to the weather, it shouldn't be too rough a crossing.'

Well now, he accepted; so it's over.

I'll be brought to trial, then imprisoned for what the magistrates choose to call the duration of my natural life. A nice turn of phrase that – four to a cell, and manacled, and subjected to the lash – yet all of it called natural.

But at least there'll be families with food enough to eat, staving off the worst of this blighted winter. Far short of what they deserve, but better than nothing.

And, most important of all, Adelaide and Elisa are on the boat. With an address to go to in Paris. A new life awaiting them. *God knows, they merit that.*

PART TWO

Paris: 1848–1850

1

On 7th January 1848, the Austrian-born Adelaide and the Irish-born Elisa completed the final stage of their journey from Cork to Corinne's house in Rue Simon le Franc.

It had taken them far longer than they'd expected, for a sudden storm in the Channel had carried the trawler *Mariette* off course, and the boat had run for shelter to the Cornish port of Falmouth. Gale-force winds had imprisoned the *chalutier* for a week and even then Captain Leguelec had been obliged to take his vessel as far east as Salcombe before daring to cross the Channel.

The passengers had reached Roscoff in time to spend a dismal Christmas in a cheap hotel waiting for the once-a-week public wagon that would take them onward to Paris. The crowded conveyance had covered the four hundred miles in twelve days, the travellers jolted along in cold discomfort.

Exhausted by the sea voyage and the seemingly endless journey aboard the wagon, Adelaide and her daughter were ill-prepared for the sight that greeted them in the *quartier* of St Merri.

The driver of the cabriolet that brought them from the wagon terminus stopped well short of their destination, announcing it was as close as his vehicle could get. 'The place you're looking for's down there. Through that arch, and it's somewhere along on the left. Fourth and fifth, though you'd best ask someone who knows their way round the warren.' Then he'd overcharged them, safe in the knowledge that foreigners never complained, and left them at the gateway to St Merri.

His description was accurate, though few animals would tolerate such a warren. Four, five- and six-storey houses leaned inwards, barring the light. Smoke poured out from narrow, red-brick chimneys, swirling beneath the overcast, or blown back on the down-draught of the wind. The air smelled vile and the open gutters stank, tanners competing with purveyors of greasy sausage, each of them discarding their unwanted scraps in the fast-running ditches of the drains. Blowzy, broad-hipped women squatted on stools or cheap kitchen chairs, the guardians of their doorways, their lips and chins stained with tobacco juice, jets of it spat at their feet. Unemployed men lounged in groups, muttering their anger at life, or roaring in disagreement, the groups swaying back at a sudden exchange of blows. Jars of colourless absinthe were guarded or shared, an empty jar always useful as a weapon. And all along the street, on either side of the gutter, children scampered and squealed, or splashed for the fun of it in the blood and offal of the drain.

Adelaide and her daughter clung tight to their bags, telling themselves the driver had misunderstood. Maybe there were *two* streets in Paris called Simon le Franc, and the one they wanted was miles from St Merri.

'I think we're lost,' Elisa quavered. 'Let's go back to the arch.'

'We will soon enough,' Adelaide told her. 'But we must first make sure we've gone wrong.'

Hesitant to approach the dull-eyed men, she asked directions from a girl who looked no older than Elisa, though this inhabitant of the warren was suckling a baby.

'You want to know where's le Franc? Want to know enough to pay a centime?'

'One for you, and one for the baby. But don't tell me lies.'

The girl weighed her chances, sensed a fairness and firmness in Adelaide's tired gaze, and said it was three streets along – 'Past the bread shop'.

Now almost penniless herself, for the journey had cost far more than she'd anticipated, Adelaide nevertheless found two centimes for the mother and her baby. Then she led her own child deeper into the warren, both of them strangely encouraged to see each off-street alleyway narrower than the last – proof surely that the city contained *another* Rue Simon le Franc.

All those twice-a-year letters from Corinne . . . The creative Madame Barachin working hand in glove with one of the great *couturiers* . . . Her husband much in demand as a talented musician . . . Her two daughters pretty as pictures . . . Her house light and airy . . .

Of course we've been misled by the cunning driver. But our own fault, too. Should have asked which Rue Simon le Franc was the one with fine houses, and not wasted money coming here.

The bread shop was filthy, its windows webbed and grimy. But the rain-streaked sign outside was enough to mark the entrance of their dead-end search.

'We'll go back to the archway, and treat ourselves to a bowl of chocolate, how's that? We've not much money left, my dear, though enough to locate Corinne. Now remind me, what was the number? *Onze bis?*'

Forced to straddle the gutter of the alley, Elisa said: 'There – nine b . . . Ten b . . . The next one. Do you want me to practise my French, Mama? *"Veuillez m'excuser, mais je cherche la résidence de Madame Barachin."* And then they'll say no, they haven't the faintest inkling – *"La moindre idée"* – and we can leave this dreadful place and find a café. *"Deux chocolats chauds, s'il vous plaît!"* And some kind of cake to eat with it? *"Un petit gâteau?"* '

Still playing with the language her mother had taught her, she stood grinning as Adelaide rapped on the door – as a lank-haired woman emerged from the gloom – as Adelaide stepped back in shock and the woman raised a hand to stifle a scream.

It was the right address after all.

Corinne Barachin made no attempt to justify her lies. She had never expected her mother and younger sister to come here, yet here they were now. And even if she'd had warning of their intended visit, what could she have done? The *quartier* of St Merri was one of the poorest in the city; Rue Simon le Franc one of the oldest; the Barachin dwelling as squalid as the rest. No more than fifteen feet wide, its walls were blotched with damp, tiny rooms piled two above two, the house all but devoid of light and air. Throughout the centuries the building had leaned and settled, windows admitting the stench and noise of the alley, thin doors dragging on buckled floorboards.

A miserable fire burned in what passed for the kitchen, children's clothes strung around the hearth, a baby crying fretfully in its plain wooden cot.

Adelaide glanced quizzically at Corinne. 'A neighbour's child?'

'No, he's ours,' she replied, shrugging. 'Born to us by surprise, you might say. Been sickly this winter . . .'

'You never mentioned *that* in your letters,' Elisa remarked. 'Told us about the spacious rooms, and how cool they were in summer, and how you were working for the great *couturiers*, and – '

'That'll do,' Adelaide told her.

' – and how you rode out to the parks in your private carriage, and how Jean-Pierre was one of the best-known musicians – '

'I said that will do!'

' – and all about your daughters, pretty as pictures, *and never as dumpy as me!*'

Elisa stopped and glared at her elder sister, her emotions tangled by the need to revenge herself for all the insults, the pretentious boasts, the outright lies – and by a deadening sense of sorrow for this woman who was young in years, yet pinched and stooped in defeat. It wasn't fair that Corinne had written what she had. But neither was it fair that all of it had to be dreams . . .

Corinne fingered wisps of lank hair, tucking them beneath a plain cambric bonnet. Then she listlessly smoothed her workaday gown, nodding as the arrows struck their mark.

'I should not have said what I did – what I wrote – and I never knew you to be dumpy. It was done without thinking. Twice a year for, how long is it? And always without thinking.' Then she whispered that she was sorry, her pale eyes filling with tears.

Adelaide waited, allowing Elisa her chance. Ten years younger than her sister, it was now the moment for Elisa to choose. Smirk in victorious disapproval, or recognize that life itself tells lies. Stand where she was, and leave the wounds open, or go forward and bandage them tight.

'What's the baby's name, Corinne? I'd need some instruction, but I wouldn't mind helping look after him. Sing him some of the songs I learned in Miss Gardiner's General Day School. So long as you don't mind him picking up words in English.'

'His name's Olivier,' Corinne told her. 'And no, I don't mind at all, Elisa. Though I doubt you'd need much instruction.' Then she smiled and extended her work- and winter-worn hands, offering them to the family she'd not seen for six long years.

Cécile and Simone were brought down from their room beneath the eaves. Scrawny and timid, their French was weak, their grasp of English even weaker. 'My husband prefers them to speak his own language,' Corinne said with another, habitual shrug. 'Though I sometimes address them in English when he's away.'

'And where is he now, my dear?'

'Jean-Pierre? Well, he's – Oh, yes, I remember. He's auditioning for a new orchestra, *L'Orchestre du Palais Royal*. If he gets the job, and there's every chance he will, he'll be one of the solo violinists. With a contract for the season. He really is brilliant, Jean-Pierre, though you can't imagine how hard he works. The life of the artist!'

She gave a short, brittle laugh, then asked about Cavan. Was he well? Why had he sent Adelaide and Elisa away in mid-winter? Were things really as bad in Ireland as the newspapers reported? 'Do you think I'll find him much changed in six years? Bound to, I suppose,

94

though I'd surely boast of him here, Senior Clerk of Shipping Affairs in Cork!'

'You might wish to blanket your boasts,' Adelaide said gently. 'Your father is likely in gaol, and committed there for life. Hurting no one – except, perhaps, a gentleman's purse – he took it upon himself to play the hero. But the story will keep till Jean-Pierre comes home. And till Elisa here learns to comfort Olivier. And you teach me the workings of your kitchen.' Then she put an arm around Corinne's shoulder and said: 'You've nothing to be ashamed of, you see. Dreams are rarely fulfilled, it seems, these days. So let's hope Jean-Pierre gets the job he went after!'

The bony, dark-suited man returned late, a battered violin-case under his arm.

Corinne had been listening for the sound of his key in the lock, and she hurried out to greet him in the passageway. Elisa and her mother exchanged a glance, hoping to hear a cry of delight as the musician told his wife he'd been accepted.

They were outside for several minutes, their voices low and urgent. Then the man entered the kitchen and gazed impassively at his visitors, saying nothing.

'It's a pleasure to meet you, Monsieur Barachin. I'm Adelaide Lynch. Corinne's mother. And this is Elisa Alicia, her younger sister. I apologize for arriving uninvited, but circumstances – '

'You speak good French,' the man said. 'But you're right. You weren't invited. It's a small enough place for the five of *us*, without two more from Ireland.'

'Yes, I appreciate that,' Adelaide said, nodding, 'and we'd only ask shelter for a while. But you'll find us a capable pair, Monsieur Barachin – '

'Oh, they are,' Corinne encouraged. 'As I told you just now, *chéri*, they can help in all kinds of ways.'

The musician admitted nothing, keeping his distance. He made no attempt to approach his calm but weary mother-in-law, and all but ignored Elisa.

The girl said: 'Corinne tells us you went for an audition today. Did it go as you wished? Get your contract?'

'What? Oh, that. Yeah, no problem. Now I've got some stuff to rehearse upstairs. See you maybe tomorrow.' It was said in slurred and gutter French, Jean-Pierre then telling his wife to bring his soup and bread to the music room. 'And fetch a jug of cider from the café.'

95

Corinne bobbed her head in obedience, then waited until he'd gone before offering Adelaide a pinched and bloodless smile. 'They're all alike, these artists. Strive for years to be recognized and, when it happens, they dismiss it with scarcely a mention. See how he answered Elisa?'

'Which orchestra is it, my dear? You told me, but I forget.'

'The one in the – now isn't that silly, I do declare it's slipped my mind too. But of course! The one in the Place Royale! *L'Orchestra de la Place Royale.*'

'What you said before,' Elisa murmured, 'was the *Palais* Royal. Is that perhaps what you meant?'

'Well, yes, you're right! That's where he'll be playing. I can't tell you what a relief it is. The security of a contract, even for just a season.'

'I'll keep an eye on the soup,' Adelaide said gently, 'whilst you fetch Jean-Pierre his jug of cider. But is that what he drinks for preference, rather than wine?'

'Wine's more expensive. It's only down in the south they drink much wine.'

Adelaide stirred the soup as Elisa cut bread, Corinne hurrying off with a heavy, earthenware pitcher.

Neither mother nor daughter voiced their thoughts aloud, though each believed that Corinne was lying again. For even artists trumpet their triumphs.

In the weeks that followed, the uninvited visitors from Ireland proved their worth.

It was Adelaide who took charge of Cécile and Simone, and nursed the infant Olivier back to health. Elisa was willing enough to help with the children, but Corinne found something else for the girl to do, a task the newcomer relished.

The truth soon emerged that Corinne Barachin, *née* Lynch, had never been employed by the city's great *couturiers*, but merely patched and mended for the inhabitants of St Merri. It was just another dream, written as reality.

Yet the task she created for Elisa was certainly astute, and made all the more successful by the twelve-year-old's gift for French.

In competition with other seamstresses, Corinne decided to offer her customers a special service. Door-to-door delivery. In future, their mended garments would be returned to them at home, those in need of repair collected, and twenty centimes added to the bill. It was a small enough sum – the price of a loaf of bread – and she estimated that all but a few would be willing to pay for the convenience.

Having recovered from her disappointment at finding the immediate area so depressing, Elisa was now eager to roam beyond the confines of Simon le Franc. Sent on three, then five, then ten deliveries a day, the girl soon learned her way around the district, her arms full of bundles, a list of addresses in the left-hand pocket of her dress, a flat leather purse in the right.

Some of the routes were boring, though on occasion she was sent through the nearby Marché des Innocents, the extensive central market that would later be known as Les Halles. This, to a girl from a country lane outside Cork, was a wild and magical kingdom.

Approached by a network of alleys, the intersections were alive with jugglers, cardsharps, fire-eaters, sword-swallowers, gaudily-robed men with performing monkeys, black-skinned men with squawking parrots, prophets who claimed the River Seine would soon rise and submerge the city, others selling flasks of 'concentrated water' before the Great Drought shrivelled the land. And, fast on their feet, the ever-present pickpockets, though the girl alert to the danger . . .

The market-place itself was filled with a thousand stalls, selling everything from sweet-scented soap to watercress – 'Good for your love-life!' – and from feathers to gingerbread – 'Good for your love-life!' – and from African charms to the salt-fish of Brittany – 'All of it good for your love-life!'

Young women made their purchases and hurried away, whilst married women stayed to slap their thighs and laugh with the vendor. Young men loitered, waited until the stall was free, then snatched at the ginger, the anchovies, the secret essence of the root found only in Siberia, concealing what they'd bought beneath a heavy, unwanted cabbage.

Elisa soon learned to spot a girl in love by the blush of her cheek; a man in love by his preference for the cabbage. It amused her to call cheekily to the girls: '*A tes amours,*' though it wasn't a thing she could say to the men – her ear clipped twice when she'd tried it.

But all was not laughter and chatter in the market of St Merri. Violence erupted without warning, and she witnessed a pickpocket skewered by a knife, a drunkard's jaw shattered by a policeman's club, a score of beggars kicked where they lay, prostitutes rejected as they propositioned a stroller.

When times were quiet, Elisa watched the knife-grinders, the leather-merchants, the delicate work of the porcelain-menders, the dripping lead of the plumbers, the plumes that rose from the coverlets and pillows of the featherers, coughing as they offered the common-place duck, or the more expensive goosedown.

Running along the side streets and into the market, the girl filled her nostrils with a thousand different scents – and smells – and stenches. Everything from the bottled perfumes of Southern France to the suffocating odour of an animal's intestines. Everything from fresh-baked bread to discarded squid. The best and the worst, and Elisa pinched her nose so as not, if possible, to mix them.

There was always the risk that a petty thief would snatch her string-wrapped bundles of clothes, but if they did they'd hear a fine Irish yell! Let 'em just try it. She'd bring St Merri to a halt.

For all the hazards, she adored the area, in and around the market, and it was clear from the first that Corinne's customers liked her younger sister. She was quite the novelty, after all, with her russet hair and pale green eyes, cheerful smile and endearing foreign accent. They held her in conversation, getting their money's worth, then paid the extra centimes without demur.

As the cold, clear January days went by, Elisa was recognized by the stall-holders, some of whom would allow her a biscuit, a lump of broken chocolate, an extra few grammes of whatever Corinne had sent her to buy for the soup. And the monkey man would give her almonds to feed to his pet, the parrot man calling to the crowd to see how his bird loved to talk to pretty girls. It was good for business, and a wide new world for Elisa.

The rented house now the province of women, Jean-Pierre Barachin left them to get on with it. The Lynch girl was bringing his wife as much work as she could handle. Adelaide was not only nursing the baby, but washing the children's clothes, teaching them games, tucking them up in bed.

Fine, he accepted. So long as they pull their weight.

Dressed as always in his tight black suit, he ate his breakfast of yesterday's bread dipped in watery chocolate, collected his violin-case and departed, not to be seen again until dusk. No matter how inclement the weather, the man remained absent, though Corinne repeated that her husband was warmer up there, near the Palais Royal, sawing away in some heated rehearsal-room . . .

'And when will his first concert be performed?' Adelaide asked. 'Perhaps he could get us tickets. Or anyway for you and Elisa. I'd be happy to stay with the children, so long as I hear all about it. And you bring back the programme.'

'No date's been fixed. It's most likely to be in – in March. Yes, that's it. Sometime in March. But isn't that Olivier squalling? Would you mind going to see?'

In the evenings, Jean-Pierre returned home, ate his soup and bread in the hutch he called his music-room, then stayed there, or went out till well past midnight. Corinne explained that her husband gave lessons, though was vague when Adelaide asked who to, and surely not around here? 'And he rarely takes his violin, I've noticed. Does he teach things other than music?'

'Oh, if only you knew him better! Knew how gifted he really is! Now before I forget, I must light the lamp at the foot of the staircase. Wouldn't do to have Jean-Pierre sprain his wrist when he comes home!'

Adelaide shook her head; no, it wouldn't. Then she told herself that whatever other sad lies her daughter had admitted, she was still stitching a fabric of fabrication for Jean-Pierre.

The rooms being so small, Elisa shared a bed with her mother, an advantage in winter, but a sure way of robbing Adelaide of her sleep.

Excited by all she'd seen in the district, the girl insisted on recounting the day's event's – or asking if her mother thought Cavan had really been sent to prison. 'I mean, I guess he has, or he'd have written by now. But he's clever, Papa. He'll talk his way out, I'd just bet on it.'

'Shhh. Go to sleep.'

'And Jean-Pierre, he's an odd one. I'd hate to be married to someone like that. Wouldn't see him all day, and *then* he goes out in the evening. And he never spends time with his children. I just hope for Corinne's sake – '

'Will you please go to sleep. And stop tugging at my nightgown.'

Elisa sighed and sank into her pillow. Then, as she dreamed, she moved her lips, mimicking the parrot who mimicked in French: '*Venez me voir! Venez me voir!*'

Every morning, and often before the grey dawn light had touched the rooftops of the city, Elisa would awake to the street sounds of St Merri. Little by little she learned to identify them, though the first, individual noises were soon joined by others, and by six o'clock all the district was awake.

First, though, came the scavenger, a lantern in one hand, burlap sack in the other. Muttering to himself, and coughing against the chill and stench of the alleys, he would pick his way through the leavings of those who had nothing to discard. Oh, a pair of rotted shoes, perhaps. A broken basket. A leather strap from which someone had forgotten to cut the buckle. A length of cord he might be able to take apart and shorten and re-plait. A jar he could scour with vinegar, then re-sell – if only he could find a cork to fit it.

A sad and lonely task, competing with the rats of St Merri . . .

At six the local church bells were rung, a flat and discordant invitation to the homeless. They could now leave their ditches and cellars, stretch their night-stiffened limbs and make their way to the lesser cold of God's houses. There'd be no bread or soup for them yet – too early – though at least they could huddle from the rain.

If the sound of the church bells offered some slight encouragement to those who had spent the night unprotected, it also brought the more fortunate from their beds. Coffee was brewed – or re-brewed for the fourth and fifth time – and laced with *eau-de-vie*. The colourless alcohol mingled with the acrid taste of the cheap, ground coffee and, with the fumes of it on their breath, the workers emerged.

Women came out to sweep the cobbles. Merchants grunted as they swung back the shutters of their shops. Costermongers and barrow boys went to their sheds; loaded their trays; trundled their handcarts to the market to buy what they hoped they could hawk in the outlying district. Lanterns were lighted in the shops, and stoves rekindled. Stiff and aching, yet always competitive, the inhabitants of St Merri came to terms with the day . . .

Well before seven – and Elisa clinging to the warmth of each precious minute in bed – the market district rang with the strident cries of the street-vendors, each tearing his throat to bellow down the others.

'*A la coque! A la coque!* Fresh eggs! *A la coque!* . . .'

'. . . *A la barque!* Get your oysters! River oysters! *A la barque!* . . .'

'. . . Nice fat mussels! Come an' get 'em! *Au gros caillou* . . .'

These, and a score of others, the scavenger long gone now, the homeless begging for their soup, Elisa and Adelaide awake and dressed, and the market-place of Les Innocents drowned by noise.

It was not just the parrot who drew the girl to the life of St Merri. It was clever of the bird to shrill: '*Venez me voir! Venez me voir!*' But the myriad sounds seemed to beckon her, and she did, indeed, wish to see what was going on in the early hours.

2

Great events meant little to those who had nothing.

The ebb and flow of power among nations mattered less than the scarcity of firewood, the increasing price of food. The world of the common people extended as far as the factories, the market stalls, the bars and *bals musettes*. What occurred beyond their own particular neighbourhood could as well have occurred in another part of the country, in another country entirely.

Yet in February 1848, the people of Paris forced the ever-insecure King Louis-Philippe to abdicate, and the last French monarch and his entourage fled to oblivion in England. Several thousand workers were killed in the uprising, and the following weeks saw the capital all but paralysed by the presence there of more than 100,000 troops. Martial Law stamped its nailed imprint on the city. A curfew was imposed; theatres and restaurants closed indefinitely, along with the corner cafés. Monarchists were denounced and hunted down.

An old name in a new guise re-emerged – that of Charles Louis Napoleon, the forty-five-year-old nephew of the great Emperor Napoleon Bonaparte. The final flirtation with the monarchy was over; '*A bas le Roi!*' There was talk of electing Napoleon president; talk of a Second Republic. There were also a thousand rumours . . .

Tucked away near the right bank of the Seine, Rue Simon le Franc was spared the bullets and sabre charges of the brief but bloody insurrection. Its occupants heard that the king had been ousted, crowns and coronets replaced by cocked hats shaped like wedges of lemon, braided or trimmed with feathers. They heard that England, staunchly monarchist, would soon declare war on France. And that Russia had already done so. And that Charles Louis Napoleon had been assassinated. Then that he'd survived. Then that the story was completely unfounded.

Rumours had it that the guillotine was once again busy, as in the days of the Revolution. And that the English were already storming inland from Calais. And that the Russians were less than a week's forced march from Paris.

The inhabitants of St Merri learned to shrug the rumours aside.

Personally, they couldn't care a damn who wore what on his head, cocked hat or jewel-encrusted crown. All that mattered was that the itchy-fingered militia were posted at every street corner, the infantrymen with fixed bayonets, officers secretly hoping for the chance to bring down a fleeing monarchist, a foreign spy, anyone who looked or acted suspiciously.

Elisa pleaded to be about her business. 'There's a pile of stuff to be delivered, Mama, and I'm not so silly as to stay out after the curfew. And so what if I'm a foreigner? I'm carrying mended clothes, after all, not messages written in code.'

But Adelaide remained firm, and was grateful for Corinne's support. 'I'm sure you see it all as rather romantic, my dear, but you'd get no further than Rue Reynard before some zealous young soldier demanded to open the bundles. He'd see the colour of your hair – '

'So I'll wear a bonnet.'

'Hear you speak – '

'I'll pretend I'm dumb.'

'Then march you off to the nearest military post for interrogation. It's hard to know what to believe these days, but France is clearly in turmoil, and we won't risk you getting hurt.'

Elisa sulked, then brightened when Jean-Pierre told them they could all sit tight, but *he* was going out. 'I couldn't care less about regiments or revolutions. To hell with the lot of 'em. This is *my* city, and I'll damn well go where I please.' Ignoring his wife's pleas for caution, he collected his violin-case and strode to the door.

'Wait!' Elisa called. 'I'll come with you. The two of us together – '

'And you with your bundles? Sorry, *ma biche*, but you wouldn't keep up.'

The street door banged behind him, and Olivier was startled awake.

Half an hour later, Jean-Pierre Barachin slapped the door with a blood-smeared hand. He trembled uncontrollably, unable to find his key in his pocket, his lips split and bleeding, tears of pain in his eyes.

The women bathed his injuries, appalled to see that two of his teeth had been snapped at the roots, and a long, almost oval bruise puffed his cheek.

'Oh, God,' Corinne wailed. 'What happened?'

It took him a while to tell them, his erstwhile arrogance reduced to sobs of self-pity. Adelaide moved back, saying nothing, leaving her

103

elder daughter to care for her husband, and her younger daughter to accept that insurrections were never romantic.

He'd got as far as Rue Aubrey le Boucher, when two young troopers had stopped him.

They'd been pleasant enough, asking who he was and where he was headed, and might they inspect his case? But Jean-Pierre would have none of it, repeating what he'd said in Simon le Franc. 'I've heard the king's gone, and someone's taken his place. There's talk of another Napoleon, so it seems. Though I'll see what he offers us artists before I bend the knee. Meanwhile, I'll thank you to stand aside. I was born in this city, and St Merri is mine!'

The first soldier had then tipped down his bayonet, revolving his rifle, and slammed the civilian in the face. The blow had caught Jean-Pierre on the cheek, sending him wheeling backwards. Instinctively turning to face his attacker, he'd been struck again, this time by the second trooper, another rifle-butt jabbed at his mouth. He'd collapsed against a drainpipe, denting the lead with his fall. Spitting blood and the bones of his teeth, he'd glimpsed the infantrymen kick at his violin-case, smashing the locks and springing the battered lid.

Then one of them had said: 'Fine. Off you go. But next time don't get clever. Next time, m'sieur, we'll furrow your bloody ribs!'

Then they'd swung their rifles upright again, standing the brass-heeled butts on the ground, and grinned as Jean-Pierre fumbled for his instrument, and was sent choking on his way . . .

'All those deemed to be worthy of arrest shall be halted with courtesy, and questioned in a moderate tone of voice. If they reply in a similar tone, and are thought to be co-operative, the military shall in no way use force, nor any threatening behaviour. However, in cases of violence, by word or deed, the military shall take such measures as they deem appropriate, keeping in mind their duty to subdue. Should a civilian be permanently incapacitated or killed, the case will be heard by a Military Tribunal . . .'

Well, he wasn't. He'd been given a lesson, that's all. And toothless or not, he could still play his stupid fiddle . . .

The presence of the troops restricted life throughout Paris, and not least of all in the alley of Simon le Franc.

Elisa moped around the house, her mother still nursing the baby and caring for the children. Corinne completed her mending, though with no new work coming in the lank-haired woman now traipsed upstairs at least ten times a day, at Jean-Pierre's beck and call.

Adelaide grew visibly tired, and her thoughts turned across the water towards Ireland, frightened for her husband. If soldiers could injure civilians in Paris, then God knows what warders could do to their prisoners, walled in an Irish gaol.

She wrote to Cavan's uncle – Lord Natesby's steward and bailiff – Conor Egan Lynch:

> I beg you to inform me where Cavan is, and how he gets on. I have yet to learn the pronouncement of the court. Was my husband severely sentenced for what he did, or did Cork rise up to defend him, as Heaven must wish?
>
> Write to me here, and tell me the best, or the worst. The pain of not knowing turns to anguish, and you can trust me to cast my eyes across the truth.
>
> Elisa is well. She skitters round the district better than anyone. Or did until the army moved in. And I'm sure she will again, when they've gone.

It was not until April that the troops were withdrawn from the city.

Jean-Pierre Barachin, once again his arrogant self, returned to his daily rehearsals, more than happy to leave the women to themselves.

Elisa asked if she too could leave, and get back to delivering the bundles. 'Give me what you've got, Corinne, and I bet I can bring you back *twice* the weight! You just see if I don't!'

With Adelaide's approval, Elisa went back to her work. Corinne's customers were glad to see the girl again, the stall-holders tossing her cubes of coloured marzipan, or dipping the scales in her favour.

The man with the monkey welcomed her, as did the man with the parrot. Her red hair was more lustrous now, her green eyes brighter. A foreigner to France, she was nevertheless a part of the Marché des Innocents, and they enjoyed her presence.

The exchange of crown for cocked hat now forgotten, life in St Merri returned to normal.

Adelaide sat with the infant and the children.

Corinne continued to patch and mend for the locals.

Jean-Pierre stayed away until dusk, though as often as not going out again, his departures unexplained.

Elisa scurried the streets, delivering and collecting, smiling as she was held in conversation by her customers, the thirteen-year-old far older than her years.

She adored what she was doing. Chose the alleyway that would take her to the parrot, the street that would curve towards the

105

monkey. Hitched her bundles and waved at her friends, then scampered on.

There could never be a market as colourful as the Marché des Innocents, she decided. Nor a *quartier* so full of contradictions as St Merri.

But Elisa had come to know it now – and embraced it.

In May, the business burgeoning again, Elisa Lynch lost her way. She'd crossed Rue Reynard, walked westwards along Le Boucher, skirted the southern edge of the market and entered Rue Coquillière, the street of the shellfish merchants. Faced with a cheese-wedge of alleys, she went left instead of right, the furthest she'd ever ventured from Simon le Franc.

She found herself in a small, tree-shaded *place*, its centre dominated by a massive, forty-foot elm. On the far side of the square was a brightly-painted café, a group of street-musicians playing outside.

Peering past the trunk of the elm, Elisa stopped to listen. She recognized the tune – '*La Fille de Bretagne*' – and wondered if she dare go across and drop a few centimes in their wicker bowl. It would mean admitting it later to Corinne, and risking her sister's anger, but they were playing so well . . .

There were two girls and two men, the girls with flute and tambourine; the men with violins tucked tight beneath their chins. The girls were in colourful gowns, the men in severe black suits. One of the violinists was bulky and bearded; the other bony, clean-shaven, his head tipping forward as he gently caressed the strings.

Elisa decided to risk Corinne's disapproval, and started across the square.

Then the tune finished with a brief tattoo on the tambourine. And the musicians waited to see if a passer-by would acknowledge their efforts.

And Elisa dodged for cover, behind the elm, her lips pinched tight to smother her surprise.

The tallest of the four, Jean-Pierre Barachin, lowered his instrument, laid his violin in its case and massaged his thin, chilled fingers, gazing around the *place* that was his Palais Royal, his open-air rehearsal-room . . .

The girl retreated, then turned and retraced her steps along the street. Her emotions mixed, she was assailed by indignation, swamped by pity. *So that's all he is! For all his arrogance and lies, he's just a fiddler, with a begging bowl at his feet. So much for the auditions. So much for his practising upstairs.*

And yet . . . He *had* played well, very well, her sister's sulky husband, and it didn't seem fair that he had to spend his days outside a café, relying on the income of tossed-out coins . . .

She decided to tell her mother what she'd seen. But say nothing to Corinne. And nothing to Jean-Pierre. As Adelaide had remarked when they'd first come to Simon le Franc, dreams are rarely fulfilled. So where was the value in tearing at the shreds?

3

The summer of 1848 brought further riots, further rumours. The Government decided to close a number of unprofitable, State-run factories, denying a livelihood to thousands of young workers. Given the choice between military service and dispersal to the provinces, they took to the streets of the capital, where for four days in June they defied Army dragoons and the troops of the National Guard.

By the time the insurrection had been crushed, more than ten thousand rioters had been killed or wounded. The barricades were dismantled. The factories remained closed.

Once again, a dusk-to-dawn curfew was imposed. Once again Rue Simon le Franc was spared the bayonets and bullets. Once again the Barachins and the Lynches waited for life to return to normal, Jean-Pierre now wise enough to stay indoors of an evening.

Adelaide busied herself with Corinne's children, Corinne herself with her mending, and Elisa with her daytime deliveries. Now regarded as a mascot by those in the market, the girl was known to them as the pretty redhead, *la belle rouquine*.

Though her time was devoted to the infant Olivier, to Cécile and Simone, to whatever tasks Corinne asked her to perform, Adelaide Katherina Lynch found her private moments filled with concern for Cavan. More than six months had passed since he'd sent her aboard the trawler, *Mariette*, and there'd still been no word from Ireland. She did her best to keep her worries to herself, though the fatigue of evening was less often rewarded with sleep. Elisa had learned not to pester her with questions about Papa, but the questions remained unanswered.

The woman now lay awake for hours at a time, her younger daughter beside her, the sounds of the district growing louder with the dawn. And Cavan, her gentle Cavan, so far away . . .

With the curfew lifted, and the troops once again withdrawn, Jean-Pierre Barachin continued with his fiction, telling the family that the concert in the Palais Royal had been set back a month or two, on account of the disturbances. Though he'd see a place was found for them in the gallery, as soon as the date was fixed. His wife said: 'The strain it must put upon these talented musicians! The months they've spent in rehearsal! We cannot imagine!'

Adelaide and Elisa nodded, merely watching as he tugged at the hem of his coat, checked the strap that now secured his splintered violin-case, then made his way from the house. He left them to believe he'd catch a cabriolet in Rue Rambuteau, though in truth Jean-Pierre had not boarded a carriage in years.

Then a messenger arrived from the nearest Postal Distribution Bureau, demanding to know if a certain Madame Adelaide Lynch was a resident of *Onze bis*, Rue Simon le Franc. With Corinne elsewhere in the house, it was Adelaide herself who answered the door, paid the man the delivery fee and was handed a dog-eared envelope, post-marked Cork, St Malo, Paris.

Written in a small, crabbed script – as if to lessen the impact of the news – the letter was from Conor Egan Lynch. A plain-speaking man, Lord Natesby's bailiff knew of no other way to soften the blow, his voice almost audible as Adelaide deciphered the scrawl.

> Dear Mistress Lynch,
>
> Set yourself for the worst. Your husband, who's also my nephew as you know, he's been killed. Stabbed with a knife in a prison brawl. Got sent up for life to Dublin Gaol, then was killed there. I don't know why. All I got was the Letter of Notification.
>
> He was a good man, Cavan, and his death has stirred the county. They talk of him as a Hero. Lord Natesby blames me too for what happened at the Warehouse, and I hear he seeks to replace me.
>
> I don't know where I'll go next, but I want to write down I'm sorry what happened to Cavan. For all he was just bald and a bunch of bones, he was stronger than me. Shall I send you word where I am when I get there? Tho' it might be best if I don't. Forgive me for that day at Kilbreen. It shames me to think back on it.

Undecided how to sign the letter, he'd finally settled on 'C. Lynch. From Cork.'

Adelaide took Elisa to their room, broke the news as gently as she could to the girl, then left the letter within reach, for Elisa to read or ignore.

They wept together, their tears of love and sorrow made astringent by the wider sufferings of Ireland, by the greed and brutality, by the senseless manner of Cavan's death. Adelaide guessed he'd been speaking up on behalf of another prisoner, and she drew what comfort she could from the distant, imagined scene . . . An old man being taunted, perhaps, or slapped and threatened . . . Then Cavan stepping forward, his voice pitched low, the tone of it calm as he addressed the bully, the enfeebled prisoner scuttling away . . .

But in Dublin Gaol, her husband had been no longer the Senior Clerk of Shipping Affairs. Just another inmate, intercession seen as unwanted interference.

A grunt of fury. The looming of the bully. The sudden appearance of a blade, honed on the stones of his cell . . .

Dear God, what a terrible waste . . .

Unaware of the letter and its contents, Corinne came to remind them that Jean-Pierre would soon be back for his soup, the girls wanted Elisa's company, and Olivier was fretful. 'It's up to us all to pull our weight, you know. *I* can't be expected – '

'We'll be down before long,' Adelaide assured her. 'Just leave us at peace for a while.'

Preoccupied with the needs of her own, younger family, Corinne Barachin failed to notice her mother's drawn features, or her sister's tear-stained cheeks. 'It's all very well to say leave you in peace, but Jean-Pierre – '

And at that, with the second mention of his name, Elisa Lynch forged a blade of her own, screaming aloud at Corinne. 'I've *seen* Jean-Pierre! I *know* what he is! He's arrogant and sulky and a liar! He's no more a member of an orchestra than you are! He's a street-musician in a square near the Rue du Louvre. Him and another, and two fancy girls. With a begging bowl on the pavement. I've seen him, Corinne! In front of the café? Under the elm tree? Or is that where the *Orchestre du Palais Royal* rehearses these days?'

Corinne stepped back, slack-jawed. But Elisa had not finished with her yet, the decency of their father's life showing up this shabby masquerade. 'You talk about pulling our weight? But who does the cooking for us all, if not Mama? Who nursed your precious Olivier back to health? Who instructs Cécile and Simone? Does your talented and artistic husband pull his weight? He couldn't pull a bell-rope!'

'So you saw him, did you? Wandered the streets when you should have been delivering the clothes – '

'And *was* delivering the clothes!' Elisa raged. 'Earning you new customers every day. Three when I started; and now how many send you their stuff to be repaired? Well, tell me, Corinne. How many?'

She glared at her sister, tears of anguish streaking her face, the blade of truth cutting cruelly at the lies. Cavan was dead, and Mama looked old, and they would surely never return again to Ireland. But neither could they go on here like this, with Adelaide cooking and nursing and teaching and bedding down the children . . . And Elisa running her constant, colourful errands . . . And Corinne saying now they must all pull their weight . . .

'Well,' Corinne admitted, 'there might be fifteen. Even twenty.'

Elisa nodded, her anger draining, and reached for the letter from Conor. But Adelaide caught it first, repeating that they'd be down before long. And see to the soup and the children.

They heard Corinne Barachin descend the narrow staircase.

'I wanted to tell her,' Elisa said. 'About Papa. Why should *she* be spared? She's his daughter, too.'

'She is,' Adelaide agreed, 'and longer than you. But I want us to have this moment to ourselves, my dear, for we might not find such privacy again. Oh, yes, we can talk in bed, but now's the best time to discuss the future – yours more than mine – for Jean-Pierre will not take kindly to being discovered.'

The girl went to crouch at her mother's skirts, fresh tears spilling as she remembered the myriad moments with her father. The books he'd bought her. The jokes he'd recited – and Papa was a terrible teller of jokes – the story lost as he floundered to find the final amusing line.

Then the toys and trinkets he'd purchased in the port. The firmness with which he'd controlled her childish tantrums. The gaze that was more corrective than any blow. The smile that made her hum with delight. The occasional light-heartedness of this otherwise serious man.

Deep within the clerk there'd been the clown; the studious volumes of his mind were interleaved with colourful sketches. Not easy to find, but there if you turned the pages . . .

'It's time you left this place,' Adelaide began. 'Raised your sights and improved your situation. You're an intelligent girl, Elisa, and you speak the language well. There's more to Paris than St Merri, and more to the world than Paris.'

Tears for her father were now chased by tears for her mother. 'You want me to leave you here? Abandon you to the Barachins?'

'But you won't. You'll find a better job nearby, then come back and see me when you're free. Corinne and Jean-Pierre are – how shall we put it? – fixed on their course. But you're still young enough

111

to turn your dreams into reality. And where would we be without dreams?'

The girl clung close to her mother and murmured: 'What were yours? When you were young in Vienna. Or had gone across to Bristol. What were yours?'

'Oh, lord, what were mine . . . ? To find myself a gentleman? A wealthy English aristocrat? Own a wardrobe of silks and satin? Snap my fingers at a dozen obedient servants? I don't know. It was probably something like that.'

'But instead you met Papa.'

'That's right. Instead of a so-called gentleman like Lord Natesby, I met your gentle Papa. And managed quite well without the finery, or the flunkeys. And I'm not sure I'd know how to go about snapping my fingers.'

Crouched at her mother's feet, Elisa asked: 'Did it matter that he was poor? That you had to live all those years in Cork? I mean, you were very young then, yet you never got the chance to travel again.'

Adelaide absorbed the question. Then she fondled her daughter's red hair and said yes, it would have been fun to travel; but no, it didn't matter that Cavan was poor. 'Money would have made him no kinder. And we know how his head used to burn in the sun, so it's as well he stayed in Ireland. But as for you, my dear . . . Until you find a Cavan of your own . . .' Then she paused and sighed, gently tilting Elisa's chin.

'. . . Until that day occurs, I believe you should – what did I say before? – raise your sights and look to the future. There are a thousand situations better than this; better than running errands in St Merri.'

'But I *like* running errands. And I won't abandon you here.'

'So you said, though you're limiting our choice. It means either you stay in Simon le Franc, or drag me along as just another valise. The truth is, my sweet, I'm too old to seek adventure. I also flatter myself that I'm needed here, though I might wish Corinne and her husband would sometimes say it was so.'

'They're the meanest couple – '

'Tut, tut, we can do without that. Anyhow, Cécile and Simone are improving in English, whilst Olivier – though I beg you not to speak of it – has twice addressed me as *Maman*.'

It was Elisa's turn to sigh. She was now thirteen, yet still young enough to tremble at a life without protection. Cavan was dead, and not all the downy wings of all the angels could bear him up and set him back on Earth. But to go on from here without either Papa or Mama . . . ? To walk the streets of Paris in search of a job . . . ? And as *what*? As a parrot's companion? A girl who'd encourage monkeys to climb a pole?

Sensing her daughter's apprehension, Adelaide said gently: 'All I ask you to do is look around. Stroll beyond St Merri. Go on south to the river – you've never even seen it yet – and explore the Ile de la Cité. Venture across the bridges. Keep to the more populous streets, and hold common sense and caution hand in hand. Time your walks so you're back home well before dark. Just lengthen your stride, that's all. Play the visitor.'

Elisa shrugged. 'All right, though I don't know what kind of job you think I can find. An Irish girl in Paris? Did a French girl ever make her way in Cork?'

'Maybe not.' Adelaide smiled. 'But an Austrian lived on the out-skirts.'

Corinne had acknowledged her father's death in Dublin Gaol with no more than a brief show of sorrow. She had not seen Cavan Lynch for seven years, and now a Barachin, she was more worried about her life in France than her father's death in Ireland.

She had pleaded with Adelaide and Elisa to allow Jean-Pierre his fiction. 'He's so terribly insecure, I can't tell you. If he learned that you'd seen him, Elisa, it would utterly destroy him. The day *will* come when he's called for an audition, and he *will* get the post, and you'll both be proud to know him. But for the moment, please, I beg you to leave him his dreams.'

Tactless and tiresome, she nevertheless remained loyal to her husband, a strength the family from Cork could fully respect. Improbable though it was, Corinne's claim was yet possible. Poets *were* discovered in their garrets, painters in their draughty studios, writers at their candlelit desks. So why not a gaunt violinist, with two teeth snapped by an army rifle, in a public square in front of a café, beneath the summer spread of an elm?

Although Elisa now accepted the wisdom of Adelaide's suggestion, it was a while before she found the courage to act. Her mother was right, of course, to say she should raise her sights. However much she claimed to enjoy running errands, she knew her life in Simon le Franc was finite. She could not live here for ever, and the break, when it came, might be sudden and tempestuous. A falling-out with

113

Corinne perhaps. An argument with Jean-Pierre, in which things were said that could never be forgotten. The longer she stayed, the greater the risk that tempers would flare, for tolerance too was finite.

And what if the Barachins told her to leave? Where would she go? What would happen to Adelaide? Too old, as she'd said, to seek further adventure, how could she start afresh in a city in which thousands of militant youngsters were unemployed and starving? Unrest was in the air, and with it talk of other bloody riots. Cast adrift on the streets, Adelaide would be bullied aside, just another nameless victim of the time.

Elisa could not and would not allow that to happen. And yet, fearing for her mother, the thirteen-year-old feared also for herself.

She made excuses. *I'm still useful here. The errands bring in a few sous every week. Enough to pay our way. Mama and me. And anyway, where would I look for work? And if the people of Paris can't find it, how will I?*

Adelaide set the subject aside, aware that the girl must find the courage within herself. As Cavan had done. 'And, Lord knows, there's much of Cavan in Elisa . . .'

4

Reluctant at first, but encouraged by her mother, Elisa walked south along Rue St Martin to the Quai des Gesvres and the Seine.

Staring at it, she did not yet realise the farther bank was just an island, another branch of the river beyond. The one she could see seemed wider than the Lee in Cork, and she hesitated before edging across the narrow Pont Notre Dame.

Open to wheeled traffic, the bridge was congested. It formed a bottle-neck between the right bank of the Seine and the boat-shaped island, carriages clashing wheel-hubs as they passed, coachmen snarling, pedestrians pressed to the heavy stone balustrades.

Here, as in the Marché des Innocents, sneak-thieves and pickpockets preyed upon the unwary. Valuables were snatched, then passed from villain to villain, or casually dropped into a dinghy below the bridge. By the time the victim had howled for help – summoned a policeman – explained his loss – by then it was far too late. The robbers had gone, the dinghy lost among fifty others, and another hand would be clawing the constable's uniformed arm.

With nothing to lose, 'Unless they're after my bonnet', Elisa made her halting way to the island. She arrived there bruised and excited, lingering on the Quai de la Corse, staring up at the high blue sky she had never seen from the confines of St Merri.

Mama was right. It's fun to play the visitor . . .

Ignoring the churches and monuments, as a thirteen-year-old will, she dodged and weaved along Rue de la Cité, crossing the island and reaching the even narrower span of the city's smallest bridge, Le Petit Pont.

Talk about a squeeze! It's a wonder the bridge can hold us. I must've collided with more people crossing the river than in the whole long length of St Martin!

The passage was difficult, elbows jabbing, parasols spearing, men's boots stamping, women treading hard with high-heeled shoes. When Paris promenades, Elisa accepted, it does so with style. They're the best-dressed folk I've ever seen. And the pushiest. No wonder they don't want a king or his court. A court would mean being courteous, and I don't see them being that.

Nudged and barged and forced to the rail, the girl eventually crossed the second branch of the river.

She made her way aimlessly along the west bank of the Seine, gazing for a while at the fine apartment buildings that encircled Place St Michel. Their entranceways were bright with awnings, ornate iron balconies festooned with flowers, broughams and fiacres jolting round the *place*.

She might have looked for a job there, and would doubtless have found one. But the brilliance of it all intimidated her, and she wandered on south into the long shallow curve of Rue Hautefeuille. Less resplendent than the riverside Place St Michel, it was nonetheless a world away from the alleys of St Merri. High Leaf Road . . . She liked the sound of the name. It seemed as good a place as any in which to make a start . . .

Elisa paused in front of a lamp-seller's window, adjusted her bonnet, fiddled with the collar of her blouse, and pirouetted to settle the folds of her long cambric skirt. An old man grinned at her from beyond the glass, then doffed an imaginary hat to show his approval. The girl curtsied, stumbling slightly on the uneven cobbles, but the lamp-seller pretended not to notice. With a wave he returned to his work among the brass containers and etched globes, the fluted chimneys and tight-woven coils of wick.

Elisa decided that, come the day she was rich enough to own a house in Paris, she'd buy all her lamps from him.

Although agencies existed for those who were seeking employment, the traditional method was simply to ask around. With more than ninety per cent of the population illiterate, the currency of communication was word of mouth. The *bureaux de placement* could, and would, send an applicant to such-and-such an address, but Elisa preferred to find her own way, enjoying her independence to the full.

She walked the length of the street, then back again, telling herself she wouldn't mind working *there*, but didn't think much of *that* house, whereas the one on the left with the big, studded door . . .

Thirteen years old, and a foreigner in France, the girl blithely prejudged the inhabitants of Rue Hautefeuille. But that was part of the fun of it. If she didn't like it here, she'd try somewhere else. There were a million streets in Paris, after all.

She saw a woman alight from a narrow, high-wheeled gig, intercepted her on her doorstep, and asked if she knew of a position vacant, perhaps as a lady's maid. 'I wouldn't wish to be just *any* sort

116

of maid, raking out the cinders and that. And I can read and write, and speak English, so I'd hope for something – '

'Hope all you like,' the woman snapped. 'But with an attitude like yours, Mademoiselle, I doubt you'd find employment here on Earth! You clearly think yourself fitted to be a handmaid in Heaven! Won't rake out the cinders, indeed. And shall we serve you champagne?'

With a snort of derision, she entered her house, and Elisa was left blushing furiously in the street.

Well, yes, the approach had been wrong. It had been a mistake to mention what she would and wouldn't do. Better to offer her services than stipulate conditions.

She tried again, this time approaching a girl who was polishing a bell and chain beside a planed oak door. 'Excuse me, but do you happen to know of anyone who – ?'

'You colour it yourself?' the maid asked. 'Stain it or what?'

'I'm sorry, I don't – '

'Your hair, what else? To turn it red like that. I went to the circus once, an' they had a clown – '

'No, it's natural.'

'Don't believe you. Lift your skirt. Pull down your drawers. Come on, no one's lookin'!'

'I told you. It's natural.'

'An' them eyes! You must've put somethin' in 'em. Green like that, it ain't normal.'

'It may not be usual here in Paris,' Elisa retorted. 'But it's perfectly normal in Ireland where I come from. It's how Irish girls are, that's all. And the men too, sometimes.'

'And where's Ireland then? I've heard my master and mistress talk about Algeria. Ireland near there?'

Elisa said no, not really, then asked if anyone was looking for a maid-servant, here in Rue Hautefeuille.

'They're always lookin' for maids. They'll be lookin' for one right here before long, 'less they treat me better than they do. But a circus-turn like you? And a foreigner? You'd better try Madame Marise. If anyone's ready for a clown, it's Madame Marise.' She smiled then at some secret joke, flicking her polishing cloth towards the southern end of the street. 'Can't remember the number, but it's on the left. Big square nails in the door. An' tell you what. If you get the job, you can come back here sometime, and we'll go to my room an' you can pull down your drawers in private. How's that?'

'We'll see,' Elisa murmured, then walked away as the maid shrilled:

'Just what I asked you!'

Along on the left . . . With the big square nails in the door . . .

It was a house she'd already judged as possible . . . Two small trimmed bushes in pots beside the step; curtained windows; a discreet brass nameplate beneath the bell: *Mme Marise Laurent-Perrone (Institutrice)*.

Oh Lord, Elisa thought. An aristocratic old dowager, strict as a magistrate, giving lessons to whey-faced pupils, and most likely with a dozen pampered cats. It was the maid's idea of a joke, saying Madame Laurent-Perrone is ready for a clown. She'll probably take one look at me, screech like an owl, then start wielding some schoolhouse cane. '*Get away! Get away! Red hair's a curse! You've the green eyes of the devil!*'

Convincing herself of the worst, Elisa stepped back into the street.

Then the studded door swung inwards, and a tall, well-muscled man held it back, though he barred the way with his arm. His hair was cropped short, his thick neck supported a tight-skinned head, hard amusement in his gaze. Someone had broken his nose and padded the flesh of his cheekbones, though it made the young man seem all the more able to deal with life's subsequent rounds.

His ears had escaped the punishment of the ring, though the hand that held the door seemed swollen, a pugilist's fist on a strong, corded arm. He was the most self-confident man Elisa Lynch had ever set eyes on.

'Saw you wondering what to do, girl. Thought I'd help sort things out.' He lounged in the doorway, a slim hip propped for support, the expression in his eyes belying the smile on his lips. 'Come here after the job, have you, girl? Well it's open, and so's the door.'

'I was told by a maid down there – '

'You was told that Madame Marise needs someone she can trust. A servant who'll be her friend. A girl like you – and, you'll set a fashion with that hair, see if you don't – who'll help make the place run smooth. That's what you should've been told.'

'What does she teach?' Elisa asked. 'I see on the plate it says "Teacher".'

The man grinned, then said Madame Marise taught her pupils anything they wished. 'She's never had one leave yet who wasn't satisfied.'

'Well, what should I do? I imagine Madame Laurent-Perrone will want to interview me, but if she's now in the middle of a lesson – '

'What you do, girl, is go over there. The Café Tourette. Then sit near the window and wait. Shouldn't be long, and I'll call you across when she's free.'

'I'm grateful, Monsieur.' Elisa bobbed. 'Perhaps you'd be kind enough to tell Madame Laurent-Perrone I can read and write, speak English and tally figures.'

'Tell her yourself,' the man said. 'Things like that, they're bound to impress her.' He grinned again, shook his bullet-like head at the ways of the world, hitched himself erect and went back inside.

5

Not sure what to order, Elisa copied a girl at a nearby table. Lemon essence and water, served with a dish of sugar and a spoon. She watched as the girl heaped sugar into the glass, stirred the drink and studied the coarse, dissolving crystals.

Elisa did likewise, thrilled that her order had been taken and brought without question. If the waiter had hesitated at all – and he had, just for an instant – it was to glance at her russet hair, not question her French.

She'd no idea how much the *citron sucré* would cost, though Adelaide had given her enough for the fare home if she found herself stranded. But surely ten times the price of a drink in Rue Hautefeuille.

Toying with her spoon, Elisa Lynch acknowledged that this was the first time she'd sat alone in a café, her gaze directed at the house across the street, her senses alert to the sounds that swirled around her.

She inclined her head this way and that, absorbing the sing-song language. A young man had joined the girl who'd first ordered the *citron sucré*, and the two of them were cooing like lovebirds. Someone else was engaged in a political diatribe, blaming all the country's troubles on the bankers, merchants, well-fed bourgeoisie. 'It's a vicious bloody cycle, is what it is! Kick the king off his throne, and we prance around, fooling ourselves we're equal. Then the prices go up, and the taxes are doubled, and we're back to where we started! I tell you, it wasn't enough to chop the aristocrats. Should've kept the guillotines busy! Lopped our way down to the workers! Call this country a republic? Shout the word in Rue de Rivoli, they wouldn't know what we meant!'

Someone offered the militant a drink, and he turned to lean on the bar, his anger refuelled with absinthe. While the lovers continued to coo, Elisa watched Madame Laurent-Perrone's curtained windows and heavy, studded door . . .

Not knowing the price of the lemon and water, she dared not order another. But half the surrounding tables were empty, the waiter loitering near a group of dice-players, the afternoon business slack in the Café Tourette.

The girl imagined her meeting with the teacher. Maybe fifty years old, Madame Marise Laurent-Perrone would appear in a dusty grey gown, her hair tied tight in a bun, a pair of spectacles perched on her nose, a long wooden pointer in her hand. She'd glare at the applicant, flicking the cane, already suspicious of the girl's red hair and green eyes.

And then I'll say: 'I'm enchanted to meet you, Madame. It's an honour and a privilege. I trust you will accept me into your household. It's kind of you, Madame. Very kind. Most kind. Too kind.' *All the required politenesses Mama said I should use.*

As for the confident brute who'd lounged in the doorway, the girl could only guess. A relative from the provinces? A general handyman? A ruffian taken in off the streets by the well-meaning Madame Perrone?

She sipped at her drink as the militant once again lectured the room. '. . . Guillotine's too quick! Let 'em suffocate with a mouthful of their own shiny coins! Bury 'em alive, I say! Drown the bloody merchants in the river! A republic means for the public, yes or no! And does anyone want to say different?' He pushed himself from the bar, blinking in search of contradiction.

Elisa watched the lovers leave, their arms entwined, their heads dipped close together. Then she saw a figure emerge from the house across the street; a man in a tight-buttoned coat, high wing-collar, tall stove-pipe hat. He left without looking back, turned north and hurried away toward Place St Michel and the river.

His ears are ringing with grammar, Elisa guessed. *He's probably regretting he didn't work harder at school. Now he's at the mercy of Madame Laurent-Perrone, the poor man!*

The door opened again, and the pugilist beckoned her from the café. For a moment the girl hesitated, unsure if she wanted to meet the *institutrice*. But if she changed her mind now, the young man might turn nasty – 'I told Madame Marise you were waiting, girl, so you just get in here, and let's have none of your nonsense.'

She paid for her drink – less than she'd expected – and left one sou as a tip. She wondered if the waiter would complain that it wasn't enough, or smirk and think her a foolish little foreigner. But he merely grunted: '*Merci, mademoiselle,*' and went back to the dice game.

The first time I ever bought a drink in a café. But I'm doing lots of things now for the first time. Like looking for work by myself . . .

She was shown into a small, over-furnished parlour, the room in keeping with her image of the grey-haired martinet. Everything was formal and slightly forbidding, dark tones predominant. The table-cloth was starched to the stiffness of plaster, the chair cushions unyielding, a cabinet filled with pewter. A group of heavy-framed paintings depicted uninspired scenes of the countryside in winter, the wreck of a galleon, the ivy-clad ruins of a temple.

I'm not going to like this place, Elisa thought. I'm not going to stay here long.

The man said: 'Cheerful, ain't it?' Then he left her to wait, closing the parlour door behind him.

She noticed a small, ormolu clock, assumed it was correct – *why not? Everything else is* – and decided she had time enough to see if other jobs were available in Rue Hautefeuille. *Anything but this! I'd rather polish glasses in the Café Tourette.*

'All right, girl. Now's the time. Madame Marise'll see you upstairs.' His broad hand on the doorknob, he leaned into the room, grinning as she was forced to brush against him. 'Occur to you to leave, did it? Wondering where else you might go? Find the place a bit gloomy, eh, bright little spark like you?'

'If you want to know the truth, Monsieur – '

'But I don't, girl, I don't. Up the stairs. First on the right. And hold on to your bonnet!'

It seemed a stupid thing for the man to say, but Elisa decided he *was* rather stupid, with his silly, self-amused smiles. Too many fights, that was it. His brain had come loose in his head.

Determined not to fidget with her bonnet, she climbed the dark, carpeted stairs, found herself on a dimly-lit landing, then tapped on the door to her right.

A muffled voice, almost inaudible, called: '*Entrez!*'

'Well, at least I can tell Mama I tried,' the girl murmured, reaching for the handle. 'And try's what she wants me to do.'

Twice the size of the parlour beneath, the room left Elisa Lynch gaping. There were tables here too; and cushions, and cabinets; carpets and heavy-framed pictures. But the tables were inlaid with mica, reflecting the light from lamps in crimson globes. The cushions turned a lean couch fat, ebony chairs into wide, welcoming nests. The pictures were bright, even garish, but none of them depicting a winter's scene, a ship on the rocks, a distant, Grecian temple. They were all of young women, and all the women naked – 'Surprised by the Hunter'; 'Her Private Pool'; 'The Rites of Spring'.

The walls were lined with imported fabrics, gold and silver thread stitched lengthways in the pattern. The ceiling portrayed the sky at night, the moon and stars picked out with pinpoints of glass.

Madame Marise Laurent-Perrone called again, her voice no longer muffled, and Elisa turned to a door at the rear of this wild, extravagant cavern. 'You the one come for the job? Let me fix these laces, an' I'll be with you!'

Then she made her appearance, gesturing at Elisa to help her.

The woman was not in any way what Elisa had supposed. She looked no more than twenty, over-dressed and over-painted, her breasts half-revealed, the skirt of her gown looped with flounces and raised to show the problem with her boots.

'Do me a favour. Tie the damn things tight. By God, but I'll be glad when the fashion's over, and we can all go back to shoes!'

Elisa stared, jerked herself from her disbelief, and laced the woman's boots.

'He was right, that Arnaud. You *are* a beauty. A touch too young, but you'll get there. And when you do, *bon sang*, you'll be something. Tell me your name.'

'It's Elisa Alicia Lynch, Madame Laurent-Perrone. You can put your foot down now.'

'Good God, what a mouthful. I'll settle for Elisa. And you'll call me Madame Marise.' She stamped to get her feet comfortable in the boots, waved the girl to one of the plump cushioned chairs, then asked if she was up to a glass of Cahors.

Without knowing what on earth the woman meant, the girl said yes.

Marise said, 'Well, maybe we'll serve it with water,' poured Elisa a measure of the heavy southern wine, then diluted it from black to pink.

Settling herself in another cushioned chair, the vibrant, colourful woman beamed at her caller. 'He *is* right. You *are* a beauty. And let me guess – about fifteen?'

'Not yet quite fourteen, Madame Laurent – I mean Madame Marise. Though I sometimes feel I am.'

'We're all what we feel,' the woman told her. 'Though I wish I could sometimes feel rich . . . Now listen. You've a fine way with French, though you're clearly not French by birth. So why don't you just tell me where you're from, and what you're after, and we'll see if we can come to some arrangement. It'd suit me well if we did, young Elisa. You look tailor-made for the job.'

Sipping her watered wine, Elisa had yet to recover from the shock of the imagined *institutrice*, and the difference between the formal parlour and this – this exotic chamber.

'I'll tell you whatever you want, Madame Marise. But why's it so gloomy downstairs?'

Blonde and buxom, the woman sat back, nodding at the points of light in the ceiling. 'Difficult for a girl like you to grasp. But appearances matter. Instruction downstairs, yet a friendlier atmosphere up here. It's the way it has to be with gentlemen students.'

'And with ladies too, I imagine. What do you teach them? Monsieur Arnaud says anything they wish, but if I could help with English – '

'Well, now! There's an idea! I bet you'd be just fine at teaching English, young Elisa. But tell me something about yourself first. Where were you born? Parents alive? Lived long here in France?'

As Elisa talked, the woman nodded. 'Seems to me you're just what I'm after. So why don't you come and join us for a while, and we'll see how things work out? Now as to your wages . . .'

Aware that domestic servants were paid between fifteen and twenty francs a month, Elisa Lynch asked for twenty. 'I know I've had no training as a lady's maid, nor indeed as a teacher, but I've a mother who's unwell, and – '

'Don't worry, you'll get your twenty. But if Arnaud asks, tell him it's fifteen. For weeks he's been looking for an excuse to demand more money, though God knows he's hardly worth what I pay him now!'

'*I* will be,' the girl said promptly. '*I'll* help you get as many students – '

'Yes, well, we'll talk about that later. In the meantime let me tell you about your other duties. And by the way, though I bet you've been asked by everyone, is that hair of yours truly red? See this?' She fingered her own, straw-blonde hair and laughed. 'The triumph of chemistry over nature, that's what this is. It's one of the things you'll have to learn, Elisa. How to keep me looking like, well, like them in the paintings there on the wall.'

She hurried back to tell Adelaide the news.

'Twenty francs a month, Mama! And with a room of my own. Madame Laurent-Perrone says I can have one afternoon a week free – she hasn't decided which yet – and that sometimes I can go out with her in her carriage. I can see I'm going to be terribly busy, what with attending to Madame Marise, that's how she says I'm to address her, and helping with the lessons. She's got a cook there, and the young man, Arnaud. Oh, yes, and I had a *citron sucré* in a café while I was waiting! The only thing is, Mama, she says I can't work there unless you give your permission. But I told her I was sure you would. After all, *vingt francs, c'est vingt francs, n'est-ce pas?* And aren't I approaching fourteen?'

Adelaide Lynch was more ill than she admitted. It was an effort to eat, a dull pain spreading across her chest, her heartbeat seeming to fluctuate. Careful not to disturb her sleeping daughter, she lay awake at nights, her thoughts cast back to her life with Cavan, then forward to all that life might hold for Elisa.

She accepted, as a fact, that she might soon die. If that were to happen – her heartspring snapping – Elisa would be alone. But better to be across the river in Rue Hautefeuille, *and terribly busy*, and with twenty francs a month of her own, than here in Rue Simon le Franc, running errands and learning nothing more than her way around St Merri.

'If you fetch me my pen and paper, my dear, I'll write a note to your future employer. But it's only fair to warn her you're sometimes given to tantrums – '

'Mama?'

' – and can, on occasion, be as obstinate – '

'Mama!'

'Oh, fetch me the materials. I'll send the lady an angel.'

Elisa smiled and embraced her mother. 'You and Papa, you were always like that. Looking so serious, then saying things that were silly. I hope I can be like that too.' Then she went to seek the means by which Adelaide Katherina Lynch would release Elisa Alicia into the care of Madame Marise.

6

Little by little she learned the truth about the house in Rue Haute-feuille.

Arnaud, she discovered, was the twenty-five-year-old son of the cook, Odile, the one-time pugilist employed as *un homme à tout faire*. It was an appropriate description, for he was required to fulfil a variety of tasks. Twice a week he carried kegs of water upstairs, to top the gravity tank that was linked by heavy lead pipes to a hand-basin and a claw-foot bath – the private domain of Madame Laurent-Perrone. He brought in the wood for the black iron range in the kitchen, organized the wine cellar, served at table if his mistress had guests to dinner in the room across from the parlour. Dressed for the occasion, he wore an olive-green suit, embroidered shirt, a flouncy silk cravat. He felt and looked ridiculous, though Elisa was careful not to be caught smiling. Make fun of Arnaud, and he'd set your head ringing with a swipe of his knuckly fist.

He drove the carriage whenever Marise demanded an outing, bullying a path towards the forested outskirts of the city. The vehicle did not, in fact, belong to her, but was hired by the hour or the day from a depot behind Rue Hautefeuille. For his role as coachman, Arnaud wore a long, crimson redingote, polished boots and a stiff, broad-brimmed hat, this outfit more to his liking.

At home, he would answer the door to the gentlemen callers, then show them into the parlour. He found this task demeaning, and told Marise that, now the girl was here, she could do it instead. 'Don't worry, I'll still be around if things go wrong.'

As they could, Elisa discovered, once she'd learned Marise Laurent-Perrone's true profession . . .

The cheerful, straw-haired young woman was not, of course, a teacher. Her so-called students were exclusively male, middle-aged and outwardly respectable. If they seemed somewhat furtive as they made their way to the house, they regained their air of pompous self-confidence once the street door was closed behind them.

'I have a rendezvous with Madame Laurent-Perrone. Please tell her that Monsieur Rémy is here.' Or Monsieur Guy, or Monsieur

Jean-Philippe. Always the first name, never the surname, yet with the transparent camouflage, Monsieur.

At twenty, the buxom Marise was one of the city's several hundred young courtesans. Despising the common prostitute, and envious of those who could count on a wealthy aristocrat as their protector, the woman was part of the world the writer Dumas had called the demi-monde. The world of those who were well above the level of the streets, though unable to catch the eye of that all-important, influential protector.

Marise was optimistic enough to believe the day would come . . . Born Marie Pierre in a village in the Vendée, she had already reached the capital, changed her name, saved enough to make a down payment on the house in Rue Hautefeuille . . . Another year spent entertaining these oh, so respectable clients, and she'd be ready to cast her line for bigger fish . . .

Also, she now had Elisa Lynch to help her. A maid of her own, and an exceptionally pretty one, too. A girl who could speak two languages, if you please! And that was a damn sight more than her competitors could offer!

Arnaud told Elisa to answer the door. 'You've seen what I do, girl, so you do the same. You treat 'em all like they owned the Bank of France, *t'as compris*? Settle 'em in the parlour, then take their message upstairs. If they've come with flowers, and most of them do, you carry 'em up to the mistress. Tells her a lot about the caller, the amount he's spent on flowers.'

Eager to prove her worth, the girl said yes, she'd do as Arnaud instructed. 'I take his hat and cane and that, see him ensconced in the parlour, then report his arrival to Madame Marise. She'll tell me what wine the gentleman might enjoy, and I'm to come back down and tell you. Then you'll go and get it from the cellar, and I'll take it up on a tray.'

'That's about it, girl. And if the gentleman fondles your hair or pats your bottom – well, you let him, you understand?'

Elisa giggled. 'Before I came . . . When *you* were greeting the callers . . . Did they fondle your hair, Arnaud?'

She reeled from the slap, tears of pain in her eyes.

'Don't you come clever with me, girl! I'm not the type as takes well to bring taunted. If we're to get along together – and I ain't convinced we will – you'd be wise to show some respect. Now get yourself ready. There's a visitor due around two.'

Elisa went to the kitchen and, keeping her scorched cheek turned away from Odile, quietly bathed it with water from the sink. *If that was just a casual slap, imagine a knuckled fist!*

Glancing across from the range, the good-natured cook asked, 'What's the problem, Elisa? You got toothache? There's a man sets up near the river twice a week, if you need him. Gives his patients opium, swears they don't feel a thing.'

'No, it's nothing. I just banged against the door.'

'Well, you watch your step. Doors around here, they've a way of swinging when you least expect it.' Then she continued stirring the rabbit in its cauldron of blood-red wine, leaving Elisa to learn for herself that Arnaud's hand was as hard as hinged wood.

The visitor arrived and said his piece. 'I have a rendezvous with Madame Laurent-Perrone. You may tell her it's Monsieur Didier.'

The girl bobbed correctly, took the caller's hat and black malacca cane, then waited for him to peel off his linen gloves.

His hair plastered tight to his skull, and with a monocle screwed into the socket of his eye, he peered at the girl and said: 'Well? Do you show me in, or what?'

'Certainly, Monsieur. But the gloves?'

'What do you mean, the gloves? I retain the gloves. It's what gentlemen do, don't you know that? It's the rule of the time, Mademoiselle. We keep our gloves.'

All right, the girl thought, so keep them. 'But the flowers, Monsieur? Is there a message to accompany them?'

The man looked confused. 'Well, tell Madame Marise – oh, tell her I await her with impatience. And bring me a glass of port wine.'

He waited until the girl turned away, and then he did what Arnaud had said the callers might do. He clumsily patted her bottom.

I must either get used to this, she thought, or go back to Rue Simon le Franc.

Couching the man's bouquet, she went upstairs. 'There's a Monsieur Didier, Madame Marise. He says he awaits you with impatience. And I'm to serve him port wine.'

'Oh, hell,' the woman said. 'I thought I'd got rid of him. Ditch-water Didier. But now he's here, let's give him his hour. *And* his port. A couple of glasses, he'll likely fall asleep. Ask Arnaud to find the cheap stuff. And just look at these flowers! Limp as he is! I tell you, Elisa, the company of gentlemen is not all a lady might wish!'

*

128

And then, the year cooling in September, Elisa returned to Rue Simon le Franc to spend her free afternoon as usual with Adelaide and the Barachins. Admitted to the house by Corinne, she was led in silence into the kitchen, the older sister telling the younger that their mother had died that morning. 'She was suffering from chest pains last night, though insisted it was nothing untoward. Then today, when she failed to join us for breakfast – ' Corinne shrugged, and made an awkward attempt to embrace the stricken Elisa.

They had nothing to say to each other now, both aware that their only link had been the impartial love of Adelaide Katherina Lynch.

The following day Cavan's widow was buried in the graveyard of the Church of St Merri.

Jean-Pierre brought his group of street musicians, the four of them playing as well as they'd ever played beneath the elm.

Marise Laurent-Perrone arranged for the grave to be banked with Arum lilies, a gesture Elisa would never forget.

Simone and Cécile clutched at their mother's skirts, the children sad because *Grandmère* had taken them to the market, then set them to sketch their memories of it, and the drawings were unfinished.

Elisa insisted on delivering a eulogy in English, not caring that the priest tapped his foot, impatient with a language he'd never learned. So what, the girl thought, it's not meant for him anyway. It's for God and the Family in Heaven, who surely know all the tongues . . .

She went back with the Barachins to their house, stayed until the stilted conversation dried entirely, then made her way south to the river, and across it to the Rue Hautefeuille.

In his gutter French, Arnaud said: 'Shame about your old lady, girl. Never mind, you're bright enough to see things through on your own. Tell you what. I've an idea as might be of interest to you. We'll talk about it sometime.'

Marise left Elisa alone in her room, then went up in the evening with two ribbon-tied boxes from a shop in Rue de Rivoli. One contained a street gown, patterned in the Turkish style, the other a matching shoulder cape, both of them trimmed with braid.

'I know it's not the time, but I thought – well, I thought it might lift your spirits. The thing is, there's a wealthy fish I've had my eye on for a while, and I happen to know he'll be riding in the park tomorrow afternoon. It'll likely impress him if he sees I've got a coachman *and* a pretty maid. But if you don't feel up to it . . . It's just that, if you do – '

'The flowers were wonderful,' Elisa murmured. 'And these

clothes . . . Oh, give me a hug, Madame Marise . . . And yes, I'll help you hook your fish.'

'Not just any old fish,' the courtesan told her. 'This one's a prize pink salmon!'

Pink he certainly was; pink to the point of being rubicund. But the colour Marise was after was the colour of his money, and she seemed happy enough as Arnaud drove the carriage back home from the park. 'Wants to come tomorrow,' she confided to Elisa, her maid-cum-chaperone.

'And you said he could?'

'*T'es folle?* Of course I didn't! I give lessons tomorrow. Then there's charity work in the evening, a banquet at eleven, a busy day's shopping on Thursday – '

'No, there isn't. Tomorrow's when I dye your hair, and what's this about giving lessons and working for charity?'

'Dear God, and I thought you were bright. It's what we say to the fish! Hook 'em, then leave 'em dangling. It's a risky game, I'll grant you that, but I'm not a fisherman's daughter for nothing – '

'Really? I didn't know you were.'

'And you don't know it now,' Marise corrected sharply. 'You just imagined what you heard.' She scowled for a moment, then laughed at her slip of the tongue; she recounted tales of other fish, and watched her young friend blush.

It was easy for Marie Pierre to be friends with Elisa Lynch. For all her experience of men – and in *that* department she'd already lost count – she seemed in many ways far younger than her years. Believing herself in control of the hook and line, the renamed Marise Laurent-Perrone was far too gullible, far too innocent, far too open ever to achieve her aims. Rue Hautefeuille was as close to the court as Marise would come; High Leaf Road as high as the steps would take her. She might think of herself as a lady in need of protection, but she had none of the skills or diplomacy of *les grandes horizontales*.

Nevertheless, it was easy for Elisa Lynch to be her friend. Seven years younger, and ignorant of the wiles of men, the girl's native intelligence closed the gap. If she blushed when Marise sought to shock her, she remembered what she'd heard. *So gentlemen did this, did they? And asked for that? And expected their women to disport themselves in such a way; misbehave in a so-and-so fashion; dress with care, then disrobe with abandon? Funny kind of fish, these men . . .*

*

130

Eight times before Christmas, Elisa made the pilgrimage to Adelaide's grave.

She went twice to see the Barachins, though the reception was chilly, Jean-Pierre absent, Corinne complaining that she'd no one to run the errands or care for the children.

'Please understand,' Elisa told her. 'I must lead my own life now.'

'Then lead it, why don't you! And stop coming here in your smart new clothes. Do whatever you do across the river, though I shudder to think what it is that earns you such braid!'

'You know what I do. I'm a lady's maid.'

'No doubt,' Corinne shrilled. 'And the lady made for the men?'

The winter passed, and with it Elisa's fourteenth birthday. She was now better fed than ever before. She grew taller, there was a hint of roundness in her hips; her breasts were cupped by the clothes Marise bought from the shop in Rue de Rivoli; her red hair lustrous, pale skin spared the blotches of disease, green eyes once again viridescent in the light.

Then one morning she whispered her shock and shame to the comforting Odile. And the cook said she'd nothing to fear, nor feel 'shamed of. They'd just wash the sheet and she'd take what was called precautions.

'*C'est le temps, ma petite. Tu es femme, tu sais. Comme Madame Marise et moi, tu es femme.*' And then, having told Elisa she was now a young woman, Odile wagged a finger and warned her about men. '*Tu te couche avec un homme – attention!* Lay with a man and he'll likely give you a baby!'

Elisa said no; a thing like that; oh, no. 'I don't know any men. Any fish. Any salmon.'

But she smiled as she left the kitchen, thrilled to know that she could, if she wanted, cast her own line on the waters.

For a while things went well for Marise Laurent-Perrone. The rubicund gentleman showed himself to be both attentive and generous,
showering the courtesan with gifts. Fresh curtains were purchased, a
canopy erected over the bed, louvred shutters made for the windows.
Unpaid bills were settled and, for the first time in her life, Marise
became the proud owner of a four-seat cabriolet, garaged in the depot
behind Rue Hautefeuille.

Monsieur Gustave seemed ready to take on the mantle of protector,
and the young woman confided to Elisa that, thanks to the salmon,
they might soon be swimming upstream. 'There's a house for sale
near the Jardin des Plantes. It's more expensive than this one, of
course, but I'm sure Monsieur Gustave would make up the difference.
So long as I make up to him!'

Arnaud pressed for a raise in pay, and got it. Odile said she needed
a new set of copper pans, and these were duly provided. Elisa asked
for nothing, though the impulsive Marise bought her a small jade
brooch, a Chinese fan and a pair of grey, buttoned boots. 'Better
than laces, eh, *ma fille?*'

Six weeks later Monsieur Gustave was arrested for embezzlement
and fraud, confessing his sins to the magistrate amid an embarrassing
welter of tears. He fell upon the mercy of the court, painting a watery
picture of himself as husband and father, until seduced by the straw-
haired siren who'd waylaid him in the forest.

For the sake of his wife and four children he was spared the rigours
of prison, the magistrate seizing the chance to deliver a broadside
against the scandalous immorality of the times. 'You have much to
reproach yourself for,' he told the accused, 'yet the court itself is
humane enough to appreciate the ease with which a weak vessel,
such as yourself, may be cracked and broken, if disturbed by the
blandishments of Sodom and Gomorrah. You will be fined the sum
of two thousand francs, and will supply the court with the name and
address of your Jezebel, along with a list of your squanderings. If
you needs take a mistress, Monsieur, take one who's happy with
trinkets.'

The embezzler dried his eyes and blinked his gratitude. The fine was equivalent to exactly three weeks earnings. He could keep his house in town, and his house in the country. His wife would forgive him, and his fellow financiers think him quite the dog. He'd make sure to send the magistrate six dozen bottles of fine wine – anonymously, of course, though as man to man.

With a plump pink hand, he denounced the owner of the house in Rue Hautefeuille.

Marise screamed at Arnaud to save her. 'Do *something*, damn you! You think yourself so tough, flexing your muscles, so kick the bastards out! Look what they're doing! They're tearing down the curtains! Christ Almighty, *they're prising off the shutters*! I don't believe it . . . What the hell have *I* done? Am *I* the fraud? Did *I* steal the money? He got what he wanted from *me*, and got it regular . . .' She turned to Elisa, and the two of them cringed together as the court officials took everything on the list.

It seemed suddenly close to Kilbreen.

Arnaud made a pretence of protecting the property, though he was far too shrewd to remonstrate with the officials. Threaten them with violence, and he'd be serving five years, his plans for the future destroyed. So he blustered and said: 'Careful there. Show a bit of respect. Mind what you're doin'. Stick within the law.'

The bailiffs ignored him. They dismantled the canopy in the bedroom, sent to the depot for the brightly painted cabriolet, then piled it high with fabrics and shutters and copperware; everything the salmon had listed.

The magistrate had told the bailiffs to make an example of this woman, this Laïs, this Jezebel. What he omitted to mention, of course, was that he too had *une petite amie*, installed in a fourth-floor apartment in the Place de la Bourse.

But where was the harm in that? So long as she continued to settle for trinkets.

As an innocent witness, Elisa learned more about the failings of the foolish Marise.

For example, she should have found herself a protector with power, not a chubby, weak-willed family man who couldn't afford to pay for his pleasures. She'd been better off with her so-called students than she was when her flag was nailed to Monsieur Gustave's fragile mast.

If *I* had a protector, Elisa told herself, I'd choose a diplomat, or someone in the Government. Or a wealthy aristocrat. Though the truth is I'd rather have a husband. Someone like Papa.

It took months for the straw-haired courtesan to recover from the loss of Monsieur Gustave. She advertised again for students, and once more dark-suited men edged furtively to her door. They brought their limp bunches of flowers, handed their hats and canes to Elisa, then perched on one of the chairs in the parlour, sipping their wine and waiting to be invited to the garish room upstairs.

Elisa Lynch was now almost fifteen, growing taller and more confident by the day. Marise regarded her as a cousin, almost as a sister, recounting intimate tales, then laughing as Elisa blushed. 'You don't believe me? You'll find out, *ma fille*. Whatever they call themselves, gentlemen or artists or what-have-you, they're basically all the same. Their wives don't understand them – heard *that* one a thousand times! Or they're frightened to offend the lady's sensibilities. Not mine, you notice, but the oh, so respectable, oh, so conventional Madame Whoever. The things they tell me their wives *won't* do, it's a wonder they ever draw close enough – '

'But why not? Being married and all. Mama used to tell me that a couple who live together in love – '

'Yes, well, your mama was special. In some ways I'm sorry I never met her.' Then she gave a cheerful, self-deprecating smile and added: 'But if she'd met *me*, you'd still be running errands round the market. Now let's see. What's the time? Ain't I got a student due at four?'

'A Monsieur Paul. The one with the moustache. He's the way I imagine a schoolmaster – '

'He *is* a schoolmaster. But I'll tell you about Monsieur Paul another time.' She gestured to Elisa to go on downstairs, then poured herself a stiffening glass of cognac, in preparation for her arduous four o'clock rendezvous.

Shortly after Elisa's fifteenth birthday, Arnaud beckoned her into the kitchen. He'd chosen the moment when Odile was out shopping, and treated the girl with uncharacteristic kindness, his wide, flattened lips stretched in a friendly smile.

'Here, girl. Take a sip of this. Raspberry cordial, fresh from the cold room. You're lookin' nice today, girl. Filled out since you come here. Grown up quite a lot, it seems to me.'

'It's kind of you to remark on it, Monsieur Arnaud, but – '

'Not too sweet, the cordial?'

'No, it's – '

'You likely don't remember,' the pugilist told her, 'But a while ago I said I'd got this idea. Seeing you now, the way you look, I thought I might bring it into the open.'

The girl said nothing, waiting for Arnaud to explain. He was what Papa would have called a three-card-tricky sort of devil, and Elisa wondered if he sought to sweet-talk her, hoping to seduce her with Odile's sugary concoction.

'You know what the word means, girl, if I say protector?'

'If you mean in its intimate details, then no, I don't. But my mother gave me instruction, and Madame Marise – '

'Yeah, well Madame Marise has gone all astray. She won't amount to nothing. But you, girl, there's a future for you, and I'm the one to see it turns out bright.' He leaned across the broad, scarred table, the muscles of his forearms straining against the tight wool sleeves of his shirt, the morning light seeming to swell the fleshy pads beneath his eyes. He looked brutal and insincere, and Elisa could see no brilliant future in the company of Arnaud.

'There's a place I know of, near the Pont d'Arcole. Overlooks the river. I've a friend who'd let us have it, an' you could be upstairs with your visitors, whilst I saw things ran smooth.' He rubbed his lips, remembering a phrase he'd been practising for weeks, then said: 'Eyes like emeralds, an' hair like rubies. You'd have 'em queueing clear along the quay!'

Elisa glanced down at her glass of cordial. Well, she thought, there's a fine, romantic thing for a man to tell his colleen. Only Arnaud isn't my man, and he disgusts me. With Odile out shopping, he abandons all loyalty to his mistress, and would set *me* up in his friend's room near the bridge. He shares this house with three women, and manages to insult us all with a single wag of his tongue. My God, what an oaf we have here!

Raising her head to gaze at him, she said: 'Listen. Listen close.'

'Doin' so, girl. Extra thoughts'd be welcome.'

'That's good. Because my first thought is that I find you a miserable, swaggering bully. As worthless as a field of rotted potatoes. A disloyal and unfaithful friend to Madame Marise, and here, if you want to know it, a ludicrous sight at table in your stupid, flouncy outfit!'

Elisa had saved the best until last, wanting to tell him that for months. But she underestimated Arnaud's reach, and the man sent her spinning from her chair. She heard him kick his own chair aside and come after her, but by then she was out of the kitchen, blood on the inside of her cheek.

She ran to her room, locked herself in, and sobbed with the pain of his blow.

So now she knew what Arnaud intended. She would keep as far away from him as possible, and hope he'd find another, more willing occupant for the room near the Pont d'Arcole.

The arrest and departure of the fraudulent Monsieur Gustave, along with the repossession of the carriage, weakened Marise Perrone's resolve to succeed in the demi-monde. She still entertained her gentlemen callers, though a listlessness drugged her days. Arnaud began to assert his own brutal authority, no longer addressing her as the mistress of the house, but as little more than a prostitute, too lazy to ply her profession. 'If you can't find clients for yourself, I'll find 'em for you. And stay off the drink. It shows in your face.'

Marise would scream invective at him, or merely shrug. 'So get me a proper protector, why don't you? I'm sick and tired of clerks who've *saved* to come here! It's a wonder they don't ask for change!'

Avoiding the arguments – and the domineering Arnaud – Elisa spent her free time in the student cafés that dotted the area. The Brasserie Andler, hang-out of writers and artists; the oddly-named Café Mariage, where the poets congregated; the Café Tabourey in Rue de Vaugirard, the favoured haunt of the debauched and brilliant Charles Baudelaire, the poet still less than thirty, yet ravaged by disease.

She found herself seated near the painter Courbet, the writer Ponsard; a dozen others who bellowed or whispered, tossed their scarves or tilted their moleskin hats.

Relieved to be away from the house in Rue Hautefeuille, Elisa was approached by a number of sallow young men, one of whom presented her with a bouquet of flowers, cunningly fashioned from newspaper. 'All I can afford,' he told her, 'though you have to admit I bring knowledge with every bloom!'

Another admirer sat scribbling, then jumped to his feet and regaled her with a fanciful poem – 'For the girl with the rays of sunset in her hair'.

Delighted by such new-found attentions, Elisa charmed them further with her foreign-accented French. *Well, this is more like it. Better than being slapped around by Arnaud.*

They invited her to the cheap student restaurants, the young men paying 30 centimes for the meal, a pitcher of cider included in the price. They talked politics and the future of France, shredded the latest literary works with critical claws, damned the past and glowered at the future – then asked her back to their garrets and their beds.

On at least two occasions she was tempted to say yes, curiosity attracting her to their slim, vibrant bodies. But she remembered the things Adelaide had told her, and Odile's advice in the kitchen, and was intelligent enough to guess that tonight's lover would seek another girl tomorrow.

As a man will ache for physical release, so too did Elisa Lynch. But it had to satisfy more than just carnal curiosity. A desire so important that it left her twisting awake in her bed – it was surely more than a gift to be exchanged in some chilly, anonymous attic.

Nevertheless, she was not averse to being kissed.

It was clear to her now that in Rue Hautefeuille the pugilist had taken full command. He roared at Marise, snarled at Odile, threatened Elisa with the lengthy sweep of his arm. 'Bunch of bloody women! We've a cook and a maid and a – whatever she is these days, and all we need are the callers. So, fine, I'll drum up the callers. And if that doesn't work, then the hell with you! I'll be off to the Pont d'Arcole!'

It was a lie, of course, for Arnaud still counted on Marise to satisfy the dwindling number of clients. He was better off here than in the two-room apartment near the bridge, though it angered him to see the courtesan growing blowzy on cognac, and the red-haired Elisa refusing to play the game. Why else were women shaped the way they were, if not to hook men?

8

In May 1850, Elisa agreed to meet a tall, languorous painter in the Café de la Rotonde, on the corners of Rue Hautefeuille and Rue de l'Ecole de Médecine. Far above the student level, the Café de la Rotonde was the meeting place of surgeons and doctors, medical scientists, lecturers and researchers, a semicircle of glass in which the critical claw gave way to the glitter of the scalpel.

By the time she'd found a seat, she realized her mistake. Glass-walled though it was, the café was dark and sombre, men were hunched forward in quiet conversation, and the room was devoid of pictures, of painters, of poets, of paper flowers. *And of any other women.*

She was the victim of a stupid, practical joke. The idiot's who'd suggested this café was probably crouched across the street, jabbing elbows with his friends, and waiting for Elisa to emerge, her cheeks as red as her hair.

But the Irish don't take kindly to being teased for the sake of a snigger, and Elisa Lynch decided to hold her ground. Catching the eye of a waiter she said: '*S'il vous plaît? Un citron sucré.*'

He saw her, pretended he hadn't and moved on.

Elisa raised her hand to a second waiter. The man looked directly at her, faltered in his stride, but turned away. Her request for sugared lemon soured in the air, and she accepted that women were invisible in the Café de la Rotonde.

All right, she fumed, so the joke's worked well. I'm in some kind of gentlemen's club, and they won't throw me out, but they won't serve me either. Won't serve me? They won't acknowledge my exist-ence!

She'd started to her feet when a voice said: 'It's not what you ordered, Mademoiselle, but it might assuage your thirst. They call it champagne, but it's probably not that either.'

She turned to see a thick-set man, his face concealed by a dark, well-trimmed beard, the hair on his head receding, his pale lips stretched in a smile. Guessing his age – *above thirty? Below forty?* – she was tempted to be rude to him, this witness to her embarrassment.

But before she could speak, the man offered her a fluted glass, beckoned for another, then rose from his chair and introduced himself: 'Regimental Doctor, *Capitaine* Xavier Quatrefages, called to Paris to await a future posting. Try it, Mademoiselle. It's only wine and bubbles.'

Now was the time to leave and sort out the painter. Catch him sniggering with his friends and slap his silly face. Then march on home . . . Back to Marise and her cognac . . . Back to Arnaud and his knuckles . . .

Or take the fluted glass and sit down again. And so what if she was the only woman in the Café de la Rotonde? What could they do to her now, the guest of this Regimental Doctor, with his unpronounceable name?

'I'll just taste it, Monsieur, how's that?'

'By all means.'

'Though it doesn't mean I can stay.'

'Quite so. You've doubtless a hundred things to do, a pretty young woman like you.'

She sipped the drink, coughed as the bubbles caught at her throat, then hurried to pronounce it quite refreshing. 'Though I've had it before. Lots of times.'

Quatrefages nodded. 'Both here and abroad, I imagine. You'll forgive me, but with your accent, your hair, your delightful green eyes – '

'I'm from Ireland,' Elisa told him, twirling the empty glass.

The man refilled it, then filled his own. He thought her one of the most beautiful girls he'd ever seen, and without reservation the most attractive he'd been fortunate enough to meet. His fellow officers sometimes escorted beautiful women, though they rarely looked twice at the sober and somewhat colourless Xavier Gaston Quatrefages.

Yet now he summoned the courage to ask the *Irelandaise* her name. 'I sense you are probably struggling with mine.'

She laughed and said yes, it was just about the most difficult – 'You'll have to write it down for me.'

'And yours, Mademoiselle?'

'Oh, mine's easy. Elisa Alicia Lynch.'

He surprised himself then by blurting an invitation to dinner, the forward thrust lost as he added: 'In a restaurant, of course . . . If you're free . . .'

She gazed at him, this stocky, middle-aged man with his hesitant manner and uncertain expression, a hand raised to his head as if to disguise his baldness. She knew who he reminded her of – Papa. Not that Papa had grown a beard, or had ever been as thick around the waist. But balding, yes, and quiet-spoken, and protective in his particular, gentle way. *Not the sort of protector Marise is after, but a man you could turn to, and count upon for comfort.*

Quatrefages was yet to learn the extent of his good fortune, already expecting to be rebuffed. After all, what would a vivacious young woman like this want with someone who was quite clearly twice her age, a man who'd offered her second-rate champagne? It was a foolish suggestion, and he waited to be ridiculed.

'Well, as you can see, I'm ill-dressed for the evening, *Capitaine* – '

'Not at all. Not at all! You're dressed well enough for anywhere, Mademoiselle Elisa. And I shall take you wherever you wish! But we can't have this *Capitaine* stuff. It's Xavier. Shall we go across the river?'

She guessed him now to be forty.

He assumed her to be at least seventeen, perhaps a year older.

She continued to draw parallels between Quatrefages and Cavan, and speculated on the life of a French Army doctor. Quite glamorous in its way. With a *képi* to hide his baldness, and a belt to hold in his stomach, the Regimental Doctor Xavier Quatrefages might cut an authoritative figure on the parade ground. And she liked the way he kept his beard well trimmed.

He treated her to a meal of oysters and lamb, slow-cooked venison, a tart soaked in Calvados, a flaky pastry seeped in absinthe. She drank a glass of white wine from Alsace, a third of a bottle of red wine from Bordeaux. Giggling at his laboured jokes, she spilled her cognac *digestif*.

She was partway drunk, and the realization scared her. But Quatrefages saw her home to Rue Hautefeuille in a fiacre, offering his hand as she entered the two-wheeled conveyance, then again as she alighted. He made no attempt to kiss her, though she wondered what *that* would be like, being kissed by a hedgehog, this *hérisson* with all his tickly bristles . . .

'So this is where you live.'

'Do for the moment . . .'

'As a companion to the elderly Madame Laurent-Perrone.'

'That what I told you? I mean, yes, that's right. But I won't be here for ever.'

Quatrefages smiled. 'I've some glimmer of hope you won't, Mademoiselle Elisa. As I hope I might take you out again.'

Unbalanced by drink, the girl caught at the low street railings. 'What? No. That's to say yes. But not from here. I'll meet you in the

Café de la Rotonde. But you mustn't come here. Madame Laurent-Perrone wouldn't like it.'

The man nodded equably. 'Very well. Then would you care to meet me on Sunday morning? I've an outing in mind you might enjoy. Or perhaps you've been on a railway train before?'

Elisa gasped with delight. 'No, I haven't! I've read about it in the newspapers, but I've never – oh, yes, Monsieur Xavier, oh, yes! I'd love to go on a railway train! Not even Madame Marise – Not even my mistress has done that!'

'Fine. Then I'll await you at nine o'clock next Sunday. But wear a tied bonnet. We'll be going at quite some speed.'

Laughing, she embraced him for his courtesy and kindness, learning what it was like to have her cheek brushed by his beard. Quite funny, really. Quite nice.

Next morning, with Sunday three days away, the pugilist told her to go up and see Marise. 'She's something to say to you, girl. Something as might get you a rise in pay.'

'I will,' Elisa agreed, 'but would you mind not calling me girl? I'm fully fifteen, and pass for more, and Odile says – '

'And what I say – *girl* – is you'll get your head bounced off the wall, you come clever with me. You've felt my hand twice. You in need of a third?'

She ran upstairs, Arnaud gazing after her, grinning at her hips and slender limbs.

The once cheerful young courtesan was now puffy and petulant, lounging in a room that smelled of liquor. 'Heard you come back last night,' she mouthed. 'Been fishing for your own pretty salmon?'

Elisa shook her head. 'If you want to know the truth, Madame Marise, I was supposed to meet a painter. But he didn't show up.'

'So you sat there in tears till midnight? Sniffing into your handkerchief? Then made your lonely way home? Come along, my cute Elisa. You cast your line wider than that.'

'I did not, as you say, cast my line. I was sitting there when a military man – '

'Don't tell me. Let me guess. He wasn't actually in uniform – '

'No, he wasn't.'

' – but told you he was a Major in the Cavalry, and due for promotion. So he took you back to his hotel room – '

'Why did you want to see me, Madame Marise? Arnaud said you'd something to tell me.' It distressed her to find the courtesan so

141

cynical, when she'd once been so ebullient. It was bad luck about Monsieur Gustave, the whimpering fraud, but if the woman stopped drinking, and found the courage to kick out Arnaud, then surely she could land another fish. It was an uncertain way of life, hoping to be a man's mistress, but Elisa didn't stand in moral judgement, she merely regretted her young friend's sudden surrender.

'Something to tell you? Yes, that's right. Tell you how you can repay the kindness I've shown you. Prove your fidelity, that's how. Not just see the clients into the parlour, but accompany them up here. You with your deep green gaze and twitching bottom! Burnished hair and French that ain't quite right! They come into the bedroom, my gentlemen callers, and who do you think they talk about, but you! Huff and puff in *my* bed, Elisa, but wheeze about my maid! So what you're to do – '

'I'm sorry, Madame Marise, but no. I'll do all I can to help you in, well, what *you* do, and it's true you've been kind to me, but I came here as your maid – '

'And stayed to make me look old, that's what you've done! Squirmed your way in, then grown in the legs, stuffing your hips and breasts with the food I've bought you! A scrawny little brat when you came here, but look at you now. Fifteen, and you'd pass for damn near twenty! But still the virgin, still the cat-play-kitten! Well, I'm telling you, *ma belle*, you've a week to decide, or you can go on back to your Major of Cavalry, and ride *his* jaunty horse! Now find me a glass. And where's that stupid bottle?'

The six-lane track led from the Place de l'Europe, later to become established as one of the city's finest stations, the Gare St Lazare.

The buildings themselves straddled a bridge, the trains on a lower level, the thirteen-year-old rails still bright, the passengers still cautious, recoiling from the noise and steam and smoke.

Xavier Quatrefages bought two first-class tickets for the eleven-mile journey to Le Pecq. 'It's worth the extra money, for at least we'll have a closed carriage. Second and Third, they're open.'

Elisa Lynch gazed wide-eyed at the ribbons of rail, buried in their oily gravel beds. She watched as boisterous young men took their girlfriends aboard, the men sporting the latest fashions, flapping trousers and broad-shouldered jackets, clothes they might have stolen from a giant. The girls were even more outrageous, their velvet skirts stitched and divided, *for all the world like breeches*!

142

Quatrefages took the tickets to a desk, waited as they were stamped and clipped and initialled, then saw Elisa aboard the train.

'The engine,' she said. 'Can it really pull these coaches?'

'Carriages,' he repeated. 'On the railway line they're carriages. But yes, sit tight, and you'll see how fast we go.'

A guard made his way along the platform, locking the passengers in. Elisa clasped her bonnet to her head and peered out of the window. Smoke was pouring from the engine, scudding beneath the arch of the station, billowing up into the sky above Place de l'Europe. *Looks to me like we're not going anywhere. And the train'll catch fire. And we'll all of us be cooked!*

She turned in alarm to the formally dressed Xavier, who drew her back to her seat. 'Don't worry. It's gathering strength. It'll jolt in a minute – there! See what I mean? – and now we're under way. Stay back from the soot, but watch the verge. When the train picks up speed it'll all be a blur. Eleven miles in thirty-five minutes, so they tell me. The fastest means of travel on earth.'

The train clattered and rocked on its way to Le Pecq, Elisa chewing her lip, unable to speak or smile. *Locked into a moving room like this . . . With dense black smoke pouring past . . . It's terrifying! But exciting, yes, and comforting to know I'm with a Regimental Doctor . . .*

In Le Pecq he bought her coffee and brioche. Then they climbed the hill to the Terrasse de St Germain, and gazed back towards the capital.

'I wish I knew it better,' Elisa mused. 'And maybe one day I will. What I think I'd like more than anything is a house in Paris with an interior yard large enough to stable a coach and horses. An upper floor for the servants. A number of rooms for my guests. A garden, of course, for vegetables and flowers. And all of it within walking distance of the river and the shops.' She turned to Xavier Quatrefages, saw the man blink, then tipped her face to the sky and laughed aloud. 'It's all right, it's only a dream. You should never have brought me up here to this wonderful *point de vue*. The chances are I'll end up in a room near St Merri, teaching French to foreigners, and English to reluctant children. Or go back home to Cork, and see if Miss Gardiner's reopened her General Day School.'

They hurried downhill to catch the *Compagnie du Chemin de Fer de Paris* train back to the city. It pleased Elisa to see trousered girls sobbing and pulling away at the prospect of this helter-skelter ride. 'Don't know what they're so worried about,' she said scornfully. 'It wouldn't

143

scare *me* if the train went twice the speed. Though I do have *you* for protection, *M'sieur le Hérisson!*'

The man had never in his life been accorded a nickname. But now he had one, and loved it . . .

9

Capitaine Quatrefages took her on other outings, shyly confiding his background to the girl. He told her he was the only child of a farming family, far away to the south in the bleak Cévennes. 'They spent every last centime to see me through school, and my father then said the most sensible thing – if this doesn't bore you, Elisa – '

'Bore me, my dear Xavier? Oh, no, you don't bore me at all.'

'Glad to hear it,' he said. 'Don't believe it, of course, seeing as you're so young and so pretty. But it grants me permission to continue. So what he said – what my father said – was that I should study hard then seek a position that would allow me free rein in France and all her dominions. Which is why I became a, well, a medical man, and joined the Army.'

Elisa Lynch loved the romance of this could-have-been peasant, who'd left the snow-swept hills of the Cévennes, studied his way to Paris, and was now no less than a military surgeon, bulky and bearded and brave.

It made her student friends seem childish, with their paper flowers and caustic chatter, their knowledge of the world confined to a few dozen Paris streets.

And he *does* remind me of Papa, she thought. He *does* seem a man one could trust.

At the end of the meal, he ordered two glasses of Armagnac, smiling as he warned her not to spill it. She promised she wouldn't, and was sipping it with care when Quatrefages said: 'Now tell me, Elisa Alicia Lynch. How'd you feel about marriage to the Army?'

'What?' she frowned. 'I don't understand.'

'Oh, I don't mean you'll be recruited,' he assured her. 'We haven't gone that far yet! All I meant was marriage to me. This farmer's son. This hedgehog who'd like to take care of you. Save you teaching those reluctant children or returning to Cork. I'm no good at this, my dear, and have never said it to anyone before. But can you hear *yourself* say aloud – "Madame Elisa Alicia Quatrefages"?'

Her emotions churning, she told him she wasn't sure. She'd need time to reflect. 'I'm flattered by your offer – '

'But you won't say yes.'

' – and I think of you as a decent, kindly man – '

'But you won't tell me yes.'

' – and feel comforted in your presence.'

'*Entendu*,' he sighed. 'But you still need time to reflect. Very well. Then why don't you take what the Army calls the *vingt-quatre*? I'll be in the Café de la Rotonde tomorrow evening. Should you care to join me, I'll assume the most beautiful girl I ever met is willing to be my wife. If not, then don't come at all, my dear. Your absence will spare us mutual embarrassment, *n'est-ce pas*?'

The girl leaned to brush her cheek against Xavier's bristly beard. 'You're a lot like my father,' she murmured. 'You know that, *M'sieur le Hérisson*?'

'I'm a lot like every girl's father,' Quatrefages shrugged. 'But in your case I'd hoped to seem younger.'

When she re-entered the house in Rue Hautefeuille, the pugilist was waiting. He caught her by the arm, hauled her close and gusted stale breath in her face. 'So it's come and go as you like now, is it? Claim you're just the maid-servant, yet think the hours are your own. Well, I tell you, girl, your wanderings are over. There's some friends of mine coming tomorrow, and you'll be upstairs to welcome 'em, you an' that damn Marise. Deny 'em what they want, and I'll show you how a coachman works his whip. Have you dancing half to the ceiling, I will. Have you screaming to shatter the glasses.' Then he shoved her violently away, flecks of his spittle on her face.

She lay fully dressed on her bed until the city clocks struck three. Easing herself from the horsehair mattress, she lighted an oil lamp, moved stealthily to the tall, mahogany wardrobe, turned the catch and opened the door in a single, sudden movement – the best way to stop it creaking. With painstaking slowness she packed her valise, pocketed the jade brooch, then laid her buttoned boots in the top of the open bag.

She faltered, imagining Arnaud in his room downstairs, the muscular brute awake and waiting to pounce. Oh, he'd love to show her how a coachman went about his task – and probably do it for the pleasure of his friends.

She stood silent, fighting her fears. Then she dug the nails of her left hand deep into her right, the pain enough to hint at the pains to come . . .

The bedroom door squealed sharply as she opened it, but it was too late to falter again. With the lamp in one hand, the unbuckled valise in the other, she crept downstairs, her stockinged feet feeling for the outer edges of the steps.

A sound came from Arnaud's room, the mutterings of his voice. 'That you, girl?'

She ran for the street door, her throat dry with fright as she thrust the lamp on to a shelf, reached to slip the upper bolt, stooped to release the lower. She heard the pugilist bellow, felt the door swing inwards, then was out and down the steps and running, trusting to her knowledge of the streets as she fled towards the only sanctuary she knew – the closed and shuttered Café de la Rotonde.

She swerved right into Rue de l'École de Médicine, left into the Rue Dubois, left again along Rue Monsieur le Prince. The cobbles punished her feet and she lost her way. But she knew she must not let Arnaud catch her again. A practised liar in many things, he'd keep his word about the whip.

She huddled in an alleyway, brushed the grit and dirt from her feet, then took the grey suede boots from her bag, fumbling with the buttons. She listened for the stamp of his own heavy heels, heard nothing and sighed with tremulous relief.

It was now about four in the morning.

Her rendezvous, if she wished to keep it, was for eight o'clock that evening.

The Army's *vingt-quatre* was reduced to sixteen, during which time she must hide from the furious Arnaud. No longer the cat-play-kitten, they might now play cat-and-mouse.

Elisa tramped her way in a circle to the left bank of the river, crossed to the Ile de la Cité, then offered her assistance to the stall-holders of the Wednesday market.

Suspicious at first, they were quickly won over by her talk of St Merri, her command of their language, her tangle of russet hair. They set her to carrying small change between stalls, the marketeers soon vying to keep her with them, aware that the girl's mere presence attracted the customers.

And so what if Arnaud finds me here, she thought. They'd throw him in the river, these *marchands*; him *and* his plaited whip.

It was June, and the day was long, but at seven that evening Elisa Lynch told her new-found friends she was leaving. They asked no questions, though assured her she'd be welcome again, then contributed their share of a full day's wage.

For an instant she was tempted to join them, enjoying their banter,

147

admiring their skills, seeing herself accepted as one of their family. After all, what was wrong with a life in the open air, every day in a different part of Paris, a circus of foodstuffs and flowers forever on the move?

But that's what it would be, of course; a circus and a circle.

And when was promotion ever won in the market?

Xavier Quatrefages had dressed for the occasion – victory or defeat. His beard trimmed by the regimental barber, he'd entered the café in uniform, his broad leather belt circled tight around his pale blue jacket, brass buttons burnished to a shine, pleated red cloth trousers tucked into polished boots. He'd worn his stiff peaked *képi* all the way to the table, ignoring the surgeons' disapproving glances. Then he'd ordered champagne – 'But I mean the real stuff tonight' – removed his cap and sat upright in his chair, gazing fixedly at the broad windows.

He heard the civilians chuckle behind his back. Heard the most famous doctors in France asking each other in theatrical whispers what their military colleague thought he was doing in La Rotonde. 'Come from the provinces, most likely. Doesn't yet know the Army's at the *other* end of the street.'

The waiter brought the champagne, and Quatrefages said: 'Yes, and another glass.'

'For another of your military colleagues Monsieur? I ask, because the *patron* would have me remind you we don't usually serve gentlemen in uniform – '

'Nor women.' Quatrefages beamed, gazing at a slim shadow beyond the heavy glass door and lurching to his feet. 'Know it for the truth you don't serve women.'

'As a matter of fact, Monsieur – '

'Well, get that second glass and let's all see! For you've got one now!'

The waiter spun round as Elisa entered the café. Then he glanced back as Xavier Gaston Quatrefages asked her: 'Well, *ma chère*? Is it yes?' And swung back as Elisa Alicia Lynch told him: 'Sure it is. And don't you look just fine!'

PART THREE

Algiers: 1850–1851

1

It was as if the high North African sun had bleached the colour from the fabric of her hopes. As if the gusting simoom had dried the juices of her desires. As if the hammer blows of heat had crushed her spirit.

But it was not just the climate, hard though it was on this woman who'd spent her childhood in the cold and damp of Ireland. It was her husband. His fellow officers. Other men's wives. And Elisa herself, of course. More than anything or anyone, it was the fifteen-year-old Madame Elisa Quatrefages.

Back in Paris, the bearded Xavier had learned that his bride-to-be was under age. She, in turn, had discovered that this-man-like-Papa was already forty-three. Naïve and love-lorn, the Regimental Doctor had taken her across the Channel to the English port of Folkestone where, on 3rd June 1850, they'd been married. In many ways more worldly than the Hedgehog, she'd convinced him that the union was a grand, romantic adventure. 'You must love me greatly, *M'sieur le Hérisson*, since you've all but abducted me, like a corsair!'

'I do,' he'd said soberly. 'And I could not envisage waiting another year to make you my wife. Nor yet another month. Oh, yes, my dear Elisa, indeed I do.'

They consummated the marriage in a hotel on The Leas, as a summer storm rattled the windows.

Xavier was nervous, inexperienced, unimaginative. Elisa feigned pleasure, though could not believe such intimate conjoining need be so – well, so singularly dull. Perhaps the next time . . . Tomorrow . . . However long it took for a man to find himself ready . . .

But the next time was the same, and all the times thereafter. Quiet and attentive by nature, his arm linked with hers when they strolled the windswept Leas, her middle-aged military husband failed to arouse her in bed.

They had returned to Paris to find orders waiting; *Capitaine* Quatrefages commanded to report to his regiment, where travel dockets would be issued, Paris – Marseilles – Algiers.

He spent a difficult hour with the *Commandant*, admitting he'd married without permission. But the senior officer had known Quatrefages for years – *a man who's good at his job, though God forbid he ever attempts a witty remark* – and offered his curt congratulations.

'I suppose you'll wish to bring the lady out with you? From your own part of the country, is she? The Cévennes?'

'Not exactly, *mon Commandant*. Though, yes, if it can somehow be arranged – '

'Oh, there's very little the Army can't arrange, *Capitaine* Quatrefages. Be a piss-poor reflection on France if her uniformed might was incapable – '

'I'll pay for her passage, of course. And for married quarters.'

'You certainly will, my dear Doctor. And for the clerk who has to contact the shipping lines. The purser who has to find your good lady a berth. The official in Algiers who must allocate extra quarters. And let's not forget the Arab girl who'll be sent to brush out the dust. Getting married, *Capitaine* Quatrefages, can do much to lighten the wallet.'

Chastened, but with only Elisa in mind, the officer had saluted, then sat in the outer office, reminding himself of his young wife's phrase – they would soon be off on another romantic adventure . . .

Too late to secure passage aboard one of the regular passenger ships, the newlyweds were given a cramped, two-berth cubicle on the steam packet *Argon*, the vessel heeling and dipping on its four-hundred-and-eighty-mile voyage from Metropolitan France to the garrison port of Algiers.

The menu in the dining saloon was beef stew, bread and coffee – and sour wine from the barrel. Twice a day, throughout the four-day crossing, it was beef stew, bread and coffee, the stew re-heated, the bread re-baked, the coffee re-boiled. And the wine turning fast to vinegar.

Elisa squirmed in agony on her bunk, her stomach vomited empty. She whimpered for Xavier to nurse her. 'You must have *something* in your bag . . . Oh, please . . . If only to let me sleep.'

He told her then he was sorry, but he'd thought she'd understood. 'Whatever I give you will be too strong. These opiates, they're for animals, didn't I make that clear? I'm a doctor, yes, but with responsibility for the horses, the mules . . .'

'Then you're not a doctor at all . . . *You're a vet* . . . '

'If you wish. Though the Army accords me the title – '

'Oh, God.' And she coughed again as the bunk heaved up on the swell.

*

152

Punishment at sea was followed by punishment on land.

Limp and dehydrated, Elisa was taken in an unsprung cart to the garrison quarters at El Biar, two miles south of the city. There, at last, Quatrefages ministered to her, keeping her body cool in the day and warm at night. He gave her purified water, well-washed dates, salt from the endless pans beyond the Sahara, then infusions of minty tea, the diet of the desert nomads.

Recovery, when it came, was quick and total. She ate ravenously, without questioning the food, drank water by the litre, spurned the blankets and demanded a mirror and comb.

Within a week of her arrival, the girl from Ireland was eager to learn about the country she'd been brought to.

With more than five-hundred-and-fifty miles of Mediterranean coastline, extending from Morocco in the west to Tunisia in the east, and a hinterland that ran south for close on four hundred, Algeria was the latest trophy on France's shelf. Invaded in 1830 – 'to repair the ravages of three centuries of wicked piracy' – it had proved both a bane and a benefit to its conquerors. Almost a quarter of a million square miles in area, it had, until the French invasion, been devoid of a single road. Camel routes, yes, though these known only to the nomads; routes that linked an oasis here with another there, the waterholes as much as two hundred miles part, and the prints of the splay-hoofed camels erased by the wind.

And yet, with the vast Sahara Desert to the south, the coastal belt could serve as fine a table as France herself. Pomegranates were grown, and mandarins and oranges and lemons. Dates and figs, fleshy olives, reeds for baskets, tobacco for the pipe and the cigar. Extensive forests supplied an abundance of wood, Arab hunters stalking them for the wild, tusky boar. Horses were raised on the plains, donkeys turned the water-wheels, goats provided milk and cheese and meat.

It was a country rich in minerals, rich in its handicrafts, yet a country sublimely ignorant of its wealth. With copper and zinc and lead still there for the taking, the shepherds were happy to graze their sheep on the lid of their unknown treasures.

Then the French sent in their fleet, their marines, their regiments of the line. They seized the ports of Algiers and Oran, blew the mud-brick forts to dust, established their presence and raised the *Tricolore* over the ruins. 'Our civilized nation will no longer accept the depredations of the African pirate. Duty demands that we call a halt to this history of blood. These vipers must be exterminated, preferably in their nests. *Vive la France!*'

It was then, with the troops still under canvas, that France acknowledged the treasure – and the traps.

A country this vast, yet without a single road? *Bon sang*, so the choice was to build 'em, or learn to ride camels.

And an enemy that could melt into the night, sleep when the desert air dropped to zero, fight when it soared to a hundred degrees at midday? *Putain de merde*, it wouldn't be quite the rabbit shoot they'd supposed.

Ill-equipped, and ignorant of desert warfare, the French troops sustained terrible losses, chasing these merciless men who fought to defend their own country. Military encampments were attacked at night, scimitars swishing in the dark. Columns were ambushed, the riders and infantry already blinded by the sun and the whip of the wind, the nomads then emerging from the dust. Prisoners were taken and tortured; not for the pleasure, but quite simply because they'd allowed themselves to be captured. If a man was a man, he should die where he fought. Or not come here at all.

With the benefits apparent, the bane of the nomads continued to halt French progress.

The coastal cities now flying the tricolour of France, the tribes to the south had yet to be subdued.

And *Capitaine* Xavier Gaston Quatrefages would be called to ride with the column.

The barracks at El Biar were as monotonous in their layout as a prison. All roads ran parallel, or at right angles to each other. A double row of trees had been planted, and died, and never been replaced. The soldiers' quarters were just small-windowed blocks of stone, the married quarters devoid of gardens, windbreaks, even a bamboo fence. Elisa had no idea why this site had been chosen, except, perhaps, that it occupied a plateau. Whether natural, or levelled, it was flat, flat, flat . . . Perfect, she decided, for a regiment of the blind . . .

The parade ground seemed the size of St Merri, men were sent to sweep it as a punishment, the red earth billowing around them, but with more red earth to be swept again tomorrow.

Less than two hundred yards from this *terrain de manoeuvres*, the house Quatrefages had been allocated was within easy earshot of the five-in-the-morning bugle. Stirring, he awoke Elisa, who was expected to light the new-fangled paraffin cooker, boil water for coffee, then see him away from the house within thirty minutes.

She murmured once: 'Just as well you've got your beard. I used to heat water for Papa, so he could shave, but it never had to be done to the call of the bugle.'

'What, my dear? What?'

'It's nothing. Stand still while I run a cloth across your boots.'

Another time, without thinking, she said: 'I can see how Madame Marise would love this! Tell her she had a caller at five! I should really write to her and – '

'What's that, my dear? Something about the teacher?'

'It doesn't matter. Cinch in your belt.'

Five o'clock every morning, and the *reveille* brought them awake. Elisa soon learned that the Army was not just as punctual as the clock, it might have invented it. Had a bugler ever overslept, she wondered, or was there always someone on hand to wake the bugler? And someone to alert the man whose duty it was to alert the strident musician? Sweet Mary, this would scarcely be the place for the layabed Madame Marise . . .

Elisa kissed her husband, brushed dust from his jacket, then closed the door behind him to keep out the wind. A waste of effort, she acknowledged, since the simoom – or was this the sirocco? – found its way through every crack and crevice. But it was an attempt, at least. And it cut out the view of the arid, treeless barracks.

Crunching sand underfoot, she peered through the living room window, from where she could see the city. Flat-roofed houses spilled down the hill to the waterfront and the port, the gritty wind blowing to obscure the view, then subsiding in a dull pink gauze. When the air had cleared she gazed out at the Mediterranean, at a dozen shades of blue. Well, she thought, you look tranquil enough from here, *Madame la Mer*, though thank God I didn't marry a Captain of Marines . . .

She made her way to the bedroom, where the coverlet and pillows were encrusted with the quartz-like grit, blown in from the desert. Get used to it, she told herself. It's part of your life here now. Even so, she shook the coverlet, slapped the pillows, then swept the drab tiled floor.

The architect who'd designed these married quarters had probably been pleased with what he'd done, the bedroom window facing south toward the high, dramatic ridge of the Massif de l'Ouarsenis. But the architect was not required to live here. Pocketing his fee, he'd most likely returned to France, boasting of the *caserne* he'd designed in North Africa. 'Can't have our conquering heroes living like the nomads, after all!'

Leaning against the window, Elisa stared at the swirls and spirals of sand. It seemed to her now that the sky was as full of lies as of reddish dust . . . Her husband neither a true doctor, nor a lover . . . this house not a home . . . the grand romantic adventure drying on the ceaseless buffet of the wind . . .

2

With Quatrefages busy in the stables and mule pens, Elisa received a visit from one of the officers' wives. Tall and imperious, the woman said: 'Madame le Tourneau. My husband is on the General Staff.' Dressed unseasonably in a dark satin gown, its high starched-lace collar looped with pearls, she extended a gloved hand, scarcely allowing Elisa time to touch it before entering the house. Preceding the younger woman into the living room, the caller then glanced at the newcomer's simple, cotton dress and remarked: 'They're a damned unreliable lot, aren't they though?'

'Madame le Tourneau?'

'Why, the shippers, my dear. The ones you've entrusted with your furniture and wardrobe. You've been here, what, ten days already, yet are still making do with – with *this*!' She raked the room with her gaze, then shook her head. 'It really is intolerable. It wouldn't surprise me at all if your stuff's in a warehouse in Oran. Or in Tunis, for all we know . . .'

'I think you misunderstand,' Elisa measured quietly. 'Captain Quatrefages and I – we brought our possessions with us. However sparsely furnished – '

'Oh, dear. Oh, I am so sorry. *Quelle gaffe!*' Her apology was accompanied by a pitying smile, the woman then peering at this newcomer to El Biar. 'You look very young to be out here, Madame Quatrefages. Come of an army background, do you? Parents originally from Quebec? There's something about your accent. Can't pin it down, but – '

'Please be seated,' Elisa murmured. 'You may find the chairs somewhat rigid, but if you wish me to recount the story of my life – '

'Good Lord, no,' the woman dismissed. 'Is that the impression I gave? I'm not here to pry, my dear, but simply to invite you to join us for coffee. The ladies of the Regiment and myself. I'd have asked you sooner, but a wife can be so terribly busy in the early days, don't you agree? Deciding where the furniture should go, and things like that. Had I known of course that you and Captain Quatrefages . . .' She smiled again and shrugged and said she'd wait whilst Elisa changed. 'Not that we dress for something as informal as morning

157

coffee. But I thought – ' Then she measured Elisa's day gown with her shameless, critical gaze, and flicked sand from the chair with gloved figures.

So now I know what I'm up against, Elisa thought. The Inquisition begins.

She excused herself, went through to the bedroom, unbuttoned her dress and donned the outfit Marise Laurent-Perrone had bought her from the shop in the Rue de Rivoli, the brightly patterned gown and matching cape with its plaited braid. She exchanged her shoes for boots, adding two inches to her height, then brushed her fine hair and protected it with a bonnet. She touched her temples and neck with perfume – a wedding gift from Xavier – then slipped her long slim fingers into gloves. She glanced once more in the mirror – and stuck out her tongue as a cheerful insult to Madame le Tourneau and the ladies of the Regiment; *the ladies in waiting*.

As Elisa re-entered the living room the woman opened her mouth, then shut it without speaking. Should have let the girl come as she was, she acknowledged. She was pretty enough before, God knows, but now she's all coloured chalks, and we're the damned blackboards.

The members of the Inquisition smiled and beamed, and prepared to 'strip her naked'.

Her French was *presque parfait*, though she surely wasn't from France?

Had she heard that the king had been deposed, and that Louis Napoleon was now President of the glorious Second Republic? Had she actually set foot in Paris? My, what a wonderful city. A person who's never been to Paris had truly never been anywhere. Though they'd love to hear where she *had* been, and how she'd managed to master their language. 'Your clothes, my dear Madame Quatrefages; they, like you, could almost pass for French.'

She sat quiet, seemingly timid, allowing the women to circle and strike. They reached to serve her coffee, leaned across to pass her biscuits and dates, brushed her arms with their fingers, cosseted this new recruit to their ranks.

Showed their teeth and bared their claws.

Waiting until she was sure she had their attention, Elisa smiled and said: 'Those are interesting questions, mesdames. *You* have clearly travelled far and wide in the world, whereas I am but a refugee from the city of Cork in Ireland. I imagine you know it.'

The women exchanged quick glances, though none of them nodded.

'Then, yes, I did find my way to Paris, and lodged in the district of St Merri during the time of the Revolution. A squalid enough area, St Merri. Though I imagine you know of it.'

The '*of* it' gave the women the chance to murmur and sigh. Everyone knew of the market quarter.

'Later,' Elisa continued, 'I spent some time with a multi-lingual *institutrice* on the Left Bank of the river; enjoyed my evenings in the cafés and restaurants there. Took boat rides on the Seine. And, oh, but I must tell you this – went on a train journey from Paris to Le Pecq, eleven miles in thirty-five minutes. I imagine you've all done the same.'

The ladies of El Biar pursed their lips and fidgeted, the silence filled by the chink of coffee cups, the flutter of fans. Furious glances were cast at Madame le Tourneau, their president having let them down so badly. What on earth had she been thinking of, encouraging them to ply this Quatrefages woman with questions, yet leaving them quite unprepared for Elisa's answers?

Infuriated by their patronizing manner, Elisa then plucked lightly at the sleeve of her gown and gazed directly at Madame le Tourneau. 'You mentioned my clothes, Madame? Said they could almost pass for French?'

'I'm sure I didn't say almost,' the woman blustered. 'I'm sure I said – '

'From Armand's in the Rue de Rivoli,' Elisa told her. 'Though I imagine you've gazed from time to time in his windows.'

She allowed the chief inquisitor to squirm for a moment, then complimented her on the delicious coffee, the biscuits that settled like feathers on the tongue. 'And please, my dear Madame le Tourneau, you must invite me again.'

In the evening, Xavier Quatrefages returned along the right-angled paths to his house. He warned his wife he might soon be called to join one of the reconnaissance columns that were extending France's reach into the Sahara. 'I'll be away for two or three weeks, maybe longer. But you've no need to feel too lonely. You must make the acquaintance of the wives and daughters. I'm sure you'll get along with them.' Then he settled himself in a chair and perused his week-old copy of *L'Echo d'Oran*. Elisa said nothing, turning instead to the kitchen. There was no point in telling him she'd already been summoned to judgement. With half the country yet to be pacified, he'd have little sympathy for wounds sustained over coffee.

They went early to bed, where they didn't make love that night. The wind dropped, and Quatrefages slept, snoring softly. Elisa lay awake until after midnight, a near-full moon bathing the room with its jaundiced light. Then she turned on her side and covered her head with the sheet, wishing herself far away.

Madame le Tourneau kept her distance. It had been a mistake to criticize the Irish woman's clothes, a more serious mistake to assume she was ignorant of politics and Paris. The ladies had had their spiteful fun, then been made to pay for it, yet they could not bring themselves to apologize to this newcomer, this child-wife, this *foreigner*.

They'd wait until Captain Quatrefages was off with his column, and Elisa stifled by boredom. Leave her alone for a week. Let her learn what it was like to be a wife without a husband, a woman denied the company of women. Teach the pretty young thing to play by the rules of El Biar . . .

For the time being, however, with Xavier occupied in the stables, Elisa swept the house, sent the sheets and linen to be laundered, polished and pressed her husband's uniform, then went to shop at the regimental store.

It was a twenty-minute walk from the married quarters, though less if you cut across the featureless, summer-brown grass.

Quatrefages had warned her she must keep to the paths. 'A silly regulation, you might think; though with upward of two thousand men in El Biar, we can't have troops milling about.'

For the first dozen times she stayed on the broad, flinty paths, the gravel destroying the soles of her shoes and bruising her feet. Arab boys were employed to carry the groceries, their own feet slapping in boiled leather sandals, though it made Elisa feel uncomfortable, returning empty-handed whilst the skinny young porters trudged uncomplaining behind.

I mean, she thought, it's not as if there *is* any grass! Seared by the sun; whipped by the wind; bring a flock of Irish sheep out here, they'd spit the stuff back!

She told herself it was a rule without reason – and finally dared to disobey Xavier's warning. The military mind was beyond her, governed as it was by a handbook of rules, the ticking of the clock, the calendar on the wall. All very well, but the hell with walking half

160

a mile on sharp gravel, when the quickest way was across the grassless square.

Taking the shortcut to the store, she sensed a shadow across her face. Intent on her shopping list, she'd failed to notice the man who strode to intercept her, but now Elisa glanced up and asked: 'M'sieur?'

'Lieutenant Chavelet, Madame. Officer of the Day. Your preoccupations have led you astray, I fear. Quite understandable, though you must allow me to escort you to the path. The lawns, I regret, are off limits.'

He was tall, his face shaded by his *képi*, his silhouette angling inwards from broad, blue-uniformed shoulders. He boasted a fine, aquiline nose, a narrow chin, and his gaze held steady, then dipped to appraise her breasts, her waist, her hips. Handsome enough to make it worth quarrying marble, she thought. And how better to get arrested?

Tilting her head, she said: 'What? You call this a lawn? You're happy to plant saplings and let them die, yet you describe this arid wasteland as – '

'I grant you,' he said wryly, 'it's not at its best today. Though it perks up with the winter rains. And yes, it's a shame about the trees. But in my experience, limited though it is, the Army wouldn't know a palm from a poplar.'

She saw him extend his right arm in courteous indication – time to go back to the path. She feared he would leave her there and return to his duties, lost among the anonymous men of El Biar.

'You may not have noticed,' she said, 'hurrying to arrest me, but I risked your famous lawn to avoid the gravel. My feet are terribly bruised by these paths. Not disfigured, of course, but certainly punished.'

'Then you shan't walk the path at all,' the young officer told her. 'You're to give me your list and go home, Madame, and I shall personally see to it that your provisions are delivered.'

'It's Madame Elisa Quatrefages. My husband is the – '

'Yes, I know.'

'The house is at the southermost end of – '

'Yes, Madame Quatrefages. And the list?'

She surrendered it, smiled as the man saluted her, then made her way back, hoping there were enough fresh lemons at home with which to make a pitcher of cordial. After all, hadn't Lieutenant

161

Chavelet said he'd deliver the things in person? And the least she could offer him was a glass of *citron sucré.*

An hour later, and Elisa answered the door.

The Arab porter swung the yoked canvas bags from his shoulders, presented her with the price-marked list, took the money she owed and bowed.

'Wait!' she called. 'Where's Lieutenant Chavelet? I thought – '

'Officer give me paper, tha's all. Officer tell me see it come safe. Officer gone be in army.'

Elisa closed the door and leaned against it, laughing at her foolish expectations. See to it personally, maybe. *But deliver the things in person?* With all the thousand duties that weighed down the broad shoulders of the Officer of the Day?

3

Quatrefages invited his wife to accompany him to a horse ranch near Merzoug, two miles east of the camp.

'It's where the regiment buys its mounts,' he explained. 'The owner's been out here for fifteen years, mating English mares with Arab stallions. And doing a damn fine job of it, let me say. El Biar now possesses some of the finest *chevaux de selles* in the region, and we're counting on three dozen more before we leave to join the column in the south.'

Elisa said yes, she'd like to visit the ranch, though Xavier had to remember she'd never ridden, except in cabriolets and fiacres. 'But I'll come for the outing.'

Jolting along in the gig beside her husband, Elisa held a scarf across her face. She turned from the wind, and asked: 'You mentioned leaving. When's that?'

'In a week or so. When we've analysed what went wrong with the scouting party.'

'You never told me – '

'Nothing much to tell, my dear. A group was sent out and got ambushed, that's all. Got themselves trapped in a wadi near Chellala. And the nomads – well, the nomads shot 'em to pieces. It's happened before; it'll happen again. The irony is – hold tight, the road's bad here . . .'

The gig lurched and dipped, and Quatrefages slowed the horse, then snaked the reins. He was a reliable driver, and the narrow, high-wheeled vehicle recovered its balance.

Elisa pulled the hood of her djellaba forward, shielding her eyes from the wind. 'Tell me,' she said. 'What was the irony?'

'Hmm? Oh, only that we lost 'em alphabetically. Artoux, Bayol, Chavelet and Sergeant Delfour. Fourteen others, though I'm told the nomads lost fifty. At least Quatrefages comes well down the list, *n'est-ce pas?*'

Elisa could think of no way to frame her question. *Chavelet? Lieutenant Chavelet? The man who'd admitted the Army didn't know a palm tree from a poplar? The handsome young officer who could well have been sculpted in*

163

marble? It wasn't true; couldn't be true; not when she'd so recently stood in his shadow . . .

'It's the devil, this dust. Ah, that's good, you're crying it out. Massage your eyes – not too hard now – we'll soon be there.'

He led the horse neatly between white-painted gate posts, tutting it along a tree-lined drive, then reining in before a wide, porticoed mansion, its two-tier balcony shaded by bamboo blinds. Elisa sat upright, weeping in silent disbelief. *It surely can't be the Chavelet I met . . .*

Then a voice growled: 'And who's this you've brought along, Captain Quatre'? Fine kind of company you must be for a lady, reducin' her to tears. It's this bloody wind, no doubt. Get her down from the cart and into the house.' The voice then rose to a bellow as the man summoned one of his lithe young ostlers to take charge of the horse and gig. '*Et plus vite que ça!*'

Elisa wiped the scarf across her eyes, clearing her vision. She peered at the owner of the voice – the owner of the ranch? – and saw a man with a pock-marked face, drink-swollen nose, his belly protruding from the inner edges of his creased, colonial jacket. A bushy white moustache drooped around his lips, white hair tangled below the brim of a battered, sweat-stained straw hat. He wore baggy trousers, held a fly-whisk in one hand and gestured liberally with the other. Muscular fingers pinched a weaving cigar.

A glance told the woman he was coarse and unlikeable, a world apart from the stylish Lieutenant Chavelet.

Yet half an hour later she knew she'd found a friend.

Xavier introduced them. 'Monsieur Framat, my dear. As I told you, he breeds and raises horses.'

'And this is your daughter, Captain Quatre'? Your wife must be a damn pretty woman to have given you a girl – '

'This *is* my wife,' the vet said sternly. 'I thought I'd told you – '

'You did, my friend, you did.' Framat chuckled. 'You just omitted to tell me what a splendid young creature she is, that's all.' Ignoring him then, the settler gazed at Elisa. 'Etienne Framat, Madame. If I didn't know it was the wind as had made you cry, I'd suppose it to be one of those tragic novels you ladies enjoy. My own wife does, for a fact. Spends half her time smiling, the other half sobbing. *And* sits up till dawn to finish the damn things. That said, you'd make a pretty good heroine yourself, seems to me. Though I leave that sort of thing to Madame Framat.' Stepping aside, he waved them into the house, the fly-whisk swirling, the cigar ash carried on the wind.

'Quite a character,' Xavier murmured. 'But you mustn't let his vulgar manners upset you.'

'I'll try not to,' Elisa replied, nodding, though she was already reappraising her opinion of Etienne Framat. Very much his own man, she decided. The Army would do well to keep in with *him*.

He directed his visitors to a pair of high-backed rattan chairs, then stumped away to fill a cut-glass jug with what looked like half the contents of half the bottles on display.

'Try this, Madame Quatrefages. It'll dry your eyes, strengthen your bones, sharpen your hearing – or kill you stone-dead where you sit. But we don't want that, so I'll cut it in half with water. As for you, Captain Quatre', you get it like it comes.'

He gave Xavier a full measure of the rust-brown liquid, then topped his own glass to the brim. 'Does nothing else, it keeps off the flies! Been married long, you two? My guess is not, the lady looking so young. A nice slim figure; sit well on a horse. Care for a ride, while Captain Quatre' and I spend an hour at business?'

Elisa sipped her drink – it was terrible, the sweetness entrenched against the sour – then told Framat she was sorry, but no, she didn't ride.

He glowered at her, jaw thrust forward, his sun-bleached eyes pinning her in her chair. 'Don't ride, Madame Quatrefages? Get yourself married to an army vet and you don't ride? Come all the way here to Algeria, a country without proper roads, no railway lines, no canals or navigable rivers, and you say in your enchanting voice you're sorry, but no, you don't ride?'

'Ease up now,' Xavier said awkwardly. 'My wife has had no occasion – '

'That right? Then it's time she did. And I'll tell you why, my dear Quatre'. I'll tell you damn well why.'

But for the moment he preferred to gulp from his glass, the edge of his bushy moustache stained by his vile concoction. Then he turned aside, crushed the end of his cigar in an ash-tray, and jabbed a stubby finger at them both.

''Cause the others do, that's why. Each and every one of 'em, an' I'm talking about the ladies of El Biar. Wives and daughters, and whoever comes to visit them. Oh, they might have to hitch their regal rumps into the saddle but, once they're up there, they ride without

165

a care. And that's how it has to be for your slender young wife, Captain Quatre'. Good God, sir, but ain't she married to the Regimental Vet?'

Xavier winced, then glanced across at Elisa. What Framat had said was true, of course. Military wives were expected to know their mounts. But tell Elisa Alicia what was expected of her, and she'd likely rebel, blind obedience low on her list . . .

'This drink,' she said. 'I regret to tell you, Monsieur Framat, but another sip and it *will* strike me dead where I sit.'

'Bloody awful,' he agreed. 'Glad to hear you admit it. I'll find you a soda.'

'And as for the riding – '

'Yes, Madame Quatrefages?'

'As for the riding, I'd be glad to catch up with the ladies. I'll report here for instruction whenever you wish. You will, I hope, treat me as any other pupil, and teach me to sit the saddle. I would like to ride as well as them all, Monsieur Framat, though most particularly Madame le Tourneau.'

'I didn't know you'd met her,' Xavier interposed. 'The chances are, she'll soon invite you for coffee. Her husband's on the General Staff – '

'So I've heard.'

'Quite an influential lady.'

'So it seems.'

'Keep in with Madame le Tourneau, and things are bound to run smoothly.'

'Yes,' Elisa murmured. 'So I imagine.'

Etienne Framat listened, then trampled the exchange. 'If your husband agrees, and it suits you to come here, I shall have you report at ten tomorrow morning. If you wish to wear a skirt, that's up to you, though I'd recommend men's breeches. It's rough ground out here, Madame Quatrefages, not bridle paths in the woods.'

Elisa might then have glanced at her husband for permission. But she didn't, nodding instead at the powerful, pock-marked settler. 'Very well, Monsieur Framat. At ten tomorrow. But, please, no more of your mixtures. I have no desire to die!'

He bellowed with laughter, reaching now for another thick cigar. 'Go along there,' he suggested. 'That corridor leads to the kitchen. Introduce yourself to Madame Framat. I'd wager she'll squawk and say you could've stepped from the pages of her books. And ask her to kit you out.

'As for you, my dear Quatre', let's talk about horses and prices. The Army wants a further three dozen steady mounts, yet offers me *this*?'

The officers and wives of El Biar were allowed the freedom of the stables. If foreign diplomats invited them to a *soirée* in Algiers, they were permitted the use of a gig; a *calèche;* a larger, four-wheeled *barouche*. If they wished to ride out to the foothills of the Massif de l'Ouarsenis they could do so, and Arab grooms would be detailed to polish the harness, curry-comb the animals, hand the reins to the rider.

Making full use of this privilege, Elisa was taken to the Framat ranch, the soldier detailed to drive her sitting stiff on the high, spring bench.

'May I ask you,' she said. 'Do you know what happened to one of our recent patrols? It was led, so I'm told, by the officers Artoux, Bayol and Chavelet. Would Chavelet be the one who's tall, somewhat thin in the face – ?'

'No idea, Madame. Officers is all much the same to me. Watch for the dip, can't avoid it.'

The gig rolling on, Elisa tried again. 'It was a sortie in the direction of Chellala. Captain Quatrefages says we lost twenty men, or thereabouts. Though the enemy lost fifty. I thought you might have heard – '

'Heard something,' the soldier dismissed, 'but it wasn't my Company. An' like I said, officers is officers.' Then he took the gig in between the gate posts, drew to a halt before Framat's mansion, and stayed where he was on the bench.

The Regulations were clear as to what the driver of a military conveyance might or might not do. '*Female passengers shall not, unless at their express request, be assisted or in any way manhandled whilst boarding or alighting from the vehicle, save in the presence of two or more female witnesses, and with the driver remaining visible to all parties. The driver may, at his own discretion, verbally offer assistance, though he shall remain at his station until such time as –* '

'It ain't that he's lacking in manners,' Framat grinned, coming down the steps to greet his new pupil. 'He's a lad what knows the rules, is all. Army's a bit strict about things like that.'

Xavier's wife said: 'The Army's strict about a lot of things, so I've noticed. Like not walking on the lush green grass at El Biar. It's something I've yet to get used to.'

Extending a strong, calloused hand, Etienne Framat said: 'If you think the Army's fenced in by rules, Madame Quatre', you just wait till you're up in the saddle. You say you want to ride better than Madame le Tourneau? Then I'll see to it you do. And likely make you loathe me in the process.'

She nodded, admitting it was possible. Yet the ugly, white-haired settler exuded confidence, and it would be worth the aches and bruises to out-ride the Inquisition.

4

Determined to avenge the losses sustained in the wadi near Chellala, the military commanders assembled a punitive force that would, it was hoped, break the back of nomadic resistance, once and for all. They'd had their fill of these desert wraiths; these silent, hard-eyed warriors with their antiquated rifles and murderous, horn-handled knives. It was time to teach them a lesson they'd never forget.

The column that set out from El Biar comprised the 4th Brigade, under the command of General de Luzy; two battalions of the 20th Regiment of the line; a battalion of native infantry; a battalion of the 9th; a squadron of scouts who could *read* the sand in a way that left the French gasping.

A second column, under General Bosquet, was to rendezvous with them twenty miles short of Chellala, the total force of three thousand men sent to make Algeria safe as far as the edge of The Endless Desert – the as yet uncharted Sahara.

The veterinarian Quatrefages was summoned to ride with the 4th.

They embraced and told each other to take good care.

'How long will you be gone?'

'I don't know. It depends. Several weeks perhaps. But you're not to be concerned. Amuse yourself with the ladies – '

'Oh, damn the ladies. Now, tell me, am I to save the papers, the ones you get from Oran?'

'I'd be grateful if you did, my dear. It's always nice to catch up with the news.'

'I shall continue with the riding lessons. By the time you return you'll be proud of me. Monsieur Framat is somewhat unremitting in his methods, though his bark's a lot worse than his bite.'

'Well, you just take good care, that's all.'

'And you, my dear Hedgehog. You, too.'

They tried their best, each striving to say what the other might wish to hear. But the exchange was stilted, intimacy absent, the marriage having become no more than a cohabitation of friends. In many ways like her father, the well-meaning vet had failed to excite Elisa as a husband. Although not yet sixteen, she hungered for passion. She craved a man's attentions, wished him to be both generous and jealous, fidgeted for a fine falling-out, then the pleasure of reconciliation.

But at forty-three, the work-weary Quatrefages knew nothing of this, preferring that his wife made the meals, made friends with the ladies, made the river of their life run smoothly.

She knew she would not miss his presence in their bed. Her dreams would not involve Xavier Gaston Quatrefages, though they might, perhaps, be peopled by the likes of Lieutenant Chavelet, or by other young officers she'd espied at El Biar . . .

Elisa had no desire to be unfaithful to her husband. It would be a mean and despicable thing to do, the hedgehog out in the desert with his horses. She was a married woman now, and would sleep alone until Xavier returned, his newspapers stacked and waiting.

Yet the dreams would come, and where was the guilt in that?

Madame le Tourneau expected Elisa to become bored and lonely, and eager to be accepted by the ladies. But the newcomer to El Biar had better things to do, reporting each morning to the Framat ranch near Merzoug.

The settler remained – as she'd told Xavier – unremitting in his methods. Several times he reduced her to tears, then wearily shook his head as she accused him of being nothing more than a brute.

'I've done everything you've told me – '

'Tried to, Madame Quatre', but you ain't done it right.'

'You don't have a single encouraging word – '

'Not out to woo you, Madame Quatre'. Out here to teach you to ride. Now dismount if you wish, or we'll try it once again.'

'All right, but I'm telling you, Monsieur Framat. This is the very last time!'

'Entirely up to you,' he said, shrugging. 'Of course, if you don't think you're good enough to out-ride Madame le Tourneau . . .'

The remark was enough to keep her in the saddle, though Etienne Framat continued to greet her faults with a growl, her progress with scarcely a grunt.

When he thought she was ready he took her on a mile-long gallop through the orchards that fringed the ranch. She stayed level with him until the final two hundred yards, then saw the stocky, white-haired rancher draw ahead. She spurred furiously to catch him, failed to do so, and arrived in the paddock enveloped in the dust raised by Framat's horse.

She knew she could not have ridden a better race. Yet here was this heavy-drinking old monster ready to make fun of her, his stained teeth bared in a grin. And now, no doubt, he'd list all her faults, tell her –

'Ride like that, Madame Quatre', you'd make Madame le Tour-neau look like she'd saddled a donkey. I damn near thought you were going to overtake me. Would that be enough encouragement for one day?'

Humming with pleasure, Elisa decided she would, after all, stay the course.

She waited in vain for a letter from Captain Quatrefages. Messengers rode back to report that General de Luzy's column had encountered stiff resistance. They'd inflicted heavy losses on the enemy, though the French themselves had suffered a number of casualties, among them more than thirty unnamed officers.

The column's single, greatest achievement had been to corner five hundred nomads in a network of mountain caves, light fires in the entrances, then suffocate the occupants. It was later revealed that the majority of those who died were women and children, old men and babies. But the Army was unrepentant. It was time that lessons taught were lessons learned.

Elisa now shared common ground with the wives, several of them fearing their husbands were among the unnamed wounded, the unnamed dead. Yet Madame le Tourneau could not bring herself to approach the red-haired foreigner, and Elisa was left to face her fears alone.

She wondered what she would do without the hedgehog. Return to Paris? To Cork? Take the pittance that would be her widow's pension, then try her luck in England? She was young enough to find another husband – *Though is that what I still want? Dull respectability? Monotonous security? And run the risk that the colours of life will fade again?*

Then Quatrefages returned unharmed. The desert heat had raised blisters round his eyes, and it was several days before he was able to read *L'Echo d'Oran*. He was granted a week's convalescence, though he insisted on making a regular inspection of the stables, assuring his wife he'd be fine in the cool and dark.

At home, he slept, or sat with the shutters closed, content to converse with Elisa if that's what she wanted, equally content to stay silent, lost within his thoughts. She told him Etienne Framat had finally commended her on her progress, and that, maybe soon, she'd have the chance to display her prowess to Madame le Tourneau.

'He said that? But it's not his place to stir up rivalry – '

'No, my dear. It's what *I* say. Show the ladies it's not just the French who can sit the saddle. When your face has healed, and you can go out in the sun, we'll ride beyond the camp and I'll show you – '

'Rivalry's a bad thing between the wives,' Xavier cautioned. 'It might be best if you tempered your feelings towards Madame le Tourneau. She's a fine and influential woman, my dear. The enemy's without, remember, not within.'

Elisa stared at him in disbelief, started to riposte, then turned away. She'd hoped that Framat's compliment would lead to one of Xavier's own, instead of which he'd applauded le Tourneau and admonished his own wife.

It occurred to her then that Captain Xavier Gaston Quatrefages shared her sense of discomfort with their marriage . . .

Nevertheless, in the months that followed, she learned to accept the routine of military life. The vet was sent out again on a ten-day sortie, returning to El Biar for most of November, then away again until mid-January, 1851. She celebrated Christmas and New Year with the Framats, having discovered by now a side to the grizzled rancher she'd not known before.

As for his wife, the good-natured Honorine, she had all but adopted the girl from County Cork, convinced that Elisa would make the perfect heroine for a romantic tale of daring in the desert. 'If only I could write,' the woman told her, 'I'd have you suffer most terribly, so I would. You'd be snatched on the high seas by corsairs – '

'But I thought that's why the French came here in the first place. To rid the North Atlantic waters – '

'Tush, tush,' the elderly Honorine dismissed. 'If I wish to have you abducted by corsairs, then by corsairs you shall be seized. Or would be, if I could manage to write down more than recipes for *couscous*.'

'You're a wonderful cook,' Elisa said tactfully. 'I've learned more about Arab dishes – '

'Then you'd be auctioned as a slave. Marched away to some mountain fastness. Rescued from there by a brave young officer who'd glimpsed you in the slave-market and sworn on his family crest that he'd search you out and find you – "Be the world as wide as the firmament". I'd have him say that. The world as wide as the firmament. It's one of the phrases I'd insist was in the story.'

Elisa grinned and embraced the *romancière manquée*. Then she hinted that the compote Honorine Framat was creating might be ready, the stew of figs and apricots and honey bubbling to the rim of the deep copper pan.

More at home now in the ranch near Merzoug than in the married quarters at El Biar, Elisa immersed herself in the role in which the Framats had cast her. She'd learned that they had both been born in the village of St Léonard-de-Noblat, the heart of the horse-breeding region of the Limousin.

'Honorine was quite the thing then,' the rancher growled. 'Lost her looks now, of course, but at least she gave me a son.'

At ease on the cool, tiled verandah, Elisa no longer feared the ugly, pock-marked Etienne Framat, seeing him now as a much kinder man than perhaps he wished others to see.

'You're no gentleman to say that, Monsieur Etienne. Your wife is a sight better looking than you. And a better cook, I've no doubt. And with ideas in her head for stories – '

'Oh, so now it's a palace revolution, is it? The women storm the citadel, eh? Pass me that box beside you, Elisa. Defend myself with a good, stinkin' cigar.'

'Tell me about your son, M'sieur Etienne. Did he stay on in the village?'

The rancher bit off the end of his cigar, spat it aside, then leaned forward in his rattan chair, seeming touchingly old in his wrinkled suit. He fumbled for a match, allowed Elisa to strike it, then sat back, puffing gouts of smoke at the overhang of the roof.

'Did he stay on in the village? Well, yes, you could say that . . . We all did till fifteen years ago . . . Then we squabbled . . . Let our mouths run quicker than our minds . . . Something you're maybe spared in green-eyed Ireland.'

'It happens in Ireland too,' Elisa murmured. 'It's why some folks call it the Land of Ire; the Land of Anger. And your son?'

The white-haired Etienne shrugged, then smoothed his moustache. 'He was married by then to a sweet young girl, and they had a child of their own. But the squabbles continued, and Laurent decided to leave. We couldn't see them go empty-handed, so we agreed to sell all we had and – Well, went our separate ways.'

Elisa hesitated, yet somehow she knew the old man wanted her to speak. 'Your son, Laurent; do you know where he is? *How* he is?'

Cigar smoke filled the air in short, erratic clouds. 'As for *how* he is, Elisa, him and his wife? Within calling distance of God, I hope, for they were both burned to death ten years ago in a stable fire. And as for where? In a graveyard near Bordeaux.'

Elisa could hear Honorine at the far end of the corridor, banging pans in the kitchen. The young woman thought the least she could do was bring the rancher a drink, but he arrested her, signalling her back into the creaking bamboo chair.

'I know you mean well, young Elisa, an' I appreciate it. But I want you to hear – well, to learn that things could've been worse. A tragedy indeed to lose Laurent and his wife. But at least their child was scooped to safety, and is married now to – what should we call him? – someone in the city?'

'You mean here, in Algiers?'

'Good God, no. I mean where *you* used to stamp around. They're in Paris, *ma fille*. And allow me to tell you, whilst the clattering goes on, that for all her talk of heroines and stories, Honorine sees you best as that selfsame child, the granddaughter she's unlikely to meet again. So you won't mind much, I hope, if she saves you from the pirates.'

Elisa glanced out at the orchard, fighting to control her emotions. Then she asked if she might have a glass of wine. 'Though none of your terrible mixtures. I'd trust you in most things, M'sieur Etienne, but not when it comes to concoctions.'

And then Honorine bustled out on to the verandah with a tray of salted fish, a bowl of olives, floury biscuits and a range of piquant sauces. She told Framat to put out his cigar – 'Kill the flies, yes, but you also kill my cooking' – then arrayed her colourful offering and sat beside Elisa.

'. . . Whilst he brings you back from the mountain fastness, the brave young officer falls in a crevice. Then a group of black-hooded men riding jet-black camels – '

'I didn't know camels were black, Honorine.'

'Well, I'm telling you, they're black! Who's writing this story, Elisa? You or me?'

174

5

It was important to Elisa to return to El Biar before dusk, in time to prepare her husband's meal. Following one of Honorine's recipes, she waited for Xavier's opinion, though the man accorded her efforts no more than a nod. 'Tell me,' she said. 'What *are* your favourite dishes? If I knew – '

He shrugged and said he was happy with whatever she chose to give him, and she certainly shouldn't go to special lengths out here, so far from Paris. 'If it pleases you to try your hand, then do so, my dear. At least I'll know you're kept busy. Not that wives can do much in a place like this. How could they? As I've often heard said, it's really only France who knows her kitchen.'

Failing to please him at the table, she attempted to do so in bed. But he was invariably too tired, or concerned about the condition of his animals, or anxious to finish one of his endless reports. He woke her once, his hand on her hip, and she turned towards him, murmuring his name. 'I regret to disturb you – '

'You haven't. I wasn't really sleeping,' said Elisa.

'That's good, because I wanted to ask you – Would it not be better to keep my uniform wrapped in cloth? I fear the night chill wilts it.'

As the months went by – her sixteenth birthday long forgotten – Elisa came to regard her husband as a man who took lodgings in the house. He was more than just a lodger, of course, though he asked only that she clean the place and feed him, send his clothes to be laundered, set fresh wicks in the lanterns, keep the newspapers piled for his return. The fact that they shared a bed at all seemed like celibate economy.

He was called to service again in the spring, and departed on two long sorties during the summer.

It was then – aware the rancher Framat had been schooling the red-haired foreigner – that Madame le Tourneau invited Elisa to accompany the ladies on an outing to the foothills. 'Though I must warn you, my dear, it's somewhat laborious. I shall well understand if you choose to stay at home.'

'On the contrary, Madame, I'd be delighted to join you. And hope not to lag too far back.'

They picked their way up the lower slopes of the Massif de l'Ouarsensis, Elisa riding tenth among eighteen. Then eighth. Then third. Then cheerfully alongside the imperious Madame le Tourneau.

'Don't exhaust yourself, my dear,' the woman measured. 'We've still a fair ride home.'

'But quicker if we raced it, what do you say? Wait for the others to catch up with us, then give our mounts their heads? *Though I shall well understand . . .* '

Her face suffused with anger, the leader of the Inquisition said the idea was stupid; pointless; dangerous in the extreme. 'It's neither the place, nor the time for such idiocies, Madame Quatrefages – '

'As you wish. But shall you mind if I try it myself?'

Without waiting for a reply, Elisa spurred her mount through the brush, and they plunged downwards, the reins snapping taut in her hands. It scared her as the horse skidded on shale, but she kept her balance, calling to the mount to please keep his. '*Come on now, stay steady. You're a fine, big beast, so you are. Plant yourself wide – like that – that's good – and look, we're nearly on the level!*'

The animal seemed to share her sense of triumph, sucking in air for its final run to the bleached white walls of El Biar. It pounded onwards, swept her in through the southern gate, and insisted on running wild across the parade ground before she could haul back its head.

By the time the others arrived, the horse had been returned to its stall in the stables, rubbed down, fed and watered. And Elisa was leaning in the shade of the high, wooden barn, a slim hand raised, as Madame le Tourneau toiled in.

It seemed like the perfect triumph, and she could scarcely wait to share it with the Framats. 'Invited me to ride with them to the foothills, but thought to make a fool of me! Probably told themselves I'd fall on my bottom in the thorns! But I didn't. Came down the ridge like the wind, and I swear to you, M'sieur Etienne, I could have slept on the straw before they ever arrived. You taught me well. Aren't you pleased?'

The rancher drew on his cigar, expelling the smoke from beneath his tobacco-stained moustache. Then he suggested she ride with them again – 'If they'll have you. And this time challenge 'em – and lose. And lose badly.'

'I don't understand.'

'Then I'll explain. What you did was fine with me, young Elisa, but the ladies'll see it quite different. From now on the sound you'll hear in the camp will be the sound of them sharpening knives. They'll be after your blood – '

'So what? You think I care about that?'

' – yours and your husband's. But mostly his.'

Disappointed by Etienne's response to her triumph, Elisa said she was sorry, but she didn't see how Xavier was involved. 'He's off somewhere in the desert. So what's it to do with him?'

The ugly Framat gazed at the girl the couple had taken as their own. 'Sit quiet,' he growled, 'and I'll tell you.'

'All right,' she said, shrugging, 'but I honestly don't – '

'*Then listen!*' The force of his breath blew the smoke into tatters, and the sound of his voice jarred Elisa back in her chair. 'You're a fine young lady, and Honorine and I, we've both grown fond of you. But you've yet to understand where you are, my girl, and it ain't back there in Paris. So . . . You're married to Captain Quatre', and that's the way it should be. But your husband's made vows before and married himself to the Army. And the Army is as devious a place to be as any civilian parliament; devious as the judiciary; devious as the church.'

'Are you saying – ?'

'I'm saying it's time you understood the game. If you annoy the likes of Madame le Tourneau, she can revenge herself on Xavier. Can't do much to *you*, of course, but she can drive a pole between the spokes of his advancement. She tugs at the ear of the generals. Stands close to the commanders. It's simply the way it is, *ma fille*. Which is why I say ride with the women again, then slow your pace.'

'If I thought it would truly help, Xavier . . .'

'It might, or might not. But I believe it's worth the trying.'

In obedience to the rancher, Elisa invited the ladies of El Biar to a picnic in a cedar grove near the camp.

She prepared the meal herself, arranged for an ice-filled box of cordials, and borrowed an awning that could be strung between the trees.

Then Madame le Tourneau sent her apologies, claiming she'd been stricken with a chill. Six others ladies pleaded a last-minute engagement. Four more found themselves variously indisposed. The others simply failed to keep the rendezvous.

They really did not like foreigners who stood in the cool of the stables, saluting them down from the slopes . . .

177

Accepting defeat at the hands of the Inquisition, and with Xavier once more away on campaign, Elisa turned again to the elderly Framats. She had already accompanied Honorine on the four-mile drive from Merzoug to the city-port of Algiers, and eagerly accepted her invitation to take tea in the French-built Government Hotel.

Leaving Etienne at the ranch, they rode in the Framats' *calèche*, two Arab servants perched before them on the bench. The women wore light summer gowns, lace-frilled bonnets and linen gloves, buttoned at the wrist. Honorine twirled a parasol, angling it so Elisa could share its shade. 'They do serve the most delicious *gâteaux* in the tea-room,' she confided. 'You must promise to keep me well away from the trolley. Or rather, prevent me from returning to it, as I most assuredly would. I often wish I'd married a *pâtissier*.'

'No, you don't,' Elisa smiled. 'You know you love M'sieur Etienne, even if he does smoke vile cigars. Now, may I ask you,' she added, 'before we take tea, can we visit the market? I do so love the smell of the fruits and spices, the colours of the fabrics they sell, the trays of jewellery and – Listen, we could say it was to sharpen our appetites for tea!'

Honorine feigned a sigh. 'Oh, very well. If we must. Though I assure you my appetite for those cakes is already honed to a fineness.'

But Elisa knew the delightful Honorine was teasing, that she was happy to stroll the length and breadth of the market, one of the Arab servants following dutifully behind, a wide, straw pannier in each hand. As his mistress stopped, pointed, haggled and purchased, the baskets grew heavier, laden down with peppers and oranges, sacks of dried beans, a length of cloth, an inlaid bowl, a bag of spices, a kilo of honey, fresh peaches, fresh dates, fresh goat's cheese wrapped in vine leaves.

He staggered, uncomplaining beneath the weight. Then Honorine reached for her purse and placed a few coins on a sack of rice in one of the panniers, telling the boy to take the shopping back to the *calèche* – 'Then get yourselves some sherbet. But nothing stronger, you understand. *T'as compris?*'

The boy grinned and lurched away, loving it when Mistress Framat tried to look stern. On the other hand, it was as well to do as she said, for no one dared risk the wrath of the woman's own master . . .

As if to prove to Elisa that tea was unimportant, Honorine took her on a walk through the alleyways of the Casbah. The women were jostled as they climbed the steps and cobbled inclines, pestered by merchants, badgered by beggars, acknowledged by fellow explorers.

178

Washing hung from lines across the streets, the alleyways turning this way and that, arches leading into deeper, darker mysteries.

'It's a bit like St Merri,' Elisa said. 'Though I didn't have to blink so much in the sunlight in St Merri.'

'We'll go left here,' Honorine told her, 'then back on down to the port. You're probably ready for tea, eh, *ma fille?*'

Elisa noticed that Honorine was now using the parasol as a cane, being too proud to admit she was tired.

'The truth is, yes, I am quite thirsty. But I'm glad we've seen what we've seen. Xavier never had time to bring me. And men don't much like shopping.'

'Only three reasons why they marry at all,' Honorine sniffed. 'One, so they can take their pleasures in bed. Two, so we give 'em their children. And three, so they've someone to do the shopping and cook what's bought and fill 'em with the energy to stir again in bed. It's a roundabout, you ask me, young Elisa. A roundabout puffing cigar-smoke.'

On their way to the Government Hotel they walked round the *place* that overlooked the port, gazing at the liners in the deepwater harbour; at the trawlers that had lurched from Spain; at the skimming dhows with their elegant lateen sails. Elisa paused, leaning on the stone balustrade, her green eyes absorbing the blue of the Mediterranean. Then she ran to catch up with Honorine Framat, who was already climbing the wide stone staircase to the tea-room of the ugly, four-storey, flat-roofed Government Hotel.

Let me guess, Elisa thought. It's the same architect who designed the barracks at El Biar. '*Can't have our civilians putting up in some waterfront bordello.*'

But once inside, she bit her critical tongue.

The hotel was cool and cavernous, its floors laid out with the finest mosaics, well-trained palms in half-barrel pots, long-bladed fans turning silently under the ceiling.

Uniformed Arabs stood waiting, the handsome young men in fez and crisp white tunics, naked feet in soft felt slippers; statues brought to life at the flick of a finger.

Honorine Framat and Elisa Quatrefages were conducted into the tea-room, where chairs were drawn out, then slipped beneath them, a bowl of rose-scented water was placed on the starched tablecloth, and warm towels set beside them.

'Don't be offended,' Honorine said. 'But they know how we Europeans tend to perspire. Well, maybe *you* don't, Elisa, but *my* chubby hands could irrigate the desert!' That said, she dipped her fingers in the bowl, dried them on the towel and turned in search of the trolley. 'Aha! Over there! And you see that thing with its layers of cream and chocolate? That's for me!'

Elisa grinned and sat back in her cushioned chair; glancing around at the occupants of the impeccable *salon*. Well-dressed gentlemen came across to greet Madame Framat, bowing as Honorine introduced them, Elisa happy to offer her own slim hand.

She heard talk of mounts to be sold or bought, compliments paid to Etienne, meetings arranged at Merzoug. The tea was served, and the trolley brought to their table. A pianist played in a corner of the room. The air was cool, and voices muted, and Elisa in her heaven . . .

'A slender young thing like you, don't be so silly! A little of this, and you *must* try a slice of the almond cake. And what's that one underneath, the one with the grapes? Well, bring it up, my man. We've not ridden in to say no!'

They left the Government Hotel at six, though neither woman was yet ready to enter the carriage. So they sat on one of the benches in the *place*, and Honorine said Elisa would have to be dragged from the galley to the slave-block. 'And whipped, of course. I'm afraid all slaves are whipped.'

'In order to pay for the tea?'

'What? No, no, of course not. I'm talking about the story. The one I plan to write.'

Elisa leaned over, kissed the woman and said Honorine could do as she wished, so long as she kept the scourgings and suchlike on paper. 'It's quite nice to be a heroine, though I'd rather be introduced to diplomats than be captured by your corsairs.'

'Well, that's fine,' Honorine said. 'But heroines have to suffer. It's not all tea and cakes, you know, if you wish to be part of the story.'

Then she asked Elisa to guide her back to the *calèche*, where she instructed the driver to take them home slowly, the rich cream *gâteaux* being not yet firmly settled in their systems.

6

One month later, the garrison camp of El Biar erupted with the showing of flags and launching of fireworks, the troops called out to celebrate the capture of Chellala.

General de Luzy was placed in command of the desert outpost, medals sent from Paris tugging at his coat.

El Biar relaxed, like pupils without their master, and Elisa watched as the soldiers ruined the grass. They played Hand Ball, and Foot Ball, and made runnels with *pétanque*, tossing the fist-sized bowls at the wooden target.

And then, abruptly, the soldiers paraded in brushed and polished uniforms, the grass was neatly trimmed, the barracks repainted, the parade ground sealed with tar.

Word had reached them that a new commander would soon take charge of the camp. A hard-nosed disciplinarian. An officer who slept with his boots on. A martinet it would be unwise to cross. Yet a man – so the rumours ran – with a weakness for women . . .

The camp to the south of Algiers slammed to attention.

And Elisa thought it as well to walk the sharp, gravel paths.

Five days after stepping ashore from the packet-boat in Algiers, the Acting-Colonel, Jean-Marie Vian Laporte, convened a military tribunal, found two young soldiers guilty of stealing their comrades' equipment – *by finding or casual opportunity* – and sentenced them to be shot.

The sentence was carried out before stunned and waxy-faced witnesses, the victims strapped to posts in the high-walled yard beside the kitchens. Their heads were sacked with canvas, the young men's cries for mercy drowned in the fusillade of shots.

'Steal another man's belt,' the colonel told his officers, 'and they'll steal another man's boots. And then it'll be his bayonet. His ammunition. His rifle.'

'But they didn't, *mon Colonel*,' one of the officers attempted. 'All those men stole was a belt an' a pair of gaiters. And they have to be shot for that?'

'You miss the point,' Laporte told him. 'The thing of it is, sir, they

181

stole. Now, I don't much care if my men steal a bag of salt or a twenty-ton cannon. What matters is the stealing. They were thieves, my dear sir, cheapjack thieves who thought to rob from their fellows. And tell me how we could raise our flag here in Algiers, if someone steals the pole?'

With the shock of the summary executions still reverberating through the camp, Colonel Laporte turned his mind to the social niceties of garrison life. He held a reception for the regimental wives and their adolescent daughters, Elisa and some forty other women invited to meet the new commander. There would be background music and a non-alcoholic fruit punch.

No one, this time, pleaded a prior engagement, or claimed to be indisposed.

Elisa stood back as the women competed for Colonel Laporte's attention, Madame le Tourneau to the fore. Watching him from the far side of the *salle de mess*, Xavier's wife thought him mean in the face, a weasel to her husband's hedgehog.

'My own dear husband,' Madame le Tourneau boomed, 'is on the General Staff. You may have heard of him, Colonel Laporte, as I'm sure he's heard of you. Two such champions of France – '

'Who's that, over there? That young woman with red hair. The one near the door.'

'Hmm? Oh, that's Madame Quatrefages. Her husband works with the mules, I believe . . . Chose to marry a foreigner . . .' She edged sideways, impeding his view, then introduced the members of her circle. By the time the fulsome presentations were completed, and Laporte had manoeuvred to peer across the room, Elisa had left the mess. She had seen all she wanted to see of the man who thought it right to execute boys of eighteen. And enough of the broad, gowned back of Madame le Tourneau.

It was a mistake, of course, to walk out on Jean-Marie Vian Laporte. He was tempted to have the woman summoned to his quarters, marched there under escort, if need be. Make an example of the insolent *rouquine*. Warn her that discourtesy hewed close to dis- obedience.

And yet he had no wish to alienate her – quite the reverse. A glimpse of Madame Quatrefages had been sufficient to arouse his interest and, with her husband nursing mules in distant Chellala . . .

Swallowing his anger, he couched the summons in terms of a

second invitation, sending a gig and two riders to collect her. If she was ill at ease in the crowded *salle de mess*, he would arrange a setting that was altogether more private.

They would dine *à deux*, in his rooms.

She thanked the subaltern who relayed the invitation, then told him no. 'Perhaps, when Captain Quatrefages returns . . .'

'I don't think you understand, Madame. Colonel Laporte is the senior officer, the *Commandant*, and it just isn't done – '

'Oh, really?' Elisa bridled. 'And what if I told you this constant damn wind makes my head ache? Would I still be expected to grace the Colonel's table?'

'I fear you would, Madame. He'd have one of the doctors make you up a tonic and – yes, I fear you would.'

'Then tell him I've nothing suitable to wear. Say I've yet to be fitted for a gown – '

'He saw you earlier, Madame. He knows you look more than presentable.' The subaltern coughed, aware it was not his place to pay compliments, yet worried the woman would send him back empty-handed. 'The thing is, Madame, the *Commandant* doesn't take kindly to being rejected. He'll accuse me – me and the escort – of failing to follow orders. Things will go hard with us. He's a man who finds it easy to make things hard.'

Elisa nodded glumly. 'So I've heard. Probably have you shot.' Then she shrugged and said: 'Very well. Allow me ten minutes, and we'll all be spared the bullets.' Turning away, she added quietly, 'Cork, then St Merri, and now out here . . . Bullets are quite the currency, so it seems . . .'

The blades of the fan revolved slowly below the ceiling, candle flames wavering in the draught. Fine, etched glasses reflected the light, silverware turned to gold. In the shadows, white-coated servants hovered like ghosts, darting forward to serve the diners, refill Laporte's glass, remove Elisa's all-but-untouched meal. Silence shrouded the table, the guest confirmed in her impression of the host. *A bright-eyed weasel, complete with sharp, nipping teeth.*

'. . . So then you took ship to Paris – ?'

'No. To Roscoff.'

'Well, yes, of course. A figure of speech. But arrived in Paris, and what then, Madame Quatrefages? Learned your way around the city?'

'Half a square mile of it, maybe. I ran errands in the Marché des Innocents. Delivering mended clothes. Would you call St Merri the city?'

Colonel Laporte laughed at the clever, expressionless way she told lies. A woman as pretty as this? Near perfect in French, and smart as a whip with her responses? 'All right, so that's the story you wish to recount. But I'm interested to know – if the question's not too intrusive – how you met your present husband, Captain Quatrefages. It's unusual for one of our officers to marry a – how to put it – ?'

Elisa gazed at him, saw the weasel replaced by the hedgehog, and decided the least she could do was fight for Xavier here, whilst he fought for France in Chellala.

'My husband – my *present* husband, as you put it – '

'So sorry. A figure of speech.'

'Yes, well, we met when he'd been sent to Dublin on the orders of the then French court. I happened to be there doing Lord knows what, buying lace I think, and Captain Quatrefages was judging livestock for the Army. He has the finest eye for horses in the business, so I'm told. Anyway, I found myself beside him at the rail . . . And we talked . . . And Cupid lodged an arrow in my heart . . . Now isn't that romantic, Colonel Laporte? *I've* gained an officer, and *you* can relax in the knowledge that your dinner guest is faithful to her husband. *Present and future.*'

Laporte reached for his wine. He struggled to keep the evening alive, testing Elisa with tales of military daring, the occasional risqué story, a few tired jokes that withered as he told them.

His small, carnivorous teeth shone in the candlelight, his bright eyes imprinting her beauty on his mind. It was hard to tell where the fiction ended, and the fact of her life began. But all that mattered was that Madame Elisa Quatrefages was here at El Biar, and the horse doctor far away.

Elisa escaped before midnight, insisting she be taken home in the gig. Laporte offered to accompany her to her door, an offer she waved aside. 'You've soldiers to do that for you, *mon Colonel.* One of the advantages of rank, don't you agree?'

'A most enjoyable evening,' Laporte grated. 'I shall look forward to seeing you again, my dear young lady.'

'As you will,' she said. 'Though I warn you – '

'Warn me of what?'

'Don't be startled. Figure of speech. Warn you my husband will likely clear the table, that's all. He's not nearly as trim as you, sir. Different in every way.'

And then, conveyed home in the gig, she thought yes, for the hedgehog was content to read his newspapers, and regard his wife as his friend. But the weasel had shown his desires were more immediate, more urgent; the rodent of El Biar prepared to snatch the red-fleeced sheep.

Quatrefages returned, again unharmed, again with his face burned and blistered. He was surprised by the urgent warmth of Elisa's welcome, almost embarrassed by the ardour of her embrace.

She told him all she knew about Laporte, believing the man would have her for himself. 'It's not just a silly boast, my dear, and I promise you he won't. But you must somehow arrange to stay here, else he's bound to invite me again.'

Then she went too far, seeing Xavier flinch as she recounted the wonderful lies she'd invented on his behalf. 'Did you know we met at the horse trials in Dublin? And that you were sent over by Louis-Philippe? Oh, he's most impressed, I assure you, my dear hedgehog. A man who travelled on the orders of the king!'

'I wish . . .' he muttered. 'I wish you had not built me up so . . . I do not enjoy these battles you undertake on my behalf . . . Well-meant, I'm sure, but not how I'd have done it . . .'

'Then I'm sorry, *M'sieur le Hérisson*. But it was done in your defence.'

'Would you make me some *citron sucré*?' he murmured. 'Then draw the shutters tight? I'll sleep here tonight on the couch, if it suits you. Leave you undisturbed in the bed.'

She did as he asked, darkening the room, then setting the jug and glass within his reach. Leaning down to kiss him, she heard him mumble something about equipment and horses, and saddlery to be ordered from Marseilles. But nothing, it seemed, that remarked his return to his wife . . .

Alone in the bedroom, Elisa set a chair near the southern window, then watched as the moon turned the sand to crystal, the hills of the high Massif to chalk, to ice. It pleased her that Captain Quatrefages was home again, and unhurt, though she'd rather he'd shared the bed with her, if only to drive off the ghosts.

Bad ones, some of them . . . Like the hulking, broad-shouldered Arnaud . . . The sharp-toothed Laporte . . . The fragmented memories of men she'd seen in Algiers . . .

185

But good ones too . . . Like the tall Lieutenant Chavelet . . . A civilian who'd paid his respects to Honorine Framat in the Government Hotel . . . A stall-holder she'd joked with in the Marché des Innocents . . .

All of them ghosts. But all of them men. And drifting into her dreams.

7

Eight days after Xavier's return, a messenger arrived at the married quarters, sweating under the sun.

'For the attention of Captain Quatrefages, Madame. I'm to wait for the Captain's reply.'

Elisa took the envelope, beckoned the soldier to wait in the cool, then brought him a mug of water. He gulped it down, thrust the mug back at her, thanked her and stood with his feet apart, arms crossed tight against his spine, rigid in the posture of what the Army calls 'at ease'.

His face still bearing the marks of the desert sun, Xavier sat in the shadows of the sparsely furnished living room, poring over his copies of *L'Echo d'Oran*. He glanced up as Elisa handed him the envelope and remarked: 'About time too! It's your pay-slip, what else? And can we ask the Framats to join us for dinner in town?'

'I don't see why not, my dear. There's a three-month backlog, so I must be worth the price of a decent dinner. Open it up, if you will. Let's see what I've earned.'

She tore the seal from the envelope, unfolded the single sheet – then blinked at its contents.

'Well, don't look so shocked,' Xavier told her. 'The Accounting Department makes all kinds of deductions. There's the rent; the piped water; the laundry bills; half a dozen contributions – '

'It's not that,' Elisa replied. 'It's not your damn pay-slip at all! What it is – well, listen, then afterwards tell me – Oh, God Almighty, just listen!'

The contents of the letter were short and precise.

Captain Xavier Gaston Quatrefages was summoned to present himself, along with sixteen fresh horses, and as many mules as were available, on the parade ground of El Biar next Friday, 9th October at 6.45 a.m. He was also to be responsible for the provisioning of the aforementioned animals, a supply wagon to contain sufficient food and water for not less than twenty days.

The paper was signed by the Commandant of El Biar, the serving colonel, Jean-Marie Vian Laporte.

And I know why *that* could be, Elisa thought, opening her hand in despair and allowing the letter to slip to the drab grey tiles.

The sores on his face not yet healed, the vet returned uncomplaining to the front.

He had brushed aside his wife's tearful outbursts, denying she was a victim of Colonel Laporte's blatant lust. 'You'd do well to present yourself at his table,' he suggested, 'and dismiss this idea that he might have dishonourable intentions. You are, after all, married to one of his officers, and I've no doubt he'll respect that.'

'And do you think,' she asked, 'that he respects you, my dear Hedgehog?'

'Why shouldn't he?' Quatrefages murmured. 'Ain't it written in the rulebook? Now come along, Elisa, you know I have no wish to leave you. But France is still at war here in Algeria and it's a war we have to win.'

Gazing despondently at him, she said fine. Then she asked herself, her lips pressed tight, if marriages also, sometimes, had to be won.

With the bearded, middle-aged vet perhaps a hundred miles to the south, Elisa was invited to dine again with Laporte. She told him no and took a leaf from Madame le Tourneau's book, pleading the onset of a chill.

But the colonel persisted, sending one of the garrison doctors to examine her. It was clear to the medic that Madame Quatrefages was nervous, though otherwise in good health, and she was forced to admit the chill had not developed.

During their second evening together, Laporte announced that Captain Quatrefages was in line for promotion. Then he reached across and laid his hand over hers, asking how it felt to know she might soon be married to a major.

'I'm sure my husband merits advancement,' she told him. 'Though I would rather have him here as a captain, than with a more exalted rank and away in the desert.'

'Of course you would,' he murmured, 'and the two things are not incompatible. As *Major* Quatrefages, his place would be here at El Biar.'

'And mine, Colonel Laporte? Where would mine be?' She stared at him, saw the whiteness of his teeth as he smiled, his gaze flicking once to the inner door of his quarters.

'These are things we might discuss in private,' he said. 'Arrangements I'm sure we could reach, you and I.' He paused, then pounced, tightening his grip on her hand and turning it as he raised it to his lips. His kiss was wet on the dryness of her palm. 'Come along now, *ma chère madame*! No need to recoil! The army is a close-knit family, after all, and we count on each other – '

'Maybe so,' Elisa retorted, freeing her hand from his grasp. 'But does membership of the family permit *incest*, Colonel Laporte? Is that what happens within the regiments of France? Or is it only here, in El Biar? And only with you?'

'Now wait – '

'I think not. Please compliment the cook on the *navarin*.'

'Surely you'll stay for coffee. I apologize if I gave the impression that – '

'Oh, yes,' she told him. 'You gave the impression as clearly as a boot-heel in clay. You find me desirable, for which I suppose I should be flattered. But I must assure you, Colonel – as one family member to another – I am not. As for the coffee, God knows my nerves are frayed enough without it.' She stood up and wiped her hand on her napkin, hoping he'd notice. What a truly disgusting creature he was.

Struggling to reassert his authority, the commandant blurted: 'I shall expect to see you again. I regret any misunderstanding, Madame Quatrefages – '

'Oh, there is none, Colonel Laporte. We understand each other perfectly well.' She ignored his attempt to assist her with her cape, opened the outer door before he could reach it, then climbed quickly aboard the waiting gig. The driver glanced back, surprised that the attractive young woman had emerged so soon from the colonel's quarters. Usually they didn't.

Laporte made a final attempt to undermine her resolve, telling her he'd convene the promotion board at the end of November. 'I'll see to it then that your husband is promoted. A fine thing to be a major's wife, eh, Madame? And you'll dine with me again next Thursday, *c'est d'accord*? Ah, yes, and there'll be tea in place of coffee!' He laughed as if to convince the driver the evening had gone well, then forced himself to raise a hand in salute as the gig rolled away.

Sweet little bitch, he thought. But she'll come. Dangle promotion in front of the husbands, it's surprising the effect it has on young wives.

Elisa let the driver take her to the house. Then she asked if he'd be willing to take her on further, a journey for which she would see he was decently paid.

'Well, I don't know as I should, Madame. I'm pretty much at the beck and call of the colonel. Like to be of service, an' that – '

'I'll pay you twenty francs for a two-mile ride.'

'And I'd have to wait?'

'No, you won't have to wait. But you won't have to say where you took me.'

The driver nodded, sharing her secret. Pretty young lady, she'd got shot of the bloody Laporte, and was now off to meet her lover. An' who could blame her? An' two miles wasn't far in the cold glare of moonlight. An' twenty francs was not to be sniffed at, neither.

'No one'll know, Madame, 'cept me. But you'll have to say – '

'Merzoug. The Framat ranch at Merzoug.'

'That's easy,' the driver grinned. 'Get you there in no time.'

Yes, Elisa thought, and if possible, sooner than that, for I'm running scared.

She found the Framats playing cards, and burst in to ruin their game. She asked Etienne if he'd pay the soldier twenty francs, and without a word the rancher crossed to a box on an inlaid table, piled coins in his hand, then stumped from the room.

Honorine drew Elisa to a couch, content to let her surrogate grand-daughter sit there and bow her head. There was a moment's silence, and then Elisa was buried in Honorine's embrace, the young wife mouthing the truth about her marriage to Xavier, the truth about Vian Laporte.

They stayed awake till dawn, Elisa talking, then Etienne advising, and Honorine saying nothing about the cigars.

The Framats learned where and why she'd been married, how and why the marriage had failed, a thousand things she would never have admitted, save here in the cool and warmth of the Framat ranch.

With the sky at last lightening to grey, then quickly to rose, to yellow, to the burnished brass of morning, Etienne Framat heaved himself to his feet, and told her that maybe the problem could be solved. 'If I've understood the thing right, *ma fille*, I've a plan as would save you both. Give you your liberty. Allow M'sieur Quatre' his future. And send bloody Laporte in search of other game. But we'll have to wait till your husband gets back.'

Her eyes ringed with weariness, Elisa said she did not wish to stay alone in Xavier's house. 'The colonel's already invited me for next Thursday, and I'm sure he intends to drag me to his bed.'

Her face drawn in by the long night's talk, Honorine Framat found the strength to say: 'Tush to that, my dear! You'll stay here. And when your husband returns, Etienne will bring him in for a chat. What kind of bedding do you like, the pink or the blue?'

True to his word, the young driver who had brought her out to Merzoug kept his mouth shut.

Colonel Laporte asked where Madame Quatrefages had gone, then thought it part of the redhead's way of teasing. She'd say never, and then no, and then maybe, and then, on the porch that opened off his bedroom, she would finally tell him yes. Oh, yes. Ah, yes . . .

Safe with the Framats, Elisa waited for news of Xavier. It was a long, unsettling wait, though she heard in mid-November that he was once again in the camp. The rancher thundered to El Biar, told Xavier they had things to discuss, man to man, and that yes, Elisa was out there at the ranch.

'I wondered where she'd gone,' the vet said, nodding. 'The house all full of grit, and the newspapers spilled on the floor.'

The women left Framat to explain his plan to his friend.

'I understand, my dear Quatre', that you're up for some kind of promotion.'

'Is that right?' Xavier beamed. 'Well, twenty years in the Army, you know – '

'But that young Elisa has caught the eye of the colonel.'

'Is that so?' Xavier scowled. 'I did warn her not to play up to the man.'

'I don't believe she did,' the rancher growled. 'I believe Laporte has chosen her for his mistress. And will – let's get this straight, my friend – send you out to die, if she doesn't submit.'

Flagging his hand at Etienne's cigar smoke, Xavier said it was all most unfortunate. But what could he do? 'I must admit to you, Monsieur Framat, I would rather have married a woman closer to my own age. But that wonderful red hair! Those luminous green eyes! Would you blame me for being entranced?'

'Don't blame you at all. But let's get back to the truth. You see her as an impediment, Quatre'. And she, herself – she's unhappy. And now, of course, we've got Colonel Laporte to contend with.'

'You said you had a plan?'

'And I do.' Then he reminded the vet that the marriage in Folkestone failed to conform to French law. 'The girl was too young when you married her. And the ceremony took place in an Anglican church, so she tells me. So you're not really married at all, M'sieur Quatre', unless you wish it to be so. No question of divorce, I'm afraid, though

191

all you'd have to say is you made a clerical error, and the union – been much of a union, has it? – the union could be annulled. Then Elisa could escape Laporte's grasping fingers. And he couldn't blame you if your wife was no longer your wife. And he'd doubtless find someone else to invite to the porch. You're a nailed-down husband in England, my dear Quatre', but not necessarily so in El Biar.'

He half expected Xavier Quatrefages to storm from the ranch, shouting that marriage was marriage, and all he desired was Elisa. But the vet thought it over, then told him yes. 'Perhaps I was taken too quickly by her looks. Perhaps she was not yet ready for the discipline of military life out here. I was flattered to find her, without knowing perhaps that she'd quickly grow bored. Her looks would attract any man around, I think, and it might be fair if I let my Elisa go.'

Then he sighed from the depths of his stomach and asked Monsieur Framat when the promotion board would sit . . .

Honorine sat with Elisa in her room. The older woman broke the news gently, then asked her if she'd care to return to Paris, and stay with the Framats' granddaughter, Ginette, and her husband, Lucien, who was something in the city. 'They've children of their own, and I'm sure you could help. And could tell me how they are. They don't write much, though I crave for news of them. And you too, Elisa. We'd hope to know how the world spins round for you.'

Her farewell to the Framats . . . blurred with tears . . .

Her farewell to Xavier . . . brave as they embraced . . . telling each other, as always, to take care . . .

She was seen aboard the passenger ship by her husband, by Honorine with her twirling parasol, by Etienne with his thrust-out jaw and vile cigar.

She imagined Madame le Tourneau watching from the rail of the Government Hotel. And Colonel Jean-Marie Vian Laporte peering through his binoculars from the hills behind the harbour. And the ghost of Lieutenant Chavelet riding down to wish her well in the future . . .

Leaving the quay, Elisa waved to Xavier and the Framats, then turned aside from Algiers and nodded to the ghost. And prayed to meet him again in another guise . . .

PART FOUR

Paris: 1852–1854

1

Elisa never really came to terms with a couple as perfect as the Dauvins.

At thirty-three, the husband Lucien was tall, conventionally handsome, successful in his career, attentive to his wife and children, devoid of snobbishness, revered by his servants, respected by his business associates, valued by his friends. He drank in moderation, smoked the occasional cigar, set the dinner table humming with his freshly minted witticisms, murmured things to his offspring that sent them into helpless giggles of mirth.

He had served for a while as a cavalry officer in both the Hussars and Cuirassiers. He was said to be practically unbeatable at cards, matching a mind for the mathematical probabilities with an ability to unnerve his fellow players. His hobbies were archery, the study of eighteenth-century French literature and his collection of clockwork, tinplate toys.

A dinner guest had once remarked: 'You have only two ways to go, my dear Lucien. You will either become the Governor of the *Banque de France*, or you'll break the bank in the Casino at Monte Carlo.'

'In other words,' he had said with a smile, 'I'll be high and dry on one bank or the other. God forbid.'

As for Ginette, she was the perfect frame for his portrait. Five years younger than her husband, the Framats' granddaughter was cool, calm, with a flawless complexion, her figure unchanged by the birth of two children, her household in Rue Caumartin running as smoothly as Lucien's toys.

She had been schooled for a while in England, then in Switzerland, spoke knowledgeably of the Escorial and of Rome, made her servants blush with pride when she praised them, or squirm with shame if she murmured her displeasure. She had a weakness for the ices sold at the Glacier Tortoni in the Boulevard des Italiens, though each indulgence was offset by a visit to the punitive Turkish Baths. She was the same weight now as she had been at sixteen.

The Dauvin children were lively and intelligent, the boy already known for his prowess at chess, the girl for her uncanny gift of memory.

From the moment Lucien and Ginette read the Framats' letter of introduction, they had made Elisa welcome. There would be no question of her earning her keep. They had room enough and to spare, and she would stay with them as their guest for as long as she liked. 'No, *better*,' Ginette corrected. 'You'll stay as our friend.'

Whatever Etienne and Honorine had written, they'd made no mention of Elisa's marriage, referring to her as 'a young lady who's known unhappiness, yet deserves all that happiness can bring'. Too polite to probe, the Dauvins asked no questions. The young *Irlandaise* was attractive, her accent enchanting, her opinions bold and refreshing. It was a pleasure to receive her.

Yet the six months Elisa spent with the Dauvins in Rue Caumartin left her faintly uneasy. Her own childhood scarred by poverty, and with memories of violence and eviction still circling – as they would forever – in her mind, she found it hard to accept that life could be this perfect, this absent of pain.

She would sometimes look at the Dauvins' daughter, and remember Biddy O'Brien, crushed beneath the hooves of the team that had drawn Lord Natesby's ram . . . Or she would watch their eight-year-old son, Lucien *fils*, hunched over his chess game, the child prodigy nodding as one of his schoolmates entered his trap. *No oatmeal biscuits here . . . Nor the smell of damp and chalk . . .*

She compared the children's father with her own, the one moving smoothly to govern or break the bank, the other – equally gifted perhaps – who'd sacrificed his freedom, and his life, so the contents of Warehouse Six could keep others from dying.

She compared too the elegant Ginette with the elegant older Adelaide, blamed Ginette not at all for being who she was, yet wondered why it was all such a lottery; *this* road scored with ruts and sewn with rocks, *that* one levelled and lighted.

Would the Dauvins have done as well in Cork? Could the Lynches have succeeded here in Paris?

And you, she thought, how well have *you* done so far? The runner of errands; a courtesan's companion; the failed wife of that poor, uncertain hedgehog. And now you're seventeen years of age, and with no more idea where to go than a cat tipped off a cart beside the Seine.

You might stand in front of a mirror and ask yourself this. What right have *you* to think the Dauvins' life too perfect? All you know of them is what you see of them now. But did Lucien perhaps nearly die of disease as a child? Might not Ginette have been the victim of some lover's callous lies? It's clear they don't know much about the guest they treat as a friend, so what do you know about *them* that you judge them too good to be true?

It had always been one of Elisa's strengths – this ability to hold the glass to her own reflection – and in doing so she murmured her thanks to the gruff, mustachioed Etienne, the capable Honorine; and to the Dauvins who'd taken her in without query or hesitation.

God knows, she accepted, am I not even now wearing one of Ginette's prettiest gowns?

Every Saturday night the children were sent to bed early – seven by the clock; seven-thirty by the time their inventive protests had been heard. Then Ginette and Elisa would prepare themselves for the evening, dressing in bodice and long, layered skirts, Ginette's of lace-trimmed velvet, Elisa's of dark shot silk. In deference to the hostess, the taller Elisa wore low-heeled shoes, scarcely more than slippers, though she pretended not to hear when Ginette asked if she'd care to have her hair combed back and pinned.

Madame Dauvin had her husband and her household, after all. But Elisa Lynch had her tumble of fine red hair, and she wasn't about to hide *that* beneath a bushel of pins and combs.

Lucien was meanwhile left to select his wines, take a dozen good cigars from the humidor, dress in his favourite bottle-green suit and pearl-grey waistcoat, curse quietly as he fiddled with his cravat, then return downstairs to steal a glass of ruby port from the decanter.

An hour later, the long, candlelit salon was alive with the sounds of animated conversation, a dozen married couples mingling with four or five of Lucien's bachelor friends, the young men glancing away from the couples at the three pretty women Ginette herself had invited. A trio of musicians serenaded the guests. Liveried servants moved discreetly about the salon, serving champagne and cakes, a dry white wine from Gaillac, savouries for those who lacked a sweet tooth. Scandalous gossip was greeted with gasps of pretended shock, a whispered exchange smothered by a sudden roar of laughter. Groups formed and dissolved, the men switching now from wine to port, the ladies fanning to clear the air of cigar smoke. The Dauvins circulated among their guests, casually drawing the threads of the *soirée* together. Their only rule was that everyone there should meet everyone else –

197

though the single men needed no urging to make the acquaintance of Elisa Alicia Lynch.

During her time with the Dauvins she had met twenty or more young bachelors, thought several of them handsome, found most of them opinionated, vain or downright boring. Why was it, she wondered, that these young Parisians felt the need to raise a vast, invisible placard above their heads, announcing their achievements and ambitions, as if that alone would hold her attention?

'. . . I'm in shipping, Mademoiselle. Mostly out of Cherbourg and Brest. Company's booming, if I do say so m'self.' A conspiratorial wink and, 'Future's in steam.'

Or –

'. . . Halfway through translating Dante. Not the first time it's been done, but my version gives more emphasis to the cosmology and angelology; let the overall theology go hang!'

Or –

'. . . Submerged in the works of Louise Florence Pétronille de la Live d'Epinay. You've read her, of course. Friend of Diderot? Baron d'Holbach? Jean-Jacques Rousseau? Amazing woman. You remember what Sainte-Beuve said about her? I really think my *critique* will be a gem.'

Or – and here things changed –

'You're the most arresting young woman I've seen outside my dreams, Miss Lynch. But tell me if you're annoyed by my efforts at English. I could have said *attractive, alluring*, but as you've already accepted, I've not much advanced beyond the "a"s!'

Surprised to be, well, yes, *addressed* in her own native language, Elisa grinned at such unexpected flattery. 'I'm not *annoyed* at all,' she said. 'You speak excellent English, Monsieur. Are you sure you're not?'

'With such an *atrocious accent*?' he queried, the two of them laughing aloud at his silly game.

His name was Régis de Broux. 'I'll admit – oh, here we go again! – to being thirty-two. I don't own ships, and I don't translate from the Italian, and I've certainly never heard of Louise Florence Who-ever-de-la-Someone. I went to school with Lucien, and was with him in the cavalry. But these days we're like chalk and cheese – or should I say cheese and chalk?'

'You were right the first time,' Elisa told him, gazing up at the man she found both entertaining and remarkably good-looking.

Nevertheless, she waited for Régis de Broux to raise his placard.

But he didn't, asking her instead where she came from and, if *she* dismissed him, would it be worth his while sailing to Cork? 'I mean to say, are there others as pretty as you over there, or did you steal the mould when you left? I tend to believe you did, Miss Lynch. I'm inclined to believe you did.'

She was about to say the mould was safe in Ireland, but Monsieur and Madame Vernier interposed to say they must leave now; it had been a pleasure to meet the Dauvins' friend – 'And you, too, Monsieur de Broux'. Madame Vernier extended her hand and Régis bowed to kiss it. *And Elisa was surprised to find herself glaring at the middle-aged lady, the shock of jealousy coursing through her veins.*

She realized then that she wanted this handsome, English-speaking Frenchman for herself. And did not care a damn what he did to earn his money. Or if he had any at all.

She started to speak, and was once again interrupted. Monsieur and Madame Heidoffe were leaving, the man offering Elisa his hand, the woman raising her cheek – *fat, powdered cheek!* – to the patient Régis.

Seizing moments between departures, Régis murmured: 'I've more questions to ask you, Miss Lynch, but it's neither the time, nor the place. Might I call on you tomorrow, at, say, ten, and take you to lunch at an inn I'm rather fond of near the river? I'm sure your time is taken up – '

'Not tomorrow.'

'Well, that's a shame.'

'No,' she hastened, not caring that her voice sounded eager. 'What I meant to say is, my time isn't taken up – not tomorrow. I'd be pleased to have lunch with you tomorrow. And beside the river – '

'*Alongside* the river?'

Delighted by his game, she smiled and said: 'And the inn *adjacent?*'

'Practically *adherent*, if that's the word to use.'

'Use it anyway,' she told him. 'After all, Monsieur de Broux, who's to *admonish* you?'

She was hugging herself in secret delight when the last guest departed. Ginette had noticed her standing close to Régis de Broux, and could easily read the girl's happiness. Very well. So *La Rouquine* had found a friend. And where was the harm in that? Yet how long, the woman wondered, would it stay as mere friendship?

2

The following day, collecting her in a gig from Rue Caumartin, Régis de Broux looked as handsome in sunlight as in the glow of last night's candles. Indeed, he seemed taller, dressed now in high, scarred cavalry boots, tight-fitting breeches, short, skirted coat and a huntsman's plain suede waistcoat. He wore a soft-collared shirt and frivolous, hand-painted stock – the casual attire of a gentleman taking his ease.

Elisa was in a full, summery skirt, wide-sleeved blouse and a small, unnecessary waistcoat. She wore calf-length boots which had taken her fifteen minutes to button, and a mannish, stiff-crowned hat. Where last night her wild red hair had tumbled free, today it was pinned to accommodate the hat. It would be the very devil if she had to take it off, but it pleased her to feel she was fittingly dressed for the outing.

'You are, in a word, quite beautiful,' the man told her. 'Bright to the eye, and devoid of all blemish. I'm working on the "b"'s.'

'Well, please don't.' She smiled. 'It's a fine, silly game, and I hope we can play it all the way to "z". But today – well, today I'd like our words to come as they will. Now tell me. Where are we going?'

'Near the Bois de Vincennes,' Régis said. 'There's talk of it being laid out as a park. Another of Napoleon's hare-brained schemes. Though for the moment it's refreshingly undiscovered. As for the inn, it's somewhat rough-and-ready, but the food, I can promise, is delicious.'

And it was.

They ate crayfish with white wine sauce; a fresh summer salad; venison cut from its charcoal spit; then goats' cheese sprinkled with herbs, and a strawberry cake, the fruit set with care upon a caramel, cream-filled mound.

Régis offered her wine, though he made no attempt to force her to drink. Far more generous than the paternal Xavier Quatrefages, he lacked the insistence of the lascivious Colonel Laporte . . .

'I've known for a while,' Elisa said, 'that the French are obsessed by good food. I still think they exaggerate, but here, today, in the forest, I can appreciate the art they apply to mere cooking. I could never have eaten like this in Ireland, of course. Nor even in Algeria.

And I'm not sure I ever did in France, before today. Would it ruin you if I asked for a *digestif*?'

The man smiled and tilted his chin, the gesture bringing a waiter to their broad-plank table beneath the trees. The waiter said: '*Qu'est-ce que je vous sers, Monsieur de Broux?*'

'They seem to know you here,' Elisa murmured. 'Bring all your ladies out to Vincennes, is that your game?'

'That's right.' He smiled. 'I've a standing order for carriages and cakes. Anyone needs to find me, I'll be here around midday. Each time with a different woman. Though I'm sure you don't really believe that, Elisa. Or do you?'

'What I believe – if you really wish to know – is that I'm staring at a most handsome fellow, and am seeking to find fault with him, but haven't done so yet . . .'

'Look harder. You will. If I shook my coat, the faults would fall on the table.'

'Very likely,' she dismissed. 'You're older than I am, and a great deal wiser, and have doubtless known women – '

'Here's the *digestif*,' he said. 'And here's my salutation.' Then he leaned forward across the scrubbed oak table and chinked his glass against hers, telling her he meant the things he'd said, 'From A to B. You *are* attractive. And alluring. And beautiful. And with a fine sense of humour. And now I intend to take you for a boat ride on the river. Let's see if you're still smiling when I miss my stroke with the oars!'

'You'd better not!' she told him, though with happiness softening her command. 'This hat – it's been lent to me by Ginette!'

'Then I'll put it behind me,' Régis decided. 'And do my best not to splash your hair. Though you might care to unpin it. As a flag to inspire the rower.'

Waved on their way by the *patron* of the inn, Régis and Elisa clambered aboard a shallow, flat-bottomed skiff, the boat tailor-made for the slow-running current of the river.

The man rowed upstream, Elisa enjoying the ripples of the water, the shards of sunlight winking between the leaves. Her attention was caught by the sudden splash of a fish, the plop of an unseen toad.

So what if he claims he comes here every day with a different woman? I can see that women would like it. But who cares who came before? Today is mine. This summer afternoon belongs to me.

Lulled by the food and wine, she gazed at the tight-drawn twill of his trousers, the pulsing of his muscles as he drew on the flat-bladed oars. She wondered what he'd be like as a lover. As dull as the hedgehog? As frantic as the colonel? Or would he, perhaps, live up to his salutation, and show her that men were not always like Xavier, not always like Laporte?

'Listen,' she said. 'I've a question to ask you. Stop rowing.'

He did so, and the skiff drifted against the current.

'Good looking as you are, Régis, surely you're married?'

'Was once,' he said, and shrugged. 'But not what you'd call married now.'

'And can tell me you don't have a mistress?'

'Word of honour. Drown where I sit. I'm not denying my past, Elisa, but there's no one I'd rather be with now than you. Now and, may I add, in the future.'

The young woman listened and believed it, then asked him to row them further upstream – 'So we're sure to be out on our own.'

Another fifteen minutes beneath the canopy of trees, and Régis de Broux guided the skiff into a small, secluded backwater, a beach-fringed tent of green and blue and gold. He assisted Elisa from the boat, hauled it on to the gently shelving bank, then removed his coat and spread it on the ground.

She stretched out at ease, waiting for the man to settle beside her . . .

He learned across, kissed her, and was ardently kissed in return. The happy young woman clung to his shoulders, then looped her slender arms around his neck. 'Is it shameless to say I want you?' she murmured. 'Would you rather I was dishonest?'

'The first does not apply,' he said. 'And the second would be clearly out of character. Aren't we here by mutual consent, *ma belle Elise*? And should shame be a prerequisite of love?'

Then his hands caressed her body, his own moving to shadow her, and their fumblings eased as slowly, gently he entered her, his strength drawn deep into the willing arch of her hips.

He made the loving last, and Elisa, now crying out, begged him to go on with it, go on and never end. 'Oh, I can't believe . . . I've never known . . . Oh, yes, please yes, it's a dream I – Ah, Régis! *Yes!*'

De Broux moaned aloud with his own masculine pleasure, no words ever known to match that moment . . . Then, slowly, his muscled arms sagged, his sigh of contentment stirring the strands of her hair. They sank as if boneless, united in their intimacy, their murmurings of affection no louder than the coursing of the river . . .

Eventually, easing apart, Régis raised himself above her and grinned down to say: 'Not often in life that a man's passions are so fulfilled, my sweet Elisa.'

'Not often in life that a girl's shameless desires are realized, M'sieur de Broux. And might we not stay here a while, then realize them again?'

They did, and it was not until dusk that Elisa was delivered back to the house in Rue Caumartin.

Ginette asked if the day had gone well, and Elisa said it had really been most enjoyable. 'Excellent food at that inn in the forest clearing. A trip up the river and – yes, it was all of it a pleasure.'

'Crowded was it, on the river?'

'Flotillas of boats! The holiday season, I suppose.'

'So little time to yourselves. What a shame. But you *did* get the chance to exchange a word with Régis?'

'Enough to be invited out tomorrow.' Elisa nodded. 'He'll be calling for me at ten.'

Ginette said good, pretending not to see the blush that suffused Elisa's cheeks. It was already more than mere friendship, so it seemed.

In the days that followed, the girl from Cork was shown half the sights of Paris. But the outings usually returned them to the inn in the forest, and from there to the beach beneath the trees. Monuments and palaces held their interest for an hour, though what mattered was to get back to the inn, then into the skiff, and upstream to their own private haven.

Elisa wondered, as any woman might, when Régis de Broux would tire of her, and recite his sad excuses.

'*Business calls me away for a while* . . .'

'*You see I'm wearing this armband? A death in the family* . . .'

'*You don't know enough about me*, ma belle. *And I'm really not worth your knowing* . . .'

These, and a hundred other ways to get out of the relationship, the man perhaps hoping for another girl on the beach . . .

But her fears were groundless, and Régis de Broux asked how she would feel if she moved from Rue Caumartin to a place he owned near the Parc Monceau? 'It was left to me by my aunt, and I could visit you there, two or three times a week. You can buy what you need from the list of shops I'll give you. You've made me yours beside the river, and it's time I made you mine. Does the thought of it appeal, *ma belle*, or would you rather stay on with the Dauvins?'

'Is it splendid?' she asked. 'With panelled doors, and velvet curtains, and statuary set in alcoves around the walls? Are the carpets from Turkey, the lanterns from Venice, all of it left by your wealthy, selective aunt?'

'No,' he admitted. 'It's just a four-room apartment in Rue de Courcelles.'

'Fine.' She grinned. 'Then that's where you'll find me. Daytime or night-time, that's where you'll find me. But beware, my love. Our bed won't be for sleeping!'

She returned to the Dauvins, her happiness still evident. 'I'm sorry to leave you like this, but you must understand – Régis wants to take me in. He has an apartment near the Parc Monceau. Forgive me for leaving – '

'We do,' Ginette said. 'We understand, and there's nothing to forgive. You are a very beautiful woman, Elisa; and Régis, himself, has undeniable charm. But there is a remark I might pass to you. A wicked remark from someone who loves you, but something you ought to know.'

Still smiling at the thought of her future home in Rue de Courcelles, Elisa asked cheerfully: 'So what? I'm to learn he's a swindler and a fraud?'

'Not at all.'

'Or has a regiment of mistresses?'

'None as I've heard of.'

'Or is married to some wild-eyed wife – '

'Come and sit beside me, Elisa – '

' – who might come bursting in with a knife – '

'Come and sit quiet, my dear – '

' – and attempt to murder us both – '

'Come over here to the couch. Sit still. Then take my hand as I tell you yes. He is. Monsieur de Broux *is* married, and has been so for the past ten years. To a woman who has a sickness of the lungs. Her condition precludes all activity, and she cannot, of course, meet the physical needs of her husband. The unutterable sadness is that as Madame de Broux grows weaker, Régis fights harder to save her. He has already taken her in a private vessel – at Lord knows what cost – to be examined by the finest surgeons in England. Brought physicians from Italy and Spain. I'm sorry to draw a cloud across your horizons, my dear, but you must understand – when you met the attentive and handsome de Broux, you met only half the man.'

Elisa sat silent, forbidding the tears to flow. Very well, so Régis had deceived her. Or anyway allowed her to believe he was '. . . *not what you'd call married now*'. Yet was it really such a shock? A personable fellow in his thirties? Didn't common sense point to the existence of a wife?

'You've no cause to be sorry,' she told Ginette. 'It was foolish of me to think it could be otherwise. And anyway – I don't quite know how to say this – I too am guilty of lies. Of withholding the truth.'

'How so?' Ginette murmured, though her expression seemed to anticipate the answer.

'These months I've been with you and Lucien . . . When you might have thought me so innocent . . . I didn't wish it to be known, but the time I spent in Algeria – '

'Was with a man, perhaps?'

'A veterinarian in the Army. Captain Quatrefages. My husband.' Then briefly, forlornly, she clutched at Ginette's hand and whispered: 'Am I not more the liar than Régis de Broux?'

It surprised her when Ginette Dauvin chuckled. 'And don't you think we, Lucien and I, might have guessed as much? Not that he was an Army man, I don't claim that. But that you were a sight more at ease with fellows than an unmarried lady could be? Attracted them like bees to pollen, yet saw half of them for the buzzing drones they are! And I'll tell you something else, if I may. I doubt you've fooled your handsome Monsieur de Broux.'

Remembering the eagerness with which she'd made love to the man on the shelving bank of the river, Elisa turned away. 'I feel like the world's finest fool,' she said. 'Of course he must have known, even then. Will you tell me what I'm to do?'

'Tell you in a phrase, my dear. Accept the gentleman's offer. Move from Rue Caumartin to the Parc Monceau. Be with him in his apartment. Then set the light of your extraordinary beauty on the darkened side of his being. Don't question the fact that he cares for his wife, but admire him because he does so. It's my opinion that women would judge men better if they made it their business to see how well the woman *before* had been treated. Is that clear, or shall I try it again when we've had a glass of muscat?'

205

'Yes, it is.' Elisa nodded. 'And thank you. But let's have one anyway, and I'll tell you about Algiers.'

The bottle three-quarters empty, Ginette was joining in on the chorus of a regimental song when Lucien returned home from the bank. He caught Elisa conducting merrily, the two women coughing, then beaming in amiable welcome.

'No, don't stop,' he said. 'I think that's one I know. "Marshal Bugeaud's Cap"?

> *As-tu vu la casquette, la casquette?*
> *As-tu vu la casquette au père Bugeaud?*

'Just allow me to change, and I'll join you. I'm a pretty fair baritone. Shiver the chandeliers . . .'

'It's as well you're leaving us,' Ginette whispered to her friend. 'Better to be whipped with a nail-studded strap, than to listen to Lucien sing.' Then she giggled, and Elisa joined her, the two of them clutched together on the couch as Lucien sniffed: 'So be it. If that's how you feel.'

3

It saddened Elisa to bid farewell to the Dauvins. The time she had been with them had proved that a family *could* be affectionate, blameless in their behaviour, courteous to their guests and warm to their friends. They had certainly made a friend of the red-haired foreigner, and she would miss them, as she missed the distant Framats.

But no magnet on earth could have held her from the four-room apartment in Rue de Courcelles, and she gazed through the window of the Dauvins' salon, not caring that she was an hour in advance of the carriage.

She did not expect Régis to come in person – he had said he'd be busy – yet suddenly there he was! A vast bouquet of flowers in his arms, he thrust them towards a delighted Ginette, told her the next time she invited him she would, please, reserve *two* places at her table, then embraced Elisa and took her away, abducting his willing victim from the house.

There are moments in life to be treasured, and here, for them both, was one.

In the carriage, he said: 'I imagine you've been told about my wife.'

'It's all right, my love. I could think you all the better – but listen.'

'Hush, now, there's nothing to say. A husband or lover in Africa? A thousand dawns and dusks before we met? So long as it's over – '

'Yes, it is. And was over, perhaps – '

'Then there's no more to be said. You see that place – no, you've missed it. The hat shop. Arranged an account for you . . . Lean over here. That one, see it, that's where they sell gowns and fabrics; leave it to you to choose . . . As for *Portal et fils*, they're the best damn grocers in the district . . .'

'Where?' she laughed. 'You'd have me look this way and that! You must give me time to discover!'

'That's right,' he grinned. 'And you've all the time you need. But tonight, if you're willing, we'll discover the apartment. And each other, once again.'

*

Blearily they saw the dawns of August and September; the softer daybreaks of autumn.

By now they'd shared their secrets, de Broux admitted that his wife was ever weaker, and unlikely to see the winter out in his family home at Rouen. 'But I've heard of a physician who's worked miracles in cases such as this, and he's agreed to come and see her.' He shrugged lightly then said: 'God knows, I remain optimistic.'

Elisa told him he must do as he thought best, though prayed they could still be together. 'If only twice a week. If only once! But please, whenever you can.'

In happier moments, the handsome de Broux took his beautiful red-haired mistress to the theatre, the concert-hall, the circus. They found themselves invited out *à deux* and, as often as he could manage it, Régis held a *soirée* at Rue de Courcelles.

The Dauvins came, pleased to see Elisa so happy, as did others who envied their host his enchanting *amie*. The men were content to gaze at her, storing fantasies for the future. The women approved of her loyalty to Régis, though from time to time felt it necessary to nudge their husbands hard. 'Look at you! Eyes gone to marble! Never seen a women with hair doused in ink?'

There were jealousies here, and joltings there, but as summer eased into autumn the lovers were wonderfully happy.

Elisa insisted they went back to the river, to the same tented bank, and they did so, eating first in their favoured inn.

Régis took her shopping, willing to buy her bracelets and brooches, and he shrugged as she said no, she'd seen nothing she fancied.

He wished to tell her to play the role. She was his mistress, *not* his wife, and should snatch at whatever was offered. But Elisa was deeply in love with her man. And was intimacy to be seen as a way of investment?

It was late October when he told her his wife found it hard to breathe, and could not survive another winter where she was.

'I must conduct her to a clinic in the south. There's one that's high up in the hills above Antibes. If she's there, I can draw on the finest doctors from Italy, or even the Swiss.'

Regretting it later, Elisa said: 'What's so wrong with the French? They're as good as anyone else, aren't they? You take her to all these other countries, or call in these foreigners, yet why don't you bring her to Paris? The English didn't do much for her; nor anyone else, so it seems. Yet now you say you must head off south – '

'Where the air is dry – '

'And will sit beside her bed – '

'If needs be – '

'And be five hundred miles from mine!'

'Now listen to me,' Régis said gently, but Elisa was not yet ready to give in.

'Why can't I come with you? You'll need a place to stay, and I could look after you. You think I'm a stranger to the mop and the broom? Frightened to soil my hands with hard work? If you believe *that*, then it just goes to show – '

'Elisa . . .'

'Oh, please take me with you . . . No one need know . . . I'll stay in our rooms all the time, if you like . . . Just so long as the two of us – '

Drawing her to him, he held her against his chest. 'You must listen to me, *ma belle*. Whatever I might wish in this matter – and yes, I would rather you were with me – my responsibilities lie now with my wife. It is no fault of her own that she's ill; and she knows I have you, knows it and reprieves me with her blessing. But you must see why I cannot take you with me. If *I* were dying, would you leave my bedside, and return to another man?'

Elisa wept quietly, aware that all her pleadings would be in vain. She heard Régis de Broux say she could stay on here for a while in Rue de Courcelles, and that before he left he would introduce her to two or three well-connected gentlemen. 'They are generous and companionable, and will offer you their protection. You must accept it, *ma belle*. It's time you hardened your heart, don't you see? If ever so slightly.'

That night they made love, Elisa then pretending to sleep in the crook of her lover's arm. Though she slept not a wink, tugging instead at the skeins of her tangled thoughts.

So it's time to harden my heart, is it? Smile at de Broux's well-connected friends, then make my choice, and accept another's protection?

Well, let's see. I certainly failed in my 'respectable' marriage to Captain Quatrefages. And my genuine love affair with Régis de Broux is soon to end. So perhaps he's right. Perhaps it is time to accept what a man can offer. Especially if the offer glints and shines.

In the morning, she said: 'I shall soon release you to your wife. But before you go, you might care to effect the first of these introductions. No point in wasting time, don't you agree? I must snare my prey whilst I can!' Her eyes were bright, her smile wide and unreal. She challenged the man to say he'd not meant what he'd told her, daring him with her brittle, glittering gaze.

But he realized he, too, must harden his heart, and said yes – in the circumstances – the sensible thing to do. 'A year from now, and all Paris will be at your knees, my sweet Elisa.'

'Nonsense!' she contradicted. 'A year from now and all Paris will be at my feet!'

She was surprised at the ease with which she climbed the uncertain ladder.

A fifty-year-old broker installed her in an apartment in the 9th Arrondissement, requesting only that she be there to receive him every Tuesday afternoon and Friday evening. He would stay for two hours each Tuesday, then take her to the theatre, the Opéra, wherever she wanted on Friday. After which they would dine in his favourite restaurant – unfrequented by his colleagues – returning to the apartment around midnight.

A fiacre would collect him at six the next morning, and the woman would be free to amuse herself until Tuesday, 3 p.m.

Employing the euphemism of the time, the broker left her 450 francs a month, 'for flowers and lace'.

At the age of eighteen, Elisa Lynch opened an account with the *Banque de France*, giggling at the thought of Lucien Dauvin, future Governor, stumbling across her name.

In May 1853, the broker made his way across the pillared hallway of the Bourse, reached to shake hands with a fellow he knew, missed the man's grasp, saw the pillars dissolve and pitched headlong to the floor. *Crise cardiaque*. Heart attack. Dead before his gold-tipped cane had finished rolling.

Elisa sent her card to the owner of the third largest munitions manufactory in France. She had met him before in the company of the broker, and she played bezique with her maid while she waited for his reply.

It came that same evening, delivered by a liveried coachman, who handed her a note in which the explosives king said: 'Much appreciate your presence at my *manoir* near Montreuil. You'll be furnished with all you need.' The note was short, but the envelope was bulky, containing as it did 2,000 francs.

The magnate's *manoir* was, in reality, a sixty-four-room château.

Elisa took her maid along, grinning when the girl said later she'd had 'to-do' with the head gardener's son, and would Madame Lynch much mind if she stayed to get married?

'Good looking, is he?'

'Well, I wouldn't say that.'

'All the better. Then maybe he'll stay at home. But good at his work?'

'Oh, yes! Each time we – well, had to-do, as it were, in the vegetable garden, he'd turn his head and tell me what was coming into season.'

Elisa said: 'Here. Take this. It's a ring I was given by the broker. Sell it, if you want to. I shan't mind. I personally find it chafes my fingers.'

Sold sensibly by her new father-in-law, it allowed the maid and her swivel-headed husband to purchase a cottage on the edge of the estate . . .

As for Elisa, she found herself offered the choice. An entire wing of the château near Montreuil, or a town house in Rue de Sevigné, within walking distance of the Seine and Ile Saint-Louis. Either would come complete with cook-cum-housekeeper, two resident maid-servants, footman and stabled conveyance.

She chose the latter – 'For I've not yet seen all of Paris!' – then discovered what was involved.

The armaments king proved as murderous as his products. It pleased him to use his fists, his probing fingers, the full, sagging weight of his body. He was callous and brutal and carelessly grotesque – then paid Elisa Alicia Lynch 2,000 francs for each dubious pleasure . . .

When the visit finally ended – the manufacturer required to demonstrate his spring-launched grenades to the Greeks – his Irish mistress returned to the capital.

The man's indecent brutalities had left her bruised and aching, yet richer by 30,000 francs. It was a way, she acknowledged bitterly, to make money, though not something she would willingly repeat. It had been for Elisa a time without affection, a hurtful and shameful – but, oh so profitable – sharing of her body.

What the man had forced her to do disgusted her, though she would not alone take the blame. For 20 francs she'd have spurned his invitation. For 200 francs she believed she'd have returned the money with his note. Yet for 2,000 francs she'd allowed herself to be bought, then re-bought fifteen times over . . .

It seems we all have our price, she thought, as the coach jolted west towards the city.

As for the magnate's offer of the house in Rue de Sevigné, a visit there might now be timely and appropriate.

She leaned forward to call to the driver, telling him to take her there. 'Yes, now. I wish to see it.'

Another fifteen minutes and the coach drew to a halt outside the house. Elisa turned in discomfort to look at it, accepting that it was indeed a very fine dwelling in which a man's mistress might live. 'But not for me,' she decided. 'Not this place, nor the wing of his château.'

Then she sucked in her lips and filled her tongue and spat at the magnate's offer. 'Now drive on,' she said. 'I've formed my opinion.'

With more money now than decent, working people would earn in a lifetime, the eighteen-year-old courtesan bathed her bruises in a claw-foot bath in the apartment she could now afford to rent in Rue du Helder, on the north side of the Boulevard des Italiens.

She used a mixture of soda and soap to enliven her skin. Imagined a bell-pull suspended beside the bath. Raised her fingers from the water and counted the rooms she'd rented; the staff she could hire; the thousands of francs left over.

The image of Corinne appeared – *Ignore it; harden your heart* – then another of Marise Laurent-Perrone – *Too bad; who ever heard of a ladder made for two?*

Other faces swirled in the steam of the bath-tub. Good men and evil. Women she'd loved, and others she'd hated. Then all the innocent children . . . the starvelings in Miss Gardiner's General Day School . . . And the children in Rue Simon le Franc . . . And the nameless ones in Algeria . . . And the nurtured ones in Caumartin . . .

Well, too bad. She'd come into money for the first time in her life, and she would now obey what her only real lover had told her. Think of herself. Massage away the bruises. Climb from the bath and stand in front of the mirror, red hair damp and green eyes glaring, seeking hard to find fault with her body.

But where was the fault to find in *that* fine figure?

Good enough for a gentle lover, an undemanding broker, a sadistic merchant, it was surely good enough for a diplomat, an aristocrat – so why not for the Monarch of the Moon?

Dreaming high, she came close.

4

The Chargé d'Affaires at the Paraguayan Legation in Paris was a career diplomat, an accomplished linguist and, when occasion demanded, a persuasive pimp.

With seemingly unlimited funds at his disposal, the tall, soft-spoken Juan José Brizuela was the darling of society. A man who would not just pay extravagant compliments to the ladies, but would pay for everything else. A *soirée* at the Legation was not to be missed, even if, supplied with an atlas, less than one in ten of the guests could have found the page containing the map of Paraguay.

Notoriously insular, and belying their claim to be part of the *haute monde*, the Parisians guessed it to be an island in the Pacific; a coastal strip at the Eastern end of the Mediterranean; a republic that shared a common border with India.

Brizuela's fine-planed features were dark, so he doubtless hailed from somewhere to the south. Africa, perhaps. In the nebulous regions of Africa. Or in the Americas – whatever *that* might mean – or in the general direction of China.

Who could say? And, frankly, who much cared?

If such wilful ignorance angered him, Brizuela was far too clever to let it show. No matter that they confused his native land with Palestine or Persia. The truth of it was, Brizuela lived the most perfect life a man could wish for. Thirty-three years old and unmarried, he had his pick of beautiful women – some of whom *were* married, *mais c'est la vie* – and was free to spend his nation's money in a way that turned his diplomatic colleagues green with envy.

Careful not to brag or boast, he knew for a fact that his budget exceeded that of Great Britain, Sweden and the Netherlands. *Combined . . .*

Once a month, unfailingly, he dispatched a ten- or fifteen-page report to his masters. It was boring to search out new phrases every time, when the gist was the same. Though where was the harm in one day's work among thirty? The thing was to let the message stand out clear.

In June 1853 he wrote: 'Admittedly less well-known than her

immediate neighbours, we are nonetheless striding more firmly in the courts of Napoleon's France. Paraguay' (he lied) 'is slowly but surely achieving the recognition Our Mighty Nation deserves. The Emperor – as he calls himself now – would, I am sure, be receptive to a visit by Our Beloved President – or by a member of Our President's Illustrious Family. I fully understand' (he crawled) 'that Paraguay lacks for nothing, though it might be of interest to see the advances made here in military *matériel*; small arms, grenades and the like. Might I humbly submit' (he slithered) 'that such a visit would be opportune? At which time I shall set Paris seething with the news. "Prepare Yourselves, for Paraguay is Coming to Inspect!" '

His month's work done, he sent off the report and went back to being Brizuela the party-giver, Brizuela the party-goer, Brizuela the part-time pimp.

This last was a task he undertook for his wealthy countrymen, here to present their credentials at the Legation, then settle down to do business with the French. It was no easy task, for the French were no fools, leaving foreigners exhausted by their guile. The Great Napoleon – not *this* one; his uncle – might once have said the English were a nation of shop-keepers. But Brizuela was convinced the French were the true *commerçants* of Europe.

Aware that his countrymen would be drained by their dealings in Paris, the sinuous Chargé d'Affaires arranged that pleasure should follow the pain. If they lost to a Frenchman at business – and who on earth did not? – they could at least enjoy the delights of a *fille de joie*. It'd cost them again, and the girl would most likely be French. But how much better to manoeuvre with a pretty young woman on satin sheets, than be outmanoeuvred in a boardroom!

Besides, business introductions were part of Brizuela's job as the Chargé d'Affaires.

But soft-spoken introductions to a pretty companion were something else. And for this he could expect a healthy gratuity – thirty per cent on top of the 'flowers and lace'.

'*Gracias, Señor*. Or, seeing as we're in Paris, *je vous remercie.*'

In September, his report of June long forgotten, Brizuela opened a packet of letters from Paraguay, noted that his bank balance had been topped up by the Government, smiled and nodded at the regularity. Then he broke the seal on another, read it – and stumbled to the window to make sure his eyesight hadn't failed. '*¡Madre de Dios!* They've taken me up on my suggestion. They're coming over!'

Not the President himself, but his son. And would Brizuela arrange an audience with the Emperor Napoleon, and with the English Queen, Victoria, and with the Spanish Royal Family, and the Crowned Heads of Italy, and with all those Majestical or Republican figures as might be present in Paris.

Paraguay would, as the Chargé d'Affaires had suggested, stride the welcoming floors of Europe. And count on the clever diplomat to make sure the footfalls were heard.

And would Brizuela ensure accommodation for the sixty-eight accredited members of the visiting entourage.

And not forget companionship for the President's son and emissary, General of the Armed Forces and Admiral of the Fleet, Francisco Solano Lopez.

His cheeks sucked tight, Brizuela sent his staff to check the shipping offices; to reserve entire floors in the best hotels; entire restaurants 'from now till whenever'; a fleet of coaches – 'Well, of course, the whole fleet! You think I want the President's son to be told he's missed one, wait for the next?'

He sat up all night, writing his first letter to the dumpy Queen Victoria, Mistress of the Realm for the past two decades, and unlikely to fit Francisco Solano Lopez into her calendar at short notice. Her Majesty had probably never heard of Paraguay. If it was not a part of the burgeoning British Empire, it was doubtless a home of monkey-men and dragons.

But send the letter anyway. And make a copy to show Lopez.

After that he wrote to the twenty-three-year-old Queen Isabella of Spain, reminding her that Spanish was the language of the Para-guayan court, so were the countries not distant cousins? It was a foolish remark, and Brizuela would pay for it later.

Then to the King of the Two Sicilies. To Pope Pius IX. To half a dozen other Heads of State. Then finally – and the letter took him more than an hour and a half to compose – to the Emperor of France, Napoleon III.

Brizuela knew, as did anyone else who had come into contact with Francisco Solano Lopez, that the young man worshipped the memory of the earlier Napoleon, and saw himself as Bonaparte reincarnate. It made the Chargé d'Affaires tremble to think what would happen if the present Emperor declined to grant Lopez an audience. This was why the letter took an hour and a half to write . . .

His fingers cramped, he abandoned the escritoire. But his work

215

was not yet over, for there were certain essential changes to be made to his quarters in the Legation.

For example, there were nineteen hand-tailored uniforms and suits to be packed away, reducing his wardrobe to six. Lopez would permit Brizuela six, but might ask where the money had come from for twenty-five!

The diplomat's personal library of erotica was stacked in a chest, along with his collection of fine French lithographs. He cleared his shelves of perfumes and pomades, thrusting them at the *femme de chambre* when she arrived. 'Do what you like with them. Are you married? Then give them to your husband.'

'My husband works for the City, M'sieur. Bit on the rough side, my husband. His job's with the gutters and drains. I can't see 'im as being the type – '

'All the more reason to douse him in scent,' Brizuela told her. 'It might not sweeten his nature, but should do wonders when he's at home.'

And then he remembered something else about Francisco Solano Lopez. The man was a lecher, a libertine, his sexual appetites insatiable. Rumour had it that the families of Paraguayan society sent their daughters abroad – not just to be schooled in Europe, but to avoid being debauched by the President's son.

So no sleep today for the diplomat. Time to change his clothes and wear his other hat. The hat of the pimp.

He eyed the courtesans in the Bois de Boulogne, in the Tuileries Gardens, in their boxes at the Opéra, at their tables in the fashionable cafés. He knew many of them by sight, several by intimate acquaintance, yet failed to find the one he sensed Lopez might most enjoy. Someone different. Attractive, of course, yet unusual. A Russian perhaps – *no, wait, are you insane? A Russian for the man who worships Napoleon? So she can giggle about the Emperor's disastrous retreat from the gates of Moscow? Wake up, you imbecile! Your job's to put him in bed with a woman, not put your own neck in the strangling rope of a garrotte!*

Frightened by the mistake he might have made, Brizuela continued his search. He grew quietly desperate, close to panic, aware that Lopez was somewhere out there, aboard the government steamship *Tacauri*, but he did not know how *far* out there, five hundred miles or five.

He visited a score of dance halls, and watched the performers lift their skirts. At other times the brazen display would have pleased him, but he was fidgety now, ignoring his wine, glancing around the smoky *bals musettes*.

Ticking off the addresses on his list, he visited one in the Jardin Mabille. Gazed bleak-eyed at the dancers. Shifted in his chair to check the customers. Missed her at first as a waiter hovered between them, then saw her and stared, though not yet daring to smile.

Seizing his chance, he moved to another table. Then he moved again, bringing himself next to hers. She was there with two other women, four other men, and it seemed to Brizuela that, whenever she spoke, the others paused to listen.

She had a mane of red hair and – he could see now – pale green eyes. Then someone said: 'You are the most terrible tease, Elisa. If I was not so good-natured – '

'But you are. And enjoy being teased, I think. After all, it's quite a novelty for the French. They normally sniff and sulk. You're far too conscious of yourselves, you know. Now as for the Germans and Austrians, they don't take offence, but insist the taunt be explained. The English, on the other hand, are quite happy to tell a story against themselves. Though maybe that's 'cause they've plenty of stories to tell!'

The woman's remarks were greeted with laughter and a smattering of applause. Brizuela found himself nodding, though not just in agreement with what she'd said. *He was nodding now because he thought her perfect for his master.* Young and attractive. Her accent enchanting. And different enough to put Lopez at his ease. The crowd would stare hard enough, God knows, at the man from Paraguay. But with the tall and vivacious redhead beside him, he might think they were staring at her.

The thing to find out now – Was she married? Was one of the four doting men her husband? Was she really no more than a faithful wife, out for an evening on the town?

Brizuela left his table and went in search of the *patron* of the Bal Mabille.

He asked the man several questions, handed him an agreed sum in coins, then resumed his seat and waited.

Fifteen minutes later the party at the next table left, though it pleased Brizuela to see that two men at least reached to settle her cape.

Another five minutes and the *patron* bent down to whisper in the diplomat's ear. Brizuela thanked him, then scribbled in his notebook. 'Madame Elisa Alicia Lynch. Born in Ireland. Seventeen, eighteen, nineteen? Rents her own apartment in Rue du Helder. Speaks French most charmingly. Lustrous copper hair. Figure faultless. Crowded around by her escorts. Was Ireland ever at war with Napoleon?'

And would it matter anyway, when Señor Lopez meets Madame Lynch?

He paid for his wine and left a hefty tip on the table. Other women called to him as he made his way from the dance hall, but tonight Brizuela flagged only a brief salute. For the first time in weeks, the Chargé d'Affaires felt the spring return to his step. He'd found the girl he was after. And wasn't the rest of it just a matter of money, since Elisa was up for sale?

Even so, he'd cut things fine, for a messenger arrived at the Legation to say the *Tacauri* had berthed at the mouth of the Seine, and Señor Lopez was on his way. He'd arrive sometime tomorrow, and would expect to be greeted by Brizuela.

Four hours in bed, and the diplomat was up again, cursing to see his rack of suits so reduced. All right, so it would have to be the blue one. And the oyster-grey cravat to go with it. *But with soap instead of perfumes?*

The Legation staff were assembled, inspected, told to stay at their desks and wait. A servant was sent to the far end of the broad, tree-lined avenue, another to stand in front of the wrought-iron gates that barred the entrance to the drive. A third was posted at the foot of the steps, a fourth within the ornate glass doors of the building.

A five-minute warning, but Brizuela did not intend to be caught by surprise.

5

Then at twenty past four, a bulbous, hooded carriage lurched towards the Legation. To be followed by another . . . Then another . . . Then fifteen more . . . And all the uniformed horsemen riding escort, swords and pistols bouncing on their hips, long plumes waving, dark eyes alert in dark-skinned faces, as Paraguay measured Paris . . .

The servants waved to warn each other. The gates were swung open, the doors hauled inwards, a bark from Brizuela bringing the staff to rigid attention.

Horses snorted, and carriages clashed wheels. Extensive though the grounds were, who on earth could have anticipated almost twenty lumbering coaches, seventy passengers, forty armed outriders and, in all, more than eighty horses?

From within the first coach, a voice boomed in disgust. 'I thought us to be better placed, from all you've told me. Seems our nation's been relegated to the suburbs, Brizuela. I'm not pleased. Not contented. Not happy at all to arrive in a peasant's front garden. Now get this door open, before I kick it out!'

The diplomat plunged to obey. It was not his job to do so, and it meant colliding with one of the servants. But if things got off on the wrong foot now –

'Accommodation has been reserved,' he blurted. 'Stabling for the horses. Restaurants booked. Theatres and music-halls I've organized a firework display – you'll see it from the riverboat I've – '

'So much for the distractions,' the voice rejected. 'But I've not come ten thousand miles for exploding candles. I am here to meet the Emperor. And his Lady. And be introduced to a lady of my own. And this evening, Brizuela, the latter.'

Then he did as he'd threatened, and slammed the toe of his solid, South American boot at the quilted lining of the door, springing the catch.

The formalities over, the diplomat conducted the President's son to a hotel overlooking the Champs Elysées, vowing to return within the hour with the *fille de joie*. 'She is the most strikingly beautiful woman,' he enthused. 'It's said she hates the Russians, and that her great hero is Napoleon Bonaparte. She speaks English and French, though she is in fact – '

'Is that what's said?' Lopez growled. 'Well, need I remind you yet again, Señor Brizuela, I'm not here for a course in foreign languages. Nor do I intend to discuss the history of Europe with a courtesan. I requested you to find me a woman with whom I might take my pleasures. Must I now spell out for you – ?'

'No, *Señor El Presidente*. She is, I'm assured, well-versed in the needs of men.'

'Then, in God's name, go and get her! No more talk. Just get her. And Brizuela?'

'*Mi Presidente?*'

'Well within the hour.'

On the journey to Rue du Helder, the diplomat felt the palms of his hands turn damp. He knew what the woman looked like, knew who she was, knew where she lived. Yet he did *not* know if she would be there.

She might be anywhere. In any of a thousand bistros or brasseries. In any of a hundred beds in Paris, or not in Paris at all. Having promised Elisa Lynch to Francisco Lopez, the pimp now sweated with fear . . .

He tugged on the bell, leaving the handle to glisten.'*Come on, come on!*'

No answer – then, yes, the creak of the Judas-port, and a maid-servant's face beyond the grille. '*Vous désirez, M'sieur?*'

'Madame Lynch; is she in?'

'You have a card, M'sieur?'

'What? Oh, yes. Here. So she *is* at home?'

The maid would neither confirm, nor deny it, but took the card and asked him to wait. At other times Brizuela would have snapped angrily at her, informing the girl that he was the Chargé d'Affaires at the Paraguayan Legation, a diplomat of some standing, and who did she think she was to leave him out here on the step? But today he just fumbled to consult his brass-case watch.

Six fifty-five. Twenty minutes of the hour had elapsed. Add another fifteen for the journey back to the Champs Elysées –

A bolt was drawn and the street door opened. '*Si vous voulez me suivre, Monsieur Briselle . . .* ' She offered to take his hat and cane, shrugged as he ignored her, then led him along a wide, panelled hallway and into a room that glowed with rich, candlelit tapestries, its size increased by the subtle use of mirrors, the sound of his boot-heels deadened by a thick Spanish carpet. He glimpsed an array of fine furniture, and would normally have paraded his knowledge, remarking on the provenance of this piece, the quality of that. It pleased him to watch the Parisians gape and nod in the face of his expertise, but now was not the moment, and the brass-case watch was ticking.

Anyway, the red-haired woman who gazed at him from the couch was Irish, and for all he knew she might yawn and say: 'Oh, really? Is that the truth?'

His hat in his hand, Brizuela bowed. 'Your servant, Madame Lynch. I'm – '

'You're the man who's name is on the card, are you not? Or is it something you stole at someone's *soirée*? Excuse my ignorance, Monsieur Brizuela, but is Paraguay down near Brazil and the Argentine, or have I confused it – ?'

'Not at all, Madame. That's precisely where it is. May I say, I'm really quite impressed – '

'Well, don't, or you'll sound insufferably patronizing. I'm quite the thing at geography, Monsieur Brizuela. Name me the nine major islands in the Mediterranean Sea.'

'Well, the thing is, Madame – '

'Never mind. One of them's slipped my mind anyway; I can only think of eight.' Composed and smiling, Elisa said: 'Tell me instead why you're here, Monsieur Brizuela. And don't be coy, for I think we've met before. Met or sat close. Was it not last night in the Bal Mabille?'

Flattered, the diplomat nodded. 'I'm surprised you remember, Madame.'

'Who wouldn't, the way you jumped from table to table, your eyes bright with looking, and your ears about coming to a point. Tell the truth, I expected a visit from you sooner. Now, be seated, Monsieur, and tell me how I can – please you. Port or wine?'

Completely off-balance, Brizuela perched on an English-style, buttoned leather chair, his hat and cane now an encumbrance, *and the watch in the pocket of his waistcoat ticking in his head . . .*

'Thank you, Madame, but neither. The reason I'm here, and time somewhat presses, is quite simply that I'd introduce you to a most important and influential countryman.'

'Of mine?' she said innocently.

'Hmm? No, of mine. A gentleman of considerable power. No less than the future President of Our Nation, His Excellency, *Maréchal* Francisco Solano Lopez.'

Elisa tipped her head to one side and listened. 'Sounds like a roll of drums,' she murmured. 'Sounds like a fanfare of trumpets. His Excellency, *Maréchal* Francisco Solano Lopez . . . Very well, Monsieur Brizuela. I've never met a future President before. So by all means bring him round. At shall we say ten?'

Close to panic, the diplomat blurted: 'Wait! You misunderstand. He expects *you* to visit *him*. I promised him you'd be there.'

No longer smiling, Elisa said: 'Well, did you now? Found the woman who took your fancy – who you supposed might take the President's fancy – then promised him I'd be there. Not quite the behaviour I'd look for in a diplomat, Monsieur Brizuela. I see you have your hat and cane, so I'll just call the maid.' Then she tossed her head in a curt show of dismissal, and reached for a small engraved handbell on a table beside the couch.

'You will be paid one thousand francs.'

'Oh, will I?' Elisa queried. 'And for what, Monsieur? For the pleasure I'm to give your faceless master, or as recompense for your own high-handed ways? Malta. That was the ninth.'

'Two thousand francs.'

'Where is that silly maid? Young, but you'd think she was deaf.'

'All right, so you won't go there. But if Señor Lopez came here?'

'I've told you. I'll receive him at ten.'

'And your price?'

'Oh, really!' she snapped. 'Your vulgarity demeans you. Four thousand – *five* thousand francs, since I can now see your own career hangs by a thread. So five thousand francs, Monsieur le Chargé d'Affaires. And I don't much care whose pocket it happens to come from.'

He left, and snarled at the driver of the fiacre to get him back to the Champs Elysées damn quick. It enraged Brizuela to think that a woman like that – *La salope! La putain!* – could dare to make demands of *El Presidente*.

It enraged him, too, that she was right. It *was* his own career that hung by a thread. And his own silk-lined pocket.

He told Lopez the woman had proved difficult. 'She knows who you are, but has changed her mind and won't come. Give me half an hour – half an hour is all – and I'll find you someone else. Someone equally – '

'Won't come?' Lopez measured. 'And why won't she come, Brizuela? She's never seen me, so you must have put her off.'

'On the contrary, Señor – '

'First night in Paris, and the woman you say you've found for me won't come? Well, I tell you, my friend. I'm not one to be rejected, sight unseen! Whatever it is you've done, or failed to do, I intend to meet this lady you've so cleverly selected. Count on you, and the battle's lost before it's fought. But tonight – did you say at ten? – then at ten I'll fight my own damn battle and – By the way, how much do they charge, these days, in Paris?'

Juan José Brizuela bit down hard to conceal his anguish. 'I'll see it's taken care of, *Señor El Presidente*. Offer her a small gift if you wish to, but as for the rest, you may safely leave it to me.'

'Least you can do,' Lopez agreed. 'And I've no doubt you can afford it, the millions we've sent you.'

Alone in the mirrored room in the Rue du Helder, Elisa wondered if she'd overstepped the mark. Brizuela *had* been patronizing and vulgar, but why else was she here if not to profit from her beauty, and the skills of her body?

Would Marise Laurent-Perrone have ejected the Chargé d'Affaires of the Paraguayan Legation? Would other pretty young courtesans – and there were plenty – have refused to visit the future President of that South American nation?

Turning to one of the mirrors, Elisa murmured: 'This is not a game at which you excel, *ma fille*. Spit at the house you were offered in Rue de Sevigné? Turn down the chance to be escorted by a man of influence and wealth? The next thing you know, the bell will ring, and the Emperor of France will ask if he might enter, and you'll tell him no, you're running a bath drawn up from the new, gas-fired boiler, and you'd hate the water to go cold. Maybe tomorrow. Around eight, *Monsieur l'Empereur*? Can't fit you in before.'

The young woman threw up her hands, admitting her own imprudent ways. Then she glanced at the clock – nine forty-six, the hand hovering as it climbed – and jumped as the bell clanged in its bracket above the door.

Elisa sat where she'd sat for Brizuela, though now she was surprised to find herself genuinely intrigued. *As tall and sleek as the diplomat? Fifty years old and dressed like a banker? Or was he callow and blotchy, the President's son but a tongue-tied youth, his virginity intact?*

She'd forgotten to ask what Francisco Solano Lopez was like. He might not even be likeable.

Dressed in a low-cut gown, the skirt clinging close to the swell of her hips in what was the latest, though not yet fully accepted, fashion, Elisa Lynch waited to meet the visitor from Paraguay.

Then the maid knocked on the door, opened it and announced, 'Monsieur Lopez, Madame.' She edged aside and a figure loomed in the doorway and Elisa whispered: 'Dear God. He could kill me at a stroke.'

6

Descriptions varied. His enemies saw him as some slouching, swaying animal, unique of its kind. His friends thought him solid and muscular, a man respected by men. Many of his past thousand women had found him ugly and brutish, though others had screamed with joy beneath him, then wept to see him leave.

On some things they were agreed. He was a magnificent horseman, a true *caballero*, as comfortable in the saddle as he was cumbersome on the ground. Generous to those he liked, he nevertheless had a savage and ungovernable temper and could, in a moment, sever the friendship of a lifetime. He had done so many times, driving his erstwhile companions into exile.

It was also agreed – though a mile beyond earshot – that his adoration of the Great Napoleon often resulted in ludicrous mimicry, his hulking frame buttoned tight in uniforms rarely seen outside a circus. Proud of his abilities on horseback, and in bed, he was sublimely unaware that, dressed in full military regalia, he resembled more the ringmaster than the future master of his nation.

To his enemies he was nothing more than a beast, never yet trained to the table, and only truly happy when spurring a mount, or spurting his seed into a woman. Paris would have a field-day with him. The wind would carry the sound of mocking laughter across the ocean and a thousand miles inland to the Court of Paraguay . . .

Yet to his friends he was exactly what that nation needed. A man with unshakeable faith in the future of his country. Physically imposing, and sexually insatiable, he also possessed an extensive library of books in both Spanish and French. He wrote poetry – did his enemies know *that*? Did he wish them to? – and had already claimed he would one day raise the flag of Paraguay above the palace of Asunción, 'High enough for all South America to see!'

Much depended on who met him, and where, and if his temper was sweet or savage at the time. Only a fool would dare predict the reactions of the twenty-eight-year-old Francisco Solano Lopez.

Elisa guessed him to be her own height, if he took off his boots. Dark-skinned, and with eyes like olive stones, he had shoulders that bulged,

and wrists that threatened to split the cuffs of his uniform jacket –
for, yes, he'd dressed as the Commander-in-Chief of the Armed Forces
of Paraguay for his visit.

Designed with the help of reference books in his library, the uniform
dripped with braid, sagged with medals, strained against the insets
of yellow and blue and beige. The buttons that looked like gold were
indeed solid gold, for his country did not lack for gold.

The sword that hung in its tasselled scabbard was studded with
jewels, the weapon forged for Bernardo de Velazco y Huidobro,
President in 1809. The holstered pistol that couched his other hip
was loaded – common practice in Paraguay – yet only loaded now
because the customs officials at the mouth of the Seine had not dared
to challenge their visitor.

The left-hand pocket of his comically coloured jacket held a poem
he intended to read to the Emperor and Empress, once that imbecile
Brizuela had arranged an audience. The right-hand pocket contained
a gift for the courtesan in Rue du Helder. He'd be glad to get rid of
it, for it spoiled the line of his jacket.

He remained for a moment in the doorway, staring at the woman
on the couch. *And why not? Been forced to drive fifteen minutes to meet her,
so let's see if she's worth it. Insolent bitch. Thank her sweet skin she's in Paris,
and not back home.*

'So you sat on your shapely arse and wouldn't come, is that what
I hear?'

'Conversing in French, are we, *Maréchal* Lopez? Well, that's a
relief. I feared it might be Spanish.'

'I have never in my life . . . Not once in my life . . . I have *never*
been summoned by a woman . . .'

'Please be seated, *Maréchal*. There, where I can see you more
directly. Summoned? Well, maybe not. You don't look like the type
who would be. But on this occasion you were. Port or wine?'

Struggling to seize the initiative, he said: 'Either. Either or both.
Drinking never affects my – abilities. Do you know where it is,
Paraguay?'

'I knew it before your Chargé d'Affaires came to call. South of
Brazil and north of the Argentine. An inland country, though isn't
there a river . . . ? That said, what do you know about Ireland,
Maréchal Lopez?'

The man stretched his lips to show his strong, white teeth. 'It *is*
as well for you you're in Paris, Madame Lynch. Taunt me like this
at home – '

226

'And you'd what?' she said cheerfully. 'Drag me off to be whipped? To be tortured? To be shot? The way you're glaring, I'd anticipate all three!' Then she came to her feet and turned towards a brass-railed table filled with various bottles and glasses. Oh, no, she thought, not the long-stem glass for Lopez. He'd snap it like a matchstick. Give him this one. Heavy as the devil, but more of a size for his hand.

She filled it with blood red port, then watched him drink it like water.

'You know why I'm here,' he stated. 'You're not as stupid as Brizuela, are you? I don't have to spell things out?'

Elisa returned to the couch and murmured that certain things were writ clear, then gazed at the man and felt suddenly afraid. *I was right. He could kill me and not know he'd done it. The strength in those arms. The power in his shoulders. And, God, just look at his face. Broad lips, broken nose, cheekbones like girders. And eyes I think would stay open to watch his enemies flayed alive. If he's half the man he looks when he sheds his ridiculous uniform –*

'Here,' Lopez growled. 'Worn by one of the High Priests in my country long ago. But you probably know that, Madame Lynch, since you seem to know everything else.' Then he leaned from his chair and half handed, half tossed her the gift that had spoiled the line of his jacket, Elisa catching it more by luck than intention.

The ornament must have hung heavy on the High Priest's arm, though it might have added weight to the downward thrust of his knife . . .

Beautifully worked, it depicted demons grinning down as earthlings died. Terrible in its detail, it shone in the candlelight of the room with a dull but glorious glow.

Elisa guessed it to weigh as much as the heavy glass that had held his port. But the glass had come from a shop in Rue de Rivoli. And the glass was only glass, whereas the amulet was a half-pound's weight of deep, historic gold.

'Dear God,' she breathed, 'it must be worth millions. Whatever the currency, millions. What do I say – ?'

'You say nothing,' he told her, 'unless I tell you to do so.' Then he moved towards her and hauled her from the couch, forcing her from the salon.

The maidservant appeared in the hallway, squealed as the uniformed monster swept her aside, then gaped as he took her mistress upstairs, Elisa appearing to struggle, though not calling aloud for help.

*

227

Less caring than Xavier Quatrefages, and less loving than Régis de Broux, the son of the President made Elisa pay the price of the pagan gold. Made her do what he wanted. Made her suffer, and smile to be his victim. Listened hard as she cried out. Kissed her sometimes, then cursed her, no words of affection ever exchanged between them – *but with a lust as pagan as that amulet discovered in the Paraguayan jungle.*

They went far beyond the strictures of morality. Far beyond the confines of the law. The woman feared that Heaven must be watching, though the man seemed happy to let the Devil perch in witness. And for all her gasps, did the woman ever complain?

The truth was, no, she did not. Dragged down to unfathomable depths by the monster, Elisa felt her body lifted by his power, by his hunger, not caring if the Devil folded its scaly wings and peered down at them. So let it, let it hiss its instructions in Lopez' ear! Tell him anything! Make him do it! Make *him* make *me*!

She was woken next morning by the sound of Lopez stamping his feet into his boots. She found it difficult to move, her slender body aching, an incredible lassitude drugging her gaze.

'Must you go now, Francisco?'

'Business,' he told her. 'But you will come to my hotel at noon. We will have lunch there. Then you will help me choose carpets for the palace. In the evening we will go to – well, wherever it is Paris goes in the evening. But not the theatre. I loathe the theatre. We'll go somewhere and watch girls dance. Brizuela is bound to know – '

'Aren't you tired?'

'Not at all. A fine night.' He nodded and repeated: 'Yes, a fine night. I shall want you for myself, Elisa, is that understood? Whatever, ah, arrangements you might have must be terminated. It is Lopez now who offers you protection.' Then he bowed abruptly and left her, and Elisa Lynch felt her eyelids close on the day . . .

In the following weeks she learned that Francisco Lopez could be as violent on his feet as in her bed. Supremely confident as a lover, the man was less sure of himself in the salons and reception rooms of Paris. Or rather, his confidence there was misplaced.

For example, he insisted on wearing his ringmaster's uniforms. Eleven had been packed in a trunk aboard the *Tacauri*, each more risible than the last. Green conflicted with yellow; scarlet with pink; lavender with a variety of cinereous greys and blues. Tight in the sleeve, and even tighter across the chest, he wore them to show his respect for Napoleon Bonaparte, then glowered when the Parisians masked their sniggers behind their remarks.

'. . . My goodness, Monsieur Lopez, but you've brought a flash of colour to our drab little party, 'deed you have! And all those medals, for one so young!'

'. . . Tell me, sir, has your country been long at war? Accoutred as you are with sword and pistol. Or do you fear an assassin might seek you out?'

'. . . Let me see now. No, don't tell me. It's off to the west of Malta, am I right?'

As his enemies had claimed, the Parisians had a field-day. *'I mean, just look at the ape! Flat-lipped, and his knuckles near the floor! It really does make one wonder what God intended, entrusting monkeys with money . . . '*

Elisa sat quiet as he roared and bellowed, venting his fury. 'For all their airs and graces, what are they but a bunch of spineless, preening *parásitos*! Oh, they know their wines and their sickly damn pastries, but what do they know of the world beyond France? Do they even know there *is* one?' He slammed his fist on a table, splintering the rosewood. Almost making Elisa smile, he said: 'Look at that. Furniture's feeble as they are.'

She nodded but said nothing, preferring to let Francisco ride his anger back to the stable. Later, perhaps, she would tell him he'd made a sufficient impression with his uniforms, and how imposing he would look in a well-cut suit. But no, not tell him; never tell him. Francisco Lopez was not a man to be told.

A letter arrived from England, via diplomatic channels, bearing the seal of Her Britannic Majesty's Government. The Chargé d'Affaires hurried to deliver it to his master, reminding him of the fulsome request he, Brizuela, had made to Queen Victoria.

'As you'll remember, Excellency, I explained in detail our wish to purchase patrol boats, artillery pieces, uniforms and weapons for the Army. You read my letter when you arrived at the Legation.'

Lopez scowled. 'What's the matter with you, Brizuela? You think my memory fails me? That it needs to be refreshed? It was, to my mind, a sycophantic piece of work, so let's hope the English queen responds to flattery. Patrol boats that cleave the water, indeed. The most accurate rifles in the world. I've come to Europe to buy *matériel*, Brizuela, and to pay for it in gold. I am not here to cheer and clap hands.'

Then he broke the seal with his heavy thumb-nail and read the reply and handed it to Brizuela. 'Something I might have missed,' he said tonelessly. 'Read it to me aloud, *mi amigo.*'

The diplomat took the paper as if it might burn the prints from his fingers. Lopez did not look pleased.

'Her Majesty thanks you for your suggestion that a representative of Paraguay seek an audience at Court.

Her Majesty regrets, however, that prior commitments preclude a meeting in the foreseeable future.

The earliest date, should it be convenient to your representative, would be in the latter half of 1856.

Her Majesty's Government offers cordial greetings to the people of Paraguay.'

Brizuela stood rigid, his dark skin bleached by fear.

'And what date are we now?' Lopez measured. 'Just in case I care to wait?'

'The tenth of March,' the diplomat told him. 'But I regret to say, we're only in '54. *¡Es increíble!*'

'No it isn't. It's clear as day. I've been belittled by Paris society, and now snubbed by the Queen of England. And, as of this moment, my friend, *I am looking for someone to blame!*'

Things went no better for Lopez with Emperor Louis Napoleon and Empress Eugénie. They did, in fact, receive the future President of Paraguay in the Tuileries Palace, though he was one of three hundred and seventy guests that night, and the Emperor's handshake was limp. As for his wife, she addressed him as Señor Lorca and asked if the climate was temperate, in Peru.

It was all Francisco Lopez could stand. He punished Elisa Lynch with his love-making, then apologized by buying her pendants and brooches. He stood aloof as she chose them. He smiled as she kissed him, then told her he was leaving to visit Spain and Italy and the Kingdom of Sicily – and she should pack; she was coming with him.

'And after that? I mean, am I to continue paying rent on my apartment?'

'I thought I'd made it clear,' he confirmed. 'You will never again need the use of coins. Henceforth you will only need me.'

It was a firm invitation; a statement, coming from Lopez. But even now, with a wild, adventurous world spread before her, Elisa reverted to character, risking all as she said; 'And when you tire of me in the sheets? Find someone who's prettier? Someone who's younger? Am I to sell up my life for that?'

'You've missed the point,' the man exploded. 'Christ, do I have to explain things to you as I do to Brizuela? You're the only woman – and you'll never hear this again from my lips – the only woman I have ever seen as a friend . . .'

Then he shrugged and looked suddenly awkward, as far out of character as Elisa Lynch was in.

Well now, she thought, there's a vulnerability in this man you would not see in his face. None of the sculpted good looks of Lieutenant Chavelet, or the urbane charm of Régis de Broux. Awkward in his manner – and his manners – yet the only man I've ever met who dared tell me I was the only woman he could count on as a friend.

It's not why Brizuela chose me – far from it. But I really feel more flattered now to be acclaimed for my friendship than for the colour of my hair.

They travelled to Spain, where Brizuela's foolish letter to Queen Isabella rebounded on the visitors. Having told her that Spanish was the language of the Paraguayan Court, and that Spain and Paraguay were distant cousins, the diplomat had set ideas ticking in Isabella's head.

A feast and an exchange of gifts in her palace in Madrid, and the flirtatious young ruler asked Lopez if *his* distant country might not care to fly the flag of *hers*. 'Same language. Same religion. You could be our best-loved colony. And we'd help finance you, of course. Set up schools and that. Send you doctors. Teach you all kinds of things – '

Far down the table, Elisa saw Lopez rise to his feet, then heard him tell the Queen of Spain she could keep her schools and hospitals. *And* her money, for she'd yet to learn that Paraguay could buy up Spain and not even bother to enter the sum in the books.

'All you do here, so it seems to me, is sell each other fruit – and baskets in which to carry it! Spain control Paraguay? I doubt you could handle the branches lopped from our trees!'

The visits to Italy and Sicily calmed him down. He fell in love with Rome, and with the workmanship of her plate, insisting Elisa choose tableware for the palace in Asunción. 'I leave the designs to you,' he said. 'You'll know what's best to buy.'

'I'm not sure I will – '

'*Si, si.* You'll know. You've an eye for fine things, for doesn't beauty recognize beauty?'

She supposed that to be a compliment – of rarity value in itself, coming from Lopez – and they made their first tentative ventures along the shopping streets of the glorious Eternal City.

She was attracted to a finely-wrought set of cutlery – silver chased with gold – then blushed as she learned the price. Buy the knife alone, she thought, it'd keep an Irish family in food for a year.

Hesitantly, she walked back to where Lopez was loitering by the door.

'What I've found, *querido*, is very expensive, and you might not approve.'

'If the form and shape please you,' he said, shrugging, 'then I approve. But please don't speak to me again of prices. I have many worries in this world, Elisa, but money is not amongst them.'

Teasing him, and testing him perhaps, she said: 'Very well. Shall I ask the salesman for forty or fifty of each? And to throw in some ladles and – '

'No,' Lopez growled. 'You misunderstand. You will ask him for a thousand.'

Elisa blinked. 'A thousand separate pieces? But that's more – '

'A thousand separate settings, *mi mujer*. As many pieces as would comprise a thousand settings. And if they're not in stock, then tell him to have them made. We are buying for the future glory of my nation, don't you see that? Now off you go. Purchase all of it. And some velvet-lined boxes in which to keep the stuff.'

She returned in a daze to the salesman, told him what she wanted and watched him stagger. His hand shook as he listed the number of fish knives, meat knives, butter knives, cake knives; spoons for soup, for coffee, for dessert, for tea, for small pastries, for the skimming of soured cream. His nerve broke once and he gaped past her at the vividly dressed Solano. 'Are you sure, Signora? Are you sure he means – ?'

'Oh, yes, I'm quite sure he means it. And *has* the means, don't trouble your mind about that. Now where were we? The forks?'

When they left the shop, Lopez and Lynch had bought thirteen thousand seven hundred individual pieces of cutlery, each of gold ornamented silver, and at a cost that exceeded the freehold value of the shop itself. The utensils were paid for in coin from Lopez' travelling treasury, his only concern that Elisa seemed somewhat pale.

The foreigners moved on, Elisa emboldened now to point at something displayed in a window, Solano grunting yes, if she thought it was right, if it was appropriate, then yes. 'Well, don't look at *me*. I've the utmost trust in you, silly woman. If you judge it's what Paraguay needs, go in and buy it!'

All thoughts of Ireland now banished, Elisa indulged in a selective yet squandering dream. A glance to left or right, and she had the power to ensure a salesman's promotion, establish a shop's reputation, leave this one to the everyday customer, and triple the profits next door. It occurred to her that she was playing a man's game now – the man choosing his companion-of-the-hour from the various *filles de joie* who paraded their charms.

'This one,' she said. 'The colour might look well in Asunción. There's a shape to the tureen . . .'

'Then buy it. The entirety. All the bowls and dishes, lids and whatever. Ask them if they have tea-sets to match. Remember, *mi mujer*, the popular drink in my country is *yerba maté*.'

Elisa nodded, aware that this refreshing, intoxicant brew was something the Paraguayans exported – at considerable profit – to the neighbouring countries of South America.

Lopez waited for fifteen minutes, brazenly staring at the pretty young girls of Rome, then nodded as Elisa said, 'You now own one thousand cups, one thousand saucers, lids for each cup and two hundred pots in which to brew your infusion. The colour is basically beige, with a pattern of red. For the same price you could have bought a *palazzo* in the Tuscan hills.'

'And still can,' Lopez smiled. 'I could buy all Tuscany itself if I wished to, my dear. But today we're just shopping for tableware. Tuscany can wait.'

During their stay in Italy they purchased paintings and tapestries, statues of Carrara marble, ikons smuggled from Greece and the Peloponnese. They bought whatever took their fancy, paid for it in coin and had it sent back to the mouth of the Seine, to be stowed aboard the broad-beamed paddle steamer, *Tacauri*.

Solano Lopez rewarded Elisa with gifts he thought might please her, the innocent vulgarity of his tastes outweighed by the value of the presents. A solid gold miniature of the Colosseum. A life-size discus-thrower in bronze, though the statue crated before ever she

233

saw it. A knee-high replica of St Peter's, fashioned in marble and packed in straw – a souvenir of their visit.

Elisa bought Solano a single, silver goblet, engraved with the words '*El Presidente – La Irlandesa*'.

He thanked her for it, then left it somewhere to be lost. He was not yet the President of his country, and regarded the engraving as bad luck. When the time came, he would be *El Supremo*, and she *La Segunda*.

But, for the moment, he was merely Don Carlos Antonio's son, and Elisa his companion.

The King of Sicily awarded Lopez the Order of St Maurice and St Lazare. At Elisa's instigation he'd reluctantly stripped his uniform of the other rows of ribbons, the washing line of his own national medals.

For several months they loitered and lingered on the shores of the Mediterranean, a couple enjoying a honeymoon free from marriage. As a lover, Francisco never flagged, and in the daytime allowed himself to be guided by Elisa, the only woman he'd admit to as his friend.

Had she deserted him then – packed and strapped her bags and returned to France, or to Ireland, or gone to any other country in the world – the red-haired mistress would have taken with her a fortune in coins and sparkling stones.

She was rich enough to set herself up in business. Rich enough to live at ease for the rest of her life.

Others would have done so, Francisco Lopez maybe shrugging. But Elisa Lynch decided to stay, for it thrilled her to have him as a lover, and pleased her to protect her protector from the arrogant ways of Europe.

And it intrigued her to imagine what might be if she went with Lopez to Paraguay, and the man was measured for the uniform of President . . .

Shivering with cold, the couple mounted the gangplank and boarded the 480-ton *Tacauri* on the morning of 4th December 1854.

The vessel was laden down with the things they had bought.

Finding a pair of boots that fitted, Lopez had ordered thirty pairs in the same brown leather. And five tinted green. And five in red. And fifteen in black, for the evenings. Enough to see him through until his next visit.

Elisa could no longer remember what she'd bought – what she'd *accumulated* – during her time with Francisco. The capacious holds of the steamship were banked high with their rape of Europe, their priceless treasures stacked as ballast, the blades of the vessel churning low in the water.

Turning towards his friend on the afterdeck, Lopez asked: 'Now we're heading out to sea, might I ask you how you feel? Seeing the world you've known recede, and the rest of it come from the atlas?'

'Oh, don't worry,' she said, grinning. 'If I don't like where we're going, I'll study the atlas again.' Then she told him above the slap of the waves and the sigh of the wind: 'But I hope the page I've found is the one we want.'

A short while later, and the captain of the *Tacouri* reached up to pull on the greasy cord of the whistle. Passenger Craft Leaving Port.

PART FIVE

Asunción: 1855–1862

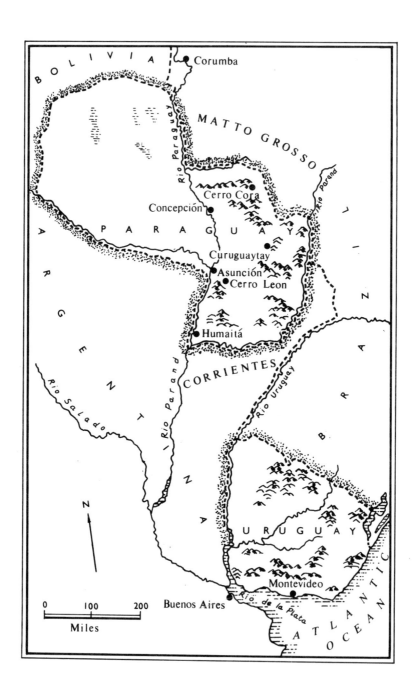

1

On the forty-third morning Francisco Solano Lopez said: 'There!' and gestured vaguely towards the west.

Standing beside him on the upper deck of the steamer, Elisa shaded her eyes with her hand, then shrugged. 'What is *there*? All I can see are whitecaps.'

'Yes,' Lopez told her. 'It's where the current meets the tide. We're approaching the mouth of the estuary.'

'Then where's the coast? I mean, if it's an estuary – '

'Oh, it is,' the man said, 'but we are not in Europe now, *mi mujer*. You will learn that things here are on a grander scale entirely. I read somewhere that those whitecaps, as you call them, extend to north and south for a hundred and sixty miles. My continent smiles wide to greet you, Madame Elisa.' The metaphor pleased him and he too smiled expansively, arms outstretched, facing the world they could not yet see.

The *Tacauri* churned onward, passing from salt water into fresh.

It had been a long and uncomfortable voyage from France to the Río de la Plata, the river of silver. The paddle steamer had been bucketed by a storm off the Azores; then an engine-room fire had left the ship without power for eighteen hours; then the ballast had shifted, killing one of the crewmen; then an epidemic of food poisoning had caused wholesale vomiting, Elisa among the victims. She prayed she would find life in Paraguay to her taste, for she had no desire to re-cross the Atlantic Ocean, none at all.

During the voyage, Solano – as she called him now – had talked to her of his country, its history, his family. As Elisa sat under an awning upwind of the three great smoke-stacks, her protector braced to keep his balance, he boasted of the life they would share in his paradise come to earth. 'It is a comparison often drawn,' Lopez told her. 'Para*guay* . . . Para*dise* . . . Even the poet Voltaire – '

'Voltaire visited your country?'

'He heard about it,' Lopez grunted. 'And what he heard inspired him.'

As the over-laden vessel had bludgeoned her way south, he'd

239

described in glowing detail the magnificent birds, eye-catching butter-flies, endless variety of plant life, every flower more brilliant than the last. 'The colours will fill your eyes,' he said. 'The sounds your ears. The scents your pretty nose. Europe will seem to you but a winter's night, *mi mujer*, when you've spent a summer's day in my wondrous country.'

'You mentioned your family, Solano. You were about to tell me more when we saw those fish jumping about, and went to the rail. I would like to know who I can count on as my friends. There's your father, Don Carlos Antonio – '

'And my mother, Doña Juana Pablo Carillo; my younger but first sister Inocencia; my younger brother Venancio; my second sister Rafaela; then my youngest brother Benigno. Of course they'll be your friends. I'll make good and damn sure they are.'

The sudden harshness in his voice had made Elisa blink. He'd told her nothing about his family during their months together in Europe, and now, aboard ship, she wondered if there might, after all, be a serpent in Solano's Garden of Eden, a worm in the family apple.

'Hard to imagine they would *not* be my friends.' She laughed. 'But better it was volunteered than conscripted, eh, Solano?'

He did not share the joke. All he said was: 'Better for *them*.'

On the forty-third evening the paddle wheels of the *Tacauri* churned in reverse, and the vessel lumbered sideways to the quay in Buenos Aires, the city of sweet air, a hundred and fifteen miles from the mouth of the Río de la Plata.

It was here that Elisa Alicia Lynch set foot, if somewhat unsteadily, on South American soil.

With a mixture of weariness and revulsion, she reminded herself that she was still nine hundred miles from her destination, the Para-guayan capital of Asunción. Weariness at the thought of another week aboard the steamer, revulsion because Buenos Aires belied its name. Drab and sprawling, the city-port of the Argentine Republic stank of fish and filth and – yes, that was it – rotted wood, the smell brought out, perhaps, by the fine summer drizzle.

Leaving Lopez to pay his respects to the Port Officials, she went back aboard, then sat in their private saloon and gazed through the rain-misted window at the few smears of light that marked the capital of the second largest nation in South America. Brazil, of course, was the greatest, but she doubted she'd ever have much to do with Brazil, far away to the north. Better just to get upriver to Solano's country, and the rainbow of sweet-scented flowers.

It was while she was sitting alone in the saloon that Elisa felt a sudden onrush of nausea, a clutching cramp in her stomach. Stooped with pain, she made her way to the primitive bathroom beside their cabin, and remained there for a while, whispering no, it can't be, I don't want it . . . *And worse, dear God, does he . . . ?*

Solano Lopez returned to the steamer with fury flaring in his eyes. Unaware that Elisa was pale and cramped, he recited his conversation with the Port Commandant, in which the Commandant had said this, and Lopez had said that, and the Commandant had sneered down his nose and informed his Excellency that a Paraguayan mail ship had caught fire and sunk in the port, and his Excellency might care to take the stranded passengers – *and* the mail – aboard the *Tacauri*.

'They're all the same, these Argentine bastards. Control the mouth of the river, and know it's our only exit to the sea, so they think they can treat Paraguay – '

'Solano . . .'

' – like some backward, backwater nation. Well, I tell you this. Each dog will have its day. God forbid, but my father will sometime die – '

'Solano . . . In those months we made love . . .'

' – and when that tragedy occurs, I, Francisco Solano Lopez, shall catch up the reins of my nation and show these *bastardos*, these *degenerados* – '

'Solano!' his mistress implored, one hand on her stomach, the other reaching towards him. 'Whatever your anger, I want you to summon a doctor. I need someone to tell me . . .'

'What?' he grunted. 'Need a doctor? What's the matter with you, woman?'

Gazing up at his blank, preoccupied stare, Elisa felt the waves of pain ebb away and said: 'Nothing. It can wait. The way it should be, perhaps. Give you your child at home . . .'

Never before had a vessel attempted to navigate the broad yet treacherous upper reaches of the Río de la Plata without the benefit of daylight. But the captain of the *Tacauri* was told to attempt it – attempt it and succeed, or be shot at the wheel if he failed – and the steamer left Buenos Aires at midnight on 16th January 1855, taking with her a confused Solano Lopez, his Irish mistress, thirty-two extra passengers from at least five countries, and the captain who had successfully navigated his ship across the Atlantic to Europe, then back to South America, yet knew if he hit a sandbar now he'd be executed by the President's son.

Female intuition told Elisa Lynch the pangs were but early warnings. It was true she felt tight in the clothes she had purchased in Paris, but her breasts were still neat, her stomach scarcely distended. Weeks, if not months, would pass before she gave birth to Solano's child, though it pleased her to know he'd reacted as he had – the man attentive to his woman, his *mujer* – and to hell with the sneering Commandant in the city of sweet air.

The captain of the *Tacauri* survived the night. He would later be promoted to Admiral, not caring that his fleet consisted of a number of fishing craft and mail packets, nor that Paraguay lay nine hundred miles upriver from the sea. Nor did he mind wearing the heavy, exaggerated uniforms issued to him by Lopez. It was enough that he'd somehow kept the steamer off the sand banks, and avoided a bullet in the brain.

The Río de la Plata forked. To the north lay Paraguay. To the south and west, Argentina. The river they were now ascending was the Río Paraná, with more than seven hundred miles still to go before Lopez would be home.

Elisa realized now that Solano had been selective in his lectures, omitting to tell her about the mosquitoes. Netting was draped over and around their bed and across the doorways, all but cocooning their quarters. Yet the high-pitched whine was everywhere, the insects attracted by the foreigner's smooth, fair skin.

He had omitted to tell her about the *yacarés*, the massive, tobacco-brown alligators that sprawled on the mud-flats, immobile and basking, then suddenly plunging forward, powering their way into the river, scaly tails lashing. She watched in horror as they snatched unwary water-fowl, or charged up the shallow banks to seize a small, spindly deer.

She saw water snakes, a squirming shoal of them, thin as her finger, but a thousand fingers entwined . . .

A combination of currents and shallows forced the *Tacauri* close to the western bank, where the smoke stacks brushed vine-strangled branches. The after deck resounded with a thump, crewmen were yelling, then running with hatchets and knives. Another snake, though this one as round as a fat man's thigh, and half the length of the steamer. Chopped dead, it took six men to lift the still-twitching body and throw it, like some great mottled hawser, into the swirling Río Paraná.

An instant later and the water boiled as the small predatory fish, the *piraña*, swarmed to strip the boa-constrictor to the bone. 'It's the blood,' Lopez told her. 'A mile away, they can taste blood in the water. Clever little devils, the *pirañas*. Sometimes, if we have to ford a river, and we know they're there, we'll shoot a *yacaré*, cut off its legs, then throw it back to be carried by the current. It attracts the *pirañas*, and then it's safe to cross. Otherwise – ' Then he grinned as Elisa turned away.

They passed the tributary of the Río Salado, then entered a one-hundred-mile-long lake. A strong, cool breeze from the south brought a few hours respite from the mosquitoes, and Elisa took the opportunity to see her new world by moonlight. Lopez stayed in the cabin that served as his study, signing papers, initialling reports, preparing to justify his fifteen-month absence from his homeland. His family would have heard about *La Irlandesa*, no question of that. The sleek Brizuela, the self-styled master of social gossip, would have slipped in a line here or there. But so what? A man had the right to choose his woman, did he not? And so long as Don Carlos Antonio approved, why care about the others? After all, Solano Lopez reminded himself, I am the second most powerful man in my glorious nation. And will one day be *El Primero*.

The steamer made its way slowly through the bright, silver-lit night, paddles scooping the water, dense vegetation silhouetted on the distant banks of the lake. Night birds whooped and cried, unseen creatures filling the air with guttural roars, piercing screams, chatterings and moans. A million creatures lived and died around her, and Elisa stood silent, allowing the sounds to come.

Well, she thought, he has so far kept his promise. A few more days – if the *yacarés* don't get me! – and we will be in his beloved Paraguay, his Para*dise* . . . His Garden of Eden, he the black-haired Adam, and I his red-haired Eve . . .

Or will he one day be what he dreams of being, the Emperor of a Unified South America, and I, perhaps, as his Empress? Quite an achievement for a colleen from County Cork . . .

What's that? A bird fallen on deck? God, but it does rain creatures around here. Enjoying the solitude and the breeze, she stepped forward,

243

intending to lift the bird from the shadows of the rail, then relaunch it towards the land.

Instead, as she stooped to collect it, she screamed as if to silence the jungle. For the bird was a dry and rustling vampire bat, its wings like tarred canvas, its teeth like needles, the blood-sucking nightmare that could scuttle along the ground, bite a sleeping man without the man ever waking, then drink and leave the wound open, quietly pumping.

Soldiers pounded in answer to her screams. The bat seemed to gather itself, foul face turned to the moon, then forced itself up and away from the deck, its night's work incomplete.

It was something else Solano had omitted from his lectures.

At dawn on the forty-eighth morning, he told her to put on her *peignoir* and accompany him to the bows. He rested a muscular arm around her shoulders and said: 'There. Over there. That's Asunción.'

Prepared in her mind for this moment, Elisa had wondered which word she would use to please him. She thought she might tell him it was splendid – breathtaking – awe-inspiring – magnificent – truly a wonder of the world.

But now the words drained like fine sand in her throat, and she viewed her future home in total silence. Paradise, it seemed, had been misplaced. Eden established elsewhere.

Seen from the boat, Asunción could claim but a single building that was more than one storey high. Pink and grey, it was the Presidential Palace, and soared to a height of, what? Twenty timid feet above the unpaved streets.

As for the streets, they led neither left nor right, but meandered round the contours of the sandstone hills, the houses constructed wherever space could be found. Buy a sackful of dice from a toy shop. Elisa decided, then dump them on an unmade bed, and there you have it – there you have Asunción.

Hovels spread away to the north and south; fishing nets stretched on bamboo poles along the mudbanks of the river. Canoes swung at their moorings. Birds flapped and chittered in the jungle to the east. The surface of the broad, brown Río Paraguay was torn by the scaly back of an alligator, the sinuous ripple of a snake.

Flags drooped in the humid air of the summer; dogs barked in the yards of the mud-brick houses.

Meanwhile, as in Buenos Aires, the ship's whistle shrilled and the

244

paddle wheels churned in reverse, and the steamer edged towards the quay.

It was now 21st January 1855.

Whatever her unspoken feelings, the twenty-year-old Elisa Alicia Lynch had reached the greatest destination of her life.

2

Who knows how, but Asunción was ready and waiting. Perhaps some tireless sailor had set out from the Río de la Plata, knowing he would earn a fortune if he could get there first and report the imminent arrival of the steamer. Perhaps the capital had been waiting for days, the troops drilled, then dismissed, the floral decorations changed each morning, the forty thousand inhabitants of Asunción ordered to assemble at dawn, then allowed home only at dusk. However the news had come, the city was prepared, and music followed the shrill of the steam-venting whistle.

Francisco Solano Lopez dressed in a Paris-tailored uniform, every awarded medal pinned to his chest. He was returning home as a man of authority – the son of his father – and not as some frock-coated businessman, in a toppling stovepipe hat. They could snigger all they liked, back there in Paris, but here, in Paraguay, he was the active commander of his nation's armed forces, and one did not smirk at the son of *El Presidente*.

Elisa dressed in a gown of lilac, with a dark blue cape, pale blue gloves, boots of blue tinted leather, a furled parasol to go with the gown, and a hat that conflicted nicely with her hair.

It was *meant* to conflict. *Intended* to make them stare. Carefully planned to show them she was different.

It was her first, enduring mistake.

She wanted to laugh at that dreadful, discordant band. Better, she thought, they should melt down their instruments and turn them into tableware. But Solano was nodding, evidently pleased by their dismal efforts, so she stood obediently beside him.

'The coaches are coming,' he said gravely. 'You will wait and I'll present you to my family.'

'Or them to me, my dear Solano.'

'Huh? Well, yes. Whichever.'

The crowd pretended to surge forward, and the soldiers pretended to hold them back. But it was clearly a pantomime, this welcome for Don Carlos Antonio's eldest son, and Elisa was forced to fight back the smile on her lips. *They really are but children. Excitable, noisy children. A bleat from a tinny trumpet and they'd be dancing around till dawn. I don't know if I could be Empress here, but I could surely run one of Miss Gardiner's Day Schools . . .*

A dozen of Lopez' soldiers in the lead, they went down the gangplank. The captain of the *Tacauri* was publicly commended for the way he'd performed his duties, and it was then that Solano Lopez murmured promotion was in the air. The captain bowed so deeply his hat fell off, though no one laughed.

Solano and Elisa crossed the cobbled Plaza de Palma, walking a traditional red carpet. But the red carpet here was more than something turned out by a mill, for this had been woven by hand. Depicting every flowering shrub in the country, and every bird – every garish parakeet – it was as fine a work of art as the Bayeux Tapestry, though just something the masters of Paraguay might walk on, scuffing it with their boots.

Ahead of them were three half-hooded coaches, the hoods of painted linen, braced with wood. Solano gestured to Elisa to stay behind him, then approached the first and peered above the door. Feeling isolated in the plaza, Elisa glanced round at the women of Asunción, the *Asuncenas*.

Dressed in shapeless white linen – the *tupoi* – they stared enraptured at the foreigner's wonderful clothes. A few of them dared to indicate things to their friends – what she wears on her feet – the *sombrilla* she carries – the colour of her hair, regard her hair, is she truly *pelirroja*? Is that how they are over there, the women; all their skins milky white and their hair the colour of hot embers?

'My father will greet you now,' Solano told her. 'And you will, please, kiss his hand.' Then he stepped aside and motioned her towards the low, closed door of the coach.

Don Carlos Antonio Lopez filled the seat. His body seemed to spread from puffy shoulders to bulbous buttocks, his face a balloon, the carriage filled with the suck and sigh of his breathing. He addressed Elisa in harsh, schoolboy French. 'So he bought you along with everything else from Paris, is that not so, Madame Lynch?'

'Brought me,' she corrected. 'He brought me here, yes, *Señor El Presidente*. But no, he didn't buy me.'

'He has plenty of other women,' Don Carlos expelled. 'You might not care to stay long. But so long as you amuse him . . .' Then he rapped with his cane and the coach lurched forward, Elisa stepping back smartly from the wheels, the President's hand unkissed.

*

After that, things continued to go badly for the foreigner.

She watched as Solano leaned into the second carriage, involved in a furious exchange with its occupants, three female voices competing to be heard. She did not understand the language – part Spanish, part native Guaraní – but the sense of it was clear. Solano wished to present her to his mother and sisters, and they did not wish to meet the *ramera Irlandesa* – his Irish whore, his Irish bitch.

'Then why in God's name did you come down here to the port?' Solano demanded.

'We wished to set eyes on her. See what game can be trapped in Europe. And now we've seen her. Pale as skinned fish. Clothes that only a dancer would wear. Or a high-priced *puta*.'

The coach was sent on, leaving Elisa to stand where she was, in the Plaza de Palma, and glimpse three black-gowned women, their ugly faces set in ugly expressions.

The third vehicle drew level, and she met Solano's brothers, Venancio and Benigno. For an instant she thought Venancio was a woman, a sister left over from the previous conveyance, for he trilled as he spoke, his hand pale and flabby, his skin kept clear of the sun.

She wondered if he might have had an accident, poor fellow, and that life had made him a eunuch. Such things could happen, after all . . . The scattering of the cards . . .

Benigno was different. As if making an effort to be different, the youngest brother was tight-jawed and unsmiling, his hand but linked bones, offered and snatched away. 'I believe you will bring my brother bad luck,' he told her. 'I do not see a halo of light, as you stand out there.'

'Oh, really?' Elisa challenged. 'Then shall I come round to the other side, Señor Benigno? Get the morning sun behind me? Blind you with my sweet, angelic appearance?'

Venancio shrilled with laughter and slapped Benigno with a soft, ineffectual paw. 'Asked for it, *mi hermano*! Asked for it, so you did!'

Once again the family carriage lurched away, and Elisa turned to Lopez to ask him what on earth she was supposed to do. The women refused to speak to her, and Benigno had already blighted her as back luck. 'You promised me I'd be welcome here. The great wide smile – '

'And so you are,' Lopez told her. 'You are welcomed by me. And no one, I assure you, *no one* will be long in saying different.' He stood there on the hand-woven carpet, quivering with anger, then escorted her to his quarters in the Palace, ignoring the well-rehearsed greetings of the crowd, and the ill-rehearsed playing of the band . . .

Elisa stayed less than a month in the Presidential Palace. It seemed that wherever she went in the crumbling, pink-washed building, she was confronted by the bleak stare of Solano's mother, Doña Juana Carillo de Lopez, or the sniffing, dismissive presence of her daughters.

It's like something from a fairy-tale, Elisa told herself. The wicked stepmother and the two hideous sisters. One day soon I'll be offered a bright, poisoned apple, or a foaming chalice. The situation is ridiculous.

Once again she asked Solano why the women disliked her so much. 'We've scarcely exchanged a hundred words. Doña Juana just sits there, glaring balefully at me, while Inocencia and Rafaela turn their heels and – '

'Understand,' he said. 'My mother is, well, why conceal the fact, she's of peasant stock, and deeply suspicious of foreigners. She does not differentiate between foreigners from abroad, or from a village a mile away from where she was born. She is narrow-minded, and unimaginative, and far too old to change. Ignore her, *mi mujer*. She'd find fault with the Madonna herself, as just another foreigner!'

'And your sisters?'

Lopez barked a laugh. 'You've seen them. With the best will in the world – *and* three bottles of fiery *caña* in my belly – I'd be hard put to call them attractive. They're not even plain. They're not even passable. They're stupid and ugly and – let's call them *infortunias*. They are jealous of you, Elisa, as a pebble might be jealous of a pearl. Ignore them, too. We'll marry them off in time. Once we've found a couple of suitable men who are blind!' He barked again, pleased by his own cruel humour. *Once we've found a couple of blind suitors* . . .

Elisa accepted Solano's explanation, and it was a while before she learned how convincingly he'd lied.

Oh, yes, Doña Juana was indeed of peasant stock, and with no space in her heart or head for foreigners. And her sweetly-named daughters were, face the truth, unfortunate in their appearance. But these limitations and handicaps had little to do with their attitude toward *La Irlandesa*.

They did not even mind that Solano had taken another mistress. After all, he'd left three behind when he'd set sail for Europe, and had already visited two of them on his return. Since manhood had first deepened his voice and put a swagger in his step, Francisco Solano Lopez had taken his women whenever and wherever he could find them.

But they had all been from Paraguay or the neighbouring nations. And when, one day, he married, he would surely marry one of South America's daughters, one of that Continent's own.

But to look at him now – the way he listened when Elisa spoke – stroked her hair with his powerful fingers – bellowed at their private jokes – turned to ask her advice – *ask advice of a woman?* – look at all that and the danger flags were flying, stiff in the wind.

Madre de Dios, but might Solano not sometime succumb totally to the spell of his red-haired *ramera*?

The family of the corpulent Carlos Antonio wrote their own fairy-tale, in which the Irish woman had come to bewitch the stocky Solano, blinding him with her raiment, seducing him with her body, enslaving him with her smile and whispered words. It would be the finish of Doña Juana Carillo, the end for poor Inocencia and the twitching Rafaela, exile or worse for the tight-jawed Benigno, the soft and flabby Venancio. None of them would dare resist Solano, least of all if Solano found the Irish witch irresistible.

Even so, the family managed to drive Elisa from the Palace.

Her protector chose a house in the Calle Independencia, a spacious, one-storey building he had for a long time admired. It belonged to an aristocratic family with ranches near Rosario and Villarrica, and it came as a shock when Solano sent them word that the house was for sale.

'First time I've heard of it,' the grandee retorted, and sent the messenger away. That evening, he chuckled over Solano's mistake, but his amusement was soon cut short by the intrusion of armed guards.

With due courtesy, the messenger repeated that the house in Calle Independencia *was* for sale, and the price would be so much, and the transfer of deeds tomorrow at eleven. And *El Mariscal* Francisco Solano Lopez sent his respects and salutations to the grandee and his family, hoping to meet them again in Rosario or Villarrica.

Then the guards ported their rifles, and the officer pinned back the flap of his holster, and a paper of agreement was laid on the table . . .

'So this is how it's done, is it?' the owner fumed. 'The way we conduct business with the Palace?'

The officer drew his pistol, held it up to the light as if to check it was clean and burnished, then murmured: 'What did I fail to hear you say, Señor? Did I fail to hear you speak against the Palace?'

Aware of his wife and children, the nobleman nodded. 'Yes. That's correct. You failed to hear me at all.' Then he leaned down to sign the paper of agreement, though he could scarcely recognize the shaky signature as his own.

Elisa exclaimed: 'But why would anyone wish to leave such fine stuff behind? I don't understand. Were they going abroad – ?'

'Very likely,' Lopez told her. 'Suddenly called abroad.'

'Well, I hope they won't miss it. I mean, look at the mirrors. The carpets. You wouldn't catch *me* abandoning such well-crafted furniture, that's for sure. It's a wonderland, Solano. How on earth did you – ?'

'Never mind that. Just install yourself here. You're far enough from the Palace not to be bothered by my family, yet near enough for me to come home of an evening.'

She smiled and said: 'Nearer than Cavan was to Adelaide, when he came back on the outside-car and up the steps and along the road to our house near Cork. I'm glad you'll be close. And I thank you for finding me such a splendid house as this.'

The man inclined his heavy head, brushing thick black hair from his eyes. 'It became available,' he growled. 'A palace to ourselves.'

And that was how she thought of it, her palace in the Calle Independencia. It delighted her to discover that a number of rooms were empty, and she used these to store the possessions they'd purchased in Europe.

Solano's suits and uniforms, and his seventy pairs of boots. His belts and embroidered epaulettes; boxes of buckles, boxes of buttons, boxes of straps and reins for his horses, boxes she'd never yet opened.

Her own hats and gowns, capes and tight-wrapped parasols, chests of shoes and trunks of silk underwear, most of it from France, but some from Spain, some from Italy, some from wherever they'd halted during their long, unmarried honeymoon.

A room for the cutlery and napery, the glasses and vases and bowls. Carefully stacked, there was space for the tea-sets, the coffee-sets, the statuettes in glass or marble, the clocks stuffed with wool – *but Solano would know of someone who could set the timepiece ticking.*

The *Tacauri* had transported a piano. Brilliant white, bearing eighteen coats of lacquer, it sat draped in a cloth, the first time such an instrument had ever been brought to Paraguay. Although she herself had never learned – the Lynches too poor in Cork; Elisa too busy running errands in St Merri; the desert winds too harsh to have such an instrument in Algiers – she had always hoped to furnish her rooms in Paris with a piano, and it pleased her to see it here now, with time for tuition and an attraction, she hoped, for any passing musician. Who knows? she thought. If Voltaire had written of Paraguay as Paradise, Hector Berlioz might one day find himself in Asunción.

She hefted a portfolio, tied with ribbons, then hid it away in secret. It contained fourteen double sheets of architectural plans, the layout and elevation of the Opera House, La Scala, Milan. Above it went the plans for the Comédie Française in Paris. And a bundle of pages she'd torn from journals and magazines; illustrations of this and that in the Old World, which she thought might be useful in the New.

Attractive though it was, this house in Calle Independencia, there was much to be done with the rest of Asunción. And all the more if Solano was to become its master. And thus the master of Paraguay.

Enjoying the house in which her protector had installed her, Elisa Lynch prepared to receive him in the evenings. It was rather like her time with Xavier Quatrefages. Like her time with Régis de Broux. But here it was altogether more exciting, what with netting over the windows, and the uncertain feeling that he'd force his way inward, advance upon her, like a returning warrior tearing his clothes to tear at hers.

She was pregnant, but aware that she need not yet deny him his advances. That would come later. For the moment she could allow Solano his way.

Three and a half months later the child was born and named Francisco, though called by its parents Pancho, Panchito, the one or sometimes the other.

Scurrilous rumours had already reached Elisa, claiming that Solano was the father of children here, children there, children in as many villages as a woman could be found. It was how Lopez was, and *La Irlandesa* had better resign herself to the fact. It might suit her to believe she was different, someone special, but let the President's insatiable son out of sight for even an hour . . .

Infuriated by these whispers, she confronted him. 'I imagine they slip from the tongues of Doña Juana, and your sisters. How you've mistresses in every town, every thatched *ramada*.'

'And you accept such stories as true?'

She waved aside the question, though noted the bluster in his voice. 'It does not matter if I believe them or not. They are common currency, Solano, and only you can change the coinage. How you behaved before you brought me here is none of my affair. But you are now the father of *my* child, and I will not be ridiculed by your family. Oh, I know your appetites are extravagant, and I'll admit you've added flavour to my own. I am also, I think, intelligent enough to see the foolishness of demanding your fidelity. You never *have* been faithful – well, have you? – so I doubt you'd change for me.'

'Now listen,' he blurted. 'You are the only true friend – '

'Maybe so,' she said wryly, 'but I've also heard that half your true friends are in exile. You could, Solano, teach fury to the devil, and that's another thing I doubt you'll ever control.' She faltered then, expecting the slap of his calloused hand, but something told her to move forward and, as she did so, Solano lowered his gaze like a freakish, penitent child.

'Very well, *mi mujer*. There will be no other women.'

'Now, for God's sake act your age! There will *always* be other women, and all I'm asking is that you behave with some discretion. I have no wish to be the object of Inocencia's twisted smile, or Rafaela's stupid grin. They would get rid of me quicker than a dog could bark, and each time you visit your mistresses I hear dogs.'

'I promise you – '

'Promise nothing,' Elisa advised him, then added: 'Well, yes, there *is* one thing you can promise me, *mi Mariscal*. That none of your other children will take precedence over Panchito. I would fight you tooth and nail if I thought that might happen. And much like yourself, Solano, the Irish are sharp in both!'

Thoroughly cowed, the all-powerful Lopez asked if he might see the infant, and lift it from its cot. Elisa said no, the child was alseep. He could hold the boy tomorrow.

'Tomorrow then,' Lopez accepted. 'That's what I'll do. Hold young Panchito tomorrow.'

3

The time Don Carlos Antonio's son had spent in Europe had inspired him with ways to make Asunción more than the huddle of one-storey dwellings that it was. In the letters he'd sent home to his father, Solano had enthused about the railway system that was spreading its web around Paris. 'It is something unknown in all the South American continent. Neither Brazil nor Argentina possess such means of communication. No one does. So Paraguay could be first!'

Elisa had spoken to him of the respect his nation would enjoy if foreign performers could be invited – *thus her folio of architectural plans; thus her piano.* Taking the idea as his own, Lopez suggested as much to the President. 'We can afford these things, heaven knows! A railway line (I'm enclosing some illustrations of a train). And imposing buildings. A theatre for example. And uniforms for the Army.'

True to his nature, Solano Lopez enclosed a great many sketches of uniforms for the Army . . .

Bridges in Spain instilled in him the desire to span the Río Paraguay. Palaces in Italy showed that a great deal could be done to embellish the drab pink Palace in Asunción. And the city streets of Europe set him thinking about roads – cobbled roads, paved roads, none of which existed in his homeland.

On those rare occasions when he'd left Elisa alone in the hotel in the Champs Elysées, he'd visited factories, consulted engineers, compiled a list of those who might be willing to help his country rise to full glory.

Paris had sniggered happily in her ignorance of Paraguay, so Lopez appealed to his father to open diplomatic channels with the Government of North America, and with all the European nations. And, reluctantly, Great Britain.

Reluctantly, because Solano Lopez still chafed at the way Queen Victoria had snubbed him. But, it had to be admitted, England and Scotland produced fine engineers, and were part of the most powerful empire on earth.

The bulbous and breathless President Carlos Antonio read the letters, and pondered over their contents. Of his three sons, Solano was the most violent, the most volatile, in every way the most dangerous. Yet Venancio was little more than a *capón*, gelded by nature, whereas Benigno twisted his bony fingers and viewed the world with cynical dislike. No matter what his spiteful, pecking womenfolk said about Solano's red-haired *ramera*, the thirty-year-old *mariscal* was the only hope for the future.

So if Solano asked for railways and bridges, artillery pieces and weapons and gunboats, a place for people to act in – damn foolish idea – and suggested chopping stones into cobbles, then laying them down as a road – well, so be it, *¿por qué non?* And it might be interesting to meet the *Norteamericanos*, the *Ingléses*. One could always listen, then take them down to the river bank and shoot them and leave the rest of it to the fish.

The first few foreigners arrived in September, the end of the Paraguayan winter. The President and Solano welcomed the *extranjeros* for what they could do for the country, Elisa for the chance to converse in English.

Among the arrivals was a specialist in railway engineering, George Edward Thompson; a Scottish surgeon who had served in the Crimea, Dr William Stewart; the distinguished American diplomat, and now Ambassador to Paraguay, Charles Ames Washburn; then a Hungarian adventurer-cum-military adviser, the Baron Enrique von Wisner de Morgenstern.

These were followed by the French Minister Cochelet and his wife; the Hon. Edward Thornton from Britain; then by ministers from Portugal, Spain and Brazil. The increasing presence of a Corps Diplomatique in the capital convinced Solano that Paraguay was right to throw open her doors and windows to the world. Although marked in every atlas, the country would now be truly on the map.

Unnoticed among the influx of foreigners was a detachment of American Marines. They had travelled from Fort Deering in Kansas via the Gulf of Mexico and along the north-eastern seaboard of Brazil, then south to Buenos Aires. They were to serve eighteen months in what the soldiers called Para Gay.

Elisa found it hard not to smile when George Edward Thompson addressed her. Stiff as a cast-iron fence rail, and with his narrow face framed by thick, bushy sideburns, he spoke from beneath a moustache a parakeet might nest in. The only thing clipped about the engineer was his voice.

She would know him for years, and would entertain an amused affection for him. But it was not until the end – the very end – that she would call him anything but Mr Thompson.

She was less sure about the Scotsman, Surgeon Stewart. There was something cunning – *would the Scots say canny?* – about him, though in time she would learn to trust him. And regret that she had done so.

As for the American Ambassador, he had all the courteous attributes of a Southerner, and the quick-witted skills of a man lifted high in the Union. He was bright, easy company, was Charlie Washburn, though clever enough to give Solano Lopez the best lines.

Yet the man who fascinated her most was the six-foot-four Hungarian, his name part Spanish, part Austrian, part Jewish; his voice the most seductive she'd ever heard. The perfect European, von Wisner was the only one of the four who might have beckoned Elisa astray. Until, that is, he had asked if she knew of a place in Asunción where he might find himself a youngster. 'Someone lithe, slim-hipped, who'd tolerate an old man like me. Do you know of a place like that, Madame Lynch, where the handsome boys go?'

She laughed with surprise and said yes, then warned him to guard his wallet.

'Please do not be offended, Madame Lynch. All ships have weak seams somewhere, do they not?'

'Indeed they do, Monsieur le Baron. And it's best to know where they are.'

Others arrived, their passage paid by Paraguay.

November saw the presence in the capital of a strutting, flamboyant Spaniard whom Solano had met in Madrid. His name was Ildefonso Barmejo, a self-acclaimed actor, novelist, playwright and poet, an artist and architect, designer of dreams, and the man who would, so he said, ensure Asunción's glorious future.

Elisa thought the man a charlatan, wrapped and ribboned, but Solano had decided otherwise. 'I forgive him the fact that he's Spanish. He clearly seeks fresh horizons, does Señor Barmejo, and I believe he'll bring great advantage to our nation.'

'Well, I think he seeks fresh coins,' Elisa told him. 'And is looking for somewhere to act in his own frothy plays.'

'If that's so, then I shall dismiss him. But I intend to give him a chance.'

So Ildefonso Barmejo joined the other arrivals, bringing with him his wife, Doña Pura.

And it was then that Elisa Lynch acknowledged some seams could never be caulked, each human vessel vulnerable to the inrush of spite or disapproval.

Having heard that Elisa had been a courtesan in Paris, and was now but one of Solano's many mistresses, Doñ Pura Barmejo refused to visit the house in Calle Independencia, cementing instead a friendship with the strait-laced Madame Cochelet. Certain standards must be adhered to, after all. And one did *not* frequent the haunts of easy women.

Aware that she had once again antagonized her own sex, Elisa bottled her anger and tapped in the cork. It was a vintage emotion. It would keep . . .

Ildefonso told the President and his son what was wrong with their quaint, yet ill-planned city. He told them in flowery reports, and on guided tours, pointing out defects here, errors there, listing a catalogue of mistakes.

Solano listened, his staff taking notes, while Don Carlos filled the seat of his carriage and wheezed.

It was a wonder to Elisa that Barmejo was not taken away and garrotted. Tied to a chair as practice for Solano's lancers. Shot dead right there in the street. But the charlatan seemed sublimely unaware of the dangers he ran, and his masters continued to nod and wheeze assent.

Ildefonso was appointed Architect in Chief. Creative Director of the Arts. Superintendent of Education. Editor of the nation's weekly newspaper, *El Semenario*.

Elisa was tempted to ask Solano if Señor Barmejo should not, perhaps, be made Governor of the National Treasury – just to see what Solano would say.

But the risk was too great. It might happen.

Meanwhile, Doña Pura bathed in the scented waters of her husband's popularity. She met Elisa at diplomatic gatherings and ignored her, her eye always caught by someone else, in another part of the room. Madame Cochelet played along, never there long enough to exchange a word with Solano's *fille de joie*.

Corked and kept cool, Elisa's vintage emotion gathered a coating of red, sandstone dust . . .

*

257

Ildefonso returned from a trip upriver to say he'd found the ideal place for the President's Summer Palace. The area he'd chosen had been staked out with flags, and it would make a pleasant trip for the ladies – an outing on the Río Paraguay.

The men would stay behind, talking roads and railways, banking and business, though the Admiral of the Fleet would give up his Sunday to command the blunt-prowed packet.

Madame Cochelet was to be the Guest of Honour. Señora Barmejo the Principal Lady. Elisa Lynch the Hostess, representing the Independent Republic of Paraguay.

'Which means what?' she asked her protector. 'Do I pin a corsage of flowers to their billowing chests? Show them to their seats on deck? Hand around the menus? Damn it all, Solano, should not *I* be the Guest of Honour? I tell you – '

'Now be calm,' he growled. 'Titles are unimportant. Just enjoy the day, then tell me about it later. It's a question of politics, *mi mujer*. Something you and I both have to learn about.'

Just twenty-one years old, Elisa's eyes flashed, then dimmed in obedience, aware that Solano was right. 'The Irish do many things well,' she said. 'But greasing the wheels of politics – ?'

The steamer flapped and fluttered with bunting, and special awnings had been erected to shield the passengers from the sun. Feathered fans were issued to the ladies as they made their way aboard, smartly-dressed crewmen directing them to where tables bore pitchers of night-cooled cordials alongside dishes of sweet, crisp biscuits.

Elisa greeted the diplomats' wives and daughter. Brazil stopped to admire her gown, Portugal to ask if the young Panchito was well, America to whisper a joke that made Elisa hold the rail in helpless laughter. Spain showed her approval for the way the steamer had been dressed, Great Britain for the smartness of the crew. Italy embraced her, and she was beginning to think things might go well after all when Madame Cochelet swept past, snatching her fan and striding away on deck.

Well, she accepted, so France – the country I love – does not love me. At least, not as represented by the Minister's buttoned-up wife.

Then Señora Barmejo came aboard and did the same, turning away as she passed Elisa, and hurrying after the distaff representative of France.

The Admiral tugged a fanfare on the whistle, and the picnic-boat drummed upriver.

Elisa Lynch stayed where she was, near the rail, wondering how best to offer herself to Cochelet and Barmejo. *A lesson in politics? Do what I said to Solano, and act like a waitress? Flatter them both and smile as they insult me? Play the hostess, but borrow an apron from the galley?*

Several miles of the Río Paraguay had slipped past before Elisa made her decision. But the swirl of the muddy waters seemed to calm her, and she told herself Solano would be proud of her humility; his woman was prepared to learn the game. Win over Madame Cochelet and Señora Barmejo, and two more wheels would be greased . . .

So she edged alongside the starboard rail, then past the wheelhouse, and stepped on to the narrow, shaded foredeck. All right, so without an apron, but willing to serve . . .

There she saw Madame Cochelet and Señora Barmejo laughing together at the head of the V-shaped setting – and the chair that might have been Elisa's tossed behind them – and heard the wife of the French Minister in Asunción saying, and saying it stridently, 'This will be an experience for my memoirs, ladies. To be the Guest of Honour of our sell-what-she-can-get-for-it courtesan!'

Señora Barmejo led the laughter. 'Oh, wouldn't it though! And from Ireland! What can young Solano be thinking about? And please, for my memoirs, too?'

Unseen by the guests, Elisa withdrew. As she backed away she heard other remarks, a further exchange between the two who so much disliked her. '. . . Not that a man would complain about her figure . . . But to bring his *petite putain* out here . . . And allow her to bear his brat . . . I mean, really . . . Oh, it's destined for my memoirs.'

As the steamer chugged sedately against the current, Elisa returned at the head of a line of uniformed waiters, each man bearing a silver-domed salver. She noticed that most of the guests looked embarrassed, though Cochelet and Barmejo smiled in welcome.

Moving between the open V of the tables, Elisa said: 'You might think yourselves spoiled today, Señoras, Mesdames. We've brought you fresh-killed boar and succulent beef; fish from the river and tender birds plucked from the trees. All the vegetables and fruits of our wondrous summer. Then cakes and sugared nuts and – wait, though. It's time to lift the covers.'

The guests leaned forward, anticipating the banquet. A meal like this on the river, and doubtless with wines kept chilled in their lead-lined containers, it was heaven. It was, without question, a sort of paradise.

259

Turning, Elisa Lynch directed the servants to stand in line, near the rail, and raise the lids of the salvers so her guests could fully appreciate the aroma of the food.

Then she told them to throw the whole lot overboard. 'I mean, now! Do it now! Covers and contents – all of it into the river! I want to see your hands empty! I want to know we've all wasted our time with this meal!'

Silver glinted as the carving knives and forks and dishes and domes were sent spinning in the air, a fortune lost in heavy, polished plate, tureens tossed out with their lids and ladles, sauce-boats and cruets scarcely making a splash in the water.

Then she turned again and re-entered the empty V of the tables and levelled her gaze at Cochelet and Barmejo.

'The breeze must have carried your voices. I heard something about your memoirs, and a sell-what-she-can-get-for-it courtesan. A woman come from Ireland. A *petite putain*. A little bitch.

'But I might also write *my* memoirs one day, should life grant me the time. And when you read them, you'll understand why I said I never served cats at my table. Whether on land, or water, *I never served cats!*'

She left the party dumb and gaping, and made her way to the wheelhouse.

'Don't worry,' she told the Admiral. 'I've seen to it there's food for you and the crew. And you won't be held responsible for what happened.'

'Viewed it all from up here,' the man muttered. 'Heard what they had to say. Ask me, Madame Lynch, I'd have kept the food aboard and tossed *them* two over, though you've no need to tell Señor Lopez.'

'How much longer until we reach the President's Summer Palace?'

'Two hours more upstream,' the Admiral informed her, 'then maybe another three back. But the passengers'll be pretty hungry – '

'Yes, won't they?' Elisa agreed. 'But let's give them their outing anyway.'

Back in Asunción, she recounted the incident to Solano. She feared a sudden display of rage, but he was smiling as he asked her to tell him again – the part where the meal had gone overboard and the guests had been left gaping – 'Tell me again.'

'I find it hard to be diplomatic when the woman of Francisco Solano Lopez is being insulted. Perhaps I should have pretended not to hear.'

'You did well,' he grunted. Then, echoing the Admiral's senti-
ments: 'Had I been there I'd have tipped the women in the river
with the dishes. Anyway, I've been told Ildefonso Barmejo's not
an architect at all. And an *un*published poet. And an *un*performed
playwright. And the closest he's ever come to a newspaper was to
buy one in the street. I've given him twelve hours to leave Asunción,
or be hanged in the Plaza de Palma.'

'It'd probably be his greatest achievement,' Elisa say wryly. 'Draw
an audience at last.'

Whilst claiming to be unskilled in diplomacy, she nevertheless con-
solidated her triumph by inviting the native-born aristocracy to a
spectacular, day-long banquet, this time dressing as the *Asuncenas*
dressed. By midnight, with torches flaring and music in the air, she
had won them over.

Madame Cochelet had been silenced. Señora Barmejo had
departed. Only the President's wife and daughters continued to glare
at Solano's foreign mistress. But even they could now feel the wind
of the future in their face.

4

Having dealt with the women, *La Irlandesa* gained the approval of the men. She showed an interest in Mr Thompson's plans for a railway; drew the dour Dr Stewart on the subject of medicine, all but promising him his own hospital; spent easy evenings with the American Ambassador, Charlie Washburn, and others with the towering Hungarian, von Wisner.

If offered refreshment, the engineer Thompson took tea, but tea from India.

The doctor preferred whisky, and allowed himself a rare smile when Elisa said the *Tacauri* had brought a crate of it, purchased in Paris, but imported from Scotland. The man sipped it and solemnly nodded approval.

The American, always genial, would have whatever was going, then one day presented Elisa with a gallon jug of bourbon. 'You might care to keep it around for me, Madame Lynch. And if you entertain any other Americans, forget you've got it, okay? Love of one's fellow countryman has its limits.'

The Hungarian adventurer was also one for tea, but his the slightly intoxicant *yerba maté*, the ubiquitous weed of Paraguay. Exported throughout South America, it ranked with tobacco and hard woods as a profitable, trouble-free crop. Gifts from God, Lopez insisted. The plants of Para*dise*.

The self-styled architect Barmejo was replaced by others who could prove they knew their job. Funds were released from the National Treasury, and Solano Lopez allowed the designers full reign. Under George Edward Thompson's supervision, a railway station was commissioned. Under Dr Stewart's, a hospital. Under von Wisner's, a barracks and arsenal, with preliminary sketches for a series of forts along the banks of the Río Paraguay.

Elisa wanted her Opera House and theatre. The corpulent President dreamed of a fine new palace, twice the size and four times the height . . . The State required fresh offices, better grouped and more imposing . . . The Church demanded a cathedral, vaulted and with stained-glass windows, an organ loft, choir stalls, comfortable seats for the ruling family, carved wooden pews for at least a thousand others . . .

Elisa added a library to her list of needs.

Solano told his father it was time the port was dredged, the quays extended, a dozen storage sheds constructed, cranes set on tramlines. And, as the centrepiece of the complex, an *Aduana*, a customs house manned by officers in uniforms he would design.

The wheezing Don Carlos Antonio agreed to everything, and the intended renewal of Asunción began . . .

Two things prevented the realization of Paraguay's dreams; ignorance and tradition.

With no building except the original palace more than one-storey high, and with the work force comprising those who were light enough to scramble round the rickety bamboo scaffolding – *boys under ten* – the New Asunción could only be built with what the boys could carry. Sun-baked, sandstone bricks.

The architects insisted on quarried stone. The Europeans pounded their fists into their palms, warning Lopez that the dream would turn to a nightmare. Good God, did he think Paris was a city of straw and red mud? Did he seriously believe it had been constructed by dwarfs on bamboo ladders? Do it properly, or leave the bricks to dissolve, and send the children home!

But Solano would not be awoken from his dream. The railway station was taking shape – lacking only the line to serve it – and the Government offices were already fifteen feet high, though as yet with only the beams to keep the walls stable.

Several hundred hovels had been razed to make room for the cathedral, and Elisa's theatre, and the intended six-storey palace. A start had been made, and Francisco Solano Lopez would not see it stopped.

The work was painfully slow. The experts from Europe attempted to communicate with a labour force of illiterate, half-starved juveniles, the materials limited to what Paraguay had always used, the methods Paraguay knew.

Children fell from the scaffolding, drowned in their attempts to dredge the port, collapsed in the heat, or perished in the cold.

Elisa asked Solano to bring men across from Ireland. 'It would serve two purposes, don't you see? Save the Irish from starvation, and give you the strength you need. Send the *Tacauri* to fetch them – '

'Oh, yes? And then what? Find they lay their hands on our women

263

so that half next year's offspring speak Irish? You just leave things to me, *mi mujer*. And tell Thompson to stop complaining, or I'll send him downriver. Him and the others, all of them.' He stared at her then, not leaving until she nodded and said as he wished it.

A year after the birth of Panchito, she bore Solano Lopez a daughter. Named in memory of Elisa's sister – *Corina* – and her mother – *Adelaida* – the infant died suddenly in 1857. Elisa blamed her death on the noise and filth and drifting dust of the so-called New Asunción, and told Lopez to find her a house outside the city.

He did so without complaint, and more than sixty child-labourers were sent by wagon to the outlying district of La Recoleta, there to build a country house for Madame Lynch. Working closely with the architect, she insisted he design a low, airy dwelling, complete with patios and inner courtyards. In full agreement, the architect married the best of Spain to the best of South America, and not a single boy was killed or injured during the construction of the *quinta*.

Meanwhile, insecure walls rose higher in the city. The mud bricks perched, unstable, or teetered in the wind. Thompson and von Wisner consulted other Europeans, aware that it was now the season of the hot, moist wind from the north – *el viento del asesino* – the murderer's wind.

It came twice and nothing happened. Then it came again, bearing hailstones the size of small onions, and the walls of the palace crumbled and ran to mud. The unroofed railway station collapsed, as did an entire corner of the customs house. The north wall of the Government offices subsided, bringing down the crossbeams. The cathedral sank into a glutinous, brown flowing river, its finely carved pews installed too early, and now smashed by the force of the storm.

The morning light showed a city in ruins. Asunción was worse now than when the hovels had clung to the sides of its sandstone hummocks.

A fortune and children's lives expended for nothing.

It was then that *El Presidente* summoned his eldest son. Before long the country would learn of the farcical tragedy. Mutterings of discontent would be heard, sparks of anger fanned to flame by those who opposed Don Carlos and his brood.

'It's time to tell them,' the old man wheezed. 'Time to tell them what you and I have long suspected.'

Frowning at the vast, sprawled figure, Solano Lopez said: 'And what's that? I do not clearly understand, *mi padre*. Since when do we tell them anything?'

Don Carlos bared his horrible, rotted teeth. 'Be bright, my son. We tell them about our enemies. How Argentina gnaws at us from the south, whilst Brazil chips away in the north. We allow the peasants their indignation, but direct it away from Asunción. Permit them their gatherings, yet turn their worthless heads towards our borders. If they want something to whine about, we'll give them the looming shadows of our neighbours. You must realize, *hijo mio*, the mass of the people are quite stupid. All people. Everywhere. They seek someone to blame for their miseries, and don't much care who it is. So we'll given them Brazil and the other one.'

'Tell them we've been invaded?' Solano queried. 'But that isn't the case – '

'Be bright,' the President repeated. 'Did I say we were yet at war? I said tell them the wolves are howling along the borders. Instruct the Hungarian, what's his name, von Wisner – yes, well instruct him to start work on the fortifications beside the river. Form a new regiment. Call it after yourself, if you wish. Just be sure word reaches all those who would march against us.' He coughed and breathed painfully, then pointed a fleshy finger at his son. 'It's the way to handle the people, don't you see that? Stifle their threats with a greater threat of our own. What's a rat in the storeroom, when the wolves might be in the yard?'

It did not seem to matter to Don Carlos Antonio Lopez that *he* was the one the peasants would think of as the rat.

When the mud of the tracks had hardened again, detachments of cavalry were sent out to spread the warning – the nation was being menaced. For the moment each man should stand firm, though volunteers might soon be required for a Regiment of National Defence. *El Presidente* was in daily contact with responsible elements in Brazil and Argentina, and prayed the dispute would be quickly, peaceably resolved. His beloved people must know that Paraguay was envied for the Paradise it was. So would God Himself not protect the country He'd chosen as His Eden?

The message had the desired effect. Frightened of imminent invasion by the South American giants, the populace forgot the drowning of Asunción.

In her flower-bedecked *quinta* near La Recoleta, Elisa felt the swell

265

of another child. Pleasing Solano, she gave him a second son and, by mutual agreement, they named him Enrique Venancio: Enrique after the boy's godfather, Elisa's friend and Solano's military adviser, the Baron Enrique von Wisner de Morgenstern; Venancio as a gesture of respect towards the Lopez family, fat and shrill and feminine though Solano's brother was.

A year had passed since the death of Corina Adelaida. It was now late summer 1858, and von Wisner had been busy supervising the construction of a fortress on the bluffs at Humaitá, close to the Argentine border. Gun emplacements dominated the river, iron sheets slipped between alternate thicknesses of brick. Watchtowers of woven cane swayed in the wind, the ground beneath them a network of trenches and bunkers, field kitchens and earth-roofed dormitories, ammunition stores and a long, pre-dug pit, in which to bury those who died resisting the giant.

Thus fiction was accepted as fact, and Humaitá stood ready to blow the enemy out of the waters of the Río Paraguay . . .

Argentine patrols reported back to Buenos Aires, where President Bartolomé Mitre and his advisers wondered if the Lopez family were flexing their muscles, prior to curling their hands into fists . . .

'I cannot believe them so insane as to attack us,' Don Bartolomé dismissed. 'For what reason would they do so? Does a parrot attack an eagle? Just keep an eye on them. They're probably playing at soldiers.'

Von Wisner returned to Asunción, then rode the few miles east to La Recoleta. He left his male companion – a quite extraordinarily handsome youth – in the capital and settled down for an evening with Madame Lynch. She had long accepted his predilections, knowing that each man's needs were different. Von Wisner remained a loyal and trusted friend, so why probe further?

'Are your children well, the boy and the baby? I found a woman near Humaitá who makes good shawls. You might care to toss them on their beds, come winter.'

A glance was enough to show her he'd dictated his demands, for the shawls he gave her portrayed the house at La Recoleta, and were sewn with small gold coins around the edges. She jumped to her feet and embraced him, the erstwhile courtesan *always* delighted by presents.

'And you, Baron Enrique? Have you finished with your fortress?'

'Well,' he murmured, his voice deep and mellifluous, 'I won't claim

266

it will last a hundred years. But, yes, it should give an invader pause for thought.'

'How soon do you think that'll be? Solano says it could come tomorrow, or in six months time – '

'As lightning could strike.' Von Wisner shrugged. 'But I, myself, have seen no evidence of aggression by our neighbour. And must ask if perhaps Don Carlos has been somewhat hasty. I'd rather you did not repeat what I say, but I don't see there's much to fear. Not yet. Not if Paraguay goes quietly about her business.'

Elisa nodded. 'Why would anyone wish to attack us? To steal our *quebracho* wood? Our tobacco? Our *yerba maté*? It seems senseless, and yet . . . The President is convinced it will happen.'

'Another thing not to repeat,' von Wisner said quietly. 'But Don Carlos will not be with us for ever. When he finally loosens his grip, *El Mariscal* will take over and, God willing, less suspicious views will prevail. Now, any chance of some tea, to go with this thin cigar?'

Elisa jerked a tasselled cord that led through rings below the ceiling, then told a servant to bring a fresh infusion of the *maté*. When the servant had gone, she smiled at the Hungarian and said: 'I meant to ask you. Do you still frequent those bars where the young – ?'

'Lord, no!' he exclaimed. 'I'm an old married man now, did you not know? In a manner of speaking, that is. His name's Fulgencio Baleriano Something y Something. An Adonis, my dear Elisa. An absolute Adonis.'

'Smoke your cigar,' she encouraged. 'Your hands are beginning to tremble.'

5

Gradually, as Don Carlos had intended, fears of invasion receded. The garrison at Humaitá was disbanded, the Regiment of National Defence never formed. The President had achieved his aim, deflecting the peasants' anger from Asunción, and they were now back on their farms or in their fields. They forgot about the ill-conceived renewal of the capital, preoccupied – as farmers everywhere – with their livestock, their crops, the seasons.

Yet both Don Carlos and Solano were determined that a new Asunción *would* arise from the rotted planks and mud bricks of the old. And in part, at least, they took Elisa's advice.

Refusing to ship labourers from Ireland, they brought them instead from their poorer neighbours, Bolivia and Uruguay. Skilled draughtsmen came from Brazil and the Argentine. Europe contributed sculptors and stone masons, the Lopez family now prepared to break with tradition. Whatever the building – palace or parade ground, cathedral or *casa* – it would be constructed of limestone, of granite, of marble. The work would be undertaken by men, not boys, and this time, whatever the weather, the structures would stand.

George Edward Thompson got his railway. It ran on a single track from Asunción to Paraguarí, forty-five miles to the east. It took six hours to complete the one-way journey and served little purpose, though would some day reach the larger, provincial town of Villarrica. But Mr Thompson's achievement elevated the clipped-voiced Englishman to the status of National Hero, *for Paraguay was the first South American country to possess such a means of transport* . . .

Don Carlos was now so obese that he had to be wheeled up a ramp to his compartment. Solano and Elisa joined him for the inaugural run. Benigno and his mother, Doña Juana, sat in another carriage, away from *La Irlandesa*. The capon Venancio and his sisters refused to come, deeming it far too dangerous.

It reminded Elisa of her trip with Xavier Quatrefages from the Place de l'Europe to Le Pecq, almost ten years earlier. But she did not mention this to Solano. The way he was pounding the sides of the velvet-lined wagon, this train was the first in all the world.

*

Cranes were erected to handle the stones that were brought by barges upriver. Quarries were mined in the regions of Paraguarí and Cordillera. The workforce from Bolivia and Uruguay cut tens of thousands of cobbles, and these were hammered into the streets of the new Asunción.

Dr Stewart got his hospital, with airy wards for those who could pay, and sixty-bed barracks for those who could not. In the first year he operated successfully on more than one hundred patients. Though three times as many died under the Scotsman's knife.

The Baron Enrique von Wisner de Morgenstern was granted a Military Academy, complete with a firing-range and subterranean arsenal – and unlimited funds for field-pieces and infantry weapons, his rank now second only to Francisco Solano Lopez.

Solano knew him for what he was, this towering, middle-aged Hungarian. Intelligent and intellectual. A man for the boys. Elisa's closest friend.

At other times, Solano would have dealt harshly with a *pederasto*; held him up to ridicule, or simply had him shot. But von Wisner was more than just a man beckoned aside by catamites. He was an accomplished military adviser. Amusing company. And safe to leave with Elisa.

Better for von Wisner that he *was* what he was, or his grey-haired head might topple with the weight of a bullet.

The President grew ever more gross.

Elisa Lynch gave Solano two more sons.

In return she got her theatre, a second *quinta* – in the hills above the mosquitoes – then a riverboat named *Irlanda*. A piano teacher was brought from Buenos Aires, a piano *tuner* brought with him. She found she had a natural aptitude for the instrument, and serenaded Ambassador Washburn and Mr Thompson and Dr Stewart and Baron von Wisner with tunes they recognized as their own.

Actors were offered unlimited fees to come from Europe and North America. Dancers too, and choirs, for whom a thirty-room hotel was built, overlooking the Río Paraguay.

She asked Solano if she was being extravagant. 'You allow me whatever I want, *querido*, but I've no wish to dig too deep in your country's purse. You must tell me – '

'Oh, I'll do better than that one day,' he promised. 'I'll take you to the Treasury and show you. Not yet. But one day soon.'

*

Now fluent in Spanish, and with a command of the native Guaraní, Elisa Lynch enjoyed her life as never before. She had no rivals, no female enemies, no errands to run as in the market of St Merri, no pompous men to make up to as in Rue Hautefeuille, no single thing she could not, if she wished to, do.

Well, yes. There was one.

Whatever Solano's views about fidelity, only insanity could make her be unfaithful. But that was all right – she had no intention of risking her future for the sake of another man. She had friends now, and authority, and was liked and respected, even loved.

The mother of five children – *though on Heaven's breast lies Corina Adelaida* – she was twenty-six years old, the favourite mistress of Francisco Solano Lopez, and who could ever be a more satisfying man than that powerful, unhandsome creature?

Madness alone could move her hips, and rock the boat. *'And listen, how many women are given riverboats of their own?'*

Shrouded by mosquito nets, Solano and Elisa were asleep in their room in the *quinta* near La Recoleta when a timid knock on the door became more urgent.

'Don Francisco . . . ? Señor Lopéz . . . ? Are you awake, Señor? I must permit myself to enter. Forgive me the intrusion, but . . .'

Solano rolled on his heavy shoulders, slid his forefinger into the trigger-guard of the pistol that always lay where he could find it, then levelled the barrel at the doorway and said: 'Enter.'

Elisa stirred beside him, asking: 'What? Is it dawn already?'

Aware of the handgun, the messenger blurted: 'From the Palace, *mi Mariscal*! I've ridden out from the Palace!'

'To tell me what?'

'To tell you he's going to God, *mi Mariscal*. Your father. May Heaven rain gently on us all. But *El Presidente – El Supremo –* he's fading fast . . .'

Fully awake now, Elisa said: 'Go and see him. And don't forget what we talked about before. You will need both keys.'

They dragged aside the shrouds of netting, Solano barking at the messenger to have a carriage ready and waiting outside. The man gasped yes and fled to the outer courtyard, knowing he'd not last long if he fumbled, no matter how much gentle rain might fall from Heaven.

Two hours later, Francisco Solano Lopez was in the overcrowded bedchamber, pushing his way past his mother, his sisters, his brothers, priests and clerics. The dying man gazed blankly as Solano loomed close. Then his bulbous chest heaved once, and he sighed the single word, 'You . . .', his breath malodorous in the room. His head flopped on the splendid, lace-trimmed pillow, and the reign of eighteen years was finally over.

Doña Juana wailed, chorused by her daughters. Venancio wept noisily as the priests intoned.

Benigno and Solano exchanged a glance of mutual distrust, the youngest brother's expression saying no, you would not dare, and Solano's saying would I not, *mi hermano*? Watch close, and you will see.

He strode to the ante-room where the government officials shuffled uncertainly, then told them what Elisa had said to him in their bed in the *quinta*. 'Don Carlos is dead. You will give me the keys. *Both* sets of keys. You will give them to me now.'

'But Señor!' they appealed. 'These things will happen later. The formalities must be observed, *excelencia*. It is not the moment – '

'You make me repeat myself. *The keys.*'

The flustered officials turned for help to Justice Lescano, the old man giving himself away as he clutched a weak, veined hand to his belt. His voice quavering, he said: 'It is true, Señor Lopez. There are many formalities – '

'And here's the first. You will – formally – surrender the keys.'

The enfeebled Lescano made one final attempt. 'The people will not approve of these methods, Don Francisco. Take it from me – '

'It's the keys I want from you, *magistrado* – that's better – thank you. Now return to your homes. The Congress will be convened later.'

He left them to mutter among themselves and walked through the Palace and out on to the steps, his progress suddenly halted by the sight of fifty armed men, Don Carlos' personal bodyguard. He thought to salute them, then gazed at what seemed to him the menacing angle of their rifles.

Oh, my God, he gaped, they are here to cut me down! Terror froze his bowels and he backed away, edging towards the shelter of the pillars.

Frantic ideas came to mind – *Promise money! Assure them of instant promotion! Grant each of them land in the Chaco!*

Award them something! Anything! Promise them anything, or you'll die . . .

271

Some fifteen abreast, the bodyguard advanced as if closing in on a target.

Francisco Solano Lopez heard himself whisper: 'Wait . . . You must understand . . . The death was natural . . . I was in no way involved, believe me . . . My father – '

Then a voice that carried better than his struck the bodyguards from the rear. 'You see him? You see your new leader? Now raise your rifles and salute *El Presidente!*'

Lopez watched in bewilderment as Elisa Lynch came striding through the ranks, the bodyguards unsettled by her presence, and by the snapped-out authority of her tone.

With this single, positive intrusion, the woman turned Don Carlos Antonio's troops into Francisco Solano's obedient defenders, the blast of their rifles spewing smoke and flame into the air as she reached the head of the steps and embraced her lover.

'Are we sure he's dead?' she asked. 'Don Antonio?'

'Yes, he's dead.'

'And you have both the keys?'

'They're here – '

'Then that's fine. We can see what's in the Paraguayan purse.'

Convinced his life had been saved by *La Irlandesa*, Solano Lopez could only sag against one of the pillars and tell her yes, they could visit the vaults any time they chose.

The next twelve hours did more to cement Elisa's position as Solano's trusted adviser than all the nine years they'd been together. Not only had the woman forced her way between the bodyguards and stood with him on the steps of the Palace, but she now took control of a situation that left Lopez strangely subdued.

Terrified by the soldiers, he found it hard to accept that the Dictator, his father, had finally agreed with God to die. It was not a thing Don Carlos Antonio would do. Don Carlos Antonio was immortal, and if immortals died, what chance for their issue, their sons?

Solano Lopez wept on Elisa's shoulder, then was gently shrugged aside.

'Now, listen,' she murmured. 'We are, I think, at a crucial moment in the history of this nation. *Your* nation, *querido*. So listen and tell me what you think.'

The powerful, dark-haired man nodded and said yes, he would listen, then leaned towards her again, rocking her slender body with the muscular bulk of his own. 'So tell me . . . I was never truly prepared for Don Carlos to die . . .'

Remembering her own father and others, Elisa said: 'All men die. It's what happens. Now stand away and listen.

'The first thing you must do, *querido*, is put troops on the streets and seal off the city. Then place the Baron von Wisner in charge of the arsenal. Then confine your brother Benigno to one of the family properties, far in the interior. He'll make trouble if he stays here, and trouble's to be avoided.

'You will further ensure that Justice Lescano is kept *incommunicado*, lest he bleats about the formalities of inheritance.'

'You seem to know more than most,' Lopez murmured. 'You seem better primed than any of us, *mi mujer*.'

His mistress shrugged the comment aside, and told him to send his other brother, the corpulent Venancio, to a trade mission abroad.

'And Don Carlos' will? Are my brothers to know of its contents? Is his widow to know? His daughters? Is there anyone – ?'

'No, not really,' his mistress told him. 'Only you, Solano – and me.'

The last word seemed to lodge in his mind, as a tap on the shoulder might leave the discolouring of a bruise . . .

Elisa made a further suggestion, hinting that Solano might care to announce it in the Congress.

The idea appealed to him and, on 16th October 1862, Don Carlos' successor *El Jefe Supremo y General de los Exercitos de la Republica del Paraguay*, Francisco Solano Lopez, told the Assembly he had a personal word to add.

'I wish due respect to be paid to one who has, from the very first, served as my counsellor, and my friend. Henceforth, it will please me to know that Madame Elisa Alicia Lynch is accorded the status and privileges normally reserved for the wife of a Head of State.' Raking the hall of the *Cabildo* with his gaze, he said: 'I make this statement without fear of contradiction. Though you are, of course, free to speak.'

But the only sounds came from his mother and his sisters, the three women gasping as they recognized they had been publicly stripped of their influence and power, rank and prestige. And that *La Irlandesa* had taken her leisurely, lasting revenge.

Nowhere in Paraguay was a gold mine to be found, nor a shallow-running river in which prospectors could pan for ore. Argentina had her fabled seams, and Brazil her long-lost mountains, pure and yellow. But Paraguay had none of these, her wealth derived from the more commonplace products of tea and tobacco and timber.

So it left Solano and Elisa blinking when the candles flared in the vaults of the National Treasury. Seventy feet long, and with the curvature of its ceilings supported by limestone pillars, the forty-foot wide vault contained rack above rack and shelf over shelf of gold coins, gold ingots, hawsers and chains of gold. Kept hidden, even from his children, the breathless and corpulent Don Carlos Antonio had played Midas in secret, transmuting the profits of Paraguay into the world's most valued metal.

It was impossible even to estimate the wealth of their landlocked republic. But the contents of the vault went beyond mere estimation. All that mattered was the dull glow that surrounded them, towered beside them, faced them wherever they turned. Richer than France? Richer than Great Britain? Richer than all of Europe?

Feeble comparisons. *They were richer than Croesus*.

Notwithstanding that she was now the First Lady in the Republic, Elisa refused to live in the Palace. Solano begged her to do so, commanded her to do so, told her he'd have her *quintas* burned to the ground.

'No, you won't.' She smiled. 'You'll do what's best for us both, and for your nation. You'll keep me here, at La Recoleta, then bring me to the Palace when it suits you. But you will *not* upset the sensibilities of our neighbours, or North America, or Europe, by parading a woman to whom you are not yet married.'

'I wrote to the Pope,' he said quickly. 'You know that, don't you? To ask His Holiness for an annulment – '

'You've written several times, as I remember, *querido*. But we've not yet had a reply.'

'There's another thing I could do,' Solano measured. 'Send some men to find this one-time husband, this Xavier Quatrefages, and – '

'And what? Have him killed? My weary military vet – you'd have him murdered? Do that, my dear, and I'd poison your next glass of *caña*! Oh, no. We'll just go along as we are. Man and woman. Husband and wife can come later. As can other, grander titles, if so we choose. But for now . . . Well, for now we shall see you established as *El Primero*. And I *La Segunda*, but in private.'

As so many times before, he could see the wisdom of her advice.

And what was five miles on the road he'd had laid between the Palace and La Recoleta – a cobbled strip that only he and she had the right to use?

In December, one of the hottest months of the Paraguayan summer, the genial American Ambassador, Charles Ames Washburn, welcomed the arrival in Asunción of a tall, quiet-spoken Bostonian, Captain Elmore Cornelius Curtin. The thirty-year-old officer brought with him four Marine troopers, less than a quarter the number Washburn had asked for.

Too accomplished a diplomat to let his feelings show, the Ambassador was nevertheless shocked by what he saw, for every man bore the scars of battle, living proof of the Civil War that now tore their homeland apart.

Although walking without the aid of a stick, Captain Curtin limped, favouring a shrapnel-torn right leg. One of his troopers was minus a thumb, another partially deafened, a third with a shattered wrist encased in a broad leather bracelet. The fourth had suffered phosphorus burns, his right eye covered by a crude, piratical patch.

It was the Union's way of telling Ambassador Washburn that he could have some of the replacements he'd requested, but must make do with war-damaged stock . . .

As long ago as July 1861, word had reached Asunción that the American Civil War had erupted in earnest. Led by South Carolina, the southern states of Alabama, Mississippi, Florida, Georgia, Texas and Louisiana had seceded from the Union, unwilling to liberate their much needed workforce of negro slaves.

The North, commanded by the angular, almost emaciated President Abraham Lincoln, native son of Kentucky, demanded the abolition of slavery, so that under the Constitution all men should be free.

The South saw no advantage in releasing 3,000,000 workers, declared themselves the Confederate States of America and elected a President of their own. Ironically, their choice was the angular, almost emaciated Jefferson Davis, native son of Kentucky . . .

The first shots of the Civil War were fired at Fort Sumter, a Union stronghold near Charleston, South Carolina. The bombardment lasted for the better part of thirty-six hours. The Union commander was forced to surrender and the Confederate flag was raised above the fort. Not a single member of the garrison was killed, the South enjoying a bloodless victory, the North determined to bring the rebels into line.

The Confederate States were soon joined by North Carolina, Virginia, Tennessee and Arkansas. The Union took comfort in the fact that they could count on the loyalty of 18,000,000 people, more than twice the population of the South.

Naval strength lay with the North, as did ninety per cent of industrial output, sixty per cent of the railway network, most of the munitions dumps, most of the stocks of fuel, of foodstuffs, of minerals and metals. Statistically, the States of the Union had every advantage over the South. Except that the newly-formed Confederacy was *there*, entrenched and determined – *'Come and get us!'*

Meanwhile, some five thousand miles away in Asunción, Ambassador Washburn's problem had also been one of statistics, though on a somewhat smaller scale.

Of his thirty strong detachment of Marines, eighteen were from the Union, twelve from the Confederacy, and these twelve now *de facto* enemies of the Government.

Barrack beds had already been shifted, the Northerners at one end, the Rebels at the other. Fist fights had broken out, and it was soon apparent that the Southerners would only stand guard with fellow secessionists, the Unionists with their brethren from the North.

Washburn discussed the situation with Surgeon Stewart, the engineer Thompson, the military adviser Baron von Wisner. He spoke to the British Minister Thornton, then to the other European diplomats, and sifted their advice.

'What the hell am I to do with them, these twelve? They've been damn good troopers, and I surely can't arrest them. Intern them here in Asunción? Commit them to a Paraguayan gaol? There *wasn't* a war when they came out here. But they're hotheads, all of 'em, and it won't be long before fists turn to firing.'

His friends and fellow diplomats voiced their opinions, but it was left to Ambassador Washburn to reach a decision.

Summoning the twelve Marines from the Rebel States, he asked if they would be prepared to serve Lincoln's Government of the Union. All of them respectfully said no. They'd been born in the South, and their place was now with the Confederate States of America. They hoped Ambassador Washburn could understand that.

'I suppose I can' – he sighed – 'so here's what I'll do. I'll relieve you of your weapons, then put you aboard a ship bound for Miami.

276

After all, Florida's one of your states, but you'll be far from the scene of action. What you do after that is up to you. If you'll take my advice, you'll keep out of the war. But you won't, of course. You'll join the first Southern regiment you can find.'

The troopers said nothing, sparing him their agreement. But they all knew it was exactly what they'd do – search out a recruiting officer on the dock, then hope to be sent to the front.

Ambassador Washburn's report was dispatched to Washington, requesting replacements. None arrived, and the war turned ever more bloody. Of the eighteen Union Marines in Asunción, seven deserted, hoping to find their own way back to North America.

Charlie Washburn sent other requests, all of them ignored, and it was not until December 1862 that Captain Elmore Curtin limped down the gangway of a packet-boat and led his damaged stock to the American Embassy.

He was placed in command of fifteen men, illness and injury reducing the turnout to ten. The weather was hot and humid, the insects ferocious, Captain Curtin unhappy to be where he was, and awaiting his recall to the States. He had already fired off a dozen letters to those he hoped might help him, pleading to be returned to his country, and to action.

Did the fact that his leg was stiff mean he couldn't ride a horse? Did the shards of shrapnel in his thigh mean he could neither give nor take orders? For God's sake, was he finished at thirty, lurching a little as he walked?

His nation at war with itself, Elmore Curtin saw nothing attractive about this dank and steaming Dictatorship, alive with its spiders and scorpions, hornets like birds, its brilliant, repulsive flowers.

From the moment of his arrival, he wanted to leave this gaudy, stinking, perfumed backwater place. Until, on 25th December, the Ambassador and his Captain of Marines were invited to enjoy a seasonal glass of bourbon at the home of Madame Elisa Alicia Lynch, in her *quinta* at La Recoleta.

After which, Elmore Curtin changed his mind.

277

PART SIX

La Recoleta: 1863–1865

1

Hot and humid, the Murderer's Wind blew from the north, torment-
ing the men who rode in the hooded Embassy carriage. Their dark
suits seemed to encase them, constricting their movements, and they
tugged at their cuffs, fingered the tight linen collars of their shirts.

Christmas in Paraguay, Curtin thought morosely. Come down *here*
to distribute presents, St Nicholas'd lose half his reindeers to the
heat. Drop dead himself, most likely, stifled in his heavy, red wool
robe.

The officer glanced at Washburn, happy to see that the normally
genial diplomat was also squirming in discomfort. 'Warm for the
time of year.' Curtin grinned. 'Not much chance of meeting carollers
in the snow, eh, Mister Ambassador?'

'I can do without your humour, Captain Curtin,' Washburn huffed.
'If humour was intended. You'd do better to think cool thoughts, my
young friend, and straighten your cravat. It amuses you to see me
dampened by this bloody awful weather, though you're pretty damn
dishevelled yourself, if you want to know.'

The men lapsed into silence, turning aside to breathe through their
mouths, the five-mile road to the *quinta* seeming like fifty.

The tall, soft-spoken Bostonian wondered what he'd find there.
His hostess, from what he'd heard, was the archetypal Irish beauty
– *all russet hair and emerald eyes, the kind a fellow could find for himself in
Boston.* Truth to tell, they were as common as beer, in Boston. Very
Irish, most of Boston. A marketable commodity up there, red hair
from the Isle of Erin . . .

And the place to be at Christmas, that's for sure. All the snow you
could shovel. Candles in the windows. Garlands on the trees. The
bite of winter in your throat and those fine fat flakes of snow drifting
lazily –

'We're here,' Washburn told him, then scowled to see the young
man dry and relaxed. How had he managed that? Taken the advice
and thought himself cool?

The carriage dipped to a halt before the *quinta*. Seniority preceding,
the American Ambassador alighted and showed his ability to rally.
He settled his stovepipe hat, whisked a handkerchief around his jaw,

adjusted the cuffs of his shirt and beamed at his hostess. He was once again the cheerful, courteous diplomat, his frock-coat seeming to lose its creases, his high, starched collar stiffened as if by magic, no bead of sweat on his hair.

'And how have you been, my dear Elisa? I could do without this wind, but – well, it's what we expect for the season.'

'I don't know how you manage it.' She grinned. 'I've no doubt your drawers are damp, Charlie, though you surely wouldn't tell me if they were. Yet here you are, cool as a lettuce. Mind over matter, is that it, Charlie Washburn? Government mind over tropical matter?'

He smiled at this woman he liked, then said: 'May I present – where is he? Ah, yes – Captain Elmore Curtin, Officer of Marines, a welcome presence on the compound.'

Curtin fought to disguise his limp, measuring his step so his left boot hit the ground just so, his right hand raised to remove the hat he'd put on for the sake of removing it.

'Madame Lynch . . . Captain Elmore Curtin, Officer of – '

'So I hear. Welcome to La Recoleta, Captain Curtin. Welcome to a room equipped with a clever, machine-driven fan. And to a tight-sealed bottle of bourbon, your tastes not too changed, I hope, since you came to Paraguay.'

She'd prepared this little speech for Washburn's companion, whoever he was, and delivered it well until almost the final phrase. But by then Elisa Lynch had seen Curtin for himself. A young man whose appearance made her falter with pleasure, her gaze returned by his own.

'Yes,' she said. 'Well, now. See if the fan's still working. Break that seal.'

The officer stared and said nothing.

Washburn edged smoothly to jab him hard in the ribs, then followed Solano's mistress into the house.

The overhead fan had been installed by the English engineer, Mr Thompson. The Captain of Marines admired it, as he admired the furnishings and decor of the room. Then he finally overrode Washburn's warning cough and said: 'But it's you who sets a visitor at ease, Madame Lynch. Leastways, does it for this fellow, come from the States.'

Invited for perhaps an hour, they stayed for three. The Ambassador sipped his bourbon and watched, aware that Elisa was much taken by Elmore Curtin, and the officer quite clearly smitten by her. The two talked of music, of horses, of historical biographies. They grinned in agreement, leaned forward if their views failed to coincide, planted grains for the future and harvested the present.

'There's some fine land to ride on around here,' Elisa said. 'When your duties permit, you might care to escort me; teach me your American ways.'

'I'd be pleased to, Madame Lynch, though don't count on me to know the tricks of Paraguay. But certainly as your escort, yes, with pleasure.'

They discussed something else, came forward in their chairs and doubled over with laughter. Washburn turned to study a Renaissance painting on the wall, his left hand raised to diminish the sound of their easy enjoyment.

Well, here we have it, he sighed. They couldn't send me an ugly, bull-nosed officer – oh, no. They had to send me *this* one, who knows all about historical-damn-biographies and has more than his share of looks. I hope to God he falls off his horse, is all, else a match might be struck, and Charles Ames Washburn accused of supplying the matchbox . . .

Still given to bouts of jealousy, *El Jefe Supremo* was uncharacteristically tolerant, not minding that his mistress and the Marine rode together on the estate that surrounded the *quinta*. They were accompanied by outriders, after all, and these men would soon tell him if the American was incorrect in his behaviour. A single report would put Solano on his guard. A second would see Captain Curtin on the next packet-boat downriver.

Elisa might well have asked herself why Solano allowed the young officer such latitude . . . Had *El Presidente* found yet another young girl, a *concubina* he kept in a house near the Palace? Was his tolerance of Elmore Curtin a way of assuaging his conscience?

Then she laughed and thought, Solano troubled by guilt? And do tomcats have feathers?

Curtin's duties at the Embassy were light, though he was forced to remind the Union troopers they were as much on American soil, here in the compound, as in their own native states. 'You wish to return and fight for the Army of the North. So do I. But the Government we have sworn to obey has sent us here, and here we will stay until our tour is over. Or Washington recalls us.'

Yes, he accepted, I have indeed changed my mind.

The more time they spent together, the more Elisa and Curtin felt the warmth of companionship spark another kind of flame. It was dangerous, and they dampened it, though the outriders must have noticed how close they rode along the bridle paths that bisected the orchards, *La Irlandesa* and *El Norteamericano*.

It fell to Elisa's oldest friend and confident, the Baron Enrique von Wisner de Morgenstern, to ask if, by chance, she'd heard the rumours.

Alone with him in one of the salons that opened on to a vine-shaded inner courtyard at La Recoleta, water bubbling from a small, central fountain, Elisa smiled gently, then asked him to move his chair. 'Whenever we're together, Enrique, I find myself downwind of your damn cigars. I don't mind at all that you smoke them, but I've no wish to sit with watering eyes – That's better. Now start again. Rumours about what? That I chatter with Captain Curtin? I tell you, the air's as thick with rumours as your smoke.'

'No, it's nothing to do with our handsome young Marine. And don't worry, I won't compete for him. Remember, I've Fulgencio Baleriano.'

'Well, that's a relief.' She grinned. '*Viva Fulgencio!*' Then she sat back in one of the fine, embroidered chairs she'd brought from Europe, and waited for the aristocratic adventurer to expound upon this particular vaporous rumour.

The towering Hungarian took his time. He knew that Solano Lopez was not the only one to possess a fiery temper. Elisa Lynch could be just as volatile, if and when she chose.

He began by explaining that Paraguay was never better positioned than now to establish herself as the centrepiece of a unified South America. As he carefully outlined the topic, Elisa yawned.

'For pity's sake, my dear Enrique. I'm as steeped in history as you are. I hear it night and day from Solano. Why else do you think we have portraits of Napoleon Bonaparte in half the rooms in the house? I *know* how Solano feels about uniting South America. So just tell me the rumours, then I'll tell you about my plans for a *bal masqué* on the plain outside Asunción. For myself, I intend to go as the goddess Diana. Solano will be – well, who else! – the Emperor Bonaparte. I've got you down as – '

'Later,' the avuncular von Wisner murmured. 'Let's talk of that later. But for now, rumour has it that the President has sent an emissary to Rio de Janeiro ... With a letter of overture to the Emperor Dom Pedro of Brazil ... A letter in which Solano Lopez asks – how to put this? – asks for the hand of Dom Pedro's daughter, the Infanta Isabel. The Palace buzzes with talk of it. I thought you should know.'

Then he turned aside and rolled the lighted end of his cigar in a bowl, not wishing to see the sudden surge of colour that suffused Elisa's cheeks. *I pray I have not lost her as a friend. It must come as a slap in the face to her, and is a sad return for her loyalty.*

When she spoke, it was in a voice bound tight against hysteria, one hand plucking aimlessly at her dark satin gown, the other twirling curls of red hair around her ear.

'Oh, that! And I thought you had something fresh for me, you old fool! You imagine I don't know what goes on in the Palace? You imagine Solano doesn't tell me? I may live out of town, my friend, but it doesn't mean I'm out of touch with events! Form an alliance with Brazil? Best thing we could do. And who do you suppose suggested it, if not me? Marry that sweet little Isabel? Smartest move Solano could ever make. Smartest move he could – wait – we must celebrate. Stay where you are. Smoke your cigar. I'll fetch us some wine. The finest from the cellar.'

Von Wisner said nothing, still watching the tobacco glow and die back to ash and fall in the bowl. His high, crimson boots were dusty from the five-mile ride to the *quinta*. But Fulgencio Baleriano would polish them for him later. He enjoyed doing things like that, did Fulgencio. Burnish the old man's buttons. Trim *Papá*'s grey hair.

The baron then grunted within the confines of his moustache, swearing dully in all the languages he knew. His oaths were directed against the insensitive, blundering Francisco Solano Lopez, who had kept his intentions secret from Elisa. *Serve the Beast right if Beauty left him tonight. With all the jewels she could carry. With all the children she could shepherd. Would it ever be less than justice if Elisa had gone by morning? Would justice be done if she had not?*

She did not go directly to the cellar, but out on to the far end of the terrace that faced east towards the ridges and jungles and swamps of Paraguay. And the two-hundred-mile-away, unseen neighbour, Brazil. Her slim body shook with the news von Wisner had brought her, and she stared as if dazed at the moonlit orange groves and orchards, her pale lips dry in the wind.

When she spoke, the words were only for herself. Herself and a sharp-eared God.

'*I have given him five children . . . I have been his lover, his friend, his*

285

comforter and adviser . . . I have been whatever he wanted, teaching him which knife to use, which vintage wine to order, which foot to start off with when he walks . . .

'*I have brought a semblance of civilization to his so-called Paradise, and now I am told he is wooing the daughter of Brazil! Well, here's to Brazil! Here! And here! And here!*'

The wide stone rail of the terrace held twenty earthenware pots, each brimming with gorgeous flowers. One by one, Elisa sent them toppling to the patio beneath, where the pots shattered, and cracked the tiles. Servants came running from the *quinta* and estate guards from the gatehouse.

When they saw she was alone and unharmed, they waited, their dark-skinned faces impassive as she completed her destruction.

'Blocking my view of Brazil,' she told them. 'I was hoping to see their celebratory fireworks. Now find the best wine and serve it in the salon. I've promised it to my friend.'

Concealing her sense of shock, Elisa Lynch played the same daring hand she'd played before, in the Rue du Helder in Paris, when the sleek Brizuela had summoned her to Solano's hotel overlooking the Champs Elysées.

She stayed where she was at La Recoleta, and waited for Solano to ride the five miles from the capital to the *quinta*. It was up to him now to explain what he'd done. Up to *El Jefe Supremo* to admit he was wooing the daughter of Brazil.

He might, of course, announce that Isabel had swooned in the face of his overtures, and the marriage was on. Or, perhaps, the Infanta might not find Solano's swagger and tombstone teeth and violent ways entirely to her taste.

Sit quiet, and let the suitor pay suit. And pray the suit wouldn't fit.

Heavy with wax-sealed ribbons, and delivered in a red leather pouch, Dom Pedro de Alcantara's reply was decently swift.

Penning lines that seared Solano's brain, the Emperor of Brazil referred to his neighbour as 'dissolute, cruel and licentious; a pretentious upstart who *has* not, and *will* not be invited to transgress our borders.' He suggested that President Lopez enjoy his concubines, whores and mistresses, foreign or domestic, but should not ever dream of an alliance with Brazil. 'You make mothers of your women as you find them, *Señor El Presidente*. Here, we still speak of husbands, and of wives.'

Rubbing salt into the wound, Dom Pedro then married the Infanta Isabel to a well-connected French aristocrat, a nephew of Louis Philippe of France, Gaston d'Orléans, the Comte d'Eu.

France and Brazil rejoiced together, breaking down their barriers as children might destroy a matchwood fence.

So far as Dom Pedro was concerned, the salesman from Paraguay had been dismissed.

So far as Elisa was concerned, she was still the First Lady in the land.

But so far as Francisco Solano Lopez was concerned, the letter burned his fingers. And where better to cool them than in the waters off Rio de Janeiro?

His rejection now common knowledge, he begged forgiveness of Elisa. 'It would not have changed things between us, *mi mujer*. You would still have been *La Segunda* – and my friend.'

Her smile like a blade between her lips, she told him not to worry. 'Though you might have thought to discuss things with me first.'

'I should have, yes. But you know what it's like, politics and that. But yes, I suppose I should have.'

'Well,' she said serenely, 'you must do what you think is best, *querido*. Leave your children abandoned . . . The deeds of this house in your name . . . A single casket of trinkets to call my own . . . You've been terribly insulted by Dom Pedro, I can see that. But it hurts me too, knowing you wooed – *and failed*.'

The last words fell like hammer blows, and he flinched. His over-tures to Brazil had cost him Elisa's respect, and he hastened to keep her beside him.

His accountants summoned to the Palace, he instructed them to draw up the necessary papers. Six *quintas*; one hundred and nineteen thousand acres of land; the titles to three river boats, and the sum of 812,000 pesos in gold – all of it in the name of Elisa Alicia Lynch, hers to hold in perpetuity, or dispose of as she wished.

It was a generous apology for his blunderings with the daughter of Brazil. But it left Elisa ever more eager to ride through the orchards with Elmore Cornelius Curtin.

With the documents duly notarized, she contacted the Scotsman, Surgeon Stewart. She remembered that he'd spoken of a banker brother in Edinburgh, and arranged for 800,000 pesos to be transferred to the Royal Bank of Scotland, interest to be paid on a long-term, ten-year investment. The dour doctor approved, reminding her that the Scots were renowned for their fine sense of business.

'Canny,' she said, and smiled. 'Isn't that what you're known as? Downright canny?'

'If that's how you like to see us, Madame Lynch,' the man replied. 'Though it's not the word I'd choose.'

At the same time she made discreet inquiries among the neighbouring states. They failed to reveal any other eligible daughters, though there were several girls who would, before long, be of marriageable age. If the danger of losing Solano – and thus, whatever his protestations, of losing everything – had receded for the moment, it nevertheless remained a threat on the distant horizon.

And then, with the American in mind, she invited him to escort her on inspection tours of her newly acquired *quintas*. 'Whenever your duties permit.'

2

The President now spent most of his time in the Palace in Asunción.

He had a damaging score to settle with Dom Pedro of Brazil; a standing army to be increased from ten to thirty thousand men; a railway line to be extended; gunboats brought upriver from Buenos Aires; batteries to be established along both banks of the Río Paraguay; thoroughfares to be laid and parks to be landscaped in the capital; a marble mausoleum to be erected, to house the mouldering remains of his father, Don Carlos Antonio Lopez.

A full agenda, and with little time to spare for the ride to La Recoleta.

Within the confines of the Embassy – American soil – Elmore Curtin wore the dark blue jacket, pale blue trousers, black boots and belt and braided blue kepi of a Federal army captain. The shoulders of his uniform jacket bore the fore-and-aft badges of rank, as did his long, bad-weather coat, with its stiff, military collar. Tall, slim, and with a pair of white-chalked gauntlets folded over his belt, he cut a fine, imposing figure.

Elisa had asked him to wear his uniform when they went to inspect the *quintas*, pouting when Curtin told her no. 'I might do so for official engagements,' he reasoned, 'but Washburn won't have us riding around in regimental garb, not during off-duty hours. It seems President Lopez is somewhat touchy about it. Won't accept foreign troops in his native land. A very proud man, your – A very proud man, *El Jefe*.'

'I'll speak to him,' she said, though she knew she wouldn't. Charlie Washburn was right. Solano had opened his country to civilians, but he would never tolerate the sight of *extranjeros* in uniform on the streets of Asunción. If he needed a military presence in the capital, he could now call on fifteen thousand of his own. Fifteen thousand and rising.

So Curtin changed into dark twill trousers, ordinary riding boots, his favourite, if scuffed, suede jacket he'd owned for ten years, grey cotton shirt and a battered, broad-brimmed hat.

Elisa revised her opinion, thinking him just as attractive like this, and dressed to match him. Boots and supple leather skirt; an embroidered cotton shirt; gaucho-style waistcoat; a tightly woven straw hat that was not yet as battered as his, but she'd work on it, punish it at home . . .

Dogged by Solano's outriders, the First Lady of Paraguay and the tall, soft-spoken Bostonian rode through the orchards and around the plantations of *mandioca* and across the low, rolling hills of the Cordillera, to the east of La Recoleta. 'What *is* that stuff?' Curtin asked. 'Is that what they use to make bread?'

She nodded, pleased to be able to instruct him. 'They dig out the roots and flake them, then dry the flakes and crush them into powder. They pound it – you must have seen them – and it breaks up into, well, yes, a sort of flour.'

'I'd have to be here a while,' he said, 'to learn about the things that spring from the soil of this wild country. There must be a thousand kinds of flowers . . . More types of fruit and berries . . . Animals out of the Ark . . . Birds you'd think could lift you off your horse . . . It sure beats the hell out of Boston, Madame Lynch – '

'And Cork.' She smiled. 'There's little here you'd expect to find in Cork, Captain Curtin.'

Chatting, or riding in silence, they trotted close along the paths, or up the shallow inclines of the hills. Solano's outriders flanked them, scouring the landscape with their dark, piercing gaze, not understanding a word of English, but alert to the tone of voice, to Curtin's chuckle, to Elisa's laugh.

They are content in their companionship, El Jefe's *woman and the damaged* Americano. *They do not touch each other, but the time might come when they feel the desire to do so. Better for them they do not, else* El Presidente *will have to be told. And better for the* Americano *that he shoots himself dead, if such a report has to be made.*

But Elisa and Curtin were not fools. They both recognized the spark was there, smouldering under the straw, yet told themselves they could bring their boot-heels down on the first flicker of flame. They were simply two people who rode well together, as much at ease in each other's company as in the high-cantle saddles.

Let the *caballistas* be as vigilant as they liked. They'd see nothing but two foreigners, unashamedly friends. Tell that to Solano Lopez and he'd nod. '*Muy bien.*'

And then, on one of their outings, this time to a *quinta* near the village of San Lorenzo, the American asked: 'If one was to keep riding east, Madame Lynch, how far would it be, give or take, before one reached the frontier with Brazil? I've studied the map, of course, but I must admit I've no more than a vague idea – '

A series of ridges and gullies had, for the moment, forced the outriders away. Perhaps for this reason, or because it was the first time Captain Curtin had mentioned Brazil, or maybe it was a combination of the two – whatever the case, Elisa Lynch found the sudden taste of bitterness on her tongue.

'Lopez hoped to marry her,' she said bluntly. 'That Brazilian bitch. Did you know of it, Captain? Surely word reached the Embassy. Even without a map.'

Surprised by her vehemence, Curtin was taken off balance. 'Well, there was some ill-defined rumour. Something about the President seeking the hand – '

'Rumours are by their nature inexact,' Elisa snapped, glancing at him, then seeming to blink in apology. An instant later and her head was turned away, though anger still soured her voice. '. . . Ten years of loyalty . . . Four surviving children . . . Then he makes a colossal fool of himself over the fish-boned Isabel . . . The man who dreams he might one day be the Bonaparte of the South American continent, and he let himself be whipped like an urchin by Dom Pedro of Brazil . . . You ask me how far it is to the frontier. Ask me again when Paraguay extends as far as Rio.'

Riding silent now, Elmore Curtin mused on her response. *An interesting outburst by Madame Lynch. Furious with Lopez for having set his cap at Isabel – a cap knocked askew by Dom Pedro – she was yet equally furious with the Emperor of Brazil for having rejected his advances. A mistress enraged because Lopez had gone behind her back? Yet a woman who shared the sting of Brazil's rejection?*

A complex lady, Madame Elisa Lynch. Or perhaps no more complex than all women, everywhere.

There was more to come.

Emerging from the shallow *cárcava*, but with the outriders forced to skirt wide of the stunted thorn trees that fringed the gully, Elisa glanced again at the tall American. Her voice now once more with its soft, easy lilt, she said, 'Whenever we're out of earshot of others, you must call me by my first name. I shall address you as Elmore. Or what's the other one, Cornelius? Whichever you prefer.'

'Cornelius?' he grinned. 'I'd shoot you out of the saddle.'

'No need,' she retorted. 'I'd choke to death on it anyway. Now listen. I've got a question to ask you. Well, there might be two or three.'

'Fire away,' Curtin told her. 'Though don't ask about the jacket. I just happen to like it, that's all.'

She could see they had maybe a minute of intimacy, two at the most, before the *caballistas* would close in again around them. So the questions had to come now.

'Are you scared by Solano Lopez?'

'Let's just say deeply respectful. On second thoughts, let's say yes.'

'Good. You'd be a fool to pretend otherwise. He's jealous, and I've no doubt he's committed murder. Knowing that, do you wish to make love to me, Elmore Curtin?'

Jesus, he thought, there've been several girls back in Boston, a couple elsewhere; but out here in the Cordillera, with this beautiful Irish woman amid the thorn trees of a country buried in the heart of South America?

It pleased him that he replied without hesitation. 'Yes, my dear Elisa. I very much do. Since the moment I set eyes on you. Yes.'

'Good,' she said gravely. 'As do I with you.'

Their mounts were on the level now, the outriders closing in.

Elmore Curtin looked ahead and murmured: 'Sure you're not influenced by the fish-boned lady from the east? Wouldn't want to be just part of your revenge.'

'Oh, but you will,' she said sweetly. 'You'll be part of many things for me, *Capitán*, just as soon as I can rid us of these slouching bandits who follow wherever I go.'

She calls him Capitán, *the outriders noted. The correct form of address for the North American. And her tone is sweet, even sugary. The tone of politeness. There'd be far more breath in her voice if she intended to deceive* El Jefe.

Unseen by humans, the bird of good fortune passed below the moon and brushed the pink-tiled roofs of La Recoleta, its shadow enough to forgive unmarried infidelity.

The mistress of a man who had bedded peasant girls and the daughters of merchants, the offspring of Paraguayan landowners, foreigners from the neighbouring nations, women he'd accosted or summoned, females he'd asked his father to call to the Palace when he was fifteen years of age and yearning – The mistress of the insatiable Francisco Solano Lopez woke beneath a roof scattered with feathers.

The first thing she learned was that, sometime during the night, her own estate guards had engaged in a short, bloody quarrel with the outriders, the President's *caballistas*.

292

One of her guards had been knifed in the chest, the blade sliding off his rib-cage. In return, one of Solano's riders had been shot in the jaw, and his face tied together with twine. The two distinct groups had retreated to their quarters, where the uniformed guards plotted a wholesale massacre of the *bandidos*, and the outriders planned to show what a well-honed blade could do to a military throat . . .

Elisa's terrified household servants begged her to impose her authority on the factions. 'The *caballistas* are nothing but trouble to us, Señora Lynch. They have none of the discipline of the guards, and say vile and terrible things to all the women. We know you must be protected when you ride, Señora, but surely *El Presidente* could replace them with men of some honour. We intend no disrespect, my lady, but these *caballistas* are no better than animals, and we fear . . . Well, we fear.'

It would have suited Elisa very well to be rid of Solano's outriders – these ugly chaperones, his vigilant spies – but she dared not simply dismiss them. To do so might arouse his suspicions, and he would anyway replace them with others. It needed a further flight by the unseen bird before she and Captain Curtin could go anywhere alone . . .

When it came it was in the form of a note from the Presidential Palace.

Francisco Solano Lopez had decided to travel upriver from the capital to the provincial town of Concepción. From there, accompanied by Baron von Wisner and the English engineer Mr Thompson, he would strike out north-east towards the border of Brazil. 'I shall be gone for a month,' he wrote. 'It is hard for you, I know, *mi mujer*, but you must miss my presence for a month. I cannot say why, but I feel an ominous movement of the earth, and I am urged to check our frontier. Pass on my embrace to our children. Amuse yourself at home, for the rains are coming. Before you know it, I shall return.'

Rereading the note, Elisa thought yes, but not for a month. Then she sat for a while in her private study, composing a letter to be delivered to Solano when he reached Concepción.

The envelope sealed with green wax, she emerged from the *quinta*, walked through the scudding winds of autumn to the long, low barracks that housed the outriders, and presented their leader with the letter.

'*El Jefe* requires you and your men to join him one hundred and forty miles upriver from Asunción. In the capital of the province of Concepción. He has need of your protection when he – '

Slouching in his stained shirt and waistcoat, holstered belts, soft leather breeches and hard leather boots, the man raised a calloused hand, palm outwards, telling her to stop. 'I myself have heard none of this, Señora. I am in the employ of *El Presidente, El Supremo* – '

'As I well know,' Elisa said wryly.

' – and receive my orders in person from – '

'Of course you do,' she said, smiling, 'and are unswerving in your loyalty. But can you not see, my trusted one, that haste has taken *El Supremo* northward? He has not said goodbye to *me* in person, he has merely sent word that you and your riders meet up with him at Concepción. Refuse to go, by all means, and I shall support you in your decision. When he returns – *if*, unprotected, he returns – we shall tell him together that you thought my word was of no value, and you refused to join the Commander-in-Chief of your nation. I'm sure President Lopez will understand. What is it, after all, but disobedience under arms?'

For all his arrogant manner, for all the knives and pistols and cartridge belts that draped his sinewy frame, the hard-eyed horseman blanched. Disobedience under arms? The one thing *El Supremo* would never forgive.

'As for me,' Elisa continued smoothly, 'you are not to spare me a thought. There are a thousand household tasks to be undertaken . . . The children to be amused . . . Diplomats to be entertained . . . I doubt I'll have time even to visit the stables, let alone ride the estate . . .'

The man said nothing, then nodded. He had no choice but to follow her instructions, taking with him his *caballistas*.

'Oh, by the way,' she added. 'It seems the riverboats are all out of service. I'm sorry, but you'll have to ride to Concepción. And hurry before the rains.' She smiled then, knowing she'd won, and bade him God Speed. A Good Journey. Safe Return.

Three hours later they were gone, her own guards grinning as they slammed the gates to the *quinta*, not caring why the *caballistas* had departed, just happy that they had. God Halt Them. Bad Journey. May They Die.

That same afternoon, Elisa Lynch sent a note to Captain Elmore C. Curtin at the American Embassy in Asunción, requesting him to escort her on an outing to a *hacienda* she thought she might purchase,

294

a mile or so beyond the south-west corner of her estate. If Ambassador Washburn would allow the Captain of Marines to leave the compound, Curtin should report to La Recoleta tomorrow at noon.

She did not raise the subject of the outriders, dispatched to join Francisco Solano Lopez . . .

3

When the Embassy troopers had been drilled for an hour, then dismissed, Elmore Curtin read the note and made his way to Washburn's quarters. The two men had forged a close friendship during the months they'd spent in the capital of this country no one knew, and the good-natured Charlie Washburn saw himself as something of a surrogate uncle to the tall, pale-haired Bostonian.

'You want a shot of bourbon, Captain Curtin? That why you're calling by?'

'Yes, sir,' the young man smiled. 'And no, sir. In that order.'

Nodding to the Marine to pour them a measure, the Ambassador queried: 'Letter from home? Or have you come to tell me Washington's finally said yes to your appeals? Are we to lose you at last to the front?'

'It's neither, sir. This isn't from the States. More local, you might say.'

'I might,' the diplomat agreed, 'if I knew what the hell it was. Now sit down. Get the weight off your leg. Local, huh? Like five miles east of here local?'

'Here's your drink, Mr Ambassador.'

'Yes, my boy, I can see you're handing me my drink. And I can also see you're stalling. So how would it be if you matched my pension – assuming the Union wins our bloody war and I get one – and I put all my money on it being from La Recoleta. No, all right, the bet's off. Your expression gives you away.'

Elmore Curtin sat erect, his right leg extended, resigned now to the cold, dull ache within his thigh. Perhaps, one day, he would have the wound reopened, and let someone who knew their business probe for the fragments of shrapnel. Or perhaps he wouldn't, for that way, so often, lay infection.

'It is, as you say, sir, from Madame Lynch. She requests that I escort her tomorrow to a *hacienda* she's thinking of buying near the edge of her present estate. If you've no objection – '

'Matter of fact, I have,' Washburn told him. 'I've got several. Now, you can tell me to mind my own damn business, which is pretty much what I'd tell *you* if our roles were reversed. But since they're not, and you're drinking my bourbon, you'd do well to hear what they are.'

Curtin nodded and thought, oh, Jesus, he's going to say no.

'Well, let's take it from the start, and hit the ground running,' the older man told him. 'Let's say you and Madame Lynch find each other companionable. Irish Boston meets Irish Cork.'

'As a matter of fact, sir – '

'Don't tell me you're not Irish! I *know* you're not Irish! I'm merely saying – Oh, Goddammit, hand me the bottle. Then sit tight and let me finish.' He reached to take it, set it beside him and forgot to charge his glass. 'Now listen. And this time do it with your lips pressed tight together. Don't worry, you'll get your day in court.'

Elmore Curtin said nothing more for a while, and wondered why he'd reacted against being Irish. There were some distinguished Irish families in Boston. And Elisa . . .

'. . . been going to La Recoleta for quite some time. So you're welcome there. So you share the same language. So she speaks of you as handsome and amusing – Christ knows why, but she does – and is clearly eager to have you escort her around. But need I remind you, my boy, *Elisa Alicia Lynch is the mistress of Francisco Solano Lopez.* A man I would not wish to challenge, not even with matches whittled to toothpicks. A man I would give way to on even the widest road. A man against whom it would be unwise to force a passage. In short, a man who is jealous, unstable and all-powerful. Say it after me, Captain Curtin. *All-powerful.'*

A rhetorical remark, the young man accepted. I'm not really required to repeat it.

Nor was he, for Ambassador Washburn had remembered his bourbon, and was busy refuelling his glass. And then, still holding the bottle by the neck, he told the Marine to go careful. 'Enjoy your outings with Madame Lynch, that's swell. Lopez knows all about it, and he's had plenty of his flea-bitten *caballistas* to play the nanny. But now that the President's up north – '

'I'm sorry, sir. What you said just then. How he *had* plenty of his riders? I mean, doesn't he still have his men at La Recoleta?'

'You see?' Washburn sighed. 'You see why *I* run the Embassy, and *you* run after the beautiful mistress of the President of the Republic of Paraguay? I got news of it hours ago. The *caballistas* have been sent north to join Lopez. Go out there again, my boy, and the lady will be waiting. And waiting alone.'

Elmore found it hard to take. To join her at the *quinta* tomorrow

– Well, sure, he could see the risks they might run, being spotted together, alone. But hadn't Charles Ames Washburn just told him that the President too had gone up north? So wasn't the coast now clear? The coast of this inland republic?

I intend to see her again, Curtin decided. To sit with her and talk and drink *maté*, and maybe, just maybe, make love. But if not make love, nor share the herbal tea, then at least to see her, for where's the danger in that?

'Stay off the tracks,' Washburn advised. 'Do what you both choose to do, Captain Curtin, but for God's sake, and the sake of North America, do it unseen. Whatever your declarations to Madame Elisa Lynch, I would rather they did not result in a declaration of war between this exotic country and ours. You got that, my boy? Or should I come across now and give your damaged leg a good kicking, then tell Madame Lynch you fell on a bar of soap?'

'There's no need, sir,' Elmore replied. 'I shall, as you say, stay clear of the well-known paths.'

Pushing himself to his feet, he saluted the worldly Ambassador and left the room, Elisa's letter in his hand.

With Solano's riders sent to meet their master in Concepción, the staff and guards breathed more easily at the *quinta*. A watch was still kept on the gates, and round the perimeter of the estate, but Elmore Curtin was admitted with a smile.

Addressing the uniformed guards, he said: 'It is my understanding that the *caballistas* have ridden to join the President. Long may they be gone.'

'Even longer, Señor,' replied one, and the other men grinned. 'We are not great believers, but light candles that they should lose their way in the jungle, and never come back. When the sun shines for them, it seems to rain for us. But today, *Capitán* Curtin, it shines, so we hope to know they are drenched.'

'And is Madame Lynch well?'

Their grins broadened out into gap-toothed smiles; they assured the American she was very well indeed, and had told them to expect a caller from Asunción, which was why they'd polished their buttons.

'You're right,' he nodded. 'They pick up the sun a treat.'

Elisa had dressed for the caller, but not for the ride. 'We can go there later,' she said with a shrug. 'Whenever we wish to. If we do at all.'

Curtin, on the other hand, having anticipated the visit to the *hacienda,* was wearing his favourite jacket, flannel shirt and dark twill trousers, and carried his broad-brimmed hat. The contrast between his chosen attire and her well-cut skirt and matching, dark silk bodice made them smile.

Elisa was clearly proud of her figure, being still as trim as any seventeen-year-old girl. Her hair had retained its lustre, her skin kept fashionably pale. Whatever the rigours of Ireland, of St Merri and the camp at El Biar, the mother of Lopez' four children wore her years lightly, and knew it. Mirrors, thank God, were not things to be avoided.

They sat in one of the ground-floor rooms that overlooked the sloping gardens to the south. A dozen men were at work out there, distant figures tending to the only extensive lawn in Paraguay. Solano had told her such a thing was impossible. Not wishing to contradict him, it had nevertheless pleased her to prove him wrong. After all, not even *El Supremo* should tell a woman from the Emerald Isle how to sow and nurture a lawn.

But Lopez was away now . . .

Elisa sat with her skirt hitched casually high . . . The American looked rather serious, as if setting words in place within his mind . . .

She asked him what he would take at this hour, and he said: 'Huh? Oh, whatever you're having. But none of those sickly cordials. I don't know. Coffee, I guess. Sure. Coffee'd be fine.'

'No,' she said. 'On second thoughts, I don't believe you want anything. Not down here. I believe you want to see the view from upstairs, Captain Curtin. I believe we both want to make our way upstairs.'

The officer emitted a low, wordless hum. Then he discarded his hat and rose to his feet and took the hand she extended and said, 'Upstairs'd be fine.'

And so it was.

Fine as she led him to her bedroom, and fine as they embraced, the two of them holding each other with foolish caution, then tighter, then clutching as if they'd been swept together in the swirling Río Paraná.

It was fine too as Elmore Curtin watched Elisa Lynch undress, the young man humming again as she revealed her taut, unblemished body. She allowed him a moment, enjoying his gaze, then murmured, 'Your turn now.'

Red-haired and naked, she tried not to smile as Elmore tugged at his belt, struggled to rid himself of his boots, cursed as his fingers slipped on a score of buttons. All the way down the front of his shirt. Four on the cuffs, then his grey cotton drawers, just buttons, bone bloody buttons . . .

He thought her quite amazing, and drew her towards him.

She thought him magnificent in his nakedness and said yes as their bodies conjoined. Then yes again, both of them breathing the word in unison, intelligent lovers lost to their animal instincts, other words indistinguishable as they hungrily fed of their passion.

Afterwards they lay close, touching, taunted by their proximity. Then they made love again, the lean young American and the smooth-limbed woman from Ireland. The glow of the sun blazed against the windows, the breeze of autumn stirring the edge of the curtains and carrying the sounds of bird-song from the forest, cawings and chitterings among a million rustling leaves.

This second time the lovers were less greedy, no longer snatching food from the table, but happy to taste, to choose, to try, before devouring the sexual feast. It would not be swept away, the first time had proved it. So why not circle, and sample, and more fully appreciate what they shared . . .

Turned on her hip now, and smiling at him, Elisa murmured, 'I could love you very easily, Captain Curtin come-from-Boston. Very easily indeed.'

Reaching to brush damp ringlets of hair from her face, he said, 'Sorry to tell you, you'll have to stand second in line – '

'Oh, I see. So there's someone – '

' – in the matter of love. Fell for you the first instant I saw you, when you invited me here last Christmas. So I fell first. Been waiting to catch you since then.'

The shadow of a rival flew away. She smiled and threatened to fall on him there and then – 'If you're man enough!' – and laughed gently as he begged her no, at least not yet. Let a guy catch his breath.

They lay side by side again in her Paris-furnished bedroom in the Spanish-style house within an easy hour's ride of the capital of this all-but-landlocked nation. Lay there naked and crossed their arms low, his right hand on the smoothness of her thigh, her left hand resting gently on the ugly – *no, not really ugly* – maze of scars that webbed the muscles of his leg. *But close to the groin. Thank God the shrapnel had not been closer.*

300

'Tell me,' she said. 'But only if you want to. Tell me how this happened.'

'This?'

Her faint, feathery pressure caused him no discomfort. '*This* . . . '

Oh, *this* had been the result of a skirmish in which – 'Well, every damn thing that could have gone wrong did go wrong. Plus a dozen others that couldn't. We're way back now, Elisa, back in '61. I'm a junior officer – still am, I guess – in the Army of the Potomac, under Brigadier-General Irvin McDowell. And we're all set to launch an attack on the Confederate forces, who are, let me tell you, only twenty-five miles south of Washington. To describe it clearly I'd need to draw you a map – '

'No maps. I don't want a lecture. I want to know where and when, my love, you got *this* . . .'

Elmore Curtin closed his eyes, went back in his mind for a while, then opened his eyes again and said, 'Bloody chaos . . . July . . . Swarms of flies, mosquitoes, you name it . . . General George B. McClellan is swinging east from Ohio with 20,000 men. He does pretty well too, chasing off the Confederates near Beverly. You want to know where that is?'

'Want to know about *this*.' The brush of her fingers, and he could half believe the shrapnel had dissolved. *Keep doing that, Madame Lynch. It surely will.*

'Anyway, encouraged by the news of McClellan's army, McDowell takes a header at the Rebels who are dug in around a railroad station called Manassas Junction, the far side of a stream known as – what's it? Bull Run River? Something like that. So on we go, with McDowell's 35,000 . . .'

Like a sleek, pampered cat, Elisa Lynch stretched in the bed and murmured, 'Then there isn't someone now?'

Curtin faltered in his story. 'What? Isn't *who* now? What the hell are you talking about?'

'Someone else. Another woman. Maybe a wife?'

'Jesus Christ!' The man erupted. 'I'm taking you step by step through a major military engagement in a war that's tearing my country apart, and you ask me – '

'Well is there?'

He paused, and let his irritation drain away, then told her, 'Not any more. The woman I'd hoped to marry died of pneumonia. She was of an established Boston family. Cosseted and comfortable and smart as a whip. Pretty as the sunrise. Fought with her father who wanted to find her a banker. Lived with me for six weeks, then went home to celebrate her mother's fiftieth birthday, and caught cold in the great stone tomb they called a mansion. And the cold lodged in her lungs and she died of pneumonia. And did so before I was ever allowed to see her again. Okay? Will that do? Does that answer your question, Madame Lynch?'

She cringed from his toneless anger, his sorrow, her own intrusive foolishness.

For a long time they stayed in stiff parallel. And even when he told her of Bull Run and the clumsy manoeuvres, of the lines stretched too wide and the flanking attacks, of the Northern Commanders too old for the job, and the luck and misfortune that governed the day, he told it in recitation, hurt more that she'd reminded him of the woman who'd died than of the hundreds who'd died around him.

'As for this – *this* – it's what you get if you stand too close to a shell when it explodes.' Swinging awkwardly from the bed he said, 'Now listen. Time I got back to the Embassy. Troopers to be drilled again. Paperwork and that.'

Elisa pushed herself upright, and extended a hand to restrain him. 'Oh, please, Elmore, please. I'm sorry for what I said. I *do* know what it is to lose a loved one. My parents. A daughter of my own out here. It was stupid of me to say what I did. But I wanted to know you felt free to come here again. That's all. Only that you'd feel free to come here again.'

The world of the past already fading, though the woman he might have married never completely forgotten, Captain Elmore Curtin turned towards her, buttoning his endless bloody buttons, and allowed his tight-drawn features to relax. He would still look serious and sober, still calm and attentive to what the world might do. But now, at last, was the vestige of a smile, and the Captain of Marines was saying yes, he too was sorry for his outburst, and he'd make himself free to see her whenever she asked him, for she surely was a flower to dull all the flowers of South America.

'Then you might come tomorrow?' she offered. 'I don't believe I'll be called from the *quinta* tomorrow.'

'Mustn't forget my hat,' he said. Then, 'Noon, if Washburn allows it.'

'Noon,' she repeated. Echoing his earlier remarks about the coffee, and coming upstairs, she said, 'Noon'd be fine.'

4

El Jefe glared as the unwashed riders came to join him at Concepción. In unprintable language he asked them what they were doing up here, deserting La Recoleta, smelling like pigs and flapping their rain-dampened letter. 'Prepare a fine answer for me, *mis amigos*, or I shall have you transmitted to the yard, to receive a bullet between the eyes. I do not understand your presence here, men I employ to escort Señora Lynch whenever she rides.'

The leader of the *caballistas* thrust the letter at him, glad to get rid of it. 'We were sent by the word of Señora Lynch to meet you here, *Excelencia*, and would have come sooner, but for the boats.'

Luckily for Elisa, Solano Lopez snatched at the letter, not hearing that final excuse. There were, of course, several riverboats still chugging the length of the Río Paraguay. But she had wanted the riders to struggle to Concepción, adding days and nights to their journey. The longer it took them to get there, the longer it would leave her with Captain Curtin, and the longer it would take Solano's suspicions to harden into jealousy, crystallize into fury.

But the letter itself gave him no cause at all for mistrust.

My sweet, heroic Solano,
   I pray you will take good care of yourself, as you stride towards Brazil. Sleep at night with the netting round you; I do not wish insects to bite my New Napoleon!
   I have commanded your *caballistas* to join you – a silly woman's whim, you might think, but my own small effort to see you well protected. Rough though they are, they kneel to you as their leader, and can shoot a scorpion – as I've seen them do – at thirty paces.
   My own estate guards take good care of *me*, and I take care of our children. Come back to me soon, *Señor El Jefe*, my own powerful protector. But send word first, so the house can be decked with flowers!

Not a bad effort – once she'd learned that he was exploring his nation's distant frontier with Brazil. And that Elmore Cornelius Curtin could be safely invited to the *quinta*.

During the month of Elisa's lapse – her lapse from grace, her lapse from fidelity to a man who had doubtless taken two or three girls with him to keep him company in his string bed in the jungle – the American and the Irishwoman met as frequently as possible.

Elisa had made love to many men before. A euphemism, of course – make love – though she had once been genuinely fond of the awkward Xavier Quatrefages, and excited by the urbane Régis de Broux. Others had been brutal, or timid, or bombastic, some as drab as the black clothes they wore, these oh, so respectable bankers and businessmen, some as lightweight in their performance as their dilettante costumes. As a courtesan she had 'entertained' her 'protectors'. 'Granted her favours' in return for 'presents'. Allowed them into her bed, for a price. Engaged in sex. Sold her body. But rarely, if ever, made love.

Had she ever loved Solano Lopez? Well, yes, she believed she had. Cared for him, certainly. In many ways protected *him*, at least against the taunts of European society. Endearing, yet unpredictable, volcanic in his anger, though given to moments of bewildered introspection, the Master of Paraguay would still turn to her, as a child to its mother, seeking comfort or advice. At times like that, she thought, then yes, it comes close to love. When the animal who has sired my children shows the same open innocence as a child. Less often, these days, though he might again. One could never know with the ever-changing cloud that was *El Jefe, El Primero, El Supremo* . . .

And then, with the pragmatism of a woman who knows men, Elisa closed the door of her mind against Lopez, crossed the room and opened another to admit the limping Captain of Marines.

With Elmore the term rang true. They had made, and would again, make love.

They did so in the house near La Recoleta. And in her other *quintas*. And in the open when the weather allowed, or when they themselves decided to hell with the weather. So long as they had Curtin's waterproof bedroll to spread on the ground, his long, heavy overcoat to warm them . . . So long as the sudden, torrential downpours didn't drown them where they lay – drowned *in flagrante delicto*! – they would assuage their endless appetites, aware that hunger would, happily, return.

In the *quintas* and the clearings, the lovers made love, and gave little thought to the calendar. Solano had said he'd be gone for a month, and Elisa could only imagine him somewhere far away to the north, in the Paraguayan jungle, near the distant Brazilian border.

Once he'd reached his destination, he'd have the long trek back to Concepción. Then the journey downriver to Asunción. A month away, if not more. And meanwhile, every day now, she had her first real lover in years.

The leaves of autumn turned. But not, for Elisa Lynch and Elmore Curtin, the leaves of the calendar . . .

Then suddenly it was over.

Elmore Curtin was on his way to the stables when Ambassador Washburn intercepted him and beckoned him to his quarters. 'A word with you, Captain. Before you ride out again. A telegraphed message – my, my, but aren't we modern these days? – that I think you might wish to read.'

Thanks to the English engineer Thompson, and dedicated work by a highly paid American consortium, Asunción was now linked with the Uruguayan capital of Montevideo.

Elmore knew that Rio de Janeiro translated into English as the January River, and Buenos Aires as the City of Sweet Air. He'd also been told that Montevideo was a corruption of the cry that had gone up from Magellan's ship, when the Portuguese explorers had sighted land in 1520. 'There! I can see a hill! *Monte vide eu!*'

But it was, the American admitted, the first time he'd heard that the thousand-mile telegraph line was in service.

Washburn handed him a flimsy sheet of grey paper. 'I'm afraid the operator here lacks a total grasp of English, my boy, though the gist of it seems clear. You're the one called *Capitán* Elme Cottin.'

The Marine limped forward and took it.

'. . . Reqest Assepted . . . Report New Olean . . . Soones Possible . . . Actin Major . . . General Merridon . . . God Blest Thee Union . . . Ent Message . . .'

The lover of Elisa Lynch rocked slightly on his feet. All right, so now, at last, he'd got what he'd hoped for, his recall to his homeland, to the war, and with it promotion. *But Jesus. To leave Elisa?*

'I notice it says the soonest possible . . .'

Washburn nodded and murmured: 'Saw that, too.'

'But who's this General Merridon – ?'

'He's actually General Cowper B. Merrydown. Fine reputation. Your appeals to return must have been passed along. Nice, though, that you're now an acting-major, Major Curtin. Let me be the first to congratulate you.'

Elmore took the Ambassador's hand, shook it without the warmth he would otherwise have intended, and said again, 'Soonest possible? Does that mean – ?'

'What it means,' Charlie Washburn said calmly, 'is that whatever you possess will be packed and stacked by the dock tomorrow morning, in time for you to catch the first packet-boat downriver. What you do between now and tomorrow at six – the sailing time's six-fifteen – is entirely up to you. You might wish to ride a while this evening. Say farewell to Madame Lynch, why not? Just so long as you're there on the dock before six – Major Curtin.'

It took the young man a moment to tighten his jaw and say yes. All right, so his appeals had met with a positive response; his prayers had been answered. But the strange thing was, how the hell had this General Cowper C. Merrydown in New Orleans, now in Union hands, heard abut Elmore C. Curtin, with connections in Boston and Washington? The Army sure had its odd little ways, but who was Merrydown to offer the limping Marine promotion?

'I shall wish to spend a while with the troopers, Mr Ambassador. And after that, well, yes, as you say, bid farewell to Madame Lynch. A most hospitable friend, Madame Lynch – '

'Don't doubt it, my boy.' Charlie Washburn nodded. 'Don't doubt you broke new ground. The two of you. Together. Now get along to the barracks, and cheer your troopers with the knowledge that you'll be leaving 'em. Then take your horse for a trot, and give Madame Lynch my best wishes.'

Acting-Major Elmore Curtin offered his hand – this time more warmly – to the avuncular Charles Ames Washburn. But the diplomat preferred to respond, 'Piss off with you, boy. The alarm rings on time, I might make it to the dock to see you leave.'

It was the longest, wildest night they had spent together, the shapely, red-haired Elisa and the man she should by rights have addressed as Major.

They indulged their physical greed, climaxing together in a storm of satisfaction, then sinking back, the woman's smooth body pressed tight against his leanness, their breath slowly settling from the shallow to the deep.

At midnight she edged from the bed, stood fresh candles in the liquid stubs of the old, then awoke him with a lingering kiss, and handed him a glass of French champagne. 'I've this plan for next week,' she told him. 'There's an amazing waterfall – the Falls of Iguazu – some distance from here, but – '

Hauled so beautifully from sleep, he said: 'Wait . . . What's this? Now listen to me, Elisa . . .'

But the woman was in no mood to hear his military excuses. He would sip the champagne – 'Well, sit up! It's not to be wasted!' – and as soon as he was awake, *man enough for the task in hand!* they would once again make love.

No euphemisms now. They would couple, conjoin and *make love*.

They did so, and Elisa used the rainbow of her skills, drawing his senses from the deepest violet to a blazing crimson, the young Marine spinning in the myriad colours of her touch. He bucked to delight her, moaned unashamedly, rose up and drove himself downward, possessing her, growling as she screamed with the arc of light, with the waxy, guttering candles . . .

Much later, a hand tugged gently on the coverlet. 'Señora Lynch? The coffee and the bread. Will you take it now, Señora?' Elisa awoke, and he was gone. There was no trace of him beyond the tangled sheets of the bed and the pleasing odour of his body. No sign of his clothes. No broad-brimmed hat discarded on a chair. Nothing now to show he had ever been there.

With a single stroke, she swept the tray and its contents aside. The servant retreated, crouching, shrivelling, scurrying from the room.

'Elmore?' she called. 'Are you out there on the terrace? Are you out there, my love? Where've you gone?' *Must be out there.* 'Elmore . . . ?'

Twisting upright in the bed, she saw on the pillow beside her an epaulette, taken from the shoulder of his foul-weather coat. And a small white card on which he had written: 'My Government has recalled me to New Orleans. As one who remains loyal to Paraguay, you will understand why I cannot desert my own country. Yet, by going, I know I am still a deserter – to the woman I very much love. Long live the United States of America. *Viva Paraguay!*'

He had hoped to soften the parting by leaving her asleep. But he could do nothing now to stop Elisa's eyes from gradually misting with tears as she stared upward, unseeing, at the high, *quebracho* ceiling.

She willed him to die before ever he reached Buenos Aires and the open sea. Alligators would do it. Or the carnivorous piranhas. Or be

307

swept overboard later, in mid-ocean, when his lean body would turn, arms extended, as he drifted downward, downward . . . Or be the first of his regiment to get shot, when the curtains would close on Curtin! Not killed outright, that wouldn't do at all. But terribly wounded, dying by inches, and in his final lucid moments calling a single name, over and over, the name of a woman far away to the south, but far too busy to listen . . .

Then she began to weep in earnest, this time praying he would live. Survive his war unscathed. Be acclaimed as a hero, honoured beyond all others, a beacon that would shine throughout the Union. And at last, the war won, he would exchange his military uniform for a diplomat's tall hat and tails. And decline the offer of a hundred other Embassy posts, preferring the one that had lately become available, on the retirement of Charles Ames Washburn.

And *Ambassador* Elmore C. Curtin would return. *Oh, God, that the man from Boston would one day return* . . .

At 5.43 that morning, Elmore Curtin alighted from the two-wheeled *coche* that had brought him to the quayside, lifted down his two leather valises, then waved his thanks to the driver. '*Un feliz viaje, Capitán,*' the man said courteously. '*El barco marchará dentro de media hora.*'

Curtin nodded. Half an hour to sailing time. Stooping, he picked up his cases and limped through the pre-dawn greyness towards the shape and sounds of the packet-boat that would be his final link with the world of Paraguay. *I am glad to have been recalled* . . . *And yet I am sorry, more than sorry, to leave Elisa* . . . *Let's face it,* he thought, *I am pretty damn confused* . . .

His leg ached, and he paused for a moment, resting the cases on the cobbles. *What's the hurry? Half an hour to go* . . .

It was then that he heard the sound of another coach clattering down the slope to the quayside. He turned to see the tall figure of Charles Ames Washburn emerging from under the hood.

'Sorry to see you go, Major Curtin. Though it's what you were always after. Back to the States.'

'That's right, sir,' Curtin admitted. 'Back to the States.'

'And the timing seems good,' the diplomat told him. 'Our volatile President's due home sooner than we thought. Day after tomorrow. Not that I'm saying you did any more than ride the hills with Madame Lynch. But we wouldn't want any misunderstandings with Señor Lopez, eh, my boy?'

Elmore Curtin's sigh showed as vapour in the cold morning air. 'This General?' he queried. 'This Cowper B. Merrydown? Did he really get my requests via Washington, Mr Ambassador?'

'How the hell should I know?' Washburn yawned. 'Listen. The captain's calling you aboard. Time to go, my young American. But keep your head down when the shells burst, if you please.'

'I will, sir. And I'll let you know – '

'That's it. Let *me* know. If there's anyone else who might care to hear how you're doing . . . Well, I'll pass the word along.' Then he clapped Curtin briskly on the arm, and the officer made his way aboard the packet-boat.

Handing his cases to one of the crew, he went to stand on the after deck. Tall and silent, his gaze was on the back-lit city of Asunción, though the image in his mind was of a cool country house some five miles beyond it. And of the woman he would never see again.

Returning to his carriage, Washburn muttered under his breath. 'Day after tomorrow? I owe you one for this, old "Coop". Getting the boy away from the Beauty, before the Beast looms large.'

5

Two days later, as Washburn had forecast, Franciso Solano Lopez disembarked at Asunción, his converted mail-boat bearing the Hungarian, von Wisner, and the Englishman, Mr Thompson.

He rode straight to La Recoleta, the Master of Paraguay genuinely eager to see his children, and to hug Elisa. 'You have missed me very much, no doubt, deprived of your man for so long. Well, I warned you you would, but you look well enough, considering your loneliness.'

'And you, too,' she deflected. 'There's an air of confidence in your manner, *querido*. Did you find what you looked for in the jungle near Brazil?'

Expecting him to say yes, he'd found it, the very thing he was searching for, it surprised her when Solano raised his hands and bellowed, 'No! Not a stake! Not a marker! Nothing at all! They've got nothing!'

'I'm not sure I understand,' Elisa told him. 'You went with von Wisner and Mr Thompson to the border; and then, when you got there – '

'We found nothing! All the province of the Matto Grosso. Unprotected. Undefended. Brazil's back door swung open, and off its hinges! Call me a pretentious upstart, would he, our neighbourly Dom Pedro? Well, he'll find me a closer neighbour than he wished for, should I choose.'

She realized then that Franciso Solano Lopez was hungry for war. A man insulted, a suitor rejected, he planned to set his own small country against the most extensive in South America. And had found the route to Rio.

She offered him wine, and settled to discuss his plans, then blinked as the man said: 'Still riding with your handsome American? Word says you do, Señora, and are gone without an escort.'

No hands raised now, and his stained teeth bared to bite, he pinned her with his dark, inflexible gaze; Brazil for tomorrow, but Elisa Lynch today.

She had burned Elmore's card, and wept to see it shrivel. Then she'd hidden the blue and gold epaulette in a wax paper wrapper in a distant part of the garden. Now she leaned towards Solano to ask him, 'Are you speaking of Captain Curtin? The one with a limp?'

'You must know I am, *mi mujer*. You must know that's who I mean.' Then he too leaned forward, daring Elisa to flinch and admit her guilt. If she did so – well, God help her if she did so, for Solano was very much a man of his country and his time, and would cruelly punish the mother of his children if she flinched.

'That know-it-all Bostonian? The kind of arrogant city-type we met in Paris? The ones you hated, remember, Solano? All talk, and you'd think he'd captured Virginia single-handed.'

'Nonetheless,' he nailed. 'Word has it Captain Curtin's been to see you.'

'Oh, he has,' she told him. 'Asked me about the horses, could he try out this one, canter about on that. Oh, sure, he's been out here, *querido*, and he'd still be here now if I hadn't begged for help from Mr Washburn. It's the Ambassador who got rid of him – dispatched him to New Orleans, I think – and Curtin was sent downriver, packed off home.'

'Not sorry he's gone?' Lopez murmured. 'Word has it – '

'*Word!*' Elisa stormed. 'Word would have me naked and in bed with him! *Word* gets people shot, my dear Solano! I would rather we backed this intangible *word* with evidence, or I might think you'd not been alone in your bed in the jungle, *word* drifting down that you weren't! Now, enough. I've our children to see to. *Or is it just word that they're ours?*'

It was a spirited display, and a chastened Solano Lopez was left to pour himself a glass of *caña*.

Even so, Elisa Alicia Lynch ensured they made love that night in the room that overlooked the terrace that overlooked the trees. Then she prayed that if she was pregnant now, the child would be dark and swarthy, and not cast in the image of a pale-haired Bostonian . . .

In the months that followed, Solano Lopez read a hundred different reports, sent secretly by the spies he'd planted in Buenos Aires, in Rio de Janeiro, in the Uruguayan capital of Montevideo. Others were dispatched from the provinces, from the ports and factories, from buildings that overlooked the parade grounds of Brazil and Argentina.

Meanwhile, disguised as merchant vessels, ships ploughed south and then west from Europe, and their crated cargoes were transferred to smaller, Paraguayan steamers in the Río de la Plata, from whence they were taken upriver to Asunción.

The first of two railway engines – ordered from 'The Metropolitan and Amalgamated Railway Carriage and Waggon Company, Ltd., Birmingham, England' – arrived in more than seventeen hundred pieces, the crates labelled 'Boiler Plate', 'Machine Tools', 'Construction Equipment', 'Spares and Miscellaneous'.

In a similar manner, rifles and phosphorous flares were imported from France; also five hundred Colt revolvers from 'The Patent Arms Manufacturing Company, Paterson, New Jersey'; along with several revolving Gatling guns – these erratic prototypes imported illegally from North America.

Military draftsmen arrived from Germany and Belgium, and were placed under the command of Baron von Wisner.

Doctors and nurses were offered a well-paid, two-year contract if they would leave their posts in Paris and Madrid, and come to staff the four field hospitals Lopez believed he might need.

Sufficiently insulted by Dom Pedro of Brazil, he chose to forget Queen Victoria's earlier rebuff, and Isabella of Spain's suggestion that Paraguay should bow to the rule of her nation. Solano thought it wise to ignore the enemies he'd made abroad. After all, he intended to make enemies of others. And these would be closer to home . . .

For Elisa, life revolved around her children, and the worrying knowledge that she was once again pregnant – *'Though by whom?'*

Panchito was now nine years old. Enrique six. The solemn Frederico almost four. Carlos Honorio just three. *And the next one? Another boy? To be seen as the son of Francisco Solano Lopez? Or as the gift of the American, Elmore Cornelius Curtin?*

Torn again, as she'd been torn by his departure, she asked God that the baby might have Solano's strong face and tar-black hair, yet grow tall and lean as the lover she'd truly loved.

When the infant was born – under Surgeon Stewart's bleak gaze – the mother who'd survived the birth lay fearing for her life.

'. . . Tell me,' she gasped. 'Is the child well-formed? Have I given him a girl this time? Has he sired another boy . . . ?'

Unwittingly, the Scotsman said: 'Well, the babe's no' like the others, tell you tha', Mistress Lynch. A child of President Lopez?'

Oh, my God.

'More like a younger brother; big, and with his fine black thatch of hair. Ya man will be pleased with this one, Mistress. I'd say you'd served him well.'

Elisa pressed her dry lips together, thanked God and asked that Curtin might forgive her for her cowardice, then sank into a long, longed-for sleep.

Piece by piece, the railway engine took shape, the line was extended, barracks constructed, fortifications raised round the looping southern border of the country, hospital tents erected, troops taught to swagger in their smart French uniforms, howitzers tested, flags unfurled, the crops brought in, *soirées* held in La Recoleta, in the Presidential Palace, on the trimmed and tree-fringed grounds of the Campo Grande.

Elisa Alicia Lynch reigned as Queen of Paraguay.

No matter that she was Solano's foreign mistress. She was the unquestioned First Lady, *La Segunda* to *El Primero*, the mother of his five male children, and pleased to see a fresh confidence in his stride.

Still earning more than ever it could spend, this inland Republic now boasted a navy of fifteen vessels, an army of sixty-five thousand, a railway that was the envy of South America, and with it – for Elisa's pleasure – a theatre and concert hall, neither of which Solano attended, unless his excuses ran dry.

'But you can't expect me to go there alone, *querido*,' she reasoned. 'How would it look – ?'

'Very well. I'll see you to your seat. But I've more on my mind than – what is it tonight? – "The Improvised Poems of Bolivia"?'

'No,' she said patiently. 'It's a French operetta, *Orphée aux Enfers*. It's good to bring creative works here. It means we're civilized.'

'Are you saying we were not?' Lopez menaced. 'Are you telling me – ?'

'No, no, *querido*, nothing of the kind. But my efforts impress the other ladies. The diplomats' wives and their daughters. Helps numb their lips when they wish to talk about Europe.'

'I'll see you to your seat,' Solano repeated immediately. 'We'll make a grand and dignified entrance. And, damn those women, I'll stay for the first fifteen minutes.'

Little by little, the political jigsaw took shape.

Argentina still regarded the inhabitants of Paraguay as little better than monkeys, the long-limbed creatures swinging down from the

313

trees, pounding their *mandioca*, scuffling to harvest their *yerba maté*, then shrieking their way back to the jungle.

A garden worth tilling, once the apes had been shot from the branches . . .

Brazil was of the same opinion. A fertile plot, watered by its broad network of rivers, Paraguay would make an excellent vegetable patch for Brazil. And an orchard. And with flowers for the *senhoras*.

'Rio is concerned that you build up your forces,' one of the spies scribbled on cheap grey paper. 'They have learned about the howitzers and the *fósforo*. Dom Pedro fidgets and grows uncomfortable.'

On the southern bank of the Río de la Plata, a second spy wrote, 'Argentina fears this constant traffic of ships from Europe, and the way they trade crates in the estuary. She is nervous of Paraguay's intentions. She might bite before she is bitten.'

Such threatening rumours were music to Lopez' ears. All right, so his neighbours suspected him. But did *he* not suspect that they, too, were about to bare their teeth?

Had not Napoleon Bonaparte felt the same, fearing for his beloved, adopted France? Bite before bitten. A good enough motto, Solano decided, for his own encircled Paradise.

6

Elisa's fifth boy was named Leopoldo Antonio. Celebrations were planned, the centrepiece to be a three-day fiesta on the Campo Grande, the extensive, landscaped park that lay on the outskirts of Asunción. The fiesta would be open to all, relays of musicians playing until their fingers bled, *caña* and *yerba maté* served night and day, singers recruited to laud *El Supremo* and his lady until their voices were reduced to a rattle. Horse races were organized. Exhibitions by the President's lancers. Displays of markmanship. Cock-fights and dog-fights. Wrestling matches, with the added spice of a deadly coral snake let loose in the ring.

The well-to-do Paraguayans – and the pale-skinned Europeans – were invited to shelter from the heat of the day in a semicircle of tents, from which most of the women never moved. Chairs and couches lined the canvas walls, a dozen kinds of fruit cordial were there to be sipped, and ice was carted in every hour from the city's only *depósito de hielo*.

The manager of the ice-making plant was later awarded a medal, having gone without sleep for thirty-seven hours, terrified that the machinery might break down.

Solano and Elisa attended the first long night of the fiesta. The President gave a speech in honour of the woman who had borne him a fifth male child, then went on to warn his countrymen that life might soon be devoid of music and song. 'Understand,' he soothed, 'I do not use this joyous occasion to cloud the skies. But the days that confront us may well be darkened, for greed consumes our neighbours. I am, as ever, in contact with those whose appetites grow large, and I hope to – ' then he paused, pleased with what was to come ' – convince them to watch their figures and eat less!'

In their hundreds, the crowd cheered, aware from his tone that he'd recited a well-turned phrase. It didn't much matter that they failed to understand it. When *El Supremo* measured his words like that, the safest thing to do was respond with cheers . . .

During the evening, Elisa found time to exchange a greeting with Mr Thompson, who was eager to tell her that the pieces had fitted. 'The train, Madame Lynch. Good as it was in Birmingham.'

'Whenever I see you,' she said gently, 'you're always alone. I know you work hard, Mr Thompson, but you really should take days off, now and then. There are several young ladies – '

He grunted, nodding dismissively. 'No doubt, Madame Lynch. But I'm happy enough as I am. A neat and tidy house. Know where things are. Tell you the truth, I'm a fellow of regular habits.'

'Oh, yes,' she smiled. 'Indeed you are, Mr Thompson. Regular as your own railway timetable. And we wouldn't want a woman holding you back 'cause she'd mislaid her purse.'

The man nodded again, this time in full agreement. Thank God for someone who understood the careless ways of her sex. Just about what they would do, mislay their purse.

She bade him good night and watched him go, his hands smoothing the flaps of his English-style jacket, then glancing down to check that the flaps were properly buttoned.

Solano veered close to ask if the evening pleased her. 'There'll be fireworks at midnight. Over there, to the north.'

Fireworks, she thought. As I once imagined I'd see above distant Rio, if Solano had won the fish-boned Isabel.

'I'll watch for them, *querido*. And yes, it does. It pleases me very much.'

'*Muy bien*. Now there are people I must speak to. I shall rejoin you later.'

'That's good,' Elisa told him. 'I shall miss you until then.'

She was not sure if she meant to tease him with what he himself had said before. But if she did, he failed to respond.

'Yes, you must,' he acknowledged, then stumped away, his power-ful shoulders swaying as he walked.

Elisa listened for a while to the piping of flutes, the strumming of magnificent, inlaid guitars, the rhythmic pounding of drums. Lan-terns fringed the Campo, drawing clouds of mosquitoes, broad-winged moths, the occasional zooming hornet. Immune now to the mosquitoes, she still feared the deadly hornet, its sting as injurious as that of any flying insect on the South American continent. 'The bee brings pain,' the saying went, 'and the wasp will make us cry. But the kiss of the hornet, the terrible hornet, and all that's left is to die.'

'A moment to spare, Mistress Lynch? Mayhap you don't, but the thought occurs . . .'

She turned to see Surgeon Stewart rocking gently on his heels. His eyes dry and watchful, he was clearly as sober as the hundreds of others were merrily, blearily drunk. '. . . You might wish to invest somewhat further in the Royal Bank of Scotland. The ten-year plan?'

'What? Oh, that. Well, perhaps, Dr Stewart, but I'm not much in the mood to discuss it now. We'll talk about it later in the week.'

'As ye wish, Mistress Lynch. Thought to remind you, is all. Fine party. Not tha' I quite grasped the import of President Lopez' speech. The bit about days being darkened. Could ye tell me, perhaps – ?'

'That, too,' she said. 'But later in the week.'

William Stewart had no choice but to bow and take his leave. His departure was no loss to Elisa, the man being altogether too strictured for her taste. Why should such a dedicated physician, as undoubtedly he was, be so unappealingly strait-laced, so perfect, so detached from all possible sin?

It was with relief that she found the tall Hungarian, the baron chewing morosely on his cigar.

'Take my arm,' his hostess told him. 'Walk me around.'

'With pleasure,' he said. 'Would you mind if we walked to Canada?'

Elisa laughed and asked why he hated these gatherings so much. 'You're supposed to be enjoying yourself, my dear Enrique. This is all to honour Solano's Irish mistress, don't forget. And his fifth strapping child. By the way, where's Fulgencio?'

'Oh, sulking back at the house, I imagine. He doesn't much like a gathering either, unless *he's* the guest of honour. If only he had a singing voice – which he hasn't. Or could play an instrument – which he can't. So he stays at home and sulks, and plans to make the rest of my night a misery – the one thing he does rather well.'

Elisa squeezed von Wisner's long, thin arm, then murmured: 'Tell me this, my dear Baron. Are we really in for dark days?'

He raised his free hand to draw it downwards over his broad, bushy moustache. The crowd eddied around them, and he steered Elisa gently from the vortex of noise, the young friend linked with the old one, the Campo clear ahead.

'Dark days?' von Wisner echoed. 'Well, yes, Elisa, they might be. *El Supremo* – '

'Oh, for heaven's sake, call him Solano. You know him as well as I do.'

'As you wish. Solano, then, was badly scarred by Dom Pedro's razored response. I don't know how he behaves when he's at home at La Recoleta, but in the Palace he all but drives his fist through the walls. He speaks endlessly of uniting South America. And speaks ominously of Paraguay's dominant neighbours, his favoured term now being: "bite before we are bitten". You ask me, Elisa, if war clouds are gathering. I can only tell you – the sky at noon seems darker than it did.'

Her last companion that night was the genial Washburn, who had arrived late from the Embassy, but determined to pay his respects to *La Segunda*.

'Stuck my head out of the carriage, but where are the fireworks?'

'You'll see them in a minute, Charlie. You'll get your unpaid money's worth.'

Then she asked him quietly what he knew she would ask; what she'd asked many times before. 'Any recent word from Captain Curtin?'

'Matter of fact,' he smiled, 'there is. It seems that *Major* Curtin was sent up north to Memphis, then went east with General Sherman and was present at the Battle of Chattanooga. Plays down his part in it, of course, though I've no doubt our young officer acquitted himself with honour. He demands to know if you're well, Elisa – '

'His actual words? Can you remember his actual words?'

'Well, let's see.' Washburn mused. 'So much comes over my desk these days – '

'Don't play games, Charlie. I'm not asking much. Just tell me what Curtin wrote.'

'Well, here,' the Ambassador told her, turning to see they were clear of the swirling crowd. 'Here's the young man's latest dispatch from the front. The last lines are for you.'

Elisa took the paper he passed her, squinting to discern the blue ink script.

You must assure me that Madame Lynch is safe and well. And that no one else yet wears the epaulette I left her. And won't for a while.

She returned the document to the Ambassador with a nod.

'Don't know what he's talking about,' Washburn murmured. 'Don't suppose you do, either.'

'None of your business anyway,' Elisa said with a grin, 'since the last lines were for me.'

Precisely at midnight, the fireworks were launched from the northern

318

hillside. Spiralling upward and seeming to die in the sky, they then exploded in starbursts and fountains, the colours etched harshly against the blackboard of the night. Rockets soared and boomed, fragmenting into drifting, flickering tinsel. Others rose, unseen by the gaping crowd, then sudden flashes and thuds made them close their eyes for an instant before the wonderful bouquets of colour left brief stains on the heavens. Fire crackers spluttered and barked, the show by no means over . . .

Then Francisco Solano Lopez showed his people something they could never yet have seen. Better than fireworks. A glimpse into the future.

From the highest peak of the northern hills, a single dull light streaked upward, reached its apogee, hung for an instant, then bathed the Campo Grande and the city of Asunción in a dreadful, intrusive glare. Children clung in terror to their parents, wives to their husbands, the men themselves agape as the harsh white flare picked them out.

Wherever they stood, they froze as the phosphorus ignited and turned the night of the fiesta into day. They cowered and blinked, then scooped their families round them and hurried to be away from it, away from the whiteness, away and back home to the friendly yellow of candlelight and lanterns.

The musicians packed their instruments. The waiters loaded their trays. Riders calmed their horses, the spirited animals whinnying with fright. Dogs that had battled to bloody victory in the ring cringed and whimpered, pleading to be thrust back in their cages. Old women cried out that they were blind; old men cursed this final, deadly firework. The glare of the devil, what else could it be? Satan's eye turned on their innocent, jaunty fiesta . . .

Solano found Elisa. 'You see! You see what it did? By God, but it's all we'd need at night, moving in on Rio! Better than daytime! See a scorpion scuttle, a man scratch his arse! I only loosed off one. But there's a crate of them left, for when we need them. Oh, what an invention! What a splendid, scorching invention!'

'We'll go home now,' Elisa told him. 'You and me, Solano, we'll go home now. Why not, after all? You've chased off everyone else.'

The fiesta finished and the tents packed away, Solano spent a few relaxing days at La Recoleta. He did not speak again of the blinding *fósforo*, but played with his children, chuckled with his baby, and shrugged as he gave Elisa a heavy silver-wrought box containing twenty ounces of gold in the form of coins.

The following day she found a new horse in the paddock; a magnificent thoroughbred, trained on the *pampas* of Argentina. The value of the horse, she decided, would perfectly match the dull yellow coins, balance their worth in the scales.

As if to please Elisa in everything – catch up with his obligations – the bullish Solano Lopez attended the concerts she'd organized in the three-storey hall beside the Palace, and fought to stay awake as he sat through another of her musical entertainments imported from Europe.

The English Ambassador Thornton wrote to a friend in London, 'You have never heard a stone snore until you have sat behind President Lopez in the theatre. We are not allowed to leave until he does, and not even his Irish girl's elbow is sharp enough to jab the stone awake. Bone against rock, it must bruise her badly, but bone against rock is what they are. As for the show, I must admit it wasn't bad.'

7

Fat and flabby, the capon-like Venancio Lopez had spent the past few months in the Paraguayan Consulate in Montevideo, from whence he dispatched secret reports to his brother Solano in Asunción.

Three years younger than *El Jefe* – and almost twice Solano's weight – the pallid Venancio was eager to be forgiven for his insulting behaviour towards *La Irlandesa* on the day she'd disembarked from the *Tacauri*. All right, so it had been a stupid thing to do, shrilling at his brother's red-haired companion; *but were two years of near exile not enough?*

Sent once to Europe and twice to Bolivia; as far south as Chile, and with a number of other trade delegations to Brazil and Argentina, the wheezing Venancio prayed he might soon return home – and this time for good.

But first he must regain favour with *El Jefe*. Prove to him that, fat though he was, he could still keep his eyes peeled, his ears pricked, his fleshy nose twitching at the faintest smell of danger. Obvious and comical on the streets of the Uruguayan capital, Venancio was intelligent enough to turn his appearance to advantage. He adopted the role of the wealthy, rotund buffoon, spilling Paraguayan money on the Uruguayan tables, playing cleverly to lose. Welcomed by the private gambling clubs, 'The Bladder from Paraguay' eased and wheezed his way among the *montevideños*, then looked and listened as he lost . . .

Late one evening, in October 1864, Venancio Lopez placed the sausages of his fingers against his bulbous, everted lips, concealing a smile at what he'd heard. He remained at the table for an hour – always losing – then giggled at his own inabilities and heaved himself to his feet. 'My purse seems somewhat depleted, señores. I fear you've outwitted me again.'

The gamblers assured him it was merely a run of bad luck. It could happen to anyone. The thing to do, perhaps, was persevere.

'Oh, I shall. You may depend on it. At the same hour tomorrow?'

'With great pleasure.' They smiled. 'We shall keep the special chair for you, Señor Lopez.' And special it was, made to order for the Paraguayan's broad buttocks.

No sooner had the door closed behind him than the gentlemen gamblers of Montevideo tapped a finger to their temples, or shook their heads and let their dark eyes roll in their sockets. What a fool he was. *Que tonto. Que necio.* One could almost believe it pleased The Fat One to lose.

But as Venancio returned in the carriage to the Consulate, beaming to himself, he murmured, 'Oh, but you will love me for this, Solano . . . Love what you read, and love me for having warned you . . . Love will perfume the air again, *mi hermano*, and you will open the doors of the Palace to me, your prodigal brother. But open them wide, dear Solano, for I do seem to stretch my suits!' Patting his belly, Venancio allowed himself a shrill, girlish laugh, then rocked back, making the government carriage bounce on its steel-ply springs.

Sealed and strapped within the diplomatic pouch, Venancio's report took a week to reach Asunción. Away when it arrived, the President was visiting his well-fortified outpost of Cerro Leon, thirty miles east of the capital. Accompanied by von Wisner and others, he was determined that Cerro Leon should become the military hub of his country's defensive network, the warehouse for its stockpiled armaments, the rallying point for the peasants who were toiling in from the countryside.

'It is not that I fear an immediate attack,' Lopez told his advisers. 'But each night I sleep less well than the night before. I hear rustlings in the forest, and the sounds always come from there – over there – from Brazil.'

His officers said yes, now he mentioned it, so did they. A well-turned phrase by his Excellency, rustlings in the forest.

'Not that we've proof of intrusion,' he admitted. 'But there's no harm in taking precautions, eh, *mis amigos*? Keep the garden clear of serpents, so to speak?'

That was it, the officers nodded. The perfect way to describe it.

Whilst assuring his compatriots they had nothing to fear, Solano Lopez continued to strengthen his fortifications, to increase the size of his army, and test the grease-wrapped weapons his agents had purchased from abroad. The summer air was filled with the crack of handguns and rifles; the dull thump of howitzer shells; the boom of field-pieces that ran back crazily on their wheels, or were embedded in cement. Accidents were frequent on the testing grounds of Cerro Leon, the screams of the wounded and dying shrilling in chorus to the guns. Engineers were kept busy, repairing or replacing the weapons;

Surgeon Stewart's team of doctors worked hard with scalpel and saw . . .

As the half-naked Guaraní Indians emerged from the forests, they were ordered to shed their simple cotton shirts, then don the magnificent uniforms Solano had purchased from France. The obedient natives squirmed and scratched in discomfort, summoned from the peace of their farms to a world they could never have imagined. A violent teeming world of thundering riders, blaring trumpets, commands bawled in a language they did not understand, sights that made them drop to their knees and grovel in prayer to their gods.

Famed for their courage in the face of natural adversity, the native Guaranís would fight the alligators of the Río Paraguay, the snakes and wild-cats of the jungle, bring their bare heels down on a scorpion or spider. But the bark and blast of weapons left them gaping, as did the noise – the constant clamour – of the camp at Cerro Leon.

Returning to Asunción, Solano Lopez spent the evening of 27th October in the Palace, sorting through a pile of accumulated papers.

He glanced at various letters of application from merchant companies in Europe and North America, seeking permission to set up trading posts in Paraguay. The Europeans addressed him with fawning flattery, the Americans with an informality that bordered on the presumptuous. *'Mister President'? 'Dear Señor Lopez'?* He tossed the letters aside. His staff could deal with them later.

Then he unstrapped the diplomatic pouch from Montevideo.

It contained a note from the Consul, in which he warned *El Presidente* of various disquieting rumours concerning the build-up of troops in Paraguay. 'They are doubtless without foundation,' the Consul wrote, 'though it would clear the air if Your Excellency issued a firm and unequivocal denial. The Uruguayans are nervous at the best of times, and are often startled by shadows.'

Lopez shrugged. Let Uruguay think what it would. Who cared if the *montevideños* slept uneasy?

He picked up a bulky envelope, recognized Venancio's neat script – strange that, from such fat fingers – and sighed as he broke the seal. What now? Another request from the overweight *eunuco*, begging funds?

He skimmed the first few lines, slowed as his eyes traversed the sheet of paper, went back and started again. This time he read his brother's words more carefully, moving the three closely written pages nearer to the lamplight, coming forward in his chair.

This was not just a plea for money, after all. Nor Venancio's usual litany of complaints about the heat, the cold, his sufferings in Bolivia, the inedible food in Chile. This, at last, was a clear and detailed report of some significance, and it held Solano's attention.

A Brazilian steamer would soon be sent upriver from the estuary of the Río de la Plata, bound for Brazil's northern province of Matto Grosso.

The vessel, the 200-ton merchantman *Marques de Olinda*, would carry the newly elected Provincial Governor, Señor Frederico Carniero de Campos; a Government Inspector of Taxes; various officials and some ninety so-called passengers. '*So-called*,' Venancio had underlined, 'because I'm informed the ship will also be transporting a considerable quantity of arms and ammunition, among them six light machine-guns. Also rough-drawn maps of Northern Paraguay, where it borders with Brazil. These, and a great amount of money, though I was unable to ascertain the true sum.

'Nevertheless, *mi hermano*, you might wish to keep an eye on that over-laden vessel. The date of her passage is uncertain, though I'd guess she will refuel at Asunción in the second week of November.'

For the first time in years, Solano spared a smile for his flabby brother. If Venancio was right, he could come back home and wheeze his way into the Pantheon of Paraguayan Heroes. Eat himself to death from the menu of his own choosing. Drink whatever he liked, and as much of it as would fill the barrel of his belly.

Just so long as the over-laden Venancio was right about the over-laden *Marques de Olinda*.

But if not, The Fat One would be chewing on heavy lead bullets, served by the Palace Guard . . .

Within hours of breaking the seal on his brother's report, the President of Paraguay was in deep discussion with his most influential adviser. Not the Baron von Wisner, nor any of his lean, muscular generals, but with the woman he'd brought from Paris, *La Irlandesa*.

He handed her the letter and said, 'Read this. Read it attentively. Tell me what you think.'

Dressed in a fine, tight-fitting gown of oyster-grey silk, but without the glitter of jewellery, Elisa suggested he say good night to their children. 'I don't like being stared at whilst I read, *querido*. So off with you, if you will.'

Solano blinked and grunted, but Elisa was already poring over Venancio's first page, her protector's presence forgotten.

Caught on the wrong foot as so often by this loyal, intelligent foreigner, the bulky Lopez faltered, 'Chance to see the children, then. Been a while. Come back down in a moment.'

She hummed, and he went off to play the father.

Reading the letter once, and then twice, Elisa glanced across the well-furnished parlour and asked herself if this might not be the chance to set Paraguay firmly where it belonged – as the centrepiece of the South American crown. It was already geographically the centre, its army as powerful now as any on the continent, *and here comes this ship . . . sneaking weapons and ammunition along the Río Paraguay . . . the easiest way Brazil can get to her province of Matto Grosso . . . establish a military presence there . . . then send its serpents into Paradise . . .*

Solano returned and said: 'Well? I'd appreciate your views – '

'Are they securely tented in? The nets tucked round them?'

'What? Oh, the children. Yes, I've seen to it they are.' Agitated by her calmness, he found it hard to talk of mosquitoes. Did the woman not realize – ?

'It's an act of provocation,' she said. 'Nothing less. A deceitful shipping of weapons under our noses. Let the *Marques de Olinda* slip by, and Brazil will send others, sneering as they use our own river to fortify their province. You ask me for my views, my dear Solano. I think you should arrest that vessel and send your customs men aboard. Show Dom Pedro we're not just lock-keepers on a canal. Not just merchants who'll fuel his ships with coal at Asunción.'

As Elisa spoke, Solano nodded, in counterpoint with her words. It was what he'd hoped she would say – arrest them – for how else could Dom Pedro de Alcantara be slapped in the face by Don Francisco Solano Lopez, the grim rejected suitor?

'But tell me this,' he pressed. 'Won't Brazil raise troops in retribution, and move against us? That most extensive nation?'

'Don't see why.' Elisa shrugged. 'They're the ones who are guilty. They're the ones who bring their guns upstream.'

8

Preparations were made in the port of Asunción, the English engineer Thompson placed in charge of refitting the 500-ton paddle-steamer *Tacauri*, the same vessel that had, ten years before, brought Solano and Elisa from Europe.

Now, her sides plated with iron, her bow reinforced, she carried Gatling guns fore and aft. With a crew of thirty, and with forty armed riflemen on deck, the *Tacauri* awaited the arrival of the *Marques de Olinda*. Give those cunning Brazilians one hell of a shock, so it would.

And then, as it happened, the boat from Brazil sailed smoothly past the ambush.

With a dozen fewer passengers than Venancio had forecast, and with an extra half-ton of coal in her bunkers, the *Marques de Olinda* churned on towards the next refuelling stop at Concepción, ignoring the port of Asunción.

The Governor, de Campos, was happy to see the Paraguayan capital slide by. What was it anyway but a maze of garish houses, this one a sickly green, that one a jaundiced yellow. The Customs House that resembled a story-book castle. The Palace on the hill that looked like a public dance hall. A vulgar little township, he decided, and one to be left alone.

Sweating beneath the awning that covered the forward deck of the steamer, de Campos leaned back in his cross-grained bamboo chair and tried to sleep. His wife and children would join him later in Corumba, the capital of the Matto Grosso province. They'd arrive by the same dismal route, of course, up these Paraguayan waterways, the Río Paraná, the Río Paraguay. The quick way, if one could say that, but how tedious; how endlessly, stickily boring . . .

Two hours later – at three o'clock in the afternoon of 12th November 1864 – the Governor was shaken from his slumbers and told that a ship was belching smoke and thrashing its paddle-wheels, and racing as if to catch them.

Drugged by the heat, and with officials swarming round him, de Campos stumbled to the afterdeck of the *Marques*, snapping his fingers for a spy-glass.

He held it to his eye, and the glass misted immediately.

'Well, what is it? Someone chasing us with a message? Does anyone recognize the vessel?'

Drawn by the sight of the larger, pursuing steamer, the so-called passengers and crew hurried to the stern. As they did so, their combined weight shifted the ballast below the single, shallow deck, and the *Marques de Olinda* lifted her bows.

The captain bellowed, and the passengers surged forward. Members of the crew yelled that pirates were out to get them, and pandemonium ensued. The ship, dipping down in the water, turned to starboard – and rammed against a sand-bank . . .

Aboard the *Tacauri*, the forward gunner raised the barrel of the Gatling and sent a long spray of bullets high into the sky, ripping the distant, innocent jungle. Incensed that the grounded vessel had slipped by them in Asunción, he was determined to prove himself as one of President Lopez' *artilleros*. Show all those aboard the *Marques de Olinda* what he could have done, if he'd depressed the muzzle by thirty degrees.

Unwittingly, the ambitious young gunner scratched a footnote in the history of South America, for the rattle of the Gatling turned suspicion into hostility, his bullets the first ever to be fired by a Paraguayan soldier in the general direction of Brazilians.

With nothing yet written on paper, it was, nevertheless, a declaration of war.

Smoke poured from her triple stacks as the *Tacauri* heaved the *Marques de Olinda* off the sand-bar.

De Campos roared at the illegality of the seizure. 'I am a Government Official! I am aboard a Government vessel! This is an acknowledged international waterway, linking my country with her northernmost province. How dare you interfere with us? How dare you drive us ashore and loose off that gun?'

He roared even louder when he realized that his ship was to be towed back to Asunción – then fell silent when they got there, standing mute as customs men swarmed aboard, quickly discovering the arms and ammunition, the six light machine-guns, the crates containing 'a great amount of money'.

For all that Venancio had lost at the tables in Montevideo, The Fat One had returned it fifty-fold to Solano. Everything the spy had said would be there *was* there. In chests, in casks, in cylindrical

327

leather tubes. All the rumours his fellow gamblers had let slip were shown to be true, even down to the rough-sketched maps of North-eastern Paraguay.

Venancio's report had been one hundred per cent correct.

Elisa had been right to say arrest the Brazilian steamer.

And Solano now nodded, pleased that he'd sent the *Tacauri* in pursuit.

Seated behind his desk in the Presidential Palace, he listened as Frederico Carniero de Campos blustered and sweated. Then *El Jefe* said: 'No. Your account does not tally with the facts, my friend,' and sentenced the newly elected Governor of the Brazilian province of Matto Grosso to imprisonment for life.

The Inspector of Taxes was regarded as a spy, and waved away to be shot. As the man reached the side-door of the room, he turned and screamed for mercy. 'I was *sent*! I was only *sent*! Oh, please God, you must spare me! I didn't want to come here, *Excelencia*! I was sick from the moment I stepped aboard – '

'Seal your teeth, man. Close your jaw.' Then Solano sighed and said why tread on beetles? He'd reprieve the insect and send him home instead.

The Inspector of Taxes was still dribbling with fear and relief when he heard Lopez say: 'On a raft of *quebracho*. Tie him down to a hardwood raft and shove him off. Let's see how well he bobs for a thousand miles.'

The next to be arraigned was the Captain of the *Marques*, a man who levelled his gaze at Solano, and made no attempt to plead for mercy.

'Did you know what you were carrying, *Capitán*?' Lopez asked him. 'I must assume you did.'

'Twenty-eight years on the rivers and at sea,' the man retorted. 'I'd be damned for a fool if I didn't.'

'So you were willing to carry weapons in secret – ?'

'What's the secret? Brazil lies to the south of you, and Brazil lies to the north. The Río Paraguay's the only way to get there, so we use the Río Paraguay. Take it overland, President Lopez, you wouldn't be talking to *me*.'

'All right,' Solano told him. 'Now stand quiet. I need a moment to think. Should I have you shot . . . ? Imprisoned till you die . . . ? Cut off your hands . . . ?'

'Seems to me,' the Brazilian interposed, 'you should make up your mind and have done with it.'

The remark was all Solano Lopez needed to enrage him. But *El Jefe* was never one to match the response of others, and with the mere lift of his hand he dismissed the captain, chuckling at the man's temerity. 'There's a sailors' hostel you can stay in near the port. You'll remain there until the next ship goes downriver. Eat and drink all you like, *Capitán*, and I'll see the bills are paid. Twenty-eight years? That's impressive. But don't waste the twenty-ninth by coming up here again.'

'And my vessel? The *Marques de Olinda*?'

'Don't be foolish, *mi amigo*. We are speaking now of the latest addition to the Paraguayan fleet. The *Francisco Solano Lopez*.'

Condemned by Venancio's term, the so-called passengers were sent to work on farms in the interior, from which none of them ever emerged.

The crew of the renamed steamship were dispatched to the manacled road-gangs, dying as they widened the paths to Humaitá and Cerro Leon.

As for the *artillero* – the ambitious young gunner who had fired above the heads of the Brazilians – he quaked in the presence of *El Supremo*.

'Tell me,' Lopez asked him, 'were we ever under threat when you opened fire? A rifle shot perhaps from the stern of the *Marques*? One of those so-called passengers with a pistol? It would please me to know that they'd fired first. I promise you, my boy, I'd believe you if you said you'd returned their fire.'

The gunner shook his head.

'Or even that you *thought* they'd fired, and reacted on the impulse?'

Unaware that his master was fighting hard to save him, the young man continued to shake his head.

'So you opened up with the Gatling gun. To try to control their panic? The way we might sound a bugle, you know, to call everyone to order?' *Oh, Christ, you ignorant youngster, nod your head* . . .

But the *artillero* denied it, and was still unaware of what he'd done wrong when the Palace Guards took him gently through the side-door and escorted him into the orchard, where an officer stepped behind him and coughed as he cocked his pistol . . .

Elisa Lynch listened calmly as Solano described the seizure of the *Marques de Olinda*. He saw no reason to tell her that Governor de Campos had been sentenced to life imprisonment, the Tax Collector set adrift on his hardwood raft, the passengers and crew dispersed to the farms and road-gangs. Nor did he mention the fate of the hapless gunner. All Elisa needed to know was that Lopez regarded Brazil's attempt to smuggle arms along the Río Paraguay as an act of provocation. 'I am not sure which angers me the most, *mi mujer*, Dom Pedro's deceit, or the way he insults our intelligence. Anyway, he has been caught *con las manos en la masa*. I shall formally sever all diplomatic relations with that ill-intentioned country, and take suitable precautions.' His deep voice was tinged with both triumph and indignation, though he merely shrugged when Elisa asked what measures he thought would be fitting.

'The bigger the bully, the more there is to chastise. Now listen. I shall be busy for a while. My time will be divided between the capital and the camp at Cerro Leon. You will embrace the children for me and – '

'Yes,' she murmured, 'I know. I must miss you.'

On the morning of 14th December, almost exactly one month after the capture of the *Marques de Olinda*, a squadron of disparate river craft steamed north from Asunción, the vessels carrying some 5,000 Paraguayan troops, smart but uncomfortable in their variegated uniforms. They were led by two of *El Supremo*'s most trusted officers, the swarthy General Vicente Barrios and the cavalry commander, General Isidoro Resquín. Cheered from the dock by a well-rehearsed crowd – who would later be rewarded with a sack of *mandioca* and a jar of *caña* – the flotilla was on its way to the Brazilian province of Matto Grosso, there to chastise the bully.

With war as yet formally undeclared between the two countries, and the province two months sailing distance from Rio de Janeiro, the Brazilians who garrisoned the small, riverside forts gazed in astonishment as the Paraguayans steamed level and opened fire.

'*In the name of God, why is this? Has Lopez gone mad? One has heard he dreams of ruling all South America, but why should he pick on us, up here in the north?*'

Taken completely by surprise, the Brazilians fled inland, abandoning the forts of Dorados, Miranda, and the provincial capital, Corumba. Panic spread, and neither General Barrios nor General Resquín were able to control their rampaging troops. Prisoners were seized, then murdered. Women were cornered and raped. Shops and houses were pillaged, lanterns kicked over and fires left to rage.

Ill-trained and inexperienced, the hitherto peaceful Paraguayans saw war as an endless series of easy victories, in which the enemy would gape in astonishment then run away, their womenfolk left as the prize.

One man who ran was the Baron Sancho de Villa Maria, the patriarch of the province of Matto Grosso. Elderly and rheumatic, the wealthy landowner escaped from his riverside mansion in Corumba, his pockets filled with the meat and bread of his unfinished dinner – and a pigskin pouch of diamonds.

Having squinted in disbelief at the invading steamers on the river, each proudly flying the flag of Paraguay, de Villa Maria struggled eastward through the jungle, hiding at first by day and walking by night, his progress lighted by the high, bright stars of December's summer.

When he realized the attackers were not riding in pursuit, he took to the trails and tributaries of Matto Grosso, paying his way with the diamonds. It was an agonizing journey for a man in his seventies, but in the final days of January 1865 he reached Rio de Janeiro. He had covered more than twelve hundred miles in forty-eight days, and gave his last three diamonds to the driver who delivered him to the Palace of Dom Pedro de Alcantara.

The men were old friends, and de Villa Maria's name was enough to gain him entry.

The Emperor Dom Pedro was horrified by the patriarch's appearance, and yelled for his physicians. 'God, but the man's been sucked half-dry by leeches! And the bites on his face! Oh, my friend, my dear old Sancho . . .'

Unaware that he was echoing the motto Francisco Solano Lopez had adopted as his own, the drained and empoisoned landowner found the strength to mutter: 'The province, too, Dom Pedro . . . Seems Paraguay has bitten off quite a chunk of Matto Grosso . . . My own increasing deafness, perhaps, but I've yet to hear that Brazil's at war with Lopez . . .'

Dom Pedro patted the old man on the shoulder, then left him in the care of the pessimistic doctors.

Shocked by what Sancho de Villa Maria had told him, the equally fragile Dom Pedro ground a bony fist against a shallow, skeletal palm. 'So that's what he's done, the salesman who dreamed of buying my daughter. Attacked our northern province without warning. Well, let me tell you this, my brutal, salacious Señor Lopez, whatever you have bitten off, it is more than you can chew. As of dawn tomorrow,

331

Brazil will move against you. And to stop you biting, we shall pull out all your teeth.'

The following day, war flags snapped harshly in the off-shore wind that gusted from the Atlantic . . .

PART SEVEN

Cerro Leon; Cerro Cora: 1865–1870

1

A score of extra rafts were constructed in order to bring back the booty from the forts and townships of Matto Grosso, the Generals Barrios and Resquín standing side by side on the fore deck of the first Paraguayan vessel to return downriver to Asunción.

Word of the incursion had reached the camp at Cerro Leon, and Lopez was on the quay to greet his victorious commanders.

'Whipped 'em well, so I hear,' he applauded. 'Taught 'em the lesson they need. Ask me, *mis amigos*, I'd say we've had done with Brazilian steamers smuggling stuff upriver. They won't try that again.'

When he learned how much had been seized from Brazil's riverside outposts, he awarded honours as a father might give candied sweets to his children. General Vicente Barrios was granted six thousand acres of grazing land in the Chaco, on the western bank of the Río Paraguay. And with it, a ten-roomed *hacienda*. General Isidoro Resquín was presented with a string of high-stepping horses, a fitting reward for the country's Master of Cavalry.

All down the line, the soldiers and sailors who had taken part in what *El Jefe* called his Campaign of the Leather Strap were recompensed with coins and flasks of *caña*. No questions were asked about rape or murder or pillage. War was war, and in war such things will happen.

Thrilled with his victory – in which fewer than fifty of his troops had been killed or wounded, and eight of those by drowning, drunk, in the river – Solano Lopez decided to wield the strap again. He would leave Brazil's broad shoulder thrashed in the north, and raise a few welts around her limbs to the south.

He sent a second force, this time commanded by Generals Robles and Estigarribia, to the frontier of Argentina, two hundred miles south of Asunción. All he'd need was Argentina's permission, and his troops could cross the province of Corrientes, then whip Brazil again.

But President Bartolomé Mitre said no. He was sorry, but no. Whatever bad blood might run between Paraguay and Brazil, it must drain through the common waterways, and not stain Corrientes. The Republic of the Argentine was a powerful, peaceable nation, and had no desire at all to be splashed with blood.

'Since much of your country shares a common border with Brazil,' he wrote, 'I would rather you jumped your *own* fences than trampled through *my* meadows.'

Had Solano's incursion into Matto Grosso been met with stiff resistance, he might have paused for breath. Reined in his army. Even spent a while at La Recoleta, discussing events with his still-shapely mistress, his intimate counsellor, his greatly valued friend.

But his troops had won too easily in the north, bolstering his confidence. So he advised Bartolomé Mitre to give way. 'You must surely have heard that my nation is not to be baulked. I wish to send my troops across the Corrientes, and you'd do well to let me do so. I have a personal score to settle with Brazil, and am eager to get there. Your permission will keep us as friends, *mi Presidente*. But a further refusal will not.'

Gentle in his manner, Bartolomé Mitre offered to mediate between Paraguay and Brazil. He would travel to Rio, to Asunción, invite both Dom Pedro and Don Francisco to Buenos Aires, if that's what they wanted. 'I shall do all I can to help settle the differences between you. But I cannot, in all conscience, grant you passage across our territory, permitting you to nip at my neighbour's heels.'

On 19th March 1865, Francisco Solano Lopez dictated four lines – more than sixty copies of which were went to Embassies and Consulates and Legations around the world.

'Barred in our attempts to confront Brazil for all her deceits, the Republic of Paraguay is forced to declare open war on both the Empire of Brazil and the Republic of Argentina. It is hoped they will seek conciliation without delay.'

The diplomats in Asunción read their copies and turned pale. What the hell was Lopez up to, pushing for a war against the two most powerful nations of South America? All right, so he had guns and grenades, he had his Guaranís, scratching their groins in their thick felt uniforms, his fortifications downriver at Humaitá, and his extensive military base at Cerro Leon. All this, and his crates of *fósforo*. And the anger he nursed against Dom Pedro de Alcantara – and now Bartolomé Mitre.

But was he serious in his intention to strike against them both?

Did he truly imagine himself cast in the mould of the Great Napoleon, as Bonaparte reincarnate? Pray God he did not, the diplomats sighed, or we're all in trouble . . .

Elated by the victories in Matto Grosso, yet enraged by President Mitre's unwillingness to let his troops 'trample the meadows', *El Jefe* sent fresh orders to Robles and Estigarribia. 'Before we whip Brazil again, we must take the strap to the Argentine. I command you to seize the province of Corrientes.'

As before, the Paraguayan forces met with little resistance, and Lopez claimed the vast southern grasslands as his own.

Within the space of four months he had driven the Brazilians from their north-western frontier, the Argentinians southward from Corrientes. It mattered little to Lopez that those extensive countries had been taken by surprise. A victory was a victory, was it not, and Paraguay was in triumphant, festive mood. 'We are invincible,' he announced in the *Cabildo*. 'They will curb their tongues in future.'

Meanwhile, another small nation was drawn into the vortex.

Her frontiers forming a clumsy square that bordered the Atlantic Ocean, the estuary of the Río de la Plata, the southern edge of Brazil, and her own flanking river, lay the import-export Republic of Uruguay. Uninvolved as yet in his neighbours' squabbles, President Bernardo Berro was horrified to discover that Uruguay and Paraguay were linked by a long-standing treaty of mutual defence.

Whatever its purpose, he was not about to implement it and earn the undying enmity of Brazil and Argentina. *Madre de Dios*, look at the map! Uruguay was but corn between two millstones. Side with the lunatic Lopez, and the stones would grind Uruguay flat!

On President Berro's advice, the treaty was buried in the archives in Montevideo. Then he contacted Dom Pedro in Rio, and Bartolomé Mitre in Buenos Aires, suggesting they form what he called 'A Triple Alliance'.

The title appealed, and the three nations planned their next move.

Washburn and von Wisner met in private, the genial American voicing the fears of all the Western diplomats. 'Jesus, my dear Baron, you think *you* can tell me what the hell is going on? What happened to all that talk about defending Paraguay against aggressors? It's Lopez who's the aggressor! He intercepts that goddam steamer, the *Marques de Olinda*, then uses it as an excuse to wreck every Brazilian fort as far up north as Corumba. *And* Corumba, their tin-pot provincial capital. Now, we both know Lopez can harbour more grudges than the port of New York – '

'Be calm,' von Wisner measured. 'What's done is done. Señor Lopez believes he has squared his accounts with Brazil – '

'Oh, sure. And squared 'em with Argentina, right, by snatching the Corrientes? I can hardly wait for Bolivia to sneeze in our direction, or for Chile to say the *maté* crop's not up to scratch. Let Lopez hear *that*, and he'd have us at war with just about everyone.' He coughed as von Wisner lighted one of his thin, vile cigars, and the two men sat in silence for a while, each aware that Solano Lopez had gone too far.

The tall Hungarian heard Washburn cough again, and twisted his long, gaunt frame, blowing smoke towards the mosquito net that covered the Embassy window. 'You're as sensitive as Madame Lynch,' he muttered. 'Though she, at least, is honest enough to complain.'

'Oh, enjoy your damn cigars,' Washburn told him. 'I'm not talking about tobacco smoke, my friend. I'm talking about the smoke and flames of war.' He rubbed his chin. 'Now, what do we do? How do we calm him? More important, maybe, how do we get him to back down in the face of Brazil and Argentina?'

'Two ways,' the baron mused. 'But don't count on Lopez ever voicing regret. No, the only two ways I can see it being done is for his troops to be roundly defeated; hurt so badly they lose the taste for battle . . . Or for *El Supremo* to listen to the person he trusts the most. And I think we both know who that is.'

The American nodded. As tall in his chair as the Baron von Wisner, he leaned forward, ignored the stinking cigar, and asked the moustachioed Hungarian which of them would go first to see *La Segunda*. 'You or me, Enrique? Me from the States, or you from Europe, going to talk about Paraguay with that red-haired lady from Ireland?'

Von Wisner said: 'You. She might listen when you tell her Lopez is stirring a whirlpool. Say what you said about Bolivia and Chile. Warn her how fast a flood can spread if the riverbanks overflow. Yes, you, I think, Señor Charlie. After all, you share the same common language, in a manner of speaking.'

The Ambassador laughed. Then he fetched his favourite bourbon and poured out two stiff measures.

'And if I can't get her to drum some sense into Lopez?'

'Then I'll tell Madame Lynch that she has only two ways to go.

She must either convince *El Jefe* he's made his point, and it's time to bend the knee, or she must gather her children and her belongings and flee the country.'

'The first would be best,' said Washburn, nodding, though both men were aware the first was unlikely.

The American's visit to the *quinta* was far from successful. Elisa welcomed him as a friend, then ejected him as nothing more than a scaremonger, demanding to know by what right he talked of floods and whirlpools, when Paraguay had administered the whipping both her smirking neighbours deserved. '*El Supremo* has been insulted, don't you see that, Mr Washburn? Called a monkey by them both! And now he has shown them how rash they've been, and how power-ful we are. You know the way out, or should do by now. But do not, if you please, attempt to find your way back in!'

The Baron Enrique von Wisner de Morgenstern fared as badly. His suggestion that *El Jefe* should bend the knee was met with a furious rebuttal, Elisa's arm extended, finger pointing, red hair swirling as she approached him. 'I thought better of you than this, von Wisner. How dare you say Solano should kneel, or that I – that *I* should desert him! He is dedicated to this country, as am I, though your own sense of loyalty seems somewhat in question. God knows, you've been well enough rewarded all these years, yet now you come striding in here with talk of submission – '

'I am saying – '

'Well, don't. Go off and bend your own damn knee in Rio or Buenos Aires. Flee back to Hungary, for all I care. But as for me, I shall remain with Francisco Solano Lopez. And remember this, my disappointing friend: if there is any kneeling to be done, it will be in the Cathedral in Asunción, on the day when Solano is crowned Emperor of South America! You will doubtless hear word of it, even in distant Hungary.'

Washburn and von Wisner met again.

'Well, now,' the diplomat began with a sigh. 'We made a fine pair of fools of ourselves with *La Segunda*, eh, my dear Baron? Quite a rarity, Elisa Lynch. She either loves Lopez more than I supposed, or truly believes his nation can defeat the Triple Alliance. Who knows? Maybe it can. On paper at least – '

'Yes, I've seen what's down on paper. If the estimates are accurate,

Brazil can put a force of twenty-five thousand in the field. Argentina, maybe half that number. Uruguay – well, no more than two or three thousand. So around forty all together. Though they're *not* all together. They're scattered across the continent. Lopez claims more than sixty-five thousand loyal troops, and all within a few days' march of the camp at Cerro Leon. Oh, yes, it looks fine on paper, Mr Ambassador. Most things can be made to look good on paper.'

'Will you stay?' Washburn asked. 'Continue to advise?'

Von Wisner nodded. 'Madame Lynch might think my loyalty's in question, but I'm vain enough to believe I'll be needed. I am also more than fifty years old, so there's an element of need on my part too. The aged war-horse scenting the smoke of battle . . .'

'The stink of his filthy cigars, more likely.' Washburn smiled. 'But yes. I also intend to remain here for a while. Look bad if America withdrew right now. But you fall over a tight-packed valise in the Embassy hallway, it'll probably be mine!'

The two men had now voiced their reasons for staying, though neither had mentioned the feeling that skirted the edge of mere reason. If Paraguay defeated the Alliance, okay, *muy bien*. If Francisco Solano Lopez was crowned Emperor, well and good. But what most concerned Charlie Washburn and the Baron von Wisner was that *La Irlandesa* should not, herself, be sucked down in the whirlpool . . .

2

Paraguay struck again at Matto Grosso, but this time the Brazilians were ready and Lopez' troops retreated, badly mauled. A second incursion into Corrientes met with similar results; the Paraguayans now learning the true nature of war. The days of easy, undeclared aggression were over. The Triple Alliance had recovered from the shock of *El Supremo*'s earlier attacks, and had now unbuckled leather straps of their own.

By the end of 1865, the Army of the Republic of Paraguay had lost more than 30,000 men, killed or captured in action, dead of starvation or disease. Recruited in haste, the bewildered peasants had been brought in from the farms and fields, forced to march about the camp at Cerro Leon, then sent into battle, where they were deafened by gunfire and blinded by the flare of blazing *fósforo*. Ill-trained and uncertain, these innocent Guaranís vomited on a diet of salted meat, their systems used only to vegetables and fruit. Weakened by dysentery, they fell victim to the greater menace of cholera and smallpox, enemies more deadly than the encircling Alliance.

Aware that his all-too-brief moment of glory had passed, Francisco Solano Lopez settled to fight a dogged, defensive war. He convinced himself that his fears had been well founded. '*They* are the invaders, not I. See how they have come to seize my Paradise!'

At home in La Recoleta, Elisa Lynch had heard several different accounts of the way the war was progressing.

The engineer George Thompson had told her, with typical British understatement, that things were not too bad, all in all, but could do with a bit of a lift. 'The natives don't know much about discipline, that's the trouble. And they're so damn vulnerable to disease.'

'Do you think President Lopez should go on with it, Mr Thompson?' *Always Mr Thompson, for he'd wince if I called him George.* 'Do you feel we can make the Alliance call off their dogs?'

'Well, there you have it, Madame Lynch,' the sandy-haired Englishman told her. 'They doubtless think Señor Lopez should call off his. Six of one, and half a dozen of the other, if you know the phrase.'

Turning away in disgust, Elisa thought, Trust the bloody English.

Ask for a straight answer, and it comes back shaped like a corkscrew. And yes, as it happens, I do know the phrase. Though in this case it's *one* of one, and *three* of the other . . .

In the *quinta*, she overheard snatches of conversation among the staff, and learned they were frightened. They knew nothing of the world beyond the hills and valleys of La Recoleta, and imagined Brazil and the Argentine as lands in which monsters roamed at large. For servant girls who had never in their lives seen Asunción or the Río Paraguay, the *quinta* and nearby village of La Recoleta was their world, and all they would ever need was contained therein. So talk of invasion brought fears of hideous creatures, rearing up on the skyline, or trampling through the forests.

On the other hand, Solano strode in to regale her with news of fresh, if invented, triumphs; of Brazilians caught in an ambush; an Argentine gunboat sunk near Humaitá; deserters pouring across to join the Paraguayan Cause. 'Each new report tops the last one, *mi mujer*. We've blockaded the river, and it won't be long before – '

'Yes,' she agreed, 'but have you not punished them enough, *querido*? Is it not now time to lay aside the belt? A simple treaty . . . I could help you write it . . . If only to get the dogs back into their kennels . . .'

'So long as they still howl, they'll need to be whipped,' Lopez stated, his strong, swarthy features set with the fixative of revenge. 'When I hear them yelp – well, maybe then. But not before. Now, bring me the children. They must hear about the gunboat that foundered downriver.'

As bewildered as the Guaranís by *El Supremo*'s belligerence, Dom Pedro of Brazil, Bartolomé Mitre of Argentina and Bernardo Berro of Uruguay convened in Buenos Aires, where they drew up a treaty of peace. It took five days, and went through eighteen detailed drafts, for the leaders of the Triple Alliance were anxious to make the dish palatable for Señor Lopez.

Nowhere in the document did the word surrender appear. At no time did the Alliance claim compensation for the deaths or destruction inflicted by their neighbour. Throughout the treaty they addressed him with respect, offering him the chance to extinguish the bonfire before it raged out of control.

'God judge us.' Bartolomé Mitre sighed. 'If he can't accept this – '

'Then it means he's warming his hands at the flames,' Dom Pedro snapped. 'And stands to get badly burned.'

Bernardo Berro nodded; it was all that was required of the Uruguayan, flanked as he was by granite millstones . . .

The three men signed and sealed the final draft, then asked the Italian Minister in Buenos Aires to deliver it to Asunción. Signor Marino Faliero agreed, delighted by the opportunity to festoon his steamer with the flags and pennants of his neutral, go-between nation.

Three days later, Lopez returned to the *quinta*, this time to tell his mistress that he'd seen off the gaudy Italian. 'All ribbons and sashes, he looked like something from a fairground.'

Elisa did not tell Solano that he too sometimes donned the trappings of a ringmaster, preferring to ask if he thought the war would continue. 'As I understand it, this Italian was empowered to bring a treaty from our enemies. If I could just look at it – '

'Nothing to look at,' Lopez dismissed. 'It's burned, and there's melted wax on the floor. We're still at war, *mi mujer*, and we'll soon be in the Río de la Plata, barging in on Buenos Aires and Montevideo. Take my word for it. This time next year we'll control all of South America! And with a crown and coronet to prove it!'

He clutched her then, not caring that his lips bruised her face. Chaining her with his arms, he lowered her to the Persian carpet brought from Paris.

As ever, the man made her cry aloud with excitement, then moan at his practised skills. Yet, when it was over, and Solano had slumped across her, Elisa thought of more than the thrust of his body, more than the demands she was ever willing to answer.

She thought now of her children. And the future. And the treaty Solano had set to the candle. She regretted the way she'd behaved with Washburn and von Wisner. Agree with them or not, she should have curbed her tongue, allowing the men time to expound their views. Instead she had chosen to see them as prophets of doom, ignoring the fact that they, more than anyone, wished *La Irlandesa* well.

She murmured: 'Impetuous fool . . .' and Solano grunted, '*¿Que dice?*'

'It's nothing,' she told him. 'I was thinking of lost friends, that's all.'

He shrugged his broad shoulders and yawned. 'What need have you of friends, *mi mujer*? You have me.' Then he turned away, leaving her to imagine a war that might, as the servants feared, bring monsters over the hills and through the forests . . .

*

343

Their appeal rejected, the leaders of the Triple Alliance had no choice but to tighten the ring. They had never wanted this war, and were anxious to see it concluded. From all they heard, Francisco Solano Lopez was edging towards madness, the man obsessed by his hero-worship of a long-dead Corsican, and by a sense of persecution that now bordered on paranoia.

It was clear to Dom Pedro and the others that *El Supremo* would never bend the knee. He must therefore be *brought* to his knees. There was no other way.

And yet, during the next two years, the war stagnated. Paraguayan troops continued to probe into Matto Grosso and, for a third time, into the province of Corrientes. They were repulsed and sustained heavy losses, though both Brazil and Argentina failed to press their advantage, allowing the survivors to shrink away.

It was not until November 1867 that a combined fleet of the Triple Alliance attempted to force a passage upriver and attack the fortress of Humaitá. If they could blast their way beneath the serried ramparts of this riverside stronghold, they could steam north and seize Asunción. After which, God willing, Lopez would finally surrender.

But Humaitá had been placed under the command of Baron von Wisner de Morgenstern, a man unwilling to shrink away. He strode the lines, towered above his officers and took time to encourage the conscripts. 'Look at me,' he told them. 'The tallest man in South America. Yet have *I* been hit by their shells or bullets? As you can see, *mis amigos*, I have not.' To emphasise the point, he scrambled on to the nearest tight-packed breastwork, and strode along it to the cheers of the heartened Guaranís. It was a calculated risk, for the Allied fleet was far below, their progress still halted three hundred yards downriver. Even so, a sudden fusillade . . . A stray shot . . .

But nothing prevented von Wisner's slow promenade, and his troops showed their terrible teeth as they roared with admiration.

Then in late December – though with Christmas to be celebrated at La Recoleta with his mistress and their children – Solano Lopez made a brief visit to Humaitá, staying the night in von Wisner's *quebracho* bunker.

'You've done well here,' Lopez commended. 'You are as fine a general as any Paraguayan.'

'Is that what I am?' the Hungarian queried. 'I thought I was just a military adviser, *Excelencia*. No one ever talked of national rank.'

'Is that so? Well, as from now you are *El General* von Wisner. There's no time to have you measured for a uniform, but here –

Here's how we'll know you.' Glancing down, Lopez twisted a ring from his finger, grunting as he wrenched it across the knuckle.

It was a magnificent band of gold, into which had been set the profile of a broad-winged condor, the vulture's eye and feathers sparkling with a dozen precious stones. A work of art, it was unique, and worth a fortune.

Von Wisner bowed and slipped it on. 'You honour me, *Excelencia*. I shall endeavour – '

'*Muy bien*,' Lopez interrupted. 'But I need something in exchange, *Señor El General*. A few of your soldiers, with your permission. You've a garrison here of eight thousand, so I'm told.'

'Scarcely six,' von Wisner corrected. 'And several hundred reduced by disease. Five would be a more realistic figure – '

'No matter. I've seen what I've seen, and I'm convinced this place can be defended by no more than a token force, with you here to lead them.' He gestured within the confines of the bunker, then told his newly promoted General he needed some troops for a sortie against Brazil. 'Lend me half the men who are fit, and – '

'*Lend?*' the Hungarian echoed. 'And how many would you borrow, *Señor El Presidente*? With the Allied fleet poised to move against us, is this really the time to weaken Humaitá?'

Lopez gazed across the rough plank table, muscles bunched in his jaw. 'Do I sense you'd place problems in my path, *mi General*? Accept my ring, then refuse a simple request? You must tell me if this is so, my old friend, so I'll know to which camp you belong. The old friends I can no longer trust, or those who still – '

'I could lend you a thousand. Maybe fifteen hundred. But, in all honesty – '

'I'll take three thousand men,' Lopez insisted. 'Twenty-five cannons and carriages. A six-horse team for each carriage, and food enough for a month. Now don't look so grim. I'm only *borrowing* them, after all. You'll get them back.'

Von Wisner knew then that the rumours were flavoured with truth. Francisco Solano Lopez was indeed edging towards madness.

3

Christmas at La Recoleta was an uncomfortable family affair. Solano assured Elisa that their country could resist the foreign invaders, and that Paraguayan regiments would march by the light of the New Year moon towards Rio and Buenos Aires.

He spoiled his children with toys, and gave his mistress a casket of washed gold filings into which she could dip her fingers – 'But lick them first, *mi mujer*, and see how it sticks!'

At night he slept badly, tormented by dreams. Thrashing between the satin sheets, he bruised Elisa with the flailing of his arms. She held him close to calm him, then eased away and lay silent, but awake, no longer convinced that Solano would ever kneel in the *Catedral de la Encarnación* in Asunción, there to be crowned the Emperor of the Continent.

It was now, for the first time, that Elisa Lynch was tempted to desert him, creep from the room and hurry her children downstairs. She had money enough banked in Scotland, and who would blame her for saving her offspring, a comfortable life awaiting them in Europe?

It was what any common courtesan would have done. What most unmarried mothers would do, with flecks of gold on their fingers. Why stay, when the cream of the dreams was turning sour? Why share the bed of a man who leaned close to insanity? Why not abandon him now, whilst he slept, and return across the Atlantic, with the coffers filled in Edinburgh, friends still alive in Paris, and Elisa perhaps remembered as the daughter of Cavan Lynch, the hero of Cork?

Yet she was unwilling to desert the man who had brought her to his exotic, self-acclaimed Eden, the father of her five young sons. Whatever her fears for the future might be, Elisa shared something in common with the Baron von Wisner de Morgenstern.

She too was not the type to shrink away.

As the New Year drenched Paraguay with its heavy, dripping humidity, Francisco Solano Lopez instructed his officers to choose one man in three, then tell them to spy on their colleagues. This

lunatic scheme resulted in mutual suspicion, the destruction of families, the tearing apart of friendships. It gave authority to those who
envied their neighbours, the chance for old scores to be settled, debts
repaid with a single, heavy bullet.

Torn from both inside and out, the seams of the nation were pulling
asunder.

With his garrison at Humaitá reduced to less than two thousand,
von Wisner was forced to withdraw to the upper ramparts of the
fortress. But even up here the breastworks were bare, and he sent
men to cut twelve-foot lengths of *quebracho* wood in the forest, strip
the branches and polish the logs to a dull black shine.

Laid in place, one end capped with metal, they resembled – at
least from a distance – the cannons Lopez had 'borrowed'. But the
logs did not spew flame or smoke, and the Allied fleet crept closer . . .

Having held the enemy at bay for three months, the Hungarian
rode north to Asunción, then east to Cerro Leon, demanding the
return of his much-needed troops. 'And with them the guns, *Excelencia*, else your capital will be at the mercy of their ships.'

Expecting a hard-fought discussion with Lopez, it astonished von
Wisner when the President shrugged and told him: 'The capital is
me, my friend. It's wherever I happen to be at the time. Asunción's
not so important.'

Then he left the Hungarian to frown in disbelief, and sent word
to Elisa and the children, telling them to pack their bags and move
to the village of San Fernando, his new-found seat of government.

At the age of thirty-three, Elisa Lynch was now pregnant for the
seventh time. The baby was not expected before September and Elisa
prayed that by then the war would be over and her family re-
established in the *quinta*.

Nevertheless, she did not voice the prayer aloud. There were too
many spies abroad these days and, although she did not truly believe
that Solano would plant informers within her own household, she
thought it prudent to speak to God without moving her lips . . .

Throughout 1868, the armies of the Triple Alliance made ponderous,
but inexorable progress. As von Wisner had foreseen, Humaitá was
seized, leaving the way wide open to Asunción.

Lopez was forced to retreat still further into the jungle. His chain of
command had snapped in several places. Messages went unanswered.
Patrols sent out to reconnoitre failed to return. Officers summoned

to his presence never arrived. Food was scarce, and he consoled himself with endless mugs of fiery, mind-distorting *caña*.

Informers came to whisper in his ear, their rumours fitting the now crazed pattern of his mind. The stories unchecked, he believed them anyway, grunting as his spies recounted what they'd heard.

They had heard, for example, that treason ran in the bloodstream of his family. That his youngest brother, the sarcastic, long-jawed Benigno, recently brought back from exile in the Chaco, was conspiring with *El Jefe*'s brothers-in-law, Vicente Barrios and Saturnino Bedoya. That a plan was afoot to assassinate Francisco Solano Lopez, then surrender Paraguay to the Triple Alliance.

Bolstered by *caña* and his own convictions, Lopez rewarded the informers, and sent his *caballistas* to arrest both Barrios and Bedoya.

Without a word to his sisters, he had the two men roped to a bench in a sunlit clearing, where they were executed by a firing-squad of twenty terrified soldiers.

Twenty was excessive, but the Guaranís were not trained to kill men who sat weeping on a bench, and they tended to miss their target.

As for Benigno and the sisters – the women now just drab, wailing widows – they were imprisoned in the latest seat of government, the village of Lomas Valentinas, there to await *El Presidente*'s pleasure.

'Deal with them later,' Lopez muttered. 'It takes no time at all to make a bench.'

Elisa stayed with him, aware that if things were bad now, far worse was to come.

He no longer spoke of a glorious future for his nation, nor of the army he would lead to the gates of Rio or Buenos Aires. His mind was corroded by the sugarcane liquor, his dark eyes dulled by distrust, Elisa herself a victim of his suspicions.

'That American,' Lopez growled. 'That Washburn you befriended. Well, you know what he's up to now, *mi mujer*? You know how your friend's turned against me?'

'I've not seen him in months,' Elisa assured him. 'I imagine he's still in Asunción. In the Embassy.'

'Oh, yes,' Lopez snorted. 'Still there, and probably cowering behind his marines. I know he's still there, and I'll tell you why. Because he has no choice in the matter! Step out, and I've snipers who'll blow off the top of his head! Your friend . . . That traitor . . .'

It took a while before Elisa could calm him, could ask what Charles

Ames Washburn had done to incur Solano's fury. 'I can't believe he's in contact with the enemy. North America is neutral.'

Solano Lopez slumped forward, spilled his drink as he poured it, then stared down at the mug. 'Not neutral enough, so it seems. What he's done – *your friend* – is to harbour a dozen men I intend to see shot. Allows them to hide in the Embassy. Refuses to evict them. Claims his compound is protected by International Law.'

'As it is,' Elisa said quickly. 'Let's not take on the United States – '

He caught the side of her face with the back of his hand, the blow so unexpected that the shock seemed worse than the pain. She grabbed at the wicker table in the earth-walled *ramada*, the flask and mug sent toppling, her own chair rocking back as she fought for balance.

And then Lopez was on his feet, howling at her never again to tell him what he should do. 'Or not do! *I* am the master here! Surrounded by traitors, by a family who'd have me murdered, by troops who desert me – All this, but *I* am the master, and it's *I* who speak for my country!'

Her cheek inflamed, Elisa Lynch thought no more of North America, or the genial Charlie Washburn. She thought now of her children. And her unborn baby. And herself. And the speed with which life had gone downhill, like an ornate, runaway carriage . . .

As she had feared, the worse came soon.

The Englishman, George Thompson, was sent to command the fortress of Angostura – The Narrow Passage – though Lopez denied him more than a weakened battalion.

Wounded in the knee, and with his ankle broken in a hand-to-hand skirmish, the man who did not like untidy young women was taken downriver as a prisoner to Montevideo, where the doctors saved the limb. He would always drag his left leg, but Mr Thompson didn't mind that, for he had met a young nurse in hospital, as neat and clean as you could wish for. They married in November 1868, and two of their five children became engineers on the Uruguayan Railway, one of the engines known for a time as *El Tomson*.

Meanwhile, in the jungle, the Scotsman, William Stewart, continued to treat the wounded. Elisa entrusted him with the casket of gold filings, the surgeon insisting that they both sign a proper receipt.

'Ye find me somewhat humourless, Mistress Lynch. That I know. But in the matter of money, ye've no reason to doubt my probity. I trust – '

'None at all, Dr Stewart,' she assured him. 'With your brother in the Royal Bank of Scotland – no, sir, not at all.'

'Hmm. Well, that's good to know. I'll have the casket sent down-river in the medical pouch. More of a sea-chest really. Painted white, and marked with a strong red cross, its contents have never been questioned. Gets the freedom of the sea, does the Medical. An' tell ye the truth, Mistress Lynch, it's brought whisky back from Scotland in its time.'

She smiled at his petty admission, then shrugged in the face of Stewart's dull, bleak gaze. *Somewhat humourless? He wouldn't even flinch if teased with feathers.*

Six weeks later – sent out to administer to the wounded on the eastern front – Surgeon Stewart was lost in the jungle, and declared to be missing or dead.

It was true that Elisa had never liked him, though she spared him a moment's thought, regretting his disappearance. A bad way for the Scotsman to vanish, his body out there to be gnawed and nibbled to the bone . . .

And how will things end for the rest of us, amid the vines and thorns of the Paraguayan jungle? Step left, and you're in a bush of poisonous briars. Step right, and a stinking swamp sucks you down, bubbles arising as the devil expels his breath.

Ride ahead, and the chances are you'll nudge a branch, lurch back in the saddle as a snake unloops from above you, mouth wide open, ready to strike.

Or a foul black tree-rat. Or the fearless spiders that scuttle and jump. Or a swarm of hornets, disturbed and intent on vengeance.

Will things end for us as they might have ended for the Scotsman? Or will they end amid the shock and blast of an ambush, our eyes still open as the bullets tear a hole in our hearts, or shatter the shell of our skulls?

Elisa kept her children enclosed in their net-draped carriages. Enrique and Frederico and Carlos in the first; Leopoldo in the second, with the newborn Miguel, and the baby's terrified nurse.

The eldest son, the fourteen-year-old Pancho, rode ahead with his father. The boy was now nearly a man, and Solano grinned as his proud young replica strained upright in the saddle, adding inches to his height.

Elisa Lynch was not sure where they were going now, though it seemed that Lomas Valentinas, under threat from the Allies, was no longer tenable. The next stop was a settlement, the name of which she found hard to pronounce. Elisa mouthed the syllables silently, Cu-ru-guay-tay.

Curuguaytay. It was even deeper in the jungle.

4

With Benigno and his widowed sisters, Doña Inocencia and Doña
Rafaela, brought along under guard – judgement yet to be pro-
nounced by Solano – the entire Lopez family zig-zagged towards the
President's next seat of government, the village of hovels in the jungle
called Curuguaytay.

Solano's mother travelled with them, the old woman wailing as
her coach lurched and swayed, banging her brittle bones against the
rigid bamboo frame. The journey was the most painful she had
ever undertaken, but the black-gowned Doña Juana had reasons for
coming. Two good reasons, though only one of which would be
confided to *El Jefe*.

When they reached the Godforsaken hideout – *seat of government,*
indeed! – Doña Juana would beg Solano to release Benigno from his
chains. She would squeeze her eyes tight until the tears came, crawl
on her knees if need be, prostrate herself in the filth, if that's what
he wanted. She would plead and whimper, imploring her eldest son
to forgive her youngest, then gabble her thanks at Solano's sweet
generosity.

After which – the second reason for suffering the agonies of the
journey – the aged crone would take Benigno aside and tell him how
he could best show his gratitude for what she'd done.

It would be by returning to Solano, swearing undying loyalty to
the leader of their nation, *then thrusting a knife blade, hard and straight,*
between Solano Lopez' ribs . . .

She had even brought a knife for that very purpose.

As for the red-haired *ramera*, the foreign cat could be skinned at
Benigno's leisure.

The gross and capon-like Venancio was also with them, his bulk
filling a carriage of his own. It amused him to think of *hermano*
Benigno in a prison cart somewhere behind, locked in with their drab
and dreadful sisters. Well, serve him right. Far too skinny. Far too
clever by half. Teach him a lesson if Solano makes him share a cell
with Inocencia and Rafaela for the rest of their miserable days. Oh,
that'd be a sight to see – a sight to avoid! The fleshless Benigno and
the two squawking widows; the supreme definition of hell.

Interspersed with the family coaches were fifteen hundred weary, ill-fed horsemen, their tattered uniforms now stiff with sweat and mud and dust. As they trampled along the thorn-webbed paths towards Curuguaytay, they attempted to herd some six thousand infantrymen into line, the exhausted Guaranís too loyal to turn for home.

For all Solano claimed, this was not an army pausing to regroup and catch its breath. It was no longer an army at all, but merely riders who feared for their lives if they disobeyed him.

Elisa rode in the first of two landaus, which were positioned in the middle of the column. From time to time, Solano dropped back to peer in through the netted windows, and ask if she and the children had everything they needed.

She wondered if she dared say to him: 'No. I'd like to return with my children to La Recoleta. I'd like food that does not pass as burning liquid through our bowels. I'd like a treaty of peace to be signed, *querido*. I'd like you to realize, at last, that the strap is broken, and that we are, all ironies apart, now on the run.'

She also wished to tell him that the water itself contributed to their weakness. He'd been feeding his troops too long on salted meat, and too long on foetid water. It was the best way she could think of to empoison a nation at war.

But she nodded, and managed a smile, and told him: 'Yes. Just get us to – wherever it is – and I'll find some *mandioca* for the children. Now ride on ahead, and resume command.'

Twenty minutes later, the landaus bucked and bounced across the bed of a shallow river, sunlight causing the passengers to squint before the coaches were dragged once again through the tunnels of the damp green jungle.

Elisa left Enrique, Frederico and Carlos moaning in sleep, and swung down from the carriage. Since leaving San Fernando, she had discarded her fashionable gowns in favour of more practical gaucho breeches and hard leather boots.

Dragging at the door handle of the coach that held Leopoldo, and her last-born, the baby Miguel, she clambered aboard. Their young nurse had been unable to prevent the clawings of dysentery, and she was blushing with shame.

'Then that's *it*,' Elisa told her. 'This journey is inhuman. It is time the caravan stopped.' Her face set in a mask that none but mothers could ever fully comprehend, Solano's mistress climbed from the coach and halted the first *caballista* who rode alongside.

'Dismount, *por favor*. I need your horse.'

The man recognized her, frowned at the hard-set mould of her expression, and decided it wasn't the time to query her needs. *Best to get off, then hold the bridle while she mounts. Anything else risks the wrath of* El Supremo.

First introduced to the saddle by the avuncular Etienne Framat on the horse-trader's ranch near El Biar, Elisa Alicia Lynch had perfected her skills out here, the pleasure enhanced by the presence of her wiry American lover, Elmore Curtin.

No matter that she was now a woman in her thirties, her lover long departed, she was still the finest female rider in the country, and was sick and tired of the illness and fatigue that drained her children. So to Hell with the journey through Paradise! The coaches had travelled quite far enough for one day.

The *caballista*'s horse was more willing than she'd expected, and she spurred it beneath the tunnel of high, tangled trees, yelling at those ahead to give way. The half-mile ride cost her a stiff-brimmed hat she'd long treasured, and her waistcoat was ripped by thorns.

She saw Solano in conversation with the Baron von Wisner, the President broad and bulky in the saddle, the Hungarian leaning over and down to hear what Solano had to say.

Unable to draw alongside them, she burst between, and both men snatched instinctively at their heavy, holstered pistols.

With scarcely a nod to von Wisner, Elisa gasped her demands to the man – her protector – with whom she'd lived for fifteen years. But today as the evening closed in, she addressed him as the father of their children, telling him that enough was enough; the children were sick; and so what if the army failed to reach the unpronounce-able Curuguaytay?

'I want the column halted now! Can't you see how the Guaranís limp and stagger? Have you no sense of mercy at all, Señor Lopez? Then come back and share the stench of our coaches, the stench of your children's bowels! Ride back and do that, and you might wish to stop where we are!'

Von Wisner said nothing. He had not regained Elisa's friendship since the day he'd been evicted from her house at La Recoleta, when she had been infuriated by his well-intentioned suggestions. *Ask Solano to bend the knee? Or abandon him and run?*

Well, no. The General who wore the Condor Ring should have

known that. You don't ever tell Madame Lynch to make Lopez bend the knee. Nor suggest the woman herself should shrink away.

Yet Elisa was here now, between them, her red hair tangled, her green eyes blazing as she called for a halt to the march. 'If I need to repeat it, enough is enough! I want my children fed and housed by sunset. *My* children, yes, but yours too, *Señor El Presidente*, since my body gave growth to your seed!'

The retreating force of cavalry, infantry and artillery reached a level, grassy clearing, twelve miles short of Curuguaytay. They guided in the supply wagons, the ammunition carts, pretending not to see the sallow camp-followers who had trudged along with the army and were weary and sorry they'd come this far.

The Guaranís slumped on the ground, covering their skinny frames with thin, colourful blankets, or their coarse white shirts, the knee-length *tupois*. Too tired to eat, they curled close to their broad-bladed knives, their bamboo lances, the guns they were frightened to fire. They whispered to their gods, asking to be allowed back home soon; their crops were long neglected, their women left at the mercy of hideous dangers.

They had fought Brazil in the east, and Argentina in the south. They had done whatever *El Jefe* had commanded. But how could a war be won if they were huddled here in the jungle? How could *any* war be won if the soldiers tramped in retreat?

At 6.35 in the morning, 11,000 troops of the Triple Alliance, led by captured scouts who knew the Paraguayan jungle, launched a sudden attack on the mile-wide clearing, raking the outposts with gunfire.

Caught by surprise, the perimeter guards were quickly overrun, though a hail of grenades from within the encampment drove the Allies back to the trees. A machine-gun chattered, as if to dominate the conversation of the rifles. Active men yelled and dying men screamed as each handthrown bomb exploded with a dull, flat thump, and filled the air with smoke and the smell of cordite. Overhead, the sky became clouded by countless screeching birds . . .

In a tent near the northern edge of the clearing, Elisa Lynch heard the first crackle of gunfire. She had slept fully-clothed, and made her children do likewise. She would never know *why* she had taken such a precaution, though its roots ran deep; perhaps they reached back to the time when Cavan and Adelaide had feared eviction from their small stone house above Cork.

It anyway saved precious minutes, and the woman was on her feet, shouting urgently at the maid to help gather up the children, Elisa herself clutching the baby Miguel.

A stray bullet buzzed like a hornet through the tent, missing a bleary-eyed Carlos Honorio by inches. The chaotic sounds of battle blew across the clearing. The maid wept and faltered. The children took their cue and trembled in tears.

Snarling at the terrified *doncella*, Elisa told her to get the children out and away to the carriages, or stay here for the pleasure of the enemy. 'Help me now, or be raped till you're dead! It's the only choice you have! You think *they* will dry your eyes?'

The girls sucked in breath and came to her senses, then herded the four young boys and followed her mistress, Elisa and her maid stooping as they ran towards the whinny of the horses. Around and above and behind them was all the insanity of battle. A man to the left looked bewildered as a bullet drilled through his chest. *Why me? Why am I do die, when I've spent my whole life farming for my family?* He fell like a puppet, cut from its strings, face down on the dew-speckled grass.

Miguel squalled, a victim of his own special nightmare – the horror of unknown sounds and the jolt of movement. Wrenched from sleep, the baby cried aloud in alarm.

Elisa turned to see that the *doncella* was with her – still herding the boys – and flinched as a line of Guaranís were cut to pieces by the panning of an enemy machine-gun. Their bodies blown back by the impact of the bullets, they were more like clowns than puppets, yet sacrificed in this grotesque and bloody circus.

And where is Solano? Where is my Protector? Where is the Ringmaster, with his broken leather strap?

Thank God there were still loyal soldiers, guarding the horses, and with the presence of mind to have hitched up a carriage. They helped Elisa and her maid lift the baby and the children aboard, then Elisa thrust the *doncella* into the overcrowded coach. 'Get them to Curuguaytay,' she shouted. 'Get them anywhere to safety!'

Twisting above the bulbous half-door of the carriage, the maid called back: 'But you, Señora Lynch? Aren't you with us? These children here, they're yours! And the baby!'

Waving urgently to the driver to leave, she thought, yes, they are mine. But so is Solano. And Pancho who fights alongside him.

The coach lurched away to the north, and Elisa turned aside, beckoning for a horse. The riot of battle seemed closer now, the

Allied troops advancing, grenades tossed ahead, the Paraguayan perimeter shrinking fast.

She snatched at the bridle of a skittish, wide-eyed bay . . . Told herself to follow her children, the obvious thing to do . . . The mother of all the future of the nation, the acceptable thing to do . . . No one would blame her, least of all *El Jefe*, so why not ram in her heels and urge the bay north, overtaking them somewhere in the jungle?

Instead, she jerked at the reins, forced the animal's head round, then charged towards the far end of the clearing, where Solano had pitched his tent. *Show him at least that the ringmaster's red-haired assistant is still in the ring.*

The skills Elisa had learned at El Biar were enough to keep her in the saddle. The confidence she'd gained from riding out here enabled her to control the terrified mount. She rode well and rode fast, skirting the northern edge of the clearing. Solano's black-tarred tent and the flag of Paraguay, flapping gently in the breeze, were in sight . . .

Then an unknown sniper took aim and squeezed the trigger of his heavy, long-barrelled rifle, and the fine, frightened bay, shot in mid-stride, stumbled forward and slid to its knees.

Elisa kicked back instinctively with her heel, to free her boot from the stirrup. She thanked heaven she was wearing breeches, not a skirt, her leg drawn up as the poor mount fell upon her.

But it rolled on a slope in the clearing, trapping her anyway, and she gasped with pain as her shoulder hit the ground, her right leg pinned by the heavy, dead weight of the handsome bay.

So much for the things I told the maid, she thought wryly. Rape *her* to death, they'll make sure *I* don't find such mercy in the grave. Oh, that hurts. My God, but a horse is heavy.

She lay there, appalled by the horrors of warfare, her nostrils filled with the stench of it, her ears with the stutter and crackle of gunfire, the myriad cries of those who would never again return to their farms . . .

The woman from Ireland waited for the men from Brazil and Argentina to shadow her face – tip down the muzzle of a pistol – lean beside her with a knife – or leave her where she was, then tug at her breeches . . .

She prayed that Francisco Solano Lopez would ride to save her. *The knight on his fine white charger, glossy teeth bared in a smile. The bullets would bounce from his armour, heads roll when he wielded his glittering sword. The maiden swept up, her slender arms around him, his gallant mount would toss its mane as it launched them to safety.*

357

Well, the bay had been gallant too, but it had died in action, and now pinned her as a prize for the Alliance. Oh, the fun they would have with *El Jefe*'s red-haired mistress. The ribald jokes they'd tell and retell later.

Then it happened. The shadow she'd feared. The blade of a knife. A hand on her shoulder.

Twisting her head, Elisa sought to bite and strike at the enemy. They would do whatever they wanted, of course, with the woman trapped firm, but she'd see to it some blood ran first, before they –

'Never mind trying to savage me,' she was told. 'Never mind that we've not been friends for a while, my dear Elisa. You just haul your leg out when I tell you. Ready? Then pull! And again. Now again. That's it. Well, massage it, woman! Decide if it's broken or not!'

Recognizing the voice, and obedient to the towering moustachioed shadow that leaned across her, Elisa dragged her leg from beneath the bulk of the bay. Then she told the man she was fine, she could move, and stumbled with him to the edge of the clearing, the Baron von Wisner supporting her, the two of them friends again, as in the past.

'We've not been this close for a while.' Elisa grimaced, hunched within the crook of his long, bony arm. 'Though I wish to God we had, Enrique, for it seems you were right. You and Charlie Washburn. We should have bent the knee.'

The distinguished Hungarian shrugged. These were things they could talk about later. All that mattered now was to hurry Solano's courageous young mistress to safety.

The battle blazing ever more fiercely around them, von Wisner assisted Elisa into the last of the family carriages.

Doña Juana had already fled the scene. The corpulent Venancio had left, shrilling his driver along. Then Benigno and the two drab sisters crowded back into their prison cart and jerked away. Though Paraguay was again losing ground, the Allies had failed to capture a single member of the Lopez family.

'Did you see Solano?' Elisa called down to the baron. 'And Pancho? Would you have me abandon them here in this nameless place? I was trying to reach them – '

'Yes, I know. But it's more important that you get away. I'll see your men are not taken.' He signalled to the driver, who crouched like a monkey on the bench, and the carriage lurched in ungainly pursuit of the others. As it swung towards the next long tunnel of trees, the woman glanced through the mud-splattered netting that covered the window, almost smiling at the sight of the tall European as he strode back into the clearing, too proud to stoop or scuttle. But there was really nothing to smile about, for she did not believe she would ever see him again.

And if Enrique dies, then why should Solano survive? The enemy are now at our throats, and the one they would cut most readily is Lopez'. Kill him here, today, the Defender of his Eden, and the serpents will writhe throughout the garden.

Kill Solano, and maybe Pancho, and another killing will follow. Doña Juana will see to it that Benigno is freed, and an hour beyond that they'll have me buried. It would suit them well to blame their defeat on a foreigner. It usually does.

Yet it was not for herself alone that she hoped Solano would live to reach Curuguaytay. There were also the younger children. Her children. But with *El Supremo* dead, not Paraguay's children any more.

5

For reasons of their own, the leaders of the Triple Alliance left Asunción undisturbed. Perhaps they believed, as Lopez believed, that the capital was *him*. Cut the throat of the man, and the city would bleed, draining down into the river.

Whatever they thought, it was bad news for Charles Ames Washburn and the dozen or so Paraguayans who'd incurred Lopez' wrath and sought sanctuary in the Embassy. Still safe on what was technically American soil, the Ambassador could not prevent Solano's loyal *caballistas* from cutting, if not throats, then all other lifelines.

The water-carts, with their two-hundred-gallon barrels, were turned away at the gates. The telegraph line that linked the Embassy with the outside world was hacked from its posts. The merchants who regularly supplied *los norteamericanos* were visited by the *caballistas*, and warned to find their customers elsewhere.

Aware that by taking in refugees he would earn the undying enmity of Francisco Solano Lopez, Ambassador Washburn had sent a long and detailed report to Washington, the message transmitted eight days before the telegraph wires came down.

Unfortunately, the Government of President Ulysses S. Grant took time to deliberate, and the reply never reached the Embassy.

Devoid of fuel for the lanterns, and with food stocks rationed, the once-genial Charlie Washburn told his Marines to stop shaving, then commanded them to set out every cask and bin and receptacle they could find, just in case it rained.

'We're in the hands of God and the clouds,' he told them. 'Lopez' miserable soldiers want us to surrender the refugees, so they can shoot 'em out of hand. That may be their way, but it sure ain't mine. So we'll just go easy on the food and the general hygiene. Washington will find a solution. In her own good time . . .'

Several of those who had fled for sanctuary to the Embassy offered to leave. If Mr Washburn's troopers would help them get over the wall under cover of night, they'd stand a fair chance of slipping away into the city. They had not come here to make trouble. They would rather take their chances –

'First guy who climbs the wall,' Washburn told them, 'I'll be there to shoot him myself. We're a young nation, our *United* States of America, but we'll start as we mean to go on. Be a sweet thing, eh, if every time we get hungry, we open the gates to the enemy? Now kneel by your bunks in prayer, or go out and do a rain dance. But so long as I hold my station here, so will you.'

The refugees cheered – a mistake as it happened, for the sound carried to the ever-alert *caballistas*. They replied by tossing dead animals into the American compound, hoping to infect the foreign air . . .

Sergeant Blackman heard it first, and rolled from his bunk. He'd missed the first few letters, but now he was out in the dawn in his long woollen underwear, blocky head tipped back and to the side, listening hard to the short, sharp blasts, and the longer mournful spelling of the message.

With a lifetime devoted to the American Marine Corps, the iron-cast soldier was not known for his grins or laughter. But a grin now stretched his lips and a growl of merriment broke free, 'You done good, Mr Morse. Buy you a beer. Buy you a whole damn crate!'

Then Sam Blackman ran to wake the Ambassador. Not caring that he had failed to snap to attention in his grey, buttoned 'coverups', the sergeant recited the message like a child.

'Word from the U.S.S. *Wasp*, Mr Washburn. "We-are-here-to-take-you-home . . . One-hour-to-reach-the-ship-or-we-assume-you-beleaguered . . . Bring-all-you-like-but-leave-the-kitchen-sink . . . Your-courage-admired . . . God-Bless-America . . ."'

Knuckling sleep from his eyes, the weary Washburn smiled at his sergeant. 'You look ridiculous, Sam, you know that? But it'll come as a great surprise to me if you don't, pretty soon, get to shake hands with President Grant. Now get your troopers ready. Wake our guests. We're leaving here in good order, and sailing downriver.'

It was what the Marine detachment wanted to hear. Breaking all records, they were dressed and armed and ready in next to no time for the walk downtown to the port, a cartridge slammed in the chamber of each rifle, their high-laced boots stamping the ground with impatience. *So Washington had finally come through. About time. But the Navy boys on the* Wasp *could stay where they were* – muchas gracias – *and leave the Marines to do the rest.*

With the Embassy staff and refugees assembled and ringed by the troopers, Charles Washburn gave the order to open the gates. 'Keep in pace with the Marines,' he told the civilians. 'If there's any firing, then drop to the ground and stay there. The thing to do now, gentlemen, is keep calm. With any luck, we'll all die of seasickness, when the U.S.S. *Wasp* hits the ocean.'

The refugees whom Lopez would have sent to the bench nodded in obedience. Better to die this morning – on their feet – than be shot like chickens on a perch.

And then, as if to show her support for her isolated compatriots, the *Wasp* stung the air with three long blasts of the horn. *Move it up there! We ain't selling tickets for a trip round the lake!*

The *caballistas* levelled their guns and hefted their knives.

The Marines had their rifles ready, each man with a target in mind, and eager to hear the sergeant give the word.

But he didn't – not yet – and the troopers halted as Washburn relocked the gate. An easy thing to do, lock the gate; but it suited him to test the lock, tug at the chain, pocket the small iron key. *Leave when it suits us to leave; not before. When America's ready, and not when Paraguay presses.*

Then the chief of the *caballistas* stepped forward and told them to surrender the civilians. 'We have decided you may leave, you foreigners. You don't belong here anyway. And the sun will revolve more smoothly without your presence.'

Sergeant Blackman's knowledge of Spanish was limited. *Muchacha* for girl, *cama* for bed, *enamorar* for love, *¿cuanto cuesta?* for the price he must pay for his pleasures. But he knew when a silver-buttoned mongrel was out to threaten him, and he'd a pretty fair idea of how to talk back to a dog.

Moving forward, he drew his heavy Colt from its holster, then snapped the finger and thumb of his leathery left hand, his troopers responding on the instant. 'Don't know what you're saying, *amigo*, but you're right in my line of march down there to the port. Now you either back off, or this here pistol blows a hole in your greasy head. And lots more holes, if your friends want to try it. But being in your place, I purely wouldn't.'

The *caballista* glared at the hard-eyed *Americano*. Then he waved the evacuees onward, as if with permission, and told them in Spanish to hurry aboard their fish-boat, and leave with the tide.

The captain of the *Wasp* had already ringed the port, and was counting the minutes until the sailors were sent to relieve the Embassy. He would lead them, of course, and if need be he'd die for his country. But at twenty-six, with a marriage planned next year in West Virginia? And how would Charlotte take to that, her man killed in this seedy, unknown city, in an all-but-landlocked country? She'd be furious. Enraged. Tell herself she'd wasted her time, plighting her troth to someone who'd allowed himself to be killed in – where was it? – *Asunción*?

So it pleased him when Charles Ames Washburn led the Marines and refugees aboard the *Wasp*.

'Sounded a long, clear message, I hope, Mr Ambassador. Got you away in time.'

'Sure you did,' the diplomat told him. 'Now shake hands with Sergeant Blackman, Captain. That's him, the one with the beard and the special perfume. Well, do it, Captain, then send us all down for a shower. Part of coming back to America, I'd say – a decent shower.'

As the U.S.S. *Wasp* steamed downriver towards the Río de la Plata and the sea, Solano Lopez, his eldest son Pancho and the Baron von Wisner rode exhausted into the village of Curuguaytay. And with all hell now to pay for what had happened.

It was obvious to *El Jefe* that someone had got word to the Allies. Else how would they have known where to come?

Someone close to the leader himself. A friend of the family. *One* of the family. And not hard to guess which one.

Not his mother, of course, though possibly Inocencia or Rafaela, his sisters seeking revenge for the way he'd sent their husbands to the bench.

Not Venancio, for the bladder had proved his loyalty in Montevideo, and was even now wheezing in the background, awaiting Solano's beck and call.

Stamping towards the hutment that would serve as his headquarters, the President of his tattered nation muttered aloud the name of the man he held responsible for the Allied assault on the clearing. '*Es Benigno*. Who else can it be but Benigno, my tight-jawed brother hissing treason through the bars?'

If it made no sense to those who were sane, it was clear enough in the distorting glass of Solano Lopez' mind. He ignored the fact that the Allies had been led there by captured scouts. Dismissed the idea that his army had trampled the jungle path flat from San Fernando and Lomas Valentinas. Ignored the truth, and found his scapegoat in the brother he'd never loved nor liked. The culprit was Benigno Lopez.

And the price of treason? Well, no more than you'd pay for a bench and a length of rope and a handful of bullets.

The village was in turmoil. Twelve miles was a long way from the clearing to Curuguaytay, though of the fifteen hundred horsemen who had ridden north from Lomas Valentinas only six hundred managed to rejoin *El Presidente.*

The task was harder for the infantry, the weakened Guaranís, and less than two and a half of the original six thousand reached the village.

Most of the cannons Lopez had 'borrowed' from Humaitá had been lost or abandoned. The weary camp-followers had surrendered to the forces of Brazil and Argentina, trading their favours for food.

The Allied commanders learned quickly that Lopez was twelve miles north, and they planned how best to encircle his shrunken force and finish the war. God knows, it was time to have done with it. Catch Lopez now and they'd snare his entire family – *and,* so it seemed, his attractive, foreign mistress. Airing their faulty English, the young officers grinned.

Elisa thanked God to see both Solano and Pancho alive. Yet a special smile was reserved for von Wisner, whose right arm was strapped where an enemy bayonet had glanced off the bone.

'You over-stayed your welcome, Enrique, so it seems. An old fool like you. Whatever were you doing playing the hero?'

'Wrong place at the wrong time,' he admitted. 'But you're not to think me infirm, Elisa. I'd have out-run a hare when I fled.'

You're a liar, she thought. It's not in your nature to run. I'll ask Solano later, and I bet he'll say you were with him until the end.

'Well, don't stand in the wrong place again, my dear Enrique. I might need you to help prise me free, from time to time.'

The Hungarian bowed, then went to organize the remnants of the army, Elisa returning to comfort her five youngest children.

They would once again sleep in their clothes, the carriages hitched to the dull-eyed horses, while this so-called seat of government was still under threat of attack. A short night's rest, and they'd be on again, ever deeper into the jungle, where the paths were not so well trampled, for there were fewer hooves and boots and naked feet to crush the thorns and the poisonous lianas.

*

Their tent left behind in the clearing – a present for the Allies – Elisa's four boys lay on the floor of a palm-roofed hovel in Curuguay-tay, shivering under a motley collection of coats and blankets. The youngsters did their best to keep the baby Miguel warm within the ring of their own skinny bodies.

The *doncella* sat in misery, a thin shawl round her shoulders, her eyelids drooping as she gazed at the saddest of fires. Elisa went to sit with her, and embraced the girl with a wing of her pleated cape. Damp and threadbare, it at least drew the maid together with her mistress. *And reminded Elisa of that terrible Irish winter when Adelaide covered her daughter with a cloak as they stumbled through the snow from the hamlet of Kilbreen . . .*

'We'll be fine,' she told the maid. 'Away from here tomorrow, and to places the President knows. I'm sure he has food stocks hidden. Fresh troops who'll fight. Clothing and whatever else we need. *El Supremo*'s our leader, after all, and we mustn't lose faith in him now.'

Doped by fatigue, the maid leaned towards her. If that's the way *El Supremo* had planned it . . . The way *La Segunda* said it would be . . . Then maybe it would . . . Maybe they'd reach a valley running with water, clear as crystal, and with *mandioca* waving in the breeze . . .

Two hundred yards away, in a narrow bamboo structure that had long served as the meeting hall of Curuguaytay, Francisco Solano Lopez watched his brother brought in in chains.

'You look like something found in a gutter, *mi hermano*. Stand there, if you will. I don't wish to catch the odour of your body.'

The slate-eyed Benigno gazed back at him. Solano was drunk – a blind man could have seen it – and didn't he appear ridiculous, his heavy body swaying on that delicate, native stool.

'Smell bad?' he retorted. 'Who wouldn't, cooped up in that cart? But no need to be squeamish, Solano. It's you who gave birth to the stench.'

The elder Lopez wrapped his hands round his stone mug of *caña*, pretended to ponder over the rim of it, then stared unblinking at his prisoner. Without preamble he said, 'I judge you guilty of imparting our whereabouts to the enemy. You know the sentence. Go away and die.'

Benigno returned a brief, wintry smile. 'Promise me something, *mi hermano*. Promise me you will live to grow very, very old. A strange request, you might think, but see it like this. The longer you stay alive, the longer I shall rest in peace. So please don't join me too soon.'

Solano watched as Benigno was led away. A few moments later he heard the ragged crackle of rifle fire. He felt no sense of relief, nor that justice had been served, but that somehow Benigno Lopez had escaped him.

When Doña Juana heard the news she screamed and fainted. Inocencia and Rafaela keened and clawed ashes from the fire, streaking their haggard faces. Venancio did not weep for his brother, though the shock set his heart pounding violently within the depths of his great, oleaginous chest. He found it hard to breathe, hard to move his hands. The pounding became irregular, a terrible coldness numbing his legs, his arms, the muscles of his jaw. He knew he must rest – *here* – *now* – and lay down where he was, in the mud of Curuguaytay's single street.

Within an hour of Benigno's execution, Venancio Lopez was also beyond Solano's reach, and the village silent but for the anguished cries of the women . . .

6

There was no question now but that Francisco Solano Lopez had relinquished all grasp of reality. When Doña Juana and her daughters begged to be allowed to return to Asunción, he accused them of cowardice in the face of the enemy. 'Cowardice and desertion; and we know what happens to those who would flee the field, eh, Señoras? You speak of Asunción, but you'll surrender to the first Allied troops you see, and it won't be long before you're pointing the way back here. If my own woman is willing to ride with her President, then so will you. Draw your courage from Elisa Lynch, Señoras. I'll ask her to give you a scrap of her clothing. You will carry it as your talisman. And the worse for you if you lose it!'

Still loyal to a cause already lost, the Baron von Wisner offered to cover *El Jefe*'s retreat. 'We are not strong enough to mount an offensive,' he told Lopez, 'but I believe I could decoy the bulk of the enemy, permitting you time – '

'What's this word you use?' Solano demanded. 'It's new to me, this word. This word *retreat*. This word is not one I have ever heard before. This word – '

'Regroup,' von Wisner corrected. 'I should perhaps have said regroup.'

'Ah, that, yes. Regroup I *do* understand, *mi General*. But the other . . .'

However, he rejected the Hungarian's offer, smiling slyly as he said, 'You're a European, after all. Might get lost in the jungle. Might be captured. Safest for us all if you stayed with the army, don't you agree?'

The army? von Wisner thought. What army? A disintegrating rabble of starved and exhausted Guaranís; enough ammunition for a fifteen-minute skirmish; horses that are dropping dead beneath their riders; soldiers who are dying wholesale from disease and untreated wounds. If retreat was not a word acknowledged by *El Supremo*, army rang like a cracked and faulty bell in the ear of von Wisner de Morgenstern.

Abandoning Curuguaytay, Lopez dragged his children, his womenfolk, his native soldiers north-east towards a hideout he remembered from long-ago hunting expeditions. A lightly wooded basin surrounded by high, protective hills, it was threaded through by a clear-running river, as close as dreams could come to Paraguay's Paradise.

He would establish his seat of government here, in the virgin valley of Cerro Cora.

Not even Elisa knew when, exactly, Solano had felt the brush of God's hand on his head. He'd kept the divine occurrence to himself for several days, humming as they made their tortuous way to Cerro Cora. Then he announced to her that the Almighty had beatified His servant, and that he, Francisco Solano Lopez, was now the Saint of Christian Paraguay.

'I thought you might have noticed the change, *mi mujer*. I find that a pale gold light surrounds me, by night as by day. Not enough to disturb my sleep, but always there, whenever I awake. I'm sure you noticed *something*.'

With tears in her eyes, his most intimate and loyal companion of almost two decades murmured yes. Afraid to displease him, she said she had indeed been aware of the clear, celestial light. It had shown in the way he'd now halted the executions, in the expression of peace that erased the furrows of anger from his brow. Oh, yes, she lied, she had noticed it, but had feared to interrupt his long communion with Heaven.

He saw her tears as soft, translucent pearls of adoration. He did not know that Elisa Alicia Lynch was weeping silently in mourning for his sanity.

But it was too late to leave him now. Too late to gather the baby Miguel and her four small boys, and throw herself upon the mercy of Allied justice. Too late to convince her eldest son, Pancho, to discard his uniform, desert his father and join her as she fled from Cerro Cora.

All dreams of the crown and coronet had vanished. The male population had been decimated, the farms, plantations and orchards left derelict. Whatever *El Jefe* might have hoped for his nation, he had brought it to the posture he himself had refused to take. Ruined, and with her lifeblood seeping into the ground, the Republic of Paraguay was on her spare, bony knees.

Brazil would later deny an intended irony, but as soon as Lopez' hideout had been located a force of eight thousand men was sent to attack it. The commanding officer was none other than Gaston d'Orléans, the Comte d'Eu, husband of the woman Solano Lopez had himself hoped to marry, his suit torn to shreds by Dom Pedro de Alcantara.

It was the last week of February 1870, the weather hot and oppressive, the air alive with wasps, mosquitoes; with clouds of plump black flies. The basin of Cerro Cora was defended by less than five hundred troops, though as many lay sprawled on the ground, dead or dying. Solano's sister Rafaela would soon die if not given salt and fruit and vegetables, though in truth the unhappy widow had no wish to live. Her husband, Saturnino Bedoya, had been among the hundreds executed on the word of the lunatic Lopez, and she prayed she might soon rejoin him. *So come quick*, Señora Muerte. *As woman to woman, don't keep your customer waiting.*

The Brazilians allowed the sun to light the sky beyond the silhouette of hills, then hurried forward in silence, stealthy with the knives and bayonets they had chosen in place of guns and grenades. They overran the pathetic southern outposts, spreading wide as they entered the valley. They did not know how much resistance they would meet, but they *did* know that the man who killed or captured *El Supremo* could retire and count his money. Put his feet up on the porch-rail of his farm. Beckon to his servants. Raise a family who'd be respected as the children of the Hero of Brazil. The soldier who had finally drawn the curtain on a mindless, five-year war.

The tropical sun soared higher, splashing light into the valley. Lopez' encampment was revealed in all its sad and scattered disorder.

Gaston d'Orléans gestured to the bugler who ran beside him, and a long, harsh blast broke the silence of the day.

The final act of the War of the Triple Alliance would be performed out here, in this hitherto insignificant basin in which the seat of government was no more than a cheap wicker stool.

Sleeping apart from Elisa, Solano had wrapped himself in a bleached linen sheet; his ecclesiastical raiment. When he heard the sound of the bugle he rolled to one side, tore himself free from the robe and stood, peering towards the south.

'But Benigno made me promise,' he breathed. 'I'm to live a long life and grow old. And anyway, what is there to fear? Brushed by the hand of God, am I not now immortal?' The thought was enough to send him striding across the encampment, thick fingers buckling his pistol belt. A final battle was to be fought and won, after which he would ride in glory to Asunción, then stand in the Palace whilst the enemy shielded their eyes against the bright, celestial glare.

There would be no more reprisals, he decided. A saint was blessed with a forgiving nature. A saint could see that Brazil and Argentina and Uruguay had been led astray by the devil. A saint could allow mere humans their petty mistakes.

Elisa was on her way back from the river, bringing water for her children, when she, too, heard the sound of the bugle. As she turned towards it she saw distant dust-clouds, the unmistakable war-cloak of galloping horses. *So here they were again, the reluctant, relentless enemy . . . Very well . . . But pray Heaven that this time would be the last, and that Solano would have the wisdom to surrender.*

'Dear God,' she whispered, as the dust-clouds swirled and spread, 'at least grant him that.'

Then the earthenware jugs were discarded, and she was running to where her children stood in a desolate group, the maidservant once again torn by indecision. As on so many other mornings, and in so many other places, the Paraguayan dawn brought pandemonium.

Lopez was lost from sight, then glimpsed, just once, astride his horse. Elisa called out to him in vain. Cloaked by fresh gouts of dust, immortality his shield, he wheeled his mount and was gone.

She felt a hand on her arm and there was Pancho, the fifteen-year-old, urging her to the carriages. 'I shall protect you, *mi madre*. Tell that girl to stop snivelling, and to bring my brothers and the baby. Come along. We've time enough. But you're not to brand me a coward, you know. It is what *El Presidente* told me to do.'

She wanted to embrace him and tell him no, he was anything but a coward. More important than that, Elisa wanted to say they must all remain here, and that Pancho should throw down the revolver he was carrying. The family of Lopez and Lynch would stand quietly together as the Allies swept through the valley.

But it was not a thing she could ask of a boy who'd already seen action as a man. If Solano had sent his eldest son to protect his mistress and children, then that's what Pancho Lopez must do, so his pride at least went untarnished.

'Do you know where General von Wisner – ?'

'Somewhere over there.' Pancho nodded. 'In charge of our only machine-gun. The Allies will have a damn hard time with *him*, that's for sure.'

They were close to the carriages, and Elisa was soon aboard with her boys, her baby, the maid, her young protector. No destination was given to the driver, for no destination had been planned beyond Cerro Cora. And had they not already come too far?

There was no real battle; just a sweeping of the ground by the Allied broom. Von Wisner fought on until the machine-gun jammed solid, then pounded a cramped left leg with his fist, forced himself to his feet, and reached for his sabre.

As he did so, a Brazilian cavalry officer rode in close, requesting him to leave the sword in its scabbard. 'You are known by reputation, General the Baron Enrique von Wisner de Morgenstern. Known and admired. Señor Lopez is fortunate to have one such as you alongside him. But please don't draw that blade, *mi General*. I would rather we took you to Rio and talked things over in my club.'

Von Wisner wiped smoke from his eyes, nodded at the rider and went back to massaging life into his leg. 'Perhaps you're right,' he said wearily. 'It would only embarrass you, watching me struggle to unship this relic of earlier days. But if I were six months younger – '

'That's right.' The Brazilian grinned, looking down at the fine old warrior with his white moustache. 'Six months, *mi General*, and there'd be all the difference. Now, tell me this, if you will. Any chance of our rounding up Lopez?'

The question went unanswered, of course, and the officer left it to others to deal with Solano. Enough that he'd found von Wisner alive, and could, as he'd promised, discuss life with him in the club in Rio de Janeiro.

7

The driver of Elisa's carriage thrashed the reins and screamed at the horses. They were still some way from the head of the valley, but the ground up here was less firm than in the south, the wheels of the coach churning mud. If only he could reach the trees . . . Find a native track . . . Get the President's woman and children into the shelter of the jungle . . .

But the animals staggered, the soft earth cloying at the carriage.

Pancho jumped out, throwing his muscular weight behind the wheels.

Elisa climbed down to help him as the driver drew the horses back, then lashed at them to haul the wagon free.

Then Elisa's son said, 'Wait. It is my belief we've been spotted. Would you please get back inside, *mi madre*. I would not care to see you wounded.'

Respecting his pride, she nonetheless begged him to cast aside his revolver. 'Do it, my love! The war is over now! But you might still, one day, inherit the mantle of your father. Guide your nation. Be a President all the world can look up to. I implore you, sink the weapon in the mud!'

'I told you to get back inside,' Pancho shouted. 'You are now under *my* protection, *mi madre*. And when *I* speak, I speak for the President! Oh, yes, here they come, the trespassers in our garden.'

Convinced that Elisa was out of danger, Solano rode humming across the river that fed the valley of Cerro Cora. Her coach had surely been carried to safety by the angels, his own horse now walking on water.

He leaned in the saddle, smiling down as the animal splashed, the river as firm to Solano Lopez as the diamonds and gold that encrusted its glittering bed.

. . . Come back here when the war's been won . . . Rake the river and take all these jewels to Asunción . . . To Paris . . . To wherever we want, the Irishwoman and I . . .

. . . Odd that they've not been raked up before . . . Idiots must have misjudged

them as pebbles . . . But idiots lack the vision of saints, seeing only stones when really they're –

'Stop where you are! Extend your arms! You are arrested in the name of the Emperor Dom Pedro de Alcantara, the President Bartolomé Mitre, the President Bernardo Berro. And in the name of all their nations. Drop your reins, Señor Lopez. It's done with now. Your lunacy's contained.'

Talk to a saint like that? he thought. But my arms have already been extended – on the Cross! They must be mad, these men on the banks of the river; mad and in need of a lesson!

Spurring his horse, *El Supremo* dragged the pistols from his holsters as he charged at the long, calm line of the enemy. Show *them* who the saint was. Show *them* who could walk on the surface of the water!

Startled by Lopez' charge, a corporal in the Brazilian Army levelled his rifle and aimed at the President's horse. The distance was no more than twenty yards, but the shot went wide – high and wide – and struck Solano Lopez in the shoulder, hurling him back into the stream.

He threw up his arms as he fell – not in surrender, but to safeguard his pistols. And came up bleeding from the water, living proof that a saint can never die. He fought for purchase on the stones, squinted in the sunlight, then stood drenched and determined as he raised his massive fists, his fingers within the trigger-guards of his weapons.

Without hesitation, the Brazilians opened fire.

Of the fifteen shots, four struck the innocent, trembling horse; seven the water, the mud, the grassy valley beyond the river. And four the body of the Master of the Republic of Paraguay.

Solano fell back again – *and came up again* – all his ebbing strength behind the cry that would secure him a place in the history of South America: *'Muero con mi Patria!'* – I die with my country!

And then he sprawled back and did not arise again, and his body was brought to the bank by the stirrings of the stream that ran down from the distant unexplored mountains.

Elisa's carriage lurched onward, though with no hope now of reaching the wooded foothills to the north. The Brazilian riders were closing on them fast, and the stocky young Pancho insisted on leaning sideways from the well of the coach, to keep watch. Ignoring his mother's pleas to discard the gun, it wavered in his hand, and he emitted a string of oaths, learned from Solano, which sounded forced and unreal on the youngster's tongue. Shifting, he braced himself against the side of the carriage, both hands now gripping the heavy American revolver.

Elisa turned to glance back through the small, horizontal aperture in the canopy. The Brazilians were almost on them, dividing to hem in the carriage from both sides. Another few yards and the chase would be over. And with it the dreams that had led to such tragic reality.

But no, not over for Pancho Lopez, not yet. Steadying the revolver, the fifteen-year-old squeezed the trigger, and grinned as a mounted sergeant jerked at the impact of the bullet. *'E viva Paraguay!'*

As the rider sagged, another spurred alongside the coach, one hand holding the reins, the other a long, quivering lance. He drove it into Pancho's chest, obedient to rules laid down by Gaston d'Orléans. 'If they wish to surrender, they may do so. If they prefer to die, then that too.'

Elisa and the *doncella* screamed together; the boys howled in terror; the infant wailed. The lancer's thrust had been text-book perfect, and Solano's eldest son might never have felt real pain. He was dead where he lay, but only now, too late, did the revolver fall to the ground, to be overrun by the mud-clogged wheels of the lumbering carriage.

The Allied commander had intended to break the news of *El Jefe's* death as gently as possible to the woman. But his troops were already yelling it loud, whooping with glee to know they could soon go home.

Doña Juana and her daughters heard it and clamped their teeth tight. It was Benigno they mourned – Benigno and Venancio – and let the devil gnaw on the bones of the crazed Solano.

But Elisa Alicia Lynch wept for them all. For the man she'd first met in the Rue du Helder in Paris. For the son she'd conceived in Europe, then given birth to here, in Solano's own country. For her only daughter, Corina Adelaida, dead at the age of eight months. And yes, without hypocrisy, for Benigno and Venancio, with whom she might, perhaps, have come to terms.

There were many others for whom tears could be shed, here in the basin of Cerro Cora. But to weep for them was to weep for every man and woman and child in Paraguay, her adopted and bloodstained nation . . .

She asked one of the Brazilians if General von Wisner had survived. 'He's tall as a tree, and with ashen hair and a white moustache. Dead or alive, you would know him if you saw him.'

374

'Been sent off down to Rio,' she was told. 'We allowed him to keep his sword. Not our usual practice. But with him . . .'

'I am grateful,' Elisa murmured. 'Except for a moment of foolishness on my part, we were inseparable friends.'

The Brazilian nodded, then saluted and hurried away. He did not wish to hear her next question – where was the body of Francisco Solano Lopez?

Her children conducted gently to the southern edge of the valley, Elisa was escorted into the presence of Gaston d'Orléans. She saw faces she recognized – the murderous gaze of Doña Juana Pablo Carillo; the drab grey features of Doña Inocencia and Doña Rafaela; three grim women who let loose with their accusations against the foreign *ramera*, the *puta*, the whore who had trapped Solano between her thighs.

'He was a good man, my son, until he met *this one* in Paris!' Doña Juana indicted. 'If he turned bad at all, it was only because of her! He had no special ambitions, my sweet Solano. But *this one*, oh, she fed him on poisoned fruits, so she did. And God knows what else she did to turn him impure. Just look at her! If I touched her now, my finger would blaze with flame! You just see! Her body all corrupt . . .'

The crone scuttled forward, a skeletal finger extended – *and the knife she'd carried so Benigno could murder his brother slipped downwards from the sleeve of her black cotton gown.*

'No more than just a poke at her and – '

Elisa saw the glint of the blade and jumped back. Doña Juana jabbed wildly, and the knife caught in Elisa's waistcoat. Brazilian guards lifted the crone away, as the air filled with her shrieks and screams of frustration.

Gaston d'Orléans shook his head and stepped forward. 'I know you were never married to Señor Lopez, Madame Lynch, but I wouldn't envy you this one as your *suegra*. Mothers-in-law can be difficult, yes, but *this one*?'

She appreciated the way he'd turned the phrase, then asked if she could now see the body of Francisco Solano Lopez – 'the man I'm supposed to have fed on poisoned fruits'.

'You have that right, Madame Lynch, though the Allies are not prepared to see him buried in Asunción. His madness has cost us many thousands of lives, as you must know, and our coffers are all but empty. See him if you wish, Madame, but don't count on a hero's burial.'

She nodded in obedience. 'Will it matter to you,' she asked, 'if he's buried here? The two of them? Solano alongside Pancho? Will you care very much if their graves are in this long, grassy valley, so far away from Asunción? I know it's quite close to the border of Brazil, *Monsieur le Comte*, but surely you can allow him to lie here in Paraguay and dream his now harmless dreams?'

Dom Pedro's son-in-law raised his eyes, and gazed round the ring of forested hills. There were worse places to be buried, he thought. And he *was* the President. And unkept graves grow over, denied their stones.

'Very well. Within the confines of the valley. I'll organize a detail.'

'Oh, no.'

'No to what, Madame?'

'No to the detail,' she said quietly. 'I'll find Guaranís to help me dig the graves. Where I'm told Solano died, near the bank of the river. This is our affair, *Monsieur le Comte*, though I'd ask you to see the dead wrapped tight in military coats, and with a priest to nudge them to Heaven. And I shall also need a spade. Why not? I come from a place where earth is dug for graves, and peat for the fires.'

The Allies kept their distance, but they could see from where they were standing that Lopez' woman meant everything she said. Sometimes with the spade, but more often now with her hands, Elisa Lynch scooped out two deep depressions in the eastern bank of the stream, dragging the earth away from the edge, then trimming the sides of the beds she was making for the fifteen-year-old Pancho, the forty-four-year-old Solano.

Among the victorious troops there was not a man who could imagine that any woman would do as much for him. It was something to see and remember, this proud and pitiful sight in which *La Irlandesa* covered the face of her son, then the face of *El Supremo*.

Dismissing the Guaranís, Elisa Lynch knelt on the red earth bank between the graves, and would not be moved from her station until dusk had laid its own sombre blanket across the valley of Cerro Cora . . .

PART EIGHT

Edinburgh; Paris: 1870–1886

1

The middle of August and it was suddenly teeming with rain, the summer storm clouds blown across from the high, stark ranges of the Grampians. The passengers on the canopied street-car grumbled – 'Allus when a person's garbed in her best' – then debated whether to stay aboard and pay the extra ha'penny, or save the money and dash to the shelter of the shops.

Armed with a stiff linen parasol, Elisa Lynch alighted from the conveyance, extended the spokes of her temporary umbrella and peered through the rain at the solid, granite building she'd come eight thousand miles to see. Well, more than just see for, whatever the attractions of this handsome and historic Scottish city, she had not travelled all this way to admire its stonework. Later, perhaps, she'd find time to visit its castle, its palace, its elegant public gardens. But business before pleasure, even though pleasure would be derived from today's affairs.

She waited for the traffic to thin, then hurried across the wide, cobbled street, lifting the hem of her skirt clear of the gutters. A liveried doorman came forward to assist her, relieving her of the parasol before ushering her into the building. 'Be bright again soon, ma'am,' he assured her. 'Be all blown over 'fore you're through.'

'I might take that as my motto,' she told him, smiling as she entered the Royal Bank of Scotland here in Edinburgh – the treasury of her wealth.

Six months earlier Elisa had been jolted south from Cerro Cora, her face besmirched by tears and blood-red mud, Solano and Pancho left to lie forever in the bank of an unknown river, and with Brazilian troopers fending off the vengeance of shrieking widows.

La puta must die! It was she who'd seduced him; she who'd shown him the Kingdoms of the World! It was this foreign harlot who'd goaded him onward, this *ramera* with her sinful limbs and swirling hair. All the fault lay with *La Irlandesa*, the whore who had enticed Señor Francisco Solano Lopez to lie with her . . .

The Triple Alliance had reasons enough to throw Elisa to the mob. But Gaston d'Orléans was a man of honour, and vengeful crowds played no part in his settling of accounts. God knows, he thought, did not *we*, the French, lop off more than thirty thousand heads in our Glorious Revolution? Did not we take our sweet revenge on poets and politicians, bankers and bakers, girls in their twenties and infirm old women who were already half-dead when we dragged them under the blade? Madame Lynch might indeed be guilty of having edged *El Jefe* along. But I've spoken with her, and watched her dig his grave with her own bare hands, and I'll not see her cast to the wolves.

Besides, I've something to tell her.

He kept the news to himself until they were twenty miles from Asunción, then had her brought to his tent, the French-born commander nodding at a plate of thin *galletas* and fresh-brewed *yerba maté*.

She declined them politely, her attractive features now drawn tight by the death of her loved ones. The aristocrat meant well, perhaps, but this was scarcely the moment to partake of tea and biscuits . . .

'Just pronounce my sentence, *Monsieur le Comte*, and allow me time to prepare. But don't fear a sudden outburst of tears; I'll see you're not embarrassed. They were all spent up there, by the stream in Cerro Corá.'

Gaston d'Orléans bowed his head in acknowledgement. 'I shall see to it you're not harmed, Madame Lynch. However, I must tell you now, you *will* be deported. Just as soon as we can arrange for a vessel to take you back to Europe. And something else . . . Punishment enough . . . You must sail without your children.'

She gasped and said: 'But wait! That's not right! What have *they* done – ?'

'Nothing yet,' the Count told her. 'But the Allies believe that if Señor Lopez' children are permitted to leave, they will, in the years to come, foment unrest. And you must admit, Madame Lynch, they would have the finest tutor.'

Having promised not to weep again, Elisa stared at him, dry-eyed. But her slender frame shook with the horror of the news, her once-manicured nails now scratching, blunted and broken, on the rim of Gaston d'Orléans' stiff camp table.

'But this much I can do for you,' he continued. 'You may leave them in your house at, where is it, La Recoleta? And you, yourself, may stay there for twenty-four hours; time enough to pack as many clothes as you can carry, and whatever personal trinkets you might cherish. Paraguay is now under Allied jurisdiction. Your children will be protected by elements of all three victorious nations. But as for you, Madame Lynch, it is best you sail away. You are, after all, the surviving companion of a man who has caused the deaths of untold thousands, of which nine in every ten were his own obedient people. There is nothing more for you here, Madame Lynch. You were simply caught up – allow me to say this – by a man who saw his reflection in a series of flawed mirrors. Are you sure you won't take a glass of *yerba maté?*'

She had asked that the twenty-four hours should run from midnight. Then she had spent the night in her room, choosing clothes she could wear when the weather grew cold in Europe. Not many, for Gaston d'Orléans had told her she must carry them – no porters now for *La Segunda* – but she tipped a variety of pendants, bracelets and brooches into a shallow leather jewel-case. Not many of these, but enough to purchase a passage from Portsmouth to London, then from London to the Royal Bank of Scotland.

Once there – well, things would be different when she gave her name to the Manager of the Bank. When she told him how the vanished Surgeon Stewart had invested her money, her jewels, her casket of shaven gold.

She'd be welcomed there, and the manager would take her ribbon-bound wallet of papers, absent himself for a while, then return to treat her as a favoured client, and with a covey of clerks cooing in attendance.

With this in mind, Elisa bade farewell to her household servants in the *quinta*. 'But I'll soon be back, you know, and I'll wish to see my children brimming with health. Perform your tasks correctly, and I might just bring you a present from Europe – something no one else possesses in all South America.'

She embraced the *doncella*, and begged her, please, not to burst into floods of tears this time. 'I am leaving you in charge of my boys, and Miguel. Your salary will be doubled, as from today. Now don't let me down. And don't let the Allied soldiers have their way with you, girl. I only want to see *five* children here in the house when I return!'

The maidservant giggled and blushed. But she was once again weeping when Elisa Lynch was summoned by the Brazilians and taken away in a gig to the port of Asunción . . .

After that followed a long and sickening journey to Europe. First the weeks on the Río Paraguay and the Río Paraná; then a ten-day delay in Buenos Aires; then they forged out into the estuary of the Río de la Plata for the veering, uncertain voyage across the Atlantic.

On 23rd June the steamship *Princeza* dropped anchor in Portsmouth, and Elisa staggered slightly as she stepped ashore. This was only her third time on English soil – actually, hard, stone cobbles – and she recalled both the first when she and Adelaide, attempting the crossing to France, had been blown back into Falmouth harbour, and the second when she'd married the avuncular Xavier Quatrefages in Folkestone.

She had not liked England then, and did not like it now; the English had such whinnying tones and arrogant ways. But she stayed long enough to spend four days in London, selling off half her trinkets. She felt she'd been cheated, though it didn't much matter, for she'd soon be up north, across the border and sipping port – or might it be whisky? – in the Manager's office in the Royal Bank of Scotland.

Agree the sum – investment plus interest – and she could not only sail back to Asunción to reclaim her children, she could purchase the steamer itself.

The liveried doorman was right. It *would* be bright again soon. And the rain clouds *would* blow over before she was through.

The slightest sounds echoed beneath the vaulted roof of this fine, imposing building. Voices were lowered to a whisper in this place which was not so much the Home of Mammon as a library, a museum, a Church of High Finance.

'Be o' service to ye, ma'am?'

She told the young counter clerk yes, she thought he might. 'My name is Lynch. Elisa Alicia Lynch. I've spent several years abroad, but have, on advice, lodged my money with you. Here – here are the relevant papers. You might wish to make sure they tally with your books. I'll be seated over there near that plant beside the window. Needs watering, by the way, if you don't mind my saying. I've seen the same species in Paraguay, only there they'd lift the roof!'

The clerk said he'd see to it. And if Mistress Lynch would not mind waiting? Then he turned away and thumbed through the papers, choking when he read the accumulated totals.

She's worth tens of thousands in sterling! By God, but this isn't for me to handle! This one's for Mister Ross!

For the first time ever, the counter clerk ventured along the corridor that led to the office of Fergus Kendall Ross, the hardwood floor turning to carpet, the Manager's mahogany door looming larger with every step . . .

Meanwhile, Elisa watched the well-dressed customers arrive and depart. Occasionally she exchanged a nod with the ladies, then she tilted her head to admire the structure of the building. *They know how to make things good and solid, the Scots. Could have done with them in Asunción. Maybe next year, when I'm back there, I'll be able to invite a few architects over and we can –*

'Mistress Lynch? I've presented your papers to the Manager, an' he'll spare ye the time in his office. Will ye follow me, Mistress Lynch?'

She nodded and did so, silently blessing Solano for his past generosity, the numerous gifts that expressed his guilt and pride, apology and prowess. He had met her as just a pretty young courtesan and paid her well for her favours. But Elisa had proved to be more than mere warmth beneath the sheets, offered more than just the spreading of sinful limbs. She had taught him a hundred things he didn't know – the way to dress for a *soirée* with the French; the way to enter a salon, and hold up his head in the presence of the unstable wigs of Europe.

And, as recompense for her tuition, her loyalty, the six sons she had given him, he'd rewarded her with land and *quintas*, with jewels and coins and a casket of fine gold filings into which she could dip her fingers. Very well, so she had lost her estates, been forced to abandon the contents of her houses. The porcelain was gone, and the elegant white piano; the cutlery and plate; the carpets and paintings; everything that could not be packed into two small valises – and the wealth Surgeon Stewart had invested for her here. Thank God at least for that, she thought. For the acumen of the Scot.

So she blinked when Fergus Ross came from behind his desk and tapped the sheaf of papers and asked if she had truly imagined she could get away with *this*?

'As a practical joke it's a poor one, Mistress Lynch. Not your real name, of course, but for the purposes of our brief discussion . . . Aye, ma'am, a poor joke, and one as does not raise a smile.'

'I'm sorry. I don't understand. As for my name, I assure you, sir – '

'I'm assured of nothing, Mistress Lynch,' the manager snapped, 'save that fraud and deceit sour the air. Ye claim to have an account with us, yet must know full well ye have not. Ye say we hold in excess of £89,000 sterling, whereas the truth reveals not a penny.'

'I repeat,' Elisa blurted. 'I don't understand.'

'Allow me to finish,' the man insisted. 'We will discuss *your* comprehension of the matter in a moment. The thing of it is, Mistress Lynch, the papers I hold are false, and a damn poor set of forgeries at that! This man Stewart, the one who claims the role of executor . . . Well, he's tried his hand at various signatures and seals, but they'd not fool a bairn, and they don't fool Fergus Ross. I'm a hard man when the subject is money, my dear lady; but I'm not, I believe, vindictive. So jus' take this ill-prepared essay in extortion, and leave Edinburgh by any means ye can. But be warned, and heed the warning. I shall circulate your description to every bank within the city, and things will go hard with ye, Mistress Lynch, if ye ever try this trick again. Now awa' with ye, foolish woman. My clerk says ye've lived abroad. Ye'd be shrewd to go back where ye came from.'

He thrust the sheaf of papers at her and was returning to his desk, shaking his head in disgust, when Elisa Lynch shrugged the clerk's hand from her arm and stepped forward to catch Fergus Ross by the sleeve, pulling the man around.

Trembling with anger – and with a deep-seated fear that perhaps he was right; *right or a greater charlatan even than Stewart* – she said, 'There is still the matter of *my* comprehension, Mr Ross. By your own invitation, we will now discuss *my* part in this affair. So sit behind your desk, sir, and I'll sit here, and we'll work out just how cleverly I've been duped. But yes, Mr Ross, my name *is* Lynch. Elisa Alicia Lynch, who was almost twenty years the companion of a South American President. Foolish in many ways, Mr Ross, but not so foolish as knowingly to bring you false papers. If I'm taking your time, I apologize. *But someone, it seems, has taken £89,000 sterling of my money. With or without the interest.* And did you not just tell me what a hard man you are about money? So be hard. Help this so-called foolish woman discover where it's gone. Do that, and I *will* bank it with you. Now what would you care to know?'

As the minutes went by, and his questions were answered candidly, the Manager realized he'd misjudged her. He offered her a glass of pale, dry sherry, concealing his smile of approval when Elisa asked if she might, instead, taste a measure of whisky.

'So the coins – and, well, the tokens of affection ye received from President Lopez – these were sometimes passed on to this Dr William Stewart, who said he'd have 'em sent on here. Is that correct?'

'They went downriver from Asunción in a medical chest. Or so I was told.'

384

'And then, sometime last year, Dr Stewart disappeared whilst in the jungle – '

'Smooth to the palette, Mr Ross, your whisky. I'm sorry? Yes. Somewhere near the border with Brazil. He'd been dispatched to what was then our front line, and was later reported as missing. Lord knows how he died, Mr Ross. There's an alphabet of ways to die in the jungle.'

Intelligent and cautious, the Manager of the Royal Bank of Scotland asked: 'And there's no one else? His family here in Edinburgh – ?'

They were with him out there. Perhaps they've returned, but what would they know of – ?'

'And nay brothers? Did he ever speak of – ?'

'No,' Elisa told him. Then she remembered something and said, 'Yes! He *did* speak of a brother. A Rory – no – a *Robert* Stewart! And I'm sure William claimed Robert Stewart was a banker. Do you think he could work for you, Mr Ross? Not here, but in another branch? You think my money's been lodged somewhere else in Scotland, and nurtured by Robert?'

Fergus Ross admitted that it was possible. Now that he knew the woman better – *an' one who'll take a dram of whisky in preference to foreign sherry* – he agreed to check with the other branches of the Royal Bank of Scotland and search out the whereabouts of Robert Stewart, banker brother of the late Dr William, lost in the dank and viridescent wilderness of Paraguay.

'Might ye be willing to return here in three days, Mistress Lynch? If Robbie Stewart's to be found, I feel sure we can find him.'

For the first time since she'd entered the panelled office, Elisa permitted herself a smile. 'For the sum of £89,000, with or without the interest that's accrued, I'd be willing to sit on the steps for three days, Mr Ross. Day *and* night, if need be.'

2

In her hotel room behind Princes Street, the claimant re-examined the sheaf of papers. Having never, until now, doubted their authenticity, she blushed with shame at both her naïvety and greed. She had *wanted* the documents to be real, convincing herself that whatever might happen, financial security awaited her here, in this 'Athens of the North'. Greed had blinded her to what now seemed glaringly obvious, the various signatures were all from the hand of Surgeon Stewart. The forgeries had not duped Fergus Ross – *'and they'd not fool a bairn'* – but they'd hoodwinked Elisa Lynch as easily as a farmhand at a fairground.

'And what,' she said dully, 'if Robert Stewart's not to be found? How then do I return to La Recoleta and my children?'

But the Manager of the Royal Bank of Scotland proved as good as his word.

'There *is* a Robert Stewart, across the Firth in Dunfermline. And, aye, he's a banker there; takes hold o' the Linen Bank of Fife.'

'Does he – did he have a brother William, Mr Ross? Were you able to find out – ?'

'A William Angus Stewart.' The Manager nodded. 'Gained his medical degree right here in Edinburgh. Served in the Crimea for a while, then sailed for – yes, Mistress Lynch, for the South American continent. It seems ye could do a lot worse than take the ferry for Dunfermline. Robert Stewart might be your man.'

'I do not in all honesty know how to thank you,' Elisa murmured, then was promptly told it was easy.

'Ye'll recoup your money, and invest a decent proportion of it with us! As ye thought ye'd done in the first place. Excellent rates of interest, here at the Royal, Mistress Lynch. Explain it all to ye later, when ye're back across from Dunfermline . . .'

The following afternoon she introduced herself to a man who in no way resembled the bleak and pious Dr Stewart. Nevertheless, the ebullient Robert assured her he was indeed his brother. 'Our faither

386

might also have wondered, Mistress Lynch, though such things happen. Now then; how'm I to help you?'

'I thought you might have recognized the name,' Elisa ventured. 'It's a question of money I entrusted to your brother. I understood he'd invested it for me with the Royal Bank of Scotland in Edinburgh, though he might instead have chosen the Linen – '

'Oh, he'd scarcely do tha'.' Robert grinned. 'Truth to tell, we don't much see eye to eye, Dr William and I. Nor do Mirren and Kirstie, come to tha'. So whatever he might have done with your money, Mistress Lynch – '

'*Stop!* Please stop.'

The good-natured Robert stepped back, his arms half-raised in surrender. 'Ye're likely right,' he admitted. 'I shouldna parade the family's wash in public.'

'No, it's not – It's what you said about not seeing eye to eye with Surgeon Stewart. But your brother is *dead*! In the Paraguayan jungle!'

'I must tell ye, the idea appeals, ma'am, so it does. But ma own evil wishes were never quite granted, an' William's come back to bore us to sobbin' again. No' here, thank God, in Dunfermline. But right over there, where ye came from this morning. Got himself a nice practice near Calton Hill. Fine area. Charges a guinea an hour. Prescribes his coloured sweeties and calls it medicine. Paradin' the family wash again, but I'm sure half the ladies go there to get their bony wrists slapped.'

Elisa sat motionless in Robert Stewart's modest version of Fergus Ross's panelled office as the full impact of his news made itself felt. The shock left her pale, though she knew now that not only was the man who had hoodwinked her throughout the years still alive, he was within her reach.

'I shall visit him tomorrow,' she said. 'Though not to have my wrists slapped. More, I think, to collect my earnings for eighty-nine thousand hours.'

When Elisa had left, the banker stood for a while, a jaunty whistle on his lips. Then he moved his feet, dancing to match the tune. 'Oh, my brother . . . What'll the ladies think tomorrow, when Mistress Elisa Lynch comes striding amongst your jars of sweeties . . . ? Oh, wait till my beloved Mirren hears this . . . An' a one – an' a two – an' a one-two-three . . .'

She called herself Mistress Macmillan. Told the nurse she'd been afflicted by headaches, and could pay whatever it took to drive them away. 'After all,' she said, 'those who save us from pain deserve payment, isn't that so? How often we ignore them when we're healthy, yet plead for their skills when we're ill. Would two guineas be sufficient for the visit? Here. I don't like falling behind with trifling debts.'

The nurse brought Mistress Macmillan a lightly drugged cordial – *make her feel the pills were taking quick effect* – and tucked a cushion behind her neck to relieve the tension. Then she sidled through to see Surgeon Stewart, beaming as she told him he must surely keep *this* one on his books. 'Two guineas down, and she doesn't like being in debt.'

Emerging from the surgery, she asked if Mistress Macmillan felt well enough to go in. 'If not, I'm sure the doctor will see you here.'

'I can manage,' the patient told her. 'But will you grant me a small favour and allow me my time with the doctor, undisturbed?'

For the amount she's paying, the nurse told herself, I could lock up and go on home. She smiled and bobbed, then skittered ahead to announce Mistress Adelaide Macmillan. The patient delayed entering the surgery until the smirking nurse had withdrawn.

It was William Stewart's practice to be seen by his patients crouched over his desk, the fingers of one hand worrying his brow, the other busy scribbling prescriptions that would serve to heal and save.

It impressed the ladies, though the timing was important, and they liked to know they'd interrupted another's salvation. So he penned out a few more words whilst saying: 'First time you've come to see me, Mistress Macmillan . . .' Then he glanced up and the words dribbled to nothing. The pen rolled aside, and a leg of his chair cracked distinctly as he jerked back in astonishment.

'I was told . . . I was told Macmillan . . .'

'I lied.' Elisa glowered. 'But then *I* was told there'd be money in the bank, Dr Stewart – jewels and coins and all the rest of it sent downriver and shipped up here. I was further told – no, stay where you are! – that my savings were secure in what Manager Ross calls the Royal. Oh, yes, I've spent time with Mr Ross. *And* with your brother, in Dunfermline. I thought you dead, Dr Stewart. Yet here you are, surrounded by pills, having somehow escaped from the horrors of the jungle.'

Born to recover, William Stewart recovered fast. 'Now look here, Mistress Lynch. Whatever the result of the war – '

'Solano died. My eldest son died. The manhood of Paraguay died. *That*, my dear Doctor, was the final result of the war. But spare your tears, and repay me my eighty-nine thousands pounds in sterling, plus the interest earned over the years. Take it from the drawer in your desk, or tell me where to find it. I've no doubt you've made a fortune of your own, you dried-up little man. But I want mine! And I want it now!'

Aware that the woman was not armed – he'd have already seen the pistol or the knife if she'd possessed one – William Angus Stewart sat back in his chair and told her he had not the slightest idea what she meant. 'Not the slightest. What money? What jewels and gold filings? What – ?'

'Did *I* say gold filings?'

'Whatever you said, I am ignorant of it all.'

'So those papers you gave me – ?'

'Not I. You confuse me with – '

'And were never entrusted – ?'

'Don't know what you mean, Mistress Lynch. If you truly believe I owe you money, then – here – here's an idea. Pick up your two-guinea fee from the desk outside. Take it, and I won't even charge you for the cordial you were served. But eighty-nine thousand pounds in sterling . . . It's all part of the headaches, Mistress Lynch. A distorting of the brain.'

After selling off more from the shallow leather jewel-case she had brought from La Recoleta, Elisa retained the services of a young lawyer, Simeon Mason. He accepted a fee of fifteen guineas, burrowed into the affair like a coal-face miner, and kept telling his client not to worry. If they couldn't prove Mistress Lynch was right, they could surely prove Dr William Stewart was wrong.

The case was postponed, held over, delayed by several months. Elisa was forced to leave the hotel behind Princes Street and seek cheaper accommodation in the old quarter near Cowgate. She spent her time walking the streets, or stretched out on her hard-sprung bed, dreaming of Solano, and of Elmore Curtin, and of the times she'd been rowed down the Seine by Régis de Broux.

Would life have been better, she wondered, if she'd stayed on in Paris, biding her time, then snatching at the chance of remarriage?

Or begged Elmore Curtin to take her with him when he went back to fight his war? But no. Not that. Captain Curtin – excuse me, *Major* Curtin – would not have had space in his baggage for a woman and her children. Their love affair had been fine, but finite. Different trumpets were sounding on different hills . . .

Then the lawyer Mason sent a note to say the case would be heard next Wednesday in the Central Magistrate's Court in the temporary chambers near the Cornmarket, and would Mistress Elisa Alicia Lynch please make herself available for a brief, pre-trial discussion?

'I'll be blunt with you,' he told his client. 'Whatever the facts of the case, as we see them, Dr Stewart can claim the loyalties of several influential ladies – '

'What have they to do with it?' Elisa queried. 'I am not bringing an action against his patients, his dinner guests. It's William Angus Stewart who's embezzled – '

'Quite so,' the young lawyer agreed. 'But a number of these women are *also* the dinner guests of the judiciary. The problem is, Mistress Lynch, that Dr Stewart is a son of Edinburgh, a gallant physician who patched up British soldiers in the Crimea, then extended his skills and abilities to South America. Moreover, my investigations reveal that at least half a dozen of his female patients are, in one way or another, related by marriage to the aforesaid members of the judiciary. Two of them are actually magistrates' wives.'

'You said you'd be blunt, Mr Mason. So far you just sound pessimistic. But I think I know where you're leading. If Dr Stewart is to be the wronged hero in all this, then the Court will need a villain. A villainess, if the word exists. A red-haired Irish confidence-trickster who came here with a satchel of forged papers. A woman who failed in her marriage to a Frenchman, then lived for all but twenty years as the mistress of a dark-skinned foreign dictator. I see you shifting in discomfort, Mr Mason, but isn't this how you fear the Court will assess it?'

Simeon Mason coughed with embarrassment. 'You are an extraordinarily honest woman, Mistress Lynch. I, personally, believe everything you've told me; and you are not, I beg you, to think my resolve has weakened. Investigations continue, and I shall fight your case to the bitter end. All I'm saying today is that – '

'That the Court of Law is a theatre, eh, Mr Mason? And that *I'm* the one with the cloak and hat, the moustache and the high-held dagger? Ireland, France, Algeria and that far-from-here Paraguay . . . Not much to stack against the unsullied reputation of Surgeon Stewart, who will probably turn up in the tartan of his clan . . .'

The lawyer was tempted to smile at her perspicacity. It was *exactly* what he thought William Stewart would do, no doubt topping off his outfit with a jaunty Tam o' Shanter.

'I repeat, Mistress Lynch, the investigations continue. You must not lose hope.'

'Losing hope,' she said wryly, 'would be relatively inexpensive, if I've already lost eighty-nine thousand pounds in sterling.

William Stewart retained the best legal minds in the city. He made sure his advocates called him to give evidence, and the Court was entertained to stories of high life and low life in Asunción. He painted a picture of Lynch-and-Lopez that brought the magistrates forward in their chairs. The squandering of their nation's money on fiestas . . . The President's ludicrous uniforms . . . The *quintas* he'd purchased for his mistress . . . *La Segunda*'s private war with Doña Juana – 'that brave and aristocratic matriarch' – and with her daughters, Inocencia and Rafaela – 'sweet-tempered ladies to whom Mistress Lynch was but vulgarity personified.

'I could describe the excesses in all their detail, Your Worships. But I know, from your intelligence, that a taste is enough to sicken you all to the stomach. Paraguay was a tragic and lawless place, Your Worships, and from Paraguay comes a tragic and lawless woman.'

William Stewart then bowed and sat down, lowering his head in modesty beneath the audible hum of approval at his performance.

Elisa turned to Mason. 'He's a brazen, bloody liar,' she hissed. 'I wish to tell how it really was! How the things that happened came about. He knows nothing, that man. He's just licking the boots of the Court.'

His eyes cast down on a crumpled sheet of paper, Simeon Mason whispered to her to wait. 'There's something here . . . If it fails, then yes . . . You may call him what you will. But allow me a moment. I need to get things in order. I've not addressed a Court like this before.'

Elisa groaned and sat back. Ahead, on their dais, were the stern, Scottish magistrates. To her left the defending barristers. Behind her the clerks and reporters and public, all of them local, and all of them eager to cheer their hero, jeer the woman who'd dressed as a Goddess for her parties on the Campo Grande. *Get rid of her quick, tha'd be the thing. See her off an' awa', an' have done wi' it. Who did she think she was to assail Dr William Angus Stewart?*

On his feet now, the inexperienced Simeon Mason let his gaze go out of focus, not daring to meet the dour expression of the magistrates. It was enough for the lawyer to stare in their general direction, then clear his throat and make himself heard above the hostile mutterings that swept around him.

'What occurred in Paraguay,' he said, 'is far beyond my reach. The plaintiff claims that a considerable sum of money was entrusted, over the years, to Dr Stewart, here present. But the truth is it's only what *she* says, and plaintiffs often lie. If I, myself, believe my client's story, you might think me foolish and taken in. I am paid to represent her, this attractive lady whom some might judge too foreign for even the impartial laws of Scotland. A failed wife. A mistress yet mother. How dare she bring Dr William Angus Stewart to the dock?'

The mutterings grew louder. How dare she indeed? Showing her russet hair without even the decency of a bonnet.

'But defendants also lie,' Mason added. 'And now is the time to ask you, Your Worships, if you, yourselves, have not been somewhat taken in.'

He lifted the crumpled paper he'd been holding and said, 'All very well to serve in the Crimea. Admirable enough to offer his skills to President Lopez. But might he not care to explain to the Court how he's linked to thirteen rented-out dwellings in the city? And to nineteen acres of public land? And to a manufactory near the Firth that produces – perhaps by coincidence – the same kind of coloured pills and tablets as are available in his surgery?

'A brave man abroad. But is it not strange, Your Worships, that all his interests in Edinburgh are in the name of friends and distant relations? And none of these said interests dated before my client entrusted him with her money? And would you not agree, Your Worships, that £89,000 would about fit the bill.

'My investigations have been thorough. The documents spell it out. The Medicine Man has cheated my client, diverting her funds to purchase properties no heroic physician could possibly afford.

'I would ask you, Your Worships, to detain Dr William Angus Stewart in this city, and that a speedy decision be reached in favour of Mistress Elisa Alicia Lynch.'

Decent and honest though they were, the magistrates dithered for days.

Then they found William Angus Stewart guilty of fraud, embezzlement and professional malfeasance. They sent two burly members of the City Constabulary to arrest him.

But the judges had dithered too long.

The thirteen rented dwellings and the public land had been sold

392

off cheap, cash in hand. The manufactory closed down and offered as a warehouse. The surgery abandoned, and the Stewart homestead snapped up for half its value.

By the time the magistrates had decided in favour of the plaintiff, the defendant and his family had fled beyond the reach of the Court, the Constabulary, and very likely beyond all Scottish jurisdiction.

Elisa had won her case, yet lost it.

And was stranded now, alone in her room near the Cowgate, fingering the last few trinkets in the shallow leather box.

Far from the land she had lived in for almost twenty years, Elisa surrendered to loneliness and despair. Her Irish family were dead or dispersed. Her South American family dead or imprisoned. There was no one. No one in all of Scotland, all of Ireland. No one she could write to or turn to, reminding them of the past.

She might, of course, appeal to her friends in Asunción. Though who were they really, these friends she invented? Who would now care what happened to the mistress of the mad Solano?

The young lawyer had done his best – won his case – then shared her horror as Stewart fled the country. So don't blame Simeon Mason. Blame the world, but not the well-meaning individuals.

Blame yourself, who else? Who else but Elisa Lynch to find fault with? Who else should be the culprit of her actions?

She huddled in bed, not sleeping, her tear-stained eyes bearing bright, blurred images:

Cavan and Adelaide . . .

Corinne and the musician, Jean-Pierre . . .

Régis de Broux who'd taken her boating on the Seine . . .

And the hedgehog . . . and the weasel . . . and countless others before she'd been summoned to meet Francisco Solano Lopez . . .

Then all the children she'd given him . . . and the friends she had made . . . and the enemies . . . and the single, unforgotten lover, Elmore Cornelius Curtin . . .

A fine cast of characters in a lifetime . . .

Yet sad if the drapes were drawn now, in this chilly little room in the Cowgate . . .

But think of it. What else to do?

Stay here, and empty the trinket chest? Or travel south to London?

Take the public coaches across country to Holyhead, then board the steamer to Ireland?

Or find the way to Dover, cross the Channel, and search out

my former protectors, those erstwhile lovers who might, perhaps, remember me?

Though God knows it would test a man's memory, seeing this red-haired woman step out of his past.

3

Whilst in Edinburgh, and now in London, Elisa had studied the newspaper reports that emanated from Paris. They made ironic reading, for France – like Paraguay – had entered into a disastrous conflict with her neighbours, and had suffered a series of crushing defeats at the hands of Prussia and her German allies.

At the Battle of Sedan, near the Belgian border, Emperor Louis Napoleon had surrendered, along with 104,000 war-weary troops. But the Prussians had pressed onward, determined to celebrate their victory in the capital itself. With the French forces shattered and fragmented, the Germanic regiments had set their sights on Paris.

And then, Elisa read with horror, the population decided to resist.

The siege lasted one hundred and thirty-one days. The might of Prussia and the German States ringed the city, sealing in almost two million inhabitants. It was winter and, when the last of the fuel stocks had been exhausted, furniture, then banister rails and floorboards, were chopped up for firewood.

When the supplies of beef and mutton had all been consumed, more exotic fare found its way on to the tables. If the tables themselves still existed. Cats and dogs were hunted to extinction. Dray horses were butchered. Then a pair of trotting horses, valued in life at 60,000 francs, and in death at 400, per carcase.

The Paris Zoo caught the eye of speculative suppliers. Deer and antelope were served. Kangaroo sold for 12 francs a pound. The two resident elephants, known affectionately as Castor and Pollux were shot with lead-tipped bullets, then offered by a restaurant on New Year's Eve as the festive dish.

The less well off contented themselves with mice, rats, birds who'd been foolish enough to winter in Paris. Squirrels were snared in the parks, though the parks themselves were soon devoid of trees, the historic woodlands cut down and burned.

Besieged by the enemy, it was still yet possible to escape. Find a man who knew his business, and judge the winds nicely, and the lucky few might rise from the heights of Montmarte in a basket suspended beneath a balloon inflated by coal gas. Sometimes they leaked; sometimes they exploded, easy targets for the German snipers.

Yet a hundred and sixty-four Parisians and foreigners floated to freedom, and smaller balloons carried more than two million letters and dispatches beyond the reach of interception.

So Elisa and London and the world learned of the four-month siege of Paris. And later of the 4,000 killed in combat, the 9,000 deported, the countless thousands who had died and been buried with the taste of reptile or rodent on their tongues . . .

She wondered if Marise Laurent-Perrone had survived; the courtesan with whom she'd lived in Rue Hautefeuille. Marise and the brutal Arnaud. Well, if anyone had, *he* would, for sure. But it had all been long ago – more than eighteen years – and Marise no longer dusted with the glitter of a *demi-mondaine*. She'd be almost forty now, and Elisa could only hope she was married, her life sedate, and far removed from the troubles of the capital.

And what of the Dauvins, Lucien and Ginette? Were they still in Rue Caumartin, the man whose friends had forecast would one day be the Governor of the *Banque de France*, and his elegant, flawless wife? Or had they, too, distanced themselves from war and revolution, and might now be found in Bordeaux, Toulouse; in the pure, bright wilderness of Canada?

There were others, and she thought of Régis de Broux. The perfect lover, he'd left her, then gone to sit with his dying, consumptive wife, somewhere near the coast – where was it? – in the hills above Antibes? *But what had he done when she'd died? Married again, and been happy all this time? Or might I still find him in Paris, and willing to see me? The idea appeals, I must admit, though it's been a long time for us both. But who knows? The world shrinks.* Le monde est petit . . .

As for her own sister, Corinne – well, Elisa would make no decisions until she reached France. She had not much enjoyed her time in the house in Rue Simon le Franc, though she did not regret having run errands in the market. An experience for *any* young girl, delivering mended clothes to the clients of St Merri.

And is Corinne still with her arrogant musician, Jean-Pierre? And their daughters as sulky as ever? Be odd if I bumped into them by accident, the two of them clinging tight to the arms of their protectors.

But a lot of things will seem odd to me, when I walk the streets of Paris. And the oddest, from all I've read, will be Paris itself.

For the moment, however, Elisa remained in London, where she placed her linguistic skills at the disposal of the British Press. Her

Spanish was faultless, her French impeccable, her English enlivened by her friendship with Washburn and Curtin. Fleet Street clamoured for her skills, and she might have remained there, this woman of considerable ability, her looks intact, and with no shortage of invitations from the writers and journalists who could say what they liked in her presence.

Her translations appeared in a wide variety of newspapers and journals, and she was offered a small apartment overlooking the crescent of Aldwych – within walking distance of *The News, The Telegraph, The Times.*

Flattered by the treatment she received, Elisa was tempted to stay.

Whatever her deep-down Irish dislike of the English, the English liked *her*. And so, deported from Paraguay, defeated in Scotland, why not fatten the purse here in London, then get *The Times* or *The News* to finance her trip back to Asunción?

She had been many things in the past, and now regarded herself as a journalist in Fleet Street. Not bad for a woman of thirty-six. A woman who could – if she wished – still crook her finger at any man in the room.

But the finger that beckoned was the finger of Paris; the city to which she'd been taken as a child; the city she'd known as an adolescent; the city in which she'd met the well-meaning Xavier Quatrefages, the romantic Régis de Broux, the anonymous black-garbed bankers and brokers, most of their faces and names now forgotten.

Start from where I started before. Where I first met the lumbering Francisco Solano Lopez. Where I carefully seduced him, and was taken up as his mistress.

Start again from where it all began a quarter of a century ago . . .

Paris – by the time Elisa reached it – was almost unrecognizable to her.

Twenty-two new boulevards now cut through the city. Entire sections of Paris had been razed, many of the slum quarters replaced with seven-storey developments. A railway line encircled the capital, trains puffing slowly round a nineteen-mile perimeter. There were twenty-seven halts; three trains in each direction every hour between dawn and dusk.

Louis Napoleon's government had also funded bridges at Solferino, L'Alma and the Pont au Change. Public riverboats chugged up the Seine, whilst omnibuses ran to forty outlying termini.

More than half the individual dwellings in Paris were now supplied with piped water. The number of street-lamps had doubled, then trebled. The area of public parkland had increased tenfold in the past few years.

Then the Prussians had won their victory, celebrated it on the Champs Elysées, taken the long-disputed territory of Alsace-Lorraine as their prize, and gone home. Even though France had been defeated in the field, Paris itself had all but escaped unscathed.

Glancing left and right at the newness of it, Elisa was driven along streets she'd never known, cheerfully overcharged by the driver – some things did not change – and deposited at the head of Rue Caumartin, fifty yards from the house in which she had once lived.

The man who answered the door might well have been Lucien Dauvin, if Lucien had not changed in two decades.

As tall as the one-time cavalry officer turned banker, the man gazed quizzically at the caller, then murmured politely: *'Puis-je vous aider, Madame?'*

'Excuse me for disturbing you, M'sieur – '

'Not at all, Madame. My wife had me trapped in the parlour, though I assure you for no more imaginative reason than to check the household accounts. Should you ask me to elope with you – though Heaven knows why you would – I'd be tempted to do so, here and now. Don't misunderstand me; I am deeply in love with my wife. But I abhor and detest doing sums!'

She found it easy to smile at his good-natured admission. 'If only they would come out to our advantage,' she suggested. 'But they rarely do.'

'Quite agree. We are, I'm convinced, considerably poorer now than when we started, just after lunch. But enough of my own weak grasp of finance. So long as you don't wish to sell me anything – '

'No, M'sieur. Only to ask if you know of a certain Lucien Dauvin. He used to live here. With his wife, Ginette.'

The man's hesitation was answer enough. 'Dauvin?' he pondered. 'I'm sure we didn't buy this place from a Dauvin. From a fellow called Toppman, I think it was. Toppman or Tapman. And I don't believe even *he* purchased it from a Dauvin. And we can't find out, because the unfortunate Toppman was drowned in a yachting accident somewhere near Sardinia. But if you'd care to come in, I'm sure my wife would be happy to – '

'Thank you, M'sieur,' Elisa declined. 'She's best left undisturbed, I think. To keep her head clear for the sums. It was, anyway, a long time ago.' Then she offered her slim, gloved hand, and the man said he was sincerely sorry, and she walked back to the head of Rue Caumartin, adding purpose to her stride, if only to let the man see she had somewhere to go.

If occurred to her later that they'd spoken of Dauvin, and of Toppman, or was it Tapman, but had never exchanged their own names.

Time then to lay aside all memories of Rue Caumartin.

The weeks that followed taught Elisa Lynch a great deal about the new Paris. She fumbled with the prices – how much they'd risen! – and was lost on the boulevards, where once she would have been at home in the sinuous alleys.

With increasing desperation, she sought out those she had known. But Marise Laurent-Perrone had left Rue Hautefeuille, according to a malicious neighbour spitting in the street as she recounted with glee the circumstances of her departure.

'*Bon débarras!* Good riddance to the fancy bitch! Grew blowzy on drink, so she did, and lost all her customers. Thought herself so high an' mighty, that Madame Perrone, but couldn't pay her debts in the end, and skulked off one night, vanishin' in the fog.'

'And the man who was her – well, her guardian? I believe his name was Arnaud. Is he still to be found in the district?'

'You speak to me about *that* one?' the neighbour howled. 'And who are you, pretty woman, to come round asking about the likes of *him*? Set your cap at him, did you; this Arnaud with his labourer's muscles, an' his big-knuckled fists? Thrilled you to get bruised by 'im, did it? The gentle come 'ere for the rough?'

'All I'm asking – '

'Well, don't. Arnaud got his throat cut in a brawl is what happened to Arnaud. You want my wishes? Nice an' slow . . . Just enough to make him bleed for hours . . . Now give me some money. I'm not here to talk for free.'

Elisa continued her search. But wherever she turned – to family, to friends, to her black-dressed protectors – she was told they'd moved on, moved away; what else did she expect after twenty years?

She had money enough, she decided, for two months of frugal living. The cheapest lodgings. Public transport. A diet of bread and wine from the markets, and soup that was boiled in cauldrons on the street, then served in chained tin mugs.

All the world talks of the past twenty years. Yet here I am counting the next sixty days.

Oh, Solano . . . How much of *your* fault was mine? Did I really lead you on towards destruction? Did my presence beside you make the difference? Would my absence have left you at peace? Ah, *querido*, what a Hell we made of your Paradise, dreaming of crowns and coronets . . . And didn't really need them, did we, since we'd gold enough in the vaults to shape our own . . .

My dear, demanding Solano . . . You would not look twice at me now, your longtime mistress, walking between the omnibus stops to save myself a few sous. But it has to be done. As does something else. A visit I never believed I would have to make, but must make whilst I still have a good gown to wear. And shoes that are yet in fashion. And a face not too pinched by the weather.

You will forgive me for doing it, *querido*, but there's nowhere else to go.

Only, now, to the château near Montreuil . . .

4

His wealth increased by the war in the Crimea, the war against Prussia, and by a dozen profitable skirmishes around the globe, the armaments manufacturer who had once taken his brutal pleasures with Elisa smiled as she was announced and entered the room. He was now in his seventies, a prisoner in his wheelchair. But his appetites were as debauched as ever; the millionaire paying well to watch others do things in which he, himself, could no longer participate. It was pleasure by proxy for Monsieur Gaétan Cravet, his victories all vicarious . . .

'I doubt you'll remember me,' Elisa began.

'On the contrary, Madame Lynch,' the man retorted. 'That red hair! Those green eyes! You were here throughout a delightful weekend in – wait, when was it? Quite some while ago.'

'Very well,' she said quickly. 'So you do. But I must tell you, Monsieur, I am not here to repeat that – *delightful* experience. But to ask for your financial support for an idea – '

'Several ideas I'd finance, Madame Lynch, were *you* there to see them run smoothly. A Private Academy for young ladies, perhaps? Or for errant women, fallen by the wayside and in need of affection. And discipline, of course. The one and the other. I fear I could only play the role of observer, though you could count on my support in every way.'

Having travelled by omnibus and on foot from Paris, Elisa Lynch was tempted to turn on her heel, leave the room and slam the door on the sight and sound of this monstrous, heavy-jowled libertine. But she had known what to expect, and now masked her disgust and said, 'I had something more ambitious in mind, Monsieur Cravet. A salon, of sorts. A gaming house. A country establishment, if you will, where the membership is restricted to the best of Paris, and their ladies. We would impose the highest fees, of course, though in return we'd supply the finest wines, the best-run tables. I have reason to believe I could manage such a place and turn it to a profit. However, if you find the thought too mundane – '

'Not at all,' Cravet told her, his expression concealing ideas of his own. 'I'm convinced you would be the perfect hostess for this *maison* you have in mind. It's just what we need at Montreuil. Some distractions after dark. Some night-life outside Paris. The scheme appeals to me greatly, Madame Lynch. But I would hope to see dancers there; frisky young creatures who'd kick up their heels and – '

'Don't worry, Monsieur. There'll be all kinds of suitable entertainment.'

'Yes, of course,' the man said doubtfully, not liking her choice of words. *But never mind. What was suitable today might seem far too staid tomorrow. And changes could always be made . . .*

However, for the moment Gaétan Cravet was willing to lend his weight and money to the scheme. His agents purchased a large country house on the edge of the forest, the building set within the centre of a high-walled estate. Elisa was offered a thirty per cent share in the partnership, and her own suite of rooms on the second floor of what was to be known quite simply as *Le Manoir*. The renovation costs could only have been met by someone as wealthy as the munitions magnate, and he rarely demurred at Elisa's extravagant suggestions.

'We must have not just one gaming-room, but three or four. Gamblers come in all colours, so I've found, and those who are happy to risk the contents of their pockets should not be inveigled into playing for stakes they cannot afford to lose. You see, Monsieur Cravet, if they lose beyond their means, then *we* lose *them*. We have yet to establish our reputation as a fair and honest place of entertainment, and I've no desire to milk our clients dry. The House will have the edge; it always does. But those who wish to play for a thousand francs – and no more – must be allowed to do so. As for those to whom a thousand francs is but *le petit monnaie*, we'll invite them into another room, where the stakes run high.'

'You appear to have made a close study of this,' Cravet approved. 'And what you say makes good sense, Madame Lynch. Let the children wager their *bonbons* – '

'Let our guests enjoy the evening at their own level,' Elisa corrected. 'We are *not*, Monsieur, setting out to steal from children.'

'Quite so,' he blinked. 'An unfortunate way of . . . But tell me this. Apart from the cards and roulette, there *will* be dancers? If I'm to be rolled in my chair of an evening to *Le Manoir*, I shall expect to see – '

'You'll see them,' Elisa assured him. 'You'll see your pretty girls, Monsieur. And dine in a restaurant that will vie with the best in

402

Paris. And get the chance to hear fine music. And meet painters and politicians; and industrial giants like yourself; and diplomats and who knows who else? As I said before, I want the best of Paris to visit us. And to return.'

His fleshy features still concealing ideas of his own, Gaéten Cravet spread the word that *Le Manoir* would open its membership list in August. He had announcements placed in every serious-minded newspaper in the city, and had brochures printed, these to be delivered to the thousand most influential financiers, aristocrats and parliamentarians in the capital. Elisa added one hundred and fifty artists, then the senior diplomats of Brazil, Argentina, Uruguay and the United States of America, plus a score of European representatives.

Not Paraguay, for the Legation in Paris had closed. But the others, yes, for she needed to cultivate their friendship, if only to learn how her children were faring at La Recoleta.

Addressing them in her prayers, she murmured: 'If *Le Manoir* is all I hope of it, I shall earn enough to sail back to Asunción and reclaim you. *Ah, mis niños.* Be patient, my boys. You must know I have never been one to quit the field.'

It was honest and clear, a claim no one would ever have denied of Elisa Lynch. An imperfect woman, she had nonetheless battled this far, and would fight on now, dressed in a gown she'd demanded from the purse of Gaétan Cravet, and wearing it well as she opened the doors to inaugurate *Le Manoir* in the forest near Montreuil.

Within weeks it was known as the place to visit, the *only* place of value outside Paris.

The menu was excellent; French for the most part, but some dishes were flavoured with the spices of Algeria, others rich with the tangy beef from South America. There was even the chance to sample the plain fare of the rain-washed British Isles . . .

The gaming-rooms – three for the moment, though the general appeal was for four – were immediately popular and stayed open until the early hours of the morning. Gamblers who lost their thousand francs merely shrugged at the night's bad luck. But they stayed to buy champagne and watch the dancers, who were quite happy to toss up their bright, voluminous skirts.

Wives were catered for in a glassed-in room bedecked with evergreen plants. Tea and infusions and cordials were served, Elisa insisting these refreshments should be free.

The wives told their husbands how well they'd been treated, and the husbands said they might visit the place again. 'Why not? Good food. A limit to the tables. And did I tell you, I met the sculptor Van Hendrik? All kinds of folk we could meet in *Le Manoir*, seems to me.'

Cravet came to watch the girls dance. It was his single pleasure, his four-wheeled chair pushed close to the stage, his swollen, old man's face tipped back, his eyes on their stockinged calves, their firm young thighs. A servant stood by to serve him champagne. The man let it run from his lips, preferring instead to twist in his chair and study the dancers.

He was well pleased with the way Madame Lynch had arranged things. *But there was still room for latitude. Girls down here on the floor, beside him. Where he could reach out and touch them. Pretty young creatures who'd squeal as he gripped their legs. Squeal and squirm . . .*

Leaving her senior partner to his pleasures, Elisa moved quietly from room to room, greeting the members and their companions.

'. . . You serve a fine meal, so you do, Madame Lynch.'

'. . . Won four hundred francs this evening, Madame! You may count on *me* to return!'

'. . . First time I ever met that composer fellow, Kavatin. Invited him to lunch tomorrow. It'll put our stock up no end, Madame Lynch. Damned if we won't come again, and trawl us an artist!'

'. . . Lost a couple of thousand this week, though I ain't complaining. This system of high and low stakes, it's a good one. Gives a man value for his money. Leaves him with the shirt on his back, so to speak. *A la prochaine, chère Madame!'*

The guests were unanimous in their approval. The establishment in the forest near Montreuil was the best they'd come across in years, and its reputation spread. Elisa shamelessly raised the membership fee, mildly surprised at the alacrity with which the Parisians opened their wallets. *Le Manoir* made a reasonable profit, then a healthy one, then one that far exceeded her expectations. Should have done this before, she told herself with amusement. I am clearly cut out to run a gambling house in the woods.

Confined to his wheelchair, Gaétan Cravet came regularly to *Le Manoir*, his place reserved below the stage where the dancers performed. He asked if they might not kick their legs higher – 'Why are they here, after all, if not to display their saucy limbs?' – then twisted his face as his servant dabbed spittle from his lips.

Meanwhile, Elisa continued to encourage the friendship of all those who could furnish news of Paraguay. The representatives of Brazil and Argentina accepted honorary membership of the house near Montreuil, informing *La Segunda* that, so far as they knew, her children were alive and in good health, though denied the right to travel beyond the estate of La Recoleta. 'The Alliance does not seek to punish your offspring, Madame Lynch. But they *do* share the name of Lopez, and our Governments cannot allow them to become the focus for rebellion. But yes, from all we hear, they are safe and well.'

She wrote to them every month, promising that one day soon she would take passage aboard a steamship and cross the Atlantic, then travel upriver to Asunción – 'and ride a high-stepping horse to the *quinta* in which you were born. It won't be long now, *mis niños*, before we can all be together.'

She convinced herself that her letters had reached La Recoleta, yet was saddened that none were answered.

Time passed, and *Le Manoir* thrived.

It took twenty-six months for Elisa to earn the sum she'd set as her goal, and she then told Gaétan Cravet that she was off to reclaim her children. 'God willing, I shall only be away for five months, maybe six. But the house runs itself now, you must agree. The staff and the croupiers are the best we could have found, and our membership list is among the most exclusive – '

'But of course you must go,' the man told her, his bloodless lips stretched wide across untreated teeth. 'Take all the time you need, Madame Lynch. We shall miss you, need I say it, but I shall personally keep an eye on things, and anticipate your return. Now arrange your departure, my dear. Pack your bags, and off with you. And here – take this – a few thousand extra in coin. Just an old man's way of showing his faith. And begging forgiveness for the excesses of that weekend, years ago.'

Elisa frowned, decided the crippled Cravet might mean it, and accepted the brass-trimmed purse. Then she thanked him and turned her thoughts to the shipping lines, the clothes she would take for a Paraguayan autumn, the presents she would buy for the seventeen-year-old Enrique and his brothers, and for all the household servants who'd stayed faithful at La Recoleta.

'And I'll find our establishment as I left it, Monsieur Cravet?'

'*Exactly* as you left it, Madame Lynch. How else could it be? Hmmm?'

405

5

On 9th February 1875, Elisa Alicia Lynch boarded an Argentine steamer in Bordeaux, and set out on the long, heaving journey to the estuary of the Río de la Plata and the port of Buenos Aires. The captain and officers knew who she was – the red-haired *Irlandesa* – but they treated the former mistress of the lunatic Lopez with courtesy. The War of the Triple Alliance was over, and Lopez was dead. And, however influential Señora Lynch might have been in the past, she was now just a passenger, an unescorted woman who stood for long periods alone at the rail, gazing out at the grey and endless Atlantic.

As a gesture of goodwill, the officers invited her to play cards. 'We understand you have a *garito* in Paris, Señora. You might care to teach us the games they play in that city.'

Cheered by their offer, she did so, her expression calm as she proceeded to win three hands in every four. A week of that, and they suggested switching to games they knew better. Elisa smiled in agreement. 'But an open hand first, señores, if you please. So I can get the hang of it.'

She then continued blithely as before, her green eyes shining as she out-played and out-scored them, eight hands in every ten.

They took pleasure in her company, and the stories she told them set the young men grinning with delight. But it was costing them a fortune to play cards with her! By the time they reached Buenos Aires they'd be borrowing from the cook!

Nevertheless, they snapped to attention as Elisa prepared to disembark from the steamer. *If life should allow me a mistress, then why not one like her? Something to think about, if I'm ever sent to Ireland.*

No sooner had she stepped ashore on the quay of the City of Sweet Air than a detachment of soldiers surrounded her, relieved her of her baggage and escorted her to the Commandant of the Port. She snapped at them in Spanish: 'In whose name do you arrest me, a civilian? My papers are in order – here – see for yourselves! Are you blind, or illiterate, or what? I have every right – '

By which time the Commandant had emerged from his office and was telling her yes, but she *was* who she was, and precautions had still to be taken.

'You came to us quite openly, Señora Lynch, and I personally see no reason to bar your progress. But you were, nevertheless, the close – perhaps the *closest* – companion of Señor Francisco Solano Lopez, and as such are a person of some account. Now don't glare at me like that, Señora. If you would simply tell me why you're here – '

'Why I'm here? I'm here to change ships, Señor. I'm here because the steamer put me ashore here, before it went elsewhere. I now wish to travel upriver to Asunción. But I am *not*, I assure you, about to re-open the war.'

The Commandant waved the soldiers back to their posts. Then he ushered Elisa into his office, gestured to a chair and returned to the far side of his desk.

'I apologize for the escort, Señora Lynch. We have never met before, and I had no idea – '

' – if I'd come ashore with a Gatling gun strung from straps round my neck? Toss a few grenades from the gangplank? Wave the flag of Paraguay and yell *'Viva Lopez!'*, though Solano five years buried? Oh, no, *Señor El Comandante*, we've not met before, so you were probably wise to whistle up your troops. I might have posed the most terrible threat; this single woman come back to wrench the limbs from Argentina . . .'

Then she shook her head and sat silent, her thoughts directed to the *quinta*, a thousand miles upstream.

She was lodged for the night in a small hotel near the port. The stench of fish and rotten wood reminded her of the first time she had come here, and she reached out to close the shutters of her room. As she did so she saw lights flicker in the street; the movement of uniformed soldiers; the glint of badges and bayonets.

Well, now, she thought, it seems the Commandant was right. I am still a person of some account in Buenos Aires. But a person to be feared by Argentina, or a person Argentina fears might be dragged from her room and killed below on the cobbles?

With the master dead, does it still remain to murder his foreign mistress . . . ?

The following afternoon, Elisa Lynch was escorted aboard a stubby British riverboat, which was laden down with reinforcing bars for construction work. On the deck was a group of Scottish and English engineers, their pale skins disfigured by the bites and stings and eruptions of myriad insects.

'Been here before?' they asked her. 'You a missionary, teaching the savages? Surprised you ain't tormented like us – the air's all full of these creatures.'

'I was here before,' she told them. 'I'm probably accustomed.'

The riverboat chugged onward, following the route Elisa had travelled twenty years ago. It was autumn now, on the Río Paraná, the Río Paraguay, and she felt some sympathy for her fellow travellers, slapping and cursing beneath the swarms of voracious mosquitoes.

One thousand miles, and a fortnight later, the riverboat edged towards the eastern bank of the river, and came to a jarring halt against the pilings of the dock of Asunción.

The engineers hurried ashore, sparing no more than a nod for their single, female companion. What they wanted now was the cool of a *cantina*, a dozen cold beers, then a shower in which to sluice the smear of crushed insects from their skin.

Elisa watched them go; bade farewell to the captain; collected her bags and returned to the cobbled waterfront of the country she had first entered as the nineteen-year-old mistress of a man who had promised her the world.

And then she was left to stand with her cases full of presents for her children until a customs officer asked if he might see such papers as would identify the visitor. He was young, but not too young to recognize the name.

'Señora Lynch? The one who was the friend of President Lopez? And now you come back *here*?' Without waiting for a reply, he turned and shouted, and soldiers came running to take her in charge.

She was held for several hours in a small, airless room in the *Aduana*.

With the country still under Allied control, various authorities were summoned to the port. They were courteous, but openly astonished by the presence of *La Irlandesa*. 'In all seriousness, Señora, did you truly believe you could re-enter Paraguay like a, well, like a tourist? I've no doubt there are some here who'd acclaim your return. But there are others who would kill you on sight, don't you realize that? The mothers and wives of all those men whom Lopez led to destruction. Paraguay lost its youth in your foolish war, Señora Lynch. The statistics are clear. Thanks to Lopez' ambitions and your

408

fidelity to his cause, there are now nine women to every surviving male. It will take God alone knows how many generations before the population of this country is brought to balance. And you think you can hail a coach at the gates of the port?'

'I have come to collect my children,' she told them. 'I have no wish – as you put it – to see the sights. I know them well enough. And, if you won't allow me to visit La Recoleta, then bring my children here. I lost one of my own in the war, if you care to remember. And buried him with my own bare hands, alongside Solano. All I ask – '

'*Lo siento, Señora*. I am sorry, but neither request can be granted.'

'You refuse me permission even to see them?'

'We refuse you permission even to stay the night ashore. There is a Brazilian gunboat at anchor in the river. She is due to return to Rio de Janeiro in two days' time. You will be put aboard that vessel and kept there until she sails. You do not seem an evil woman, Señora, and there are many, perhaps, who would sympathize with your plight.'

With a note of desperation in her voice, Elisa said, 'I own certain properties out here. I would have them transferred – '

'They have *been* transferred,' the authorities told her. 'Back to their original owners, or their heirs. You own nothing here any more, Señora Lynch. It was not Lopez' place to offer them to you, nor ever yours to accept. He asked too much of the world, did Francisco Solano Lopez, unwilling to accept that he owned a luxuriant part of it anyway.'

Elisa said: 'May I leave some money with you? Not much, but if banked for my children – '

'*Lo siento, Señora*. It will be confiscated as a matter of course, then returned to the near-empty coffers of Paraguay.'

'And the presents I brought them? Do you plan to seize them too?'

'All but your personal effects, Señora. And your ticket of return to distant Europe. We regret such severity and, within the confines of this room, wish you well in the future. But you gave your allegiance to a man who made undeclared war on several nations, and at the cost of many tens of thousands of lives.'

'Do you think I should have deserted him?' Elisa blurted. 'Taken his gifts and fled? He was kind to me, in his way. We were friends for a long time. Lovers, of course, but *friends*!' Then she came to her feet and kicked at the bags, offering their contents for confiscation, and shouted through spilling tears that she had not had many true friends in her life; *and how many did they?*

The sailors aboard the Brazilian gunboat erected a canvas shelter on the after deck, concealing Elisa's presence from the banks of the Río Paraguay.

She was allowed to sit out there while the vessel prepared to sail downriver. Raising her eyes from a book, she gazed unseeing at the tight-woven wall, lost in her memories of the city and the *quinta*.

She accepted now that she would never see Asunción again.

Never see the screeching parakeets in the trees, nor the snakes that lay unmoving within the tangle of the vines. The monkeys would swing and jabber in the upper branches, the armadillos snuffle through the undergrowth, tusky pigs snort and squeal as they dashed from a hundred dangers, wild cats coughing in the purple darkness of the jungle.

She would return to *Le Manoir* and smile at her guests, assuring Gaétan Cravet that the dancers could lift their skirts ever higher, if that's what he wanted. And she'd save her money and maybe, in the not-too-distant future, offer for sale her thirty per cent share in the establishment near Montreuil, then catch the ferry to her native city, and purchase a small, white-washed house within sight of the Lee.

Go back to where you were born, why not? It's a powerful magnet, and you've seen enough of the world.

France and Algeria, Spain and Sicily, the gaping mouth of the Río de la Plata and the rivers and hinterland of Solano's self-styled Paradise.

Then Edinburgh, London, Paris and Asunción; and back to Le Manoir *to refill your empty purse for the final time.*

You have lost El Presidente, *your protector. Lost your fortune. Lost your children. You fought to win, yet lost everything but your looks and your Irish courage.*

So, all right. We'll open a fourth gaming-room. Set off fireworks to mark the National holidays. Hold occasional fancy-dress gatherings. Landscape the grounds and ensure that the house in the forest near Montreuil is unsurpassed as a place of entertainment. A few more years of that and then, yes, perhaps home to Ireland.

6

The cabriolet that brought Elisa from the railway station in Paris rocked to a halt before the high-walled entrance to *Le Manoir*. It was seven o'clock on a fine June evening, and gigs and barouches were parked at the far end of the drive.

Yet the gates themselves were chained and padlocked.

Frowning, Elisa alighted from the vehicle, paid the driver and went to tug at the rope beside the entrance. The bell swung in its bracket on top of the wall, summoning the guardian, Valentin, from the tiny, one-room gatehouse.

As the old man hobbled towards her, Elisa snapped: 'And what's this? Are we now so over-subscribed that we must keep the place locked? Has the house been robbed in my absence, M'sieur Valentin, and the chain's for our security? Will you tell me what's going on?'

'Welcome back, Madame Lynch,' the guardian muttered, fumbling to twist the key in the weighty padlock. 'You're home earlier than expected, Madame. Another month at least, so I was told.'

'Answer my question. What is the meaning of – ?'

'Monsieur Cravet's instructions, Madame. He's in there now. Forgive me, but I think you'd best ask him.'

'You may count on it,' she said brusquely, edging between the gates. 'Now leave them open, M'sieur Valentin, if you please. This is a licensed place of entertainment, not an asylum for the insane.'

Valentin mumbled something as she started along the drive towards the manor, and she glanced back to see him surreptitiously slipping the hasp of the padlock through the chain. A moment ago locked out, she was now locked in.

She wondered what Gaétan Cravet had been up to since her departure for Bordeaux in early February. What in hell had he done to *Le Manoir*? What had he *undone*?

Suspicion made her hurry. But, as she approached the house, she saw two men lounging in the doorway. They wore the boots and breeches and thigh-length jerkins of common labourers, the sleeves of their woollen shirts rolled high on burly forearms. They reminded her of the slab-fisted Arnaud, the pugilist from Rue Hautefeuille. Her

411

suspicions deepened, and she hurried from the drive to the cover of the trees.

It was too late. The men had seen her, and shouted at her to stop, one of them striding down the steps. Elisa decided to follow a route that she knew would bring her round to the back of the house and the kitchen. She still had her leather valise, though lightened by all she'd been forced to leave in Asunción. She heard her pursuer bellow again, but now she was on a narrow path flanked by high box hedges, sounds of strident music away to her left, the man's voice fading, the kitchen no more than twenty yards ahead.

She expected to be swallowed by steam and smoke. Greeted by the cooks and serving girls. Deafened by the clatter of plates, the rattle of pans and trays, by all the backstage sounds to *Le Manoir*'s restaurant.

Everything was there, as she remembered it. But the plates were now stacked on the shelves and sideboards, the ovens unlit, and a single roast turned on a spit, where a few months ago there'd been six. As for the vast central table, once groaning beneath the weight of a dozen chosen dishes, well-polished cutlery, shimmering glasses and bottles of wine selected from the *cave* – it now held platters of bread and cut cheese, pale, jointed wildfowl and beef, sliced carelessly thick.

Where the kitchen in the house near Montreuil had once vied with the kitchens of Paris, it now seemed the perfect canteen for men such as those who had been lounging in the doorway.

Elisa slid her bag across greasy flagstones. Then she glared in disbelief at the few remaining members of the staff, and extended a finger at the cook she had thought she could trust, the ever-cheerful Colombe.

'Oh, Madame,' the woman gasped. 'Thank God you are back!'

'As you see.'

'Have you heard – ?'

'I've heard nothing. And now, since you seem less busy than usual, Mistress Colombe, I might as well hear it from you. What exactly has become of this place? No; better. *What has this place become?*'

Colombe surrendered to tears, her story garbled, her chubby features sagging as Elisa's hardened. The serving girls backed away and would have fled. But Elisa said: 'Oh, no, you don't, *mes filles*. My return is unannounced, and that's how I want it, for the moment. Now stand back from the door, at least until I've seen things for myself. You were saying, Mistress Colombe . . . ? You were telling me of the changes made in *Le Manoir* . . .'

Five minutes was enough. Five minutes that left Gaétan Cravet's partner ashen with anger, horrified by the garbled account, yet anxious now to test the truth of it; plumb its depths.

But the truth was already there, of course, on Colombe's tear-streaked face. A wonderful cook, she could never have advanced herself in the world by the use of deceit, the practice of lies. All she'd told Elisa *had* to be true. The rest would merely illustrate the words.

Removing her gloves, then her bonnet and cape, Elisa Lynch made her way along the corridor that led left to the restaurant, right to the first of the gaming-rooms.

No sound at all came from beyond the soft-sprung door of the dining room. She pushed it open, saw deserted tables, withered plants, grime and webs on the windows. Just as Colombe had told her. The menu had been withdrawn.

She went right and into the first of the three gaming-rooms, each arranged to cater for the individual gambler. Shouts and the pounding of fists were there to welcome her, the green-baize card tables now replaced by three clicking Wheels of Fortune, three girls in scanty costumes spinning the wheels, three men standing by to scoop up the losers' money from the counter.

She watched for a while, only now truly accepting Colombe's tearful story. The wheels revolved, and the customers roared, and the women who were with them shrieked to encourage the painted number their escorts had chosen. Thin metal blades clicked and ticked against the circle of whirling nails, the gamblers gaping as the wheels slowed, cursing the bloody thing to stop *now*, then cursing again when it didn't.

She recognized no one from the past. The aristocrats were absent, the diplomats departed, the gentlemen no longer there with their wives or mistresses. The room had become but a roofed-over fairground, and she made her way across it, jostled as she went.

The second of the three rooms was now given over to dice pits, the players hunched forward on low benches, their companions left to stand behind them, eyes smarting from the rising clouds of tobacco smoke.

But the cursing continued. And the jostling.

Elisa waited for a game to finish, then dodged between the outbreak of arguments and went through into what the cook had warned her would be the worst.

Another pit, but this one octagonal, rough-cut planks hammered on to posts to keep in the wild, blinded cockerels that leapt and squawked, their scaly legs strapped with lovingly-sharpened spurs.

In here, the men and women were on their knees. No need to stare up, as at the Wheels of Fortune. No need to lean forward, as over the dice pits. Here they could crouch on the planks and scream at the flustered, eyeless birds, handkerchiefs ready to wipe at the spatter of blood . . .

After this, it came as no surprise to Elisa to learn that the theatre, too, had changed for the worse. She scoured the chamber in search of Gaétan Cravet, then gazed at the dancers who, performing in obedience to a thick-fingered pianist, were discarding their petticoats, their stockings, feathers hitched to replace their drawstring underwear. They cavorted for the pleasure of the impassive assembly, though they were as impassive themselves as those below the stage.

One more room, and then she would confront her crippled partner.

This last was the glassed-in sanctuary for the wives – the Tea Room – in which they could relax whilst their menfolk skidded cards across the baize.

But the baize had gone. And so, too, had the Tea Room, thick curtains now strung from a skein of wires, the sounds from each narrow cubicle telling Elisa all she needed to know. Men grunted, and young girls squealed. The place had been turned, on the cheap, into a brothel, and she closed the door on it, her green eyes harder than emeralds.

She found Gaétan Cravet in what might once have become the fourth gaming-room in *Le Manoir*. But now the man had made it over as his office, and was seated there, in his wheelchair, in discussion with a tall, gaunt, blue-gowned woman who quickly withdrew her hand from his shoulder as Elisa Lynch strode in.

It was good to see Cravet blink, and hear the sudden screech of the wheels as he jerked back in his chair. Good to see his expression dissolve and reform itself, the man clearly taken by surprise. And good to startle the woman – whoever she was – and watch her collide with the wall.

'As Monsieur Valentin said at the gate. Home earlier than expected, eh, Monsieur Cravet? Though God knows what difference it would have made if I'd come a month later. June or July, you've ruined this place anyway. So just give me my thirty per cent of the share and I'll leave you to your vile and disgusting designs. Who's this, by the way? This lady who seems to have banged her head on the wall?'

As Elisa spoke, she advanced towards the desk that was now the centrepiece of the office, her voice nailed flat. 'Introduce me, why don't you? She might wish to know how we rack the wines in the *cave*. The correct form of address for a diplomat. The care with which we must hang up their hats and coats. Now, come along. Introduce me, Monsieur Cravet. Or – if you won't do that – dig in your drawer for the thirty per cent of our understanding.'

She was almost within arm's reach of him when he asked, 'What thirty per cent, Madame Lynch? You have papers that confirm this? And why should I pay you anything, my dear, when all you do is travel?'

'We had an agreement – '

'Dreams aboard your ship, I'm afraid. Dreams brought about by the lulling of the waves. But thirty per cent of *Le Manoir*? And all the arrangements now made by Madame Bazin, here? Oh, no. I'm sorry, Elisa. But I don't think you could ever claim you were part of *this* house, as it is.' Then he grinned as Madame Bazin hooked her hand on his shoulder again, and the two of them sighed in unison, waiting for the Irish woman to bite at her lip and leave.

She returned to the kitchen and collected her valise.

Colombe asked if things would be as before. If proper meals would once again be served. But all Elisa could do was embrace her, then pick up the case and make her way back to the gates, handing coins she could scarcely afford to the lonely Valentin, the night to be spent in a cheap hotel in the village of Montreuil.

At the age of forty, having flown so high, Elisa Lynch was now again spiralling downwards, her glossy wings tattered by the world . . .

She sold off the last of her jewellery; a brooch of Spanish silver, and a finely worked Venetian pendant, both gifts from Solano Lopez. They went for less than a third of their true value, but Elisa was in no position to complain. It was a buyer's market, and she needed the money to live.

She rented two street-level rooms in a house in Rue Faidherbe, and there, in a gesture of defiance, she stood her shallow, empty jewel-case on a rickety wall shelf, the lid of the case propped open. Its velvet lining bore the marks of the rings and clasps it had once contained, and it would stay there, she decided, as a reminder of how things had been.

'After all,' she told herself. 'I can always wear them from memory.'

There was no question now of returning to Ireland; no question of travelling anywhere beyond the expanding city of Paris. She would stay here in the Rue Faidherbe and think how best to earn a living . . . *But doing what?*

She was an excellent rider, and understood horses. So why not set up a *centre équestre*? But where would she find a backer for such a scheme, a man who'd be willing to finance the purchase of land, the construction of stables, the careful selection of mounts? A nice idea, but altogether too ambitious.

Very well. Then why not run a gaming-house? Make a modest start, and maybe, in time – But not here, in Rue Faidherbe. If she wished to operate the place with style, then someone – this mythical backer – would have to open his wallet to the seams. Install her in a town house in one of the wealthy *arrondissements*. Pay whatever was needed for a hard-to-get city licence. Underwrite any losses – always possible – and shrug if the tables were turned.

An attractive thought, but not feasible.

'Your wings are torn,' she murmured aloud. 'You will never again fly so high.'

It was not until August, when she was passing a newsvendor's stand in the Boulevard Voltaire, that Elisa thought of the thing she *could* do, and do from home.

Paris was now – well, had always been, but was now more than ever – a cosmopolitan city. The racks on the news-stand proved it, the wire grilles jammed with journals and papers in French, in Spanish, in English, in Italian.

And don't I speak three of them almost to perfection? And can write in them all? *And could therefore likely teach them?*

She returned to her rooms and seated herself at a worm-ridden table near the window. And wrote words that might appeal on a printed card. And went to talk to a printer, charming his price in half with her smile and her stories.

Then she walked the streets of the capital, her heels blistered in unmended shoes, delivering the cards to all those she remembered from the early days of *Le Manoir*, when the house near Montreuil had been worth the hour's ride out.

> A Knowledge of Languages is of Inestimable Value.
> Mme Elisa Alicia Lynch, residing at
> 17 Rue Faidherbe, Paris 11ᵉ, offers
> instruction to Young Ladies.
> English (and American parlance). Spanish
> (with knowledge of South America). French
> (for those lately come to this city).
> Fees by arrangement. Hours 10–12; 2–6.
> Sundays reserved for individual tuition.

The response astonished her.

Not only were household servants sent to deliver the replies, but aristocrats and diplomats came in person, bringing their wives. They were openly upset to see Madame Lynch in her large but austere rented rooms, though she told them she was fine where she was, and would let them know if she cared to change her address.

'We witnessed the sinking of *Le Manoir*, in your absence,' the parents sympathized. 'You ran a fine house there, Madame Lynch, and it doesn't seem fair.'

'It isn't,' she agreed. 'But where is it written, and by whom, that Life is Fair? Now here's the price I'm asking, and let's see how it goes with your daughter. If she wishes to learn, I can teach her. If she doesn't – ' Then she took their money, and excused herself as she stepped to the next room to lay it in the shallow, open jewel case.

It was uphill work from the start. Profitable in terms of cash, but disastrous when it came to the pupils attempting to pen grammar, or mimicking Elisa's intuitive accent. The truth was that the adolescent girls were bored, their futures already charted on a map they did not need to read. Their fathers provided for them now, in the parental mansions of Paris. And their mothers would find them husbands, who would provide for them in the future. So why study Spanish? Why entertain English? The line ran straight from *Papa* and *Maman* to *Le Mari*, and with provisions stocked for life.

Elisa persevered for eighteen months, though her patience finally snapped in the face of their unconcealed yawns. Hurling aside the cloth she used to clean the blackboard, she asked one of her mid-week classes why in God's name they bothered to come.

'You are delivered here within the studded velvet of your coaches, gowned in silk and with no more to carry than a couple of text-books – *when and if you remember them*. I do my best to instruct you in the language, but it doesn't seem to get through. You resist it, Mesdemoiselles. You just sit round the table and study your nails. Do you not – may I ask you – think knowledge of any value? Is it better to be ignorant than inquiring? Is it better to stare at the clock over there, than wonder what makes it tick? Is your world really contained within the borders of France, the *arrondissements* of Paris?'

Two of the young women giggled, then gasped when Elisa told them the class would finish early. 'Out you go! *Allez-vous en!* Out on the street with you! And so what if it's raining? Don't tell me you've never felt rain!'

She herded the whining pupils from the room and into the drizzle of Rue Faidherbe. Then she slammed the door behind them, and shrugged at the loss of income. Too bad. If she'd *wanted* to teach those who yawned, she'd have set up her blackboard on the banks of the Río Paraná and instructed the *yacarés*, the alligators that stretched their jaws as they wallowed in the blood-red mud.

Her anger dissipated, Elisa reluctantly sat down to write letters of apology to the parents of those she'd evicted from the classroom. 'I regret my outburst, though must ask that you speak with your daughter. As I told you, I am willing to teach her, but question her willingness to learn.'

What she'd wanted to say was: 'Willing to teach her, but who can draw blood from a stone?'

Wondering how many of the girls she would see again, she was gazing out at the gusts of rain that brushed the street when an old man stepped from the far side of Rue Faidherbe, his malacca cane raised like a sabre in the face of a churning *calèche*.

418

Foolish old man . . . Tottering off the pavement . . . Waving his stick as if he owned the street . . . Get himself run flat, so he would . . . And look at him now, caning the side of the carriage . . .

Elisa Lynch shook her head, and turned again to the letters she would have to send to the five angry parents.

Then she felt her body jolt – her head jerk back – her eyes stretched wide as she looked for him again, that militant civilian.

Papers fluttered and the pen splashed ink. The chair toppled over as she snatched her cape from a hook, and ran for the door. The rain invited itself across the threshold as she sped out into the street.

Oh, no . . . Not here . . . Not after all these years . . .

But find him, and find out . . .

Look the crusty old fool in the face, then smile and say sorry, I mistook you for . . . And come back inside to mop up the ink and finish those letters.

She hurried to the corner of Rue Faidherbe and Rue Chanzy, and wasted seconds peering left and right. Then she saw him again, striding north towards the Rue de Charonne. She told herself that maybe it was, maybe it wasn't, but who was Elisa Lynch to flinch from the rain?

She tracked him along Faidherbe. Then, splashing through the mud in her thin leather house-shoes, she moved faster than the man could totter on his cane.

And was waiting at the corner as he turned it. And said to him in English: 'Well, here's a sight! You and me. Colliding together like this.'

Then she wept with delight, her face turned upwards to his, her old friend found after all this time; and the towering Hungarian raised a hand to dash drops from his eyes, and pretended it was only the rain.

The Baron Enrique von Wisner de Morgenstern was in his seventies now, the brass-topped cane no more mere affectation. He leaned on it as he blinked at her, then with clumsy courtesy guided her to the shelter of an awning.

'Well, now Elisa. I'd not have bet money on this. Are you visiting the city? Married, are you? Those boys of yours – '

'No,' she said, 'and no, and no again. Where you thrashed at that carriage . . . I live across from there. Alone. I run a language school. Or did until this morning, when I evicted half my pupils. I was writing to their parents when I looked out through the window and saw you directing the traffic. Oh, Mother of God, it is good to meet you again, Enrique. Have you time to come back with me, or are you on your way somewhere else? And with the handsome Fulgencio Baleriano?'

'My, my,' the old man growled in approval. 'You still remember that?' Shaking rain from his hair he said: 'Lost touch with him near the end of the war. I'm told he took up with a Brazilian officer, and was happily placed under house arrest in São Paulo.' Then von Wisner turned and jabbed his cane towards the western end of Rue de Charonne and told her: 'Neighbours without knowing it, so it seems. Bought a place along there. Taken care of by the very devil of a housekeeper. Stump the streets to get away from her. Use this stick on the coaches and wish them all to be her.'

'Listen,' Elisa invited. 'Lose my pupils or not, I was paid last week. I've coal for the stove, fresh mantles for the gaslights; and there's a bakery that would heat up some pies while we wait. If you can spare the time – '

'No need for such *politesse*, you silly woman. You go and wait your turn in the bakery, whilst I purchase brandy and wine. But don't ask for *caña*. Not even Paris knows a damn thing about *caña*.'

She smiled and took his arm, her head spinning with pleasure at the incredible coincidence of their meeting, von Wisner not minding at all that his progress was stabilized on one side by the malacca cane, and on the other by the longtime friend he had found again.

With careless extravagance, Elisa Lynch bought two brimming pies, one mutton, one Normandy beef, and a small bag of garish, sugared buns. The baker hurried to hold open the door of his shop and wish her *'Bonne journée'*.

The Baron von Wisner lurched to meet her, a long arm curled round a canvas sack of bottles. 'Give you the thing without any bloody handles! Probably hope you drop it, then go back for more.'

'It's there.' She nodded the direction. 'Across the street to the right. The Internationally Renowned Language School, to which spoilt young ladies flock for the chance to yawn.' Then they crossed the Rue Faidherbe, bottles clinking, Ireland and Hungary reunited on this dismal day in Paris.

Von Wisner stooped as he entered the house, stooped again as he entered the drawing-room-cum-schoolroom. Elisa set the food on the table, rescued the bottles and told him to sit where he wanted. 'None of the chairs are much made for leisure, but that one there might

420

suit you. Came from a shop in Rue Chanzy. Give it a kick, and the back reclines – well, a bit.'

The baron lowered his frame into the chair, as his hostess fed the stove. She knew she was being excessive – *this much kindling? This much coal?* – but the penny-pinching no longer mattered, not today.

Coincidence is as much a part of life as a rendezvous missed. A random bullet is as likely to strike you dead as to spare you by inches. Disease could swarm in your blood, yet leave you immune, as all those around you die.

Ignorance and innocence and pure blind luck were among the many ingredients of that coincidental meeting in the rain in the heart of the 11th *Arrondissement* of Paris on that February day in 1877.

But the baron *had* lashed in irritation at the carriage, and Elisa *had* looked up from her letters to see him do it. And she had hurried out in time to catch him, coincidence forced to convergence.

'Don't think much of the beef,' he groused. 'Far too salty.'

'Are you warm enough, Enrique? If you're not, I could always set the house alight.'

He scowled to see her standing with coal dust on her hands, then said he was sorry. 'Getting irritable with the years. Meal's fine. And your room's a damn sight warmer than it ever is in Charonne.'

He finished his slice of pie to please her, then winced as he came to his feet, to uncork a bottle of the best the vintner could sell him. Filling their glasses carefully, his two hands grasped the bulbous black container, the better to conceal the shaking of age . . .

Elisa recounted her life since Cerro Cora. Told von Wisner how she'd buried Solano and their eldest son with her own bare hands. Then been deported from *El Jefe*'s landlocked Paradise. Sailed to Portsmouth. Travelled to Edinburgh. Fought and lost her case against Surgeon Stewart. Worked for a while in London. Sought the backing of Gaétan Cravet and managed *Le Manoir* in the forest.

'Heard about it,' von Wisner nodded. 'Thought I might go there, then decided it was too damn far for my haunches. But on reflection, a pity I didn't.'

'On reflection,' Elisa echoed softly, 'you'd have liked it then, I think, in the early days.'

They sipped at the vintner's best wine, and the Baron von Wisner de Morgenstern told his only female friend that he, too, had travelled – 'But without much by way of result. You might or might not know

I was forced to surrender in the valley of Cerro Cora. A coward's way out – '

'Don't say that, Enrique – '

' – sabre half stuck in its scabbard – '

' – you are not shaped for cowardice – '

' – and falling about, with a young Brazilian warning me not to unsheath it. Dear God, but what a pantomime I must have presented . . .'

Elisa saw the warrior slouch, as he held his honour to the mirror.

Then she grinned mischievously and asked, 'Not so handsome then, this Brazilian? Not your type, Enrique? Not the kind *you* could have gone to São Paulo with?'

An instant later he laughed and slid his boot-heels across the floor. 'Likely it was that,' he acknowledged. 'Likely I wasn't scared at all by the threat of his pistol, but didn't take to his looks.'

As the coal-fired stove glowed and beat back the damp, the woman extended her glass. The drizzle of rain had become a steady downpour, pattering on the windows, and she left von Wisner to serve her with wine whilst she closed the brass-ringed curtains.

'Did you go back to Hungary, my old friend? Is there no one there? Your family – ?'

'Oh, yes. But no one of my persuasion, *ma chère*. No one who needs the presence of a man with a weakness for men. I went back, and they were kind to me, and even invited women to keep me company at the table. But the uniform doesn't matter, nor the medals, once the ladies learn they've been wasting their time on a – '

'Rue de Charonne? And what number is it? And when shall I be invited?'

The questions brought him alert. He told her forty-three; and whenever she wished; whenever she could take time off from her school.

'But I must warn you, Elisa. My housekeeper is something of a harridan, and might not think well of your visit.'

'Then why do you let her keep house for you? Why do you keep *her*?'

Von Wisner sighed. 'I'm an old and irascible ex-soldier, *ma chère*, with neither the ability nor inclination to shop or cook or – '

'Tomorrow,' Elisa said firmly. 'I shall call on you tomorrow, after my classes. You may expect me at six-thirty.' Then she smiled and added: 'Harridans come in all colours, Enrique, didn't you know that? Even some, so I've heard, with red hair!'

422

8

Anticipating the worst, the aged warhorse was nonetheless intrigued to see what would happen.

In command of the house, and thus in military terms holding the high ground, was the well-entrenched Madame Bertille Sauret, backed by her slatternly niece. They would know how best to strengthen their defences, judge the moment to counter-attack, manoeuvre so the enemy had no chance to establish a foothold on the carpets of the dwelling in Rue de Charonne.

On the other hand, he knew Elisa Alicia Lynch, and could remember, even now, the sight of *La Segunda* riding across the clearing at Curuguaytay, her life at risk as she spurred to rejoin *El Primero*.

Watch out, Madame Sauret, von Wisner thought. And you, too, Yvette. My friend has faced far greater dangers than you.

At five o'clock, as usual, the Hungarian settled himself in a corner of the small, poorly heated parlour, and peered at the foreign reports in *Le Figaro*. This time, he decided, I'll keep out of the line of fire.

The bell rang at six twenty-eight. Madame Sauret came to the door of the parlour and asked: 'Who would this be, Monsieur le Baron? I've already set Yvette to making the soup, so I hope you've not invited another of your cronies in from the park. In my opinion – '

'Be good enough to see who it is, Madame Sauret, then we'll know. And I hope there's some meat in the soup tonight. You tell me you buy it, but it seems to dissolve in the boiling.'

The domineering housekeeper snorted and went to deal with the caller. Doubtless another stoop-shouldered relic who would claim he'd fought battles in faraway places, then stay until he'd finished a bottle of wine. Not that von Wisner cared, of course. Generous as the day was long, the old baron. But it ate into the budget. And, more important, into Madame Sauret's profits.

Her mouth open to tell the man that now was not the moment – Monsieur le Baron was at table – the housekeeper stared at the woman who stood on the doorstep, her bonnet tied with a bow Madame Sauret herself had often tried to fashion, but had always failed.

'Excuse me for disturbing you, Madame. But would this be the residence of General the Baron Enrique von Wisner de Morgenstern? We met by chance last afternoon.'

'And if it is?' Sauret scowled. 'No one told *me* – '

'*Ah, quelle joie!*' Elisa bubbled. 'Perhaps you'd give him my card, Madame. His memory's not what it was and – well, you know, just to remind him.'

Madame Sauret felt the corner of the card jabbed into her palm. Instinctive curiosity made her glance down at it, by which time the breezy Elisa had slipped past her and inside.

'We call this city civilized,' she prattled, 'and Lord knows, they charge us enough for piping the gas.'

'What?'

'The lights here in the hallway, Madame! The pressure must be down again, it's so gloomy. Or maybe the taps are stuck. Let's see now . . . But no! They're not at all! They weren't full on, Madame. And see how it brightens the entrance!'

She beamed at the housekeeper, loosed the bow of her bonnet, then lifted it from her head, and tossed her hair. 'You have a block for it, Madame? To hold its shape? This rain's a terrible thing for hats, don't you find?'

'No, we – '

'Never mind. Off you go with my card. I'll just wait here and make what I can of these paintings. The dust, I imagine, is on the *inside* of the glass. Else someone – ' and she wagged a playful finger – 'someone's been derelict in their duties!'

Madame Sauret moved back, her shoe heel tapping twice to correct her balance. Who *was* this woman, this Elisa Alicia Lynch who offered a Knowledge of Languages of Inestimable Value? And dared to fiddle with the gas jets, expect her frivolous bonnet to be blocked, criticize the state of the paintings – *then tell me to be off and present her card!*

'You wait here,' she snapped, enraged as she heard herself echo what Elisa had just said. 'And I'll thank you to leave things alone.'

'Terrible habit,' Elisa admitted. 'Interfere with everything.'

The housekeeper turned, and the caller wiped away her flighty expression. Be a hard nut to crack, Enrique's gaoler. But she'd stick with the role she'd created, and see how things went.

With undisguised reluctance, Madame Sauret returned to say: 'It seems the Baron will see you. In there.' Then she caught Elisa's arm, her fingers tightening like claws. 'He's a sick old man. Visitors upset him. Ten minutes is all he can take.'

424

'Ten minutes? I'll only need five.'

'That's good.'

'By which time I'll have him waltzing round the floor!' Raising her arm, she disengaged Sauret's claws, then sang her way into the parlour, wondering why she had never chosen acting as a profession.

The warhorse watched her, then hid his smile behind *Le Figaro*. He'd heard everything Elisa had said in the hallway – *and all of it calculated to infuriate the harridan* – but was not yet sure what part she'd found for him. He had never forgotten *La Segunda*, but had never spoken of her to Madame Bertille Sauret. So Elisa would have to lead him now. Let him know what he was to her. Old friend, or new-found fossil. Her long-lost uncle, or –

'Well, you don't look so sick to me, Monsieur le Baron. Your housekeeper calls you a sick old man – Oh, you're still there, Madame? Still in the doorway?'

Her teeth clamped tightly behind her lips, the woman said: 'All I *meant*, Madame Lynch, was that the Baron von Wisner was not to be over-excited. Now allow me to bring you some tea; I believe there's some left.'

'Splendid.' Elisa clapped. 'And honey, if you have it. There are few things as refreshing – '

'No, we haven't.'

'*Tant pis*. The tea as it comes then. And a scuttle of coal for the fire perhaps? The baron's fingers are shaking, can't you see that? The way his newspaper trembles? Now then, Monsieur le Baron. About this question of studying English . . .'

So that's it, Sauret acknowledged. The old fool's growing bored, and the Lynch woman's sold him on the idea of learning a language. And will doubtless charge him handsomely for it. Which will bite into the profits . . .

The door closed and von Wisner raised a hand. 'Wait,' he whispered. 'There's a floorboard that – You hear it? Means she's gone to the kitchen. But as for your tea – '

'Don't worry, Enrique. I can see the acid fumes rising from it now.'

She did what she could to resuscitate the fire, then knelt on the carpet, close to the man's bony knees, and told him it was time to take stock of events. 'I may be wrong, but I believe you're being cheated, my dear Enrique. Perhaps you don't care, and perhaps you can afford it – '

'Which is why I lean on a cane? For the pleasure of stumbling?

425

Oh, no, *ma chère*. I am maybe as you, yourself, these days. Leafing through the wallet in the hopes of finding a crumpled note? Shaking the purse and praying to hear it chink? I'd not lie to you, Elisa. The money seems to disappear these days like sand down a funnel.'

She placed her hands on his knees – *Oh, lord, yes, they were bony* – and murmured: 'Here's what I suggest.' She told him quickly, her voice kept low, then grinned conspiratorially when his own hands covered hers.

Yvette brought the tea and set it heavily on a ringed, unwiped table.

Elisa came to her feet and glanced at von Wisner, who nodded permission.

'Bring two more cups,' she invited. 'Then will you and the house-keeper please join us? Your master would like to have a friendly, family gathering. Oh, and there's something else you can bring us, Mademoiselle.'

'We ain't got no cakes.'

'Of course not. But you will have the books – '

'I don't read,' the maid blurted, then stood dumb and slack-jawed as Elisa continued.

'The ones that contain the accounts of all expenditures, invoices, taxes, bills, costs and whatever else you'd like to call them. Madame Sauret will surely have quite a stack of them by now. It'll give us something to talk about over tea.'

The slattern blinked. Something was wrong here. *This* red-haired woman couldn't surely be the same red-haired woman who her aunt said had interfered with the gas jets. *This* red-haired woman seemed to know exactly what she was doing!

Elisa kept her school going, if only to honour her contracts with the parents. But with Bertille Sauret and her niece, Yvette, questioned by von Wisner, and shown to have cheated him for years, then dismissed with a roar by the furious Hungarian, Elisa's life was brought simmering to the brim. Not only had she to instruct her tiresome pupils, but she now had to find the time to buy food and cook it in Rue Faidherbe, or hurry it to the stove in Rue de Charonne.

Von Wisner arranged for a laundress to collect his clothes and linen, and insisted that a florist deliver a bouquet of flowers to Elisa's door on alternate Friday evenings.

They met at irregular hours, but every day. And then, in the first

426

week of May 1877, the towering Hungarian brushed at his magnificent moustache and mumbled behind it.

'Can't hear a thing,' Elisa told him. 'Are you speaking to me, or
to your buttons?'

'All I was saying . . . That maybe now would be the moment . . .'

'Which reminds me. I thought I might close the school. Be rid of
the yawners. Save the rent and move in here. Get to grips with your
damn great stove. Be odd, perhaps, a woman who's slept with men
for money, and sometimes for love, and on occasion for the simple
need to sleep. Yet would now keep house for you. An ill-tempered
old creature, with a courtesan to brush the lint from your clothes?
Now what were you saying, Enrique? What did you think would suit
the moment – *querido*?'

He knew how precious that single word was to her – reserved for
Solano alone – and he thought it best to jab his cane on the carpet
and come to his feet and bow in her direction and say yes, she'd
spoken his wishes aloud.

And everything in her room upstairs had been washed and aired
and ironed.

They lived as a married couple might have lived, had they been
thirty years together. And bickered as couples will do.

Von Wisner encouraged Elisa to find herself a husband – 'You're
still a fish to be hooked, *ma chère*. There's many a man who I'm sure
would take you on.'

'I could likely count them in their thousands.' She smiled. 'But so
long as I skin you at cards – And see? Full suit! You lose again!'

Lose or win, von Wisner marked her forty-fifth birthday with the
presentation of a drab brown envelope.

'And what's this?' she queried. 'You couldn't have tied it with a
ribbon?'

'Open it, woman; open it. By God, but it's all the crust and no
contents with females! You'd think I'd give you an *envelope*? Just open
it.'

She did so and gazed at the printed, stamped and initialled slips
of paper. And turned her head so her tears wouldn't smear them.
And told him he wasn't just a one-time fool, but two.

Two tickets for passage on the steamer *La Bailadora*, sailing from
Bordeaux to Montevideo, from where they would have to find their
own way up to Asunción. But First Class Cabins. Both to leeward

of the hot summer breeze. And Heaven knows how much of the old man's savings squandered on such kindness.

'You'll probably die on the voyage,' she told him. 'I'll probably come back alone.'

'However it happens. With me or your children. We'll see.'

They were taken to Montevideo in high style, the Atlantic running smooth.

A few days there and they transferred to a well-run Uruguayan steamer, the War of the Triple Alliance never mentioned.

Von Wisner and Elisa slapped at the mosquitoes, their immunity worn off, and the customs officers let them through without question when they reached the shed in Asunción.

'I am going to see them!' Elisa exclaimed. 'They'll be unrecognizable, those boys. But it won't take long before – '

'Not long at all,' her companion agreed. 'But don't expect too much, my dear. It has, after all, been quite a while since you left La Recoleta.' Nodding, neither of them mentioned that it had really been more than ten years.

As the carriage bucked east, Elisa pointed to plantations she remembered, orchards she'd known as saplings, once bare hills that now wore a fine green wig.

Then the driver hauled at the reins, swung the team, and jumped from the bench to tie the traces.

'La Recoleta, Señor, Señora. The monster Lopez kept a mistress here. Rose red hair like yours, Señora. And crucified the peasants in the garden there. And held orgies in the upper rooms – and such things as I would not repeat in the presence of a lady. Or a gentleman. Sixty pesos, I'll show you around.'

'No,' Elisa told him, but the denial not for the money. Just no, because the *quinta* was empty and overgrown, her children gone, and the stories all untrue.

All but the first. The first undeniable. He *had* kept a mistress here, and here it was she'd made love to Elmore Curtin, hurled the flowerpots from the wall in her anger, entertained the ebullient Charlie Washburn, raged at Solano's *caballistas* and screamed to the painted beams as she'd jerked her boys into the world . . .

But she told the driver no, this vine-strangled ruin held nothing for her, and she'd rather pay him his sixty pesos to see her safe back to the city.

*

With von Wisner's help, she inquired as to the whereabouts of Enrique Venancio and Frederico and Carlos Honorio and Leopoldo and the last born, Miguel. But no one seemed to know any more. And clearly no one cared.

She was never a woman to let her spirits flag, this daughter of Cork. But her heart could be damaged, fissured, even broken, and she struggled to protect it.

Responsible for von Wisner, she returned to Rue de Charonne, where she lifted the frames from the paintings, and polished the glass, and hung them back on their hooks.

Brought men in to dismantle the stove and clean it.

And let herself be known again in the district as someone not to be fooled with; a customer who would pay a fair price; but never one to be tricked.

It was a long time later when the Baron von Wisner beckoned her within earshot and said: 'Listen to this. *Le Figaro*'s correspondent in New York. "We regret to report the heroic death of General Elmore Cornelius Curtin (54) who gave his life – " '

'I don't want to hear it,' Elisa dismissed. 'I don't want to hear it.'

'But what he did – '

'I've told you, Enrique. I don't want to hear it.'

'But he saved a dozen lives, sailing his yacht from – '

'I have told you!' Elisa stormed. 'I don't wish to hear it. I have no wish to know what he did, nor how he died. Nor anything else about him. Nothing at all.' Then she shrank away and concealed her brow with her hands, her heart pounding hard as she thought of him in the orchards and mansion of Paradise . . .

That very same night – Elisa Lynch now scarcely more than fifty years of age – she apologized to von Wisner for her outburst concerning Elmore Curtin. She chinked glasses with the baron and told him he was to see to the turning off of the gaslights in the hall.

Then she made her way to her room and sat on the edge of the bed, regretting she'd not asked how Curtin had done it, saving those lives.

All right, so she'd find out the truth tomorrow.

Though she'd have to beg for the news, of course, for the baron hated interruptions.

She tossed back her hair . . . Stared for a moment, unblinking, at the mirror . . . Then she felt the need to lie down, a sudden siphoning in her lungs, her breath drawn away, her body left limp on the coverlet fresh from the laundry.

'Oh, Lord,' she murmured, as she faded. 'He won't even know where his soup bowl – '

But he did, and the bowl was still unwashed in the kitchen when the black-dressed official muttered his condolences and turned to the question of payment.